TRAITORS

TRAITORS

KRISTINE KATHRYN RUSCH

MILLENNIUM
An Orion Book
LONDON

This edition first published
in Great Britain in 1993 by
Millennium
An imprint of Orion Books Ltd,
Orion House, 5 Upper St Martin's Lane
London WC2H 9EA

A CIP catalogue record for this book is available
from the British Library

ISBN: (Csd) 1 85798 054 9
(Ppr) 1 85798 055 7

Millennium
Book Twenty-Five

Typeset by Deltatype Ltd, Ellesmere Port, Wirral
Printed and bound in Great Britain by Clays Ltd, St Ives plc

For Kevin J. Anderson
because Diate has always been his favorite.

Acknowledgements

Thanks on this book go to Paul B. Higginbotham for his enthusiasm about an early draft, to Nina Kiriki Hoffman for her valuable advice, to Dean Wesley Smith for forcing me to think about setting and history, and to Deborah Beale for her insightful rewrite suggestions.

Author's Note

Most Kingdom names have Spanish pronunciations. Diate, for example, is pronounced Dee-ah-tay, with the accent on the second syllable.

PART ONE

Chapter 1

Class C ocean-going cruise ships had large under-the-seat storage compartments. Diate's sister had told him that when she signed onto her post almost two weeks before. A bit of training, and she would have been on the ship instead of him. She would have ridden up front or in one of the booths, entertaining passengers, instead of lying in the storage compartment itself.

He hated it in there. The interior was made of unfinished wood. Splinters dug into him. His shoulders spanned the width only when he remained on his side, with his knees pulled up to his chin. The first day he suffered leg cramps so bad that he could hardly keep quiet. The second day the pains subsided, but the ache remained. This morning, the cramps had started again, but his training had taken over. He didn't utter a sound. It probably wouldn't have mattered if he had. Silence was the least of his worries.

He needed food.

The slit between the seat top and the storage bin sent light into his prison. Sometimes he watched the shadows pass, and sometimes he listened to the low hum of the ship. Occasionally the choppy ocean added a rocking rhythm to the the ship's gentle forward movement, and gave him something new to concentrate on.

Each time the ship had docked at a small island, he had worried that someone would find him. But so far, no one had.

He had picked a seat storage unit in a back room, thinking no one would use it. The lack of use had been a blessing. He had been able to sneak to the bathroom just off the storage compartment several times without being seen. Each time, he got a little worse: dizzy, unable to stand quickly, but at least he was stretching his cramped muscles. Once, as he peed, he heard another passenger in the corridor, and he hid in one of the stalls until the passenger left. No one else had come close to him.

But he hadn't realized that the lack of use was also a problem. He got bored. He examined the compartment in minute detail to keep himself awake. When he slept, he talked. He had done that since he was a small child. He was afraid of doing it here, and only allowed himself to nap when the slit between the lid and the bin had gone dark.

Sometimes he reviewed the ship's plan in his head, just to keep his memory fresh. A Class C cruiser was large and capable of carrying three small Vorgellian air shuttles on its main deck. The passengers haunted the upper decks, and the lower decks were reserved for storage and engineering. He was glad the storage was down low. It kept the traffic in this part of the ship to a minimum. He wouldn't be able to sneak out of the storage compartment at all if he were on an upper deck.

He slid an arm to the water stash near his head. At least he brought enough water for the journey. He kept the water in goatskin bladders he had stolen from a house near the port. He had tucked the bladders into his duffel, along with his paints, dance clothes and extra toe shoes. He had hung onto the duffel throughout the entire long trip.

Diate permitted himself a small sigh. Three more days until Rulanda. Then he would have to sneak off the ship and somehow explain his presence to the Rulandan authorities. Maybe they would grant him asylum. They certainly wouldn't send him back. Rulanda was a luxury resort, and would do nothing to offend potential guests. The incident would be hushed and he would be safe until he thought of his next step.

Slowly he brought a goat skin to his lips and sipped the wooden straw he had left in the opening. The water's warmth eased the dryness in his throat, but made his stomach rumble. He had eaten all his rations, even though he had tried to do so sparingly. He had to get food.

He needed a plan.

He had to be careful. This far away from the Kingdom, he might be safe, but he doubted it. The captain could do anything to a stowaway. He had heard stories about the ways stowaways were treated. Most were indentured. Vorgellian captives became little more than servants. If he got caught, he wanted to be indentured because his other choice was worse.

The captain would imprison him, and send him back. Home. To the Kingdom.

The copper stench of blood rose from the house. His father's body, in pieces on the path, led the way like grotesque bread crumbs. His sister, sprawled on the porch, arms and legs extended, and inside, his brothers, his mother, and the baby, eyes open, their blood mingling into the copper river sopping his toe shoes . . .

He twisted his head, wishing he could move. Wishing he had left the memory behind when he snuck on board the ship. Hard to believe he had come home to that only a week before. Only a week since Myla had tried to warn him, since he had left her dance studio without removing his shoes, since he had run the short distance to his home.

He had been running ever since.

The dance had served him well. It had given him stamina when he thought he would collapse, strength when he needed one more push, agility to crawl into the smallest spaces to hide.

For six days.

When it got dark, he would search the other bins. If he didn't find food there, he would risk going into the kitchen. He had to keep himself awake, and somehow, he had to stretch before that. He had managed to keep the blood flowing in his legs, but the cramping when he stood would be unbearable.

Footsteps outside made him breathe shallowly. He tried to lean farther into the wooden side of the bin as if that would protect him. Splinters pierced his back. A thin trickle of warm blood ran down his skin.

'. . . do not believe in Kingdom magic,' a male voice said behind the creak of the double doors. 'It is not a true Talent. It has no biological base.'

'Outsiders don't determine Kingdom Talents,' a female voice said. 'Besides, magic sells as well on Rulanda as music does on Vorgel.'

'This is not Rulanda.'

The footsteps, ringing on the metal floor, grew closer. The storage bin shook each time a foot went down. Diate thought ships had to be sturdier than this. Didn't the Vorgellians build them to last?

'Then you should have no fear of checking if her predictions were right.'

The voices were directly above him. Diate believed in Kingdom magicians. He was six when the Queen's read him. *This boy is a*

3

great Talent, the magician had said. *And within him, he carries the seeds of destruction.*

She had been right. He had destroyed his entire family.

The man and woman blocked the light coming in through the slit. The floor creaked, as if someone had shifted weight, and then a hand covered the slit in front of his eye.

The lid flew up and Diate blinked at the brightness. Perfume and musk mingled in the dry air.

'Shit,' the man hissed. His slender build and almond eyes marked him as a Vorgellian. His dark, work-stained uniform indicated he was a lesser crew member, not one of the Captain's personal staff.

The woman standing beside him was not much older than Diate. She was taller than the Vorgellian, and she wore thigh-high suede boots, tight black pants and a loose, ruffled white shirt. The red caste mark on her right temple marked her as part of the Kingdom. A Trader. With enough power to get a Vorgellian crew to do her bidding.

'Get out,' she said. It took Diate a moment to realize that she was talking to him.

Diate pushed himself up on his arm. It shivered beneath him. He sat up, and a wave of dizziness washed over him. He clutched the metal lip of the bin.

Her gaze had already taken in the thin blue lines that marked Diate's forehead. Talents did not stow away on cruise ships. Only runaways did. Runaways whose entire family had been slaughtered.

'Not much of a dancer now, are you, boy? See what a Talent comes to when it mingles with traitors?' She knew who he was. His heart started pounding rapidly.

'My father was not a traitor,' Diate said. His voice sounded raspy. It hurt against the back of his throat. He had not spoken in nearly a week.

'No.' She crossed her arms in front of her, her light eyes mocking him. 'He was a minor Talent. A poet, if I remember right.'

'He didn't like what the government was doing to my sister.'

The woman shrugged. 'She didn't have your gifts. The system can only provide for Talents.'

Diate's eyes were finally adjusting to the brightness. The room was smaller than he remembered. The six long, padded seats were

4

spaced evenly apart and on the shiny metal walls hung costumes, clothing and shipboard entertainment packs. Double doors led out on each side, except behind him.

'You know this person?' the Vorgellian asked.

'I know of him,' she said. 'Remember the documents security gave us when we boarded? He's the missing rebel.'

The Vorgellian let air through his teeth and sat on a seat across from Diate. The padding wheezed under the Vorgellian's weight. 'We have never had a stowaway. I thought it was not possible.'

'The boy's smart,' the woman said. 'You don't get to his level of proficiency without some kind of brain.'

'The captain will not be happy.' The Vorgellian stood. 'I will bring him here.'

He rose, spun on one foot, and marched toward the double doors. He struck them with the heels of both hands, the gesture betraying the anger that his stance had not. The doors swung back and slammed against the outside wall.

Diate's body shook, but the dizziness had retreated a little.

'Get out,' the woman repeated.

Her tone brooked no objection. He gripped the edge of the bin so hard the metal dug through his fingers. He took a deep breath and pulled himself forward, willing his body to work as he instructed. His muscles ached, a tight, painful ache he had never felt before. Each movement added to his dizziness. He swung one leg over, then the other, and stood before her.

He was taller than she was. The crown of her head revealed a thousand different hair colors, blending into one. She managed to watch him without tilting her head up. Her nose was small and upturned, her features delicate. With half an effort, he could knock her aside and run.

But he had nowhere to go.

'You realize stowing away violates the International Trade Agreement the Kingdom has with the Vorgellians? You no longer belong in our jurisdiction. You belong in theirs.'

Diate had known it. He had hoped he wouldn't get caught.

'But you're a Talent,' the woman said. 'And I don't think the Kingdom wants to give you up. I'm going to contact the Queen, and see what she wants done with you.'

The Queen. Diate closed his eyes. He had been her favorite, even after his father had begun his campaign. She would put her

5

hand on Diate's head and smile at him. *You're not crazy like your father, Emilio. You will bring a great glory to my Kingdom.* Tearing his body to pieces and leaving those pieces on a path wouldn't be good enough. She would do something else, something even crueler to show the other Talents what happened when one betrayed her.

His knee buckled beneath him and he collapsed on the floor. His body had never betrayed him like this before. Spasms ran through both legs. He leaned forward, clutched the backs of his knees, and stretched. Cries rose in his throat and he stifled them, but he couldn't stop the pain-tears from coursing from his eyes.

'Look how pathetic the rebel's son is,' the woman said. She watched him for a moment, then walked away. He watched the fringe on her soft boots move to its own personal rhythm. She opened the doors gently, and pulled them quietly shut behind her.

The metal floor was cold. He remained in the pike position for a long time after the spasms left, stretching his body. The ship gave him no more cover. They would search him out, find him, and torture him. He would have to do what they wanted, until he thought of something else.

With an agility he didn't feel, he rolled up, and extended one leg out behind him. He put his knee down, and his other leg forward, stretching his Achilles tendon and his back. He brought his arms up, and his back leg in, feeling the pull on his muscles. They hummed. The tight ache was easing. He was regaining control. He stepped into first position as the door opened.

The Vorgellian who had found him entered, followed by another Vorgellian. The new man was taller and huskier, with a darker suit, dark skin and the trademark almond eyes. He waited in the door frame.

'The stowaway,' the Vorgellian said. His words were clipped. Lillish was not a language he knew well.

The other Vorgellian came into the room. He walked around Diate, grabbing an arm, poking his ribs. Diate did not move under the physical onslaught.

'You are quite thin,' the Vorgellian said.

His Lillish was better than his companion's, but it still lacked the flow of a native Kingdom member.

'I would like to eat,' Diate said.

'In due time.' The Vorgellian nodded to his companion, and

6

spoke in a language Diate did not know. The companion left, closing the door behind him.

The Vorgellian sat on the bench and patted the seat beside him. Diate sat down, wincing as his partially stretched muscles tightened up again. The padding felt soft after those long hours trapped in the bin. The Vorgellian stared at him, and Diate stared back. He had never seen one up close. The Vorgellian's skin was smooth and had no facial hair. His eyes had an extra fold in the outer corners to give them the almond shape. His nose was as delicate as a woman's. Diate had heard Traders complain that Vorgellians were impossible to recognize, impossible to read. But this Vorgellian wore his emotions like a shield. Beneath the curiosity was a lot of sadness.

'What purpose does a Talent have aboard my ship?'

'I am no longer a Talent.' Diate worked to say the sentence. Until a week ago, being a Talent had been the greatest joy in his life.

The Vorgellian raised a hand and traced the blue marks on Diate's forehead. The Vorgellian's fingers were warm. 'One cannot deny one's self.'

The gesture made him tremble. No one had touched him since he found his family. 'They murdered' – the words brought back the smell, thick and coppery – 'my family. They want to kill me.'

The Vorgellian shook his head. 'You are their wealth. The Kingdom values wealth. I have read the papers they sent about you. I do not think they wished to harm you until you tried to leave them.'

Diate clenched his fists. He could never dance for them again. Each action would have brought back his father's voice. *The Talent system destroys people. By elevating Talents, and forcing the rest to a hard-scrabble existence, we are ensuring the downfall of this place. Someday the people will rise up against this oppression. Someday they will understand that the Talents are not their gods, but their destroyers.*

'You have disappeared.' The Vorgellian's hand slid down to Diate's cheek and then off his face.

Diate started. He was still present. He had no magic powers. Then he understood what the Vorgellian meant. The Vorgellian had seen him get lost in the memory. No one had ever read him so clearly.

'I have no wish to hurt you,' the Vorgellian said. 'You have suffered enough. I must give you to the Kingdom, but until then, I will treat you well.'

7

A thread of hope mingled with the hunger in Diate's stomach. He swallowed, and forced the hope away. The Vorgellian could not save him. The Vorgellian had taken pity on him in his last days.

'I am Sehan,' the Vorgellian said. 'Come with me. I will feed you.'

On the main deck, the cruiser had few corridors. The shuttle bays took up a large area, and most of the deck remained open to the sky, in case a shuttle needed to take off. Inside, away from the bay, booths lined the walls and chairs dominated the centers. This was where the poorest passengers rode out the trip.

Fake walls separated eating areas from viewing areas. Large portholes that ran the length of the deck reflected the stars and the darkness of the ocean. Diate had never been on a ship. He had traveled between islands on the Kingdom's only shuttle. The darkness extending forever fascinated him.

'You do not realize until you come here how very small we are,' Sehan said. 'And how very small our problems. The world has a place for all of us. If the Kingdom did not know about you, you would be able to find your place.'

A few passengers sat in the booths near the walls. One young man had a large duffel bag tucked under his head like a pillow. His feet hung off the edge of the booth. A woman worked behind a counter, her hair tucked under a hat. Near her, four people sat at a table, talking and laughing. They had clear glasses filled with an amber liquid that Diate had never seen before. As he and Sehan passed beside them, Diate's legs wobbled. The area smelled of stale food, old grease, and spices.

He had never been so hungry in his life.

Sehan clasped his shoulder, keeping Diate upright. 'We will take you to a better place,' he said.

They walked around the kitchen to an elevator. Sehan pressed a button and a small light went on. Diate gaped at his surroundings. He had only read about this kind of technology. The Kingdom had little of it. Technology was too expensive and the Kingdom only cared about imports they could resell. The Vorgellians said the Kingdom members lived in primitive conditions. But the Talents and Traders studied everything from technology to languages, so that they could thrive on other islands. Diate had never learned

8

Vorgellian. His sister had. They figured, between the two of them they could learn every language in the world.

He had never expected to be alone.

The light went off, and the doors swung open, revealing a box-like room. Sehan stepped in and Diate did the same. The little room was hot. Sehan pressed another button on the control panel, and the doors swung shut. The elevator rose. Diate's already precarious balance failed him, and he stumbled against the railing lining the walls.

'The body does not like to be cramped in such a small place,' Sehan said with a smile.

Diate did not smile back. 'Why are you being so nice to me?'

Sehan's smile faded. He clasped his hands behind his back. 'In all the years my people have serviced the Kingdom, we have never had a stowaway. Many have tried, and all have failed to board. Except for you. You are smart. You knew how to avoid security, pass the sensors, and where to hide.'

Diate thought for a moment about what Sehan said. Respect. Sehan was talking about respect. And he admired Diate – not just Diate's dance.

'Can you help me get away from the Kingdom? They'll kill me, you know.'

Sehan did not look at him. 'I will do as I can.'

The elevator stopped and Diate stumbled again. No amount of study could prepare him for the odd feelings that accompanied the new technologies. The doors slid open, and Diate had to use the railing to get his balance before following Sehan out.

They stepped into a corridor. It took a minute for him to compare the physical area with the map he had memorized. He was on the fourth deck where his sister would have performed, if she had lived.

The air was cooler here, and smelled of processing. The walls were white. The dark blue carpet was thick and plush, and the people who passed them were Vorgellian, but not in uniform. As Diate and Sehan walked down the corridor, they passed doors but no passengers.

His stomach growled, noticing the smell of roast beef before his mind did. The smell grew stronger as they walked forward. They went up four stairs to an open area filled with fake plants and wood benches. The restaurant. The one his sister had said convinced her to join the ship.

9

The room had the same open view of the night sky as the main deck, only the layout here accentuated the sight. Four steps down led into a dining area filled with clear tables and chairs. The dishes were clear also, as were the sideboards and the work surfaces. Everything reflected the starry darkness. The people and the food itself were the only solid things in the room.

In the daylight, the restaurant would be light and airy. It would capture the warmth of the sun and the pale blue of the ocean. His sister had said this restaurant was the most beautiful place she had ever seen.

Diate liked the smells better. The roast beef dominated, because it steamed on a plate near the door. But Diate also caught the odors of sautéed onions, mild spices, and Erani coddles. His mouth filled with water, and it took all of his restraint to remain beside Sehan.

Music flowed in the background, soft enough to hide under human speech. The notes were delicate – an ancient harp, Diate guessed, and looked for the source of the sound. A minor Talent sat on a raised platform behind the roast beef, plucking at a harp almost twice her size. Minor Talents thrived on cruise ships. They had captive audiences, and received a living wage for their work. Kara would have danced here, even though their father wanted to stop her. She would have been confined to cruise ships for the rest of her life, making little money and having no family. And she had been willing to do that, to dance.

A wave of dizziness passed through him. Sehan touched Diate's arm, to steady him and to lead him to a table. They sat in a corner away from the beef and the harpist.

The chairs were light, and had the smoothness of plastic. A waiter followed them, and Sehan ordered in Vorgellian. 'I have ordered a little of many bland things,' he said. 'The stomach does not like food after it has been starved. You must reaccustom yourself slowly.'

Diate believed his stomach wanted as much food as it could get. But he didn't complain as the waiter set down a dish covered with rice. The rice had a slight spice to it, and was the most delicious meal Diate had ever eaten.

He felt someone walk up behind him. Sehan's gaze moved up, and Diate turned. The woman wore a flowing silver gown, with bell-like sleeves. The gown covered her feet and made her look as if she were floating. Her hair matched the gown, and she had a small silver caste mark on the bridge of her nose. The magician. The one who had found him, probably.

'He's not as ferocious as I thought he would be,' the magician said.

Sehan sighed. 'Sit down, Torrie.'

She slid over a chair and perched on its edge like a small china doll. 'He was in the Lower A Deck, Storage Compartment D.'

'You have spoken to Lanu,' Sehan said.

'Of course,' Torrie said. She still had not looked directly at Diate. 'But I have unnerved you, haven't I?'

'There are many things in this life that we can not see,' Sehan said.

The waiter whisked away Diate's empty plate and brought him another, filled with a white gruel. He also set a plate filled with bright greens in front of Sehan.

'You need a magician aboard this ship,' Torrie said.

Diate stopped eating for a moment. 'As a full Talent, you're volunteering?' He couldn't block his question, even though he knew he shouldn't speak. Her actions were unheard of. Full Talents had no need to serve in places like a cruise ship. They were in demand everywhere they went.

'See?' Torrie said, without facing Diate. 'I told you he is a smart child.'

'I am surprised at you, Torrie,' Sehan said. 'I would think the boy is someone who can help your fight. I thought you admired his father.'

'His father is dead.'

'Ideals live on.'

'With coaxing.'

Diate felt as if he could leave the table and no one would miss him. He scraped the last bite of gruel from his dish, surprised to find himself full. The waiter, as if he knew, took the dish away, but did not bring another.

'The boy has a good point.' Sehan leaned forward, ignoring his greens. 'Why would a full Talent want to serve on my ship?'

'I was not asking for myself,' she said. 'I know of minor Talents who could serve you well.'

'I see,' Sehan said. 'You wish to test magicians on my ship, and if the test works, you will try to link more magicians with navigation.'

11

'I do believe you owe me a favor. You would never have found the boy without me.' She stood and nodded to him. 'I'll leave you to your dinner now.'

Sehan watched her walk away. 'I like it better,' he said, 'when she does me no favors at all.'

Sehan gave Diate a cabin on the lowest deck, with the new crew members. Diate had stood at the door for a long time, remembering the layout. An elevator down the corridor led to the upper decks. He was as far from the captain and the valued passengers as he could be.

The cabin was small, but seemed roomy after the storage compartment. The walls were white, without portholes. A regulation issue bed stood in the center, flanked by two tables. A door leading to a small bathroom opened on the left, and inexpertly done portraits hung on the walls. Diate didn't like all the poorly painted eyes staring at him. He reached up to take one of the paintings down, but found he couldn't dislodge it.

He sat on the edge of the bed and sighed.

The dizziness had faded, replaced by an overwhelming headache. He had to stretch his muscles, then sleep. Sehan promised him food, but decided that it was probably best if Diate did not leave the cabin again. The request seemed odd for Sehan, who had been kind before the magician turned up. Now he acted as if Diate posed a danger to the rest of the ship. He would receive his meals at regular intervals, and Sehan would provide books, if Diate preferred.

He wanted fiction books, which he doubted he would get on a Vorgellian ship. He asked for nothing, just in case they surprised him. He didn't want to lose himself in a fantasy if he only had a few days to live. He needed to spend all of his waking hours on planning an escape.

The fact that he had survived this long was a small miracle. The Kingdom's security guards were ruthless and they had been searching for him. He had slipped through the gates at the port by walking at another man's side as if that man were his father. By comparison, getting on the ship had been easy – he waited until the Vorgellian maintenance people took their break, and then walked in the open hatch and ran to the storerooms.

He wished he could thank Kara. The game they had played as he helped her memorize parts of the ship – *And where could a slim dancer hide? he had asked. Lower A Deck, Storage compartment D, she had answered* – had given him a complete knowledge of the cruiser. The only thing he hadn't counted on was a Kingdom member with enough authority to override Vorgellian custom. He had expected, if he had been found, to be sent on a slaver or to work as an indentured servant – anything to keep him away from the Kingdom itself.

But his luck had only stretched so far. He couldn't face the Queen. Not after what she had done. Even if she were civil to him, he would want to kill her. When he closed his eyes, he saw his family in their death tableau. He couldn't even remember the sound of his sister's laughter –

The door slid open and Lanu, the Kingdom member who had found him, stood there. Her arms were crossed over her ruffled shirt.

'Much better than a storage compartment, isn't it, boy?'

Diate didn't say anything. His mouth had gone dry. He didn't want her anywhere near him. His aching muscles tensed.

She came in and let the door swing shut behind her. 'The cruise ship will stop on Rulanda. You and I will get off there, and take a freighter back to the Kingdom. The Queen wants to see you herself.'

'Is she going to kill me?' Diate couldn't stop the words from leaving his mouth. He wasn't sure if he wanted to know the answer.

'She won't let you dance, at least not as a Talent. She won't be able to trust you to travel. And if you can't be a Talent, what's the point of living?'

Diate had never seen anyone with eyes as cold as Lanu's. They chilled him. He made himself sit still, even though he wanted to back as far away from her as he could.

'Well, now that we know what's going to happen,' he said, trying not to let fear into his voice, 'you can leave me alone.'

'Be nice to me, boy,' she said, 'because I hold your future.'

'Hold it?' He dug his fingers tightly into the bed. The blanket scratched his palms. 'You've already decided it. Sehan would give me a second chance. Why won't you?'

She smiled, but the movement didn't warm her eyes. 'Sehan is sentimental. I am not. Your kind of courage doesn't impress me, especially when you could have saved your entire family a long time ago. Or don't you remember?'

Diate remembered. He had thought about it ever since the coppery scent hit him near his home. The Queen had made him an offer. If he stopped his father from speaking out, she would give Diate the best post in the industry. His family would have to separate, of course, and vow never to see each other again, so that they would not contaminate each other. But she considered that a small price to pay for the rewards both Diate and the Kingdom would receive.

Diate didn't want his family to separate. They were wonderful together. And his father was harmless.

Or so he had thought.

Lanu smiled, just a little. For the second time that day, he felt as if someone could read his mind. 'You see,' she said. 'You could have prevented it all.'

A shiver started inside his stomach that took all of his dancer's strength to control. 'Why do you hate me so much?'

She stared at him for a moment, and her smile faded. Then she leaned back against the door. 'I am not a Talent,' she said. 'I have had to work for everything I have, and I will never rise above my station. You could have had it all, boy. For nothing. And you chose to throw it all away for a little bit of loyalty, a little bit of love, things that would not matter to you ten years down the road. I am not fond of Talents, boy. I am even less fond of Talents who give up everything on a whim.'

Diate's hands dug deeper in the bed. 'What happened to my family was not a whim.'

'Wasn't it?' she asked. 'Your father didn't think of any of you. He only thought of himself, and his own glory. And you, you fell for it all.'

The shiver had traveled through all his muscles. Small spasms played a random pattern across his back. 'You hate me because you think I was stupid.'

Her smile returned. 'Exactly,' she said, and let herself out of the room.

The door slammed shut behind her, and Diate released the rigid control with which he held himself. Shakes and tremors ran through him. The spasms in his back traveled to his chest and arms. He flopped on the bed, and felt the rough blanket against his skin.

14

He hadn't been stupid. He hadn't.

Even though he might have been able to save them.

He should have asked them. It was their choice, not his. And he hadn't said a word.

They wouldn't have wanted him to save them. The cost would have been too great.

The cost was greater than any he ever would have dreamed of.

They would have hated him, but they would have been alive.

They would have been alive.

A hand over his mouth pulled him out of a sound sleep. He pushed and thrashed, choking. The blanket wrapped around his legs. The room was dark – so dark that he could see nothing, not even the person who held him in place. The hand over his mouth smelled of leather, a scent that made him think of home. He didn't like to have the comforting smell associated with such terror.

They were going to kill him here. Quicky and violently, like they had killed his family. And they wouldn't even give him the opportunity to beg for his life.

Another hand clamped his shoulder and a long body leaned against him, pinning him to the bed.

'Quiet. It is me.' Sehan's flat, odd accent.

Diate stopped struggling. His heart was pounding against his chest. Sehan wouldn't kill him. Sehan had promised to help him.

'Do not move. Just listen. In fifteen minutes, the shuttle will leave this ship for Golga. It will land in the Port City to deliver some wine we picked up yesterday. I will leave your door open. If you can find your way to the shuttle, then you will have a chance. They hate the Kingdom in Golga, but if you get through and cover that caste mark, you might be okay. It is the best I can do for you. It is all I can do for you. If you get caught, I will deny any knowledge of this. Do you understand?'

Diate swallowed. His throat was dry. He nodded once.

'Good. I will leave. You must count to thirty before you stand up. That way we will not be seen together.' Sehan released Diate. 'Good luck.'

Diate took a deep breath. His mouth hurt from the pressure of Sehan's hand. Sehan slid through the door and left it open. Light from the corridor flooded the room, giving the furniture a gray, almost invisible quality. Diate counted, and did his warm-up stretches. Fifteen minutes was barely enough time to make it to the shuttle bays. Sehan did not make it easy for him.

When he reached thirty, Diate went to the door, and looked both ways. The corridor was empty. A few yards away was a core stairway for staff members. He remembered it from the map he had memorized. He was afraid to try the doors, afraid to wake someone up. But he had never used an elevator, and didn't want to try with time so short.

Finally he passed a door in the right position. He turned the knob and shoved the door open. It revealed a platform that led to a ladder hidden in a small, circular shaft. Warm air rose, fueled by an invisible breeze. The shaft smelled of oil and plastic. Diate walked to the edge, gripped the ladder, and started up.

He played a march tune in his head, moving his feet and hands in time to the music. The march would keep his movements constant. If he hurried, he had more opportunities to hurt himself, to slip or miss a rung. He tried not to think of the time deadline, but it insinuated itself into the tune in his head.

Step.

Step.

Another minute.

Step.

Step.

Out of time.

The tune repeated itself three times before he reached the top. He yanked open the door on the main level, and found himself in a shuttle bay, like the one the Queen used near her palace in the Kingdom's only city, Tersis. This bay had no windows, only large oversized doors that blocked his entry to the flight deck. Two shuttles were directly in front of him. The third sat in the distance.

Only one had its running lights on, and he hurried over there, as a large bang echoed in the room.

The shuttle's door was open. The pilot reached out and yanked Diate aboard.

'Thought you weren't going to make it, kid,' the pilot said.

She pressed the control and the door slid shut. Through the windshield, Diate saw the bay doors rising, revealing the darkness beyond. His heart continued its panicked rhythm. What would have happened to him if the doors had opened when he was outside the shuttle?

The pilot resumed her seat. She was half his size with delicate hands and ebony skin. Her blue, almond-shaped eyes marked her as Vorgellian.

Of course. Only Vorgellians knew how to operate the shuttles.

'Sit down and strap in,' she said.

Diate took the seat behind her and looked for a strap. Finally she reached around and pressed a lever. Two heavy bands of cloth bound his lap and chest, leaving his hands free.

'We got a few hours,' she said. 'So try to relax.'

Relax? How could he relax? He could barely control his breathing. He had escaped the Kingdom twice in one week. And each time, he had gone somewhere worse. He had heard stories of Golga. The Golgoth enjoyed executions. People said the Golgoth laughed while Kingdom members burned alive.

Diate shut his eyes. Sehan believed Diate could pass. Diate hoped Sehan was right.

Chapter 2

Diate's first view of Golga came through the windshield of the shuttle. Dawn had broken over the ocean. They were high enough that Diate saw dozens of small islands dotting the choppy water, their long black shadows stretching out in the distance. Some of the islands were merely oversized rocks. Others were large enough to support settlements, although most did not.

The number of islands grew as they got closer to Golga. The shuttle had backtracked the ship's passage, flying over the Kingdom just before the sun had risen over the horizon. Diate was glad. He didn't want to see the trees and the low hills from the air. He especially didn't want to see Tersis and the shining towers of the palace reflecting the sun.

The shuttle's mechanical hum made conversation difficult. That was fine with Diate. He needed to watch, and think, and absorb.

An island twice the size of any he had ever seen appeared before the shuttle. It had true mountains, large and gray, touched with jagged white caps that he assumed were snow-covered. For a moment, he thought that was all he would see, then the shuttle flew over them, and the mountains tapered down into a lush greenness.

No trees graced the surface. Only measured plots outlined by brown lines he assumed to be roads. An occasional tiny building stood on the plots. As the shuttle dipped lower, Diate saw a rail line and a huge electric plant.

Diate clasped his hands together. The bucolic vision did not soothe him. Instead, the fear he had been fighting almost strangled him. Golga and the Kingdom had been enemies for over a century. They did not battle in the traditional sense. They interrupted each other's trade, spied on each other's businesses, and made plans for overthrowing each other's governments. Defectors were killed.

Nothing is ever easy, Myla had told him when he complained that a dance move was too hard. *Everything in life will give you a trial.*

The shuttle banked and left the electric plant behind them. The roads got wider, and from the side window, he could see an electric railcar chugging below. It looked like one of his brother's toys.

People did live down there. People who killed Kingdom members.

He glanced around the shuttle, wondering how he could have felt safe here, even briefly. He sat in the seat beside the pilot. Behind them, rows and rows of boxes were stacked tightly together. The cabin smelled faintly of wine. He had seen other shuttles. This one was tiny compared to them.

Yet the pilot expected him to hide when they landed. He saw nowhere to go.

They banked again. As the shuttle lowered, the mechanical hum grew. He kept his gaze focused on the windshield. A large, gray city rose before him. Towers stood in the distance, flanked by the ocean. Golga was an island, but it was a large island. On this side, no mountains blocked the natural port. He had seen pictures of Golga's harbor, which was, in fact, a large inlet, twice the size of any other harbor on the settled islands. On the far sides of the inlet, the mountains tapered down into small hills that disappeared into the water.

The city seemed to go on forever. As the shuttle lowered, he saw row after row of matching homes. The homes got smaller as they got closer together, until they became two-story buildings with balconies. Apartment buildings. He had heard of them, but never seen them.

In the center of the city, four tall rectangular buildings stood around a wide expanse of green. On the other side of the grass and trees stood an even taller building, which looked from the sky like an oversized skull. The Golgoth's palace. Diate had seen pictures of that too.

If he wasn't careful, he would die there.

They flew over the palace. Diate's knuckles turned white as he pressed his hands even tighter together. Finally, he could see the harbor. It was filled with ships of all shapes and sizes. Large port buildings blocked entry to the water itself. And to one side, various oddly shaped buildings stood behind a large fence.

The pilot pulled up the wire that had been dangling below her chin. A small black rectangle fit in front of her mouth. She pushed a button on the console, then spoke into the rectangle. She wasn't talking to Diate.

He had heard of such communications devices, ones that allowed the words to travel great distances, but had never seen them. He stared at her for a moment, then turned his attention back to the window.

The shuttle flew over a flat open surface tucked between the edge of the coastal mountains and the open harbor. As they got closer, Diate saw the familiar gleaming metal of a Vorgellian structure. Even the Golgans bought their technology from the Vorgellians. Diate had always thought the Golgans could do anything.

'I thought this was a rich place,' he said.

The pilot laughed. She put her hand over the mouthpiece. 'It is,' she said. 'They just don't believe in beauty.'

The shuttle lowered until it hovered above the concrete expanse. The bay doors were sliding open. Diate's throat tightened. He didn't even speak the language here, and he had left all of his possessions on the Vorgellian ship.

He had no plan. How would he survive with no plan?

'I cannot acknowledge you once we land,' the pilot said. She had to shout above the noise. 'I will deliver my wine and leave the doors open. You must get out yourself, and not be seen. There are guards, but they usually pay more attention to the shipments. Wait a few minutes, and then get out. Their attention should be on me at that point.'

Diate nodded. He was trying to make himself breathe easily. He had made a mistake coming here. He should have tried to talk Sehan into sending him away as a prisoner of the Vorgellians. Or sneaking him to Rulanda. At least on Rulanda, there were other Kingdom members, Talents who might have helped him out. On Golga, he would be alone, and an enemy of the state.

He didn't even have any money.

The pilot eased the shuttle into large bay doors and it bumped to a stop. Diate clung to his belts for reassurance. He had experienced rougher landings, but had always known what would happen once he landed.

The interior of the bay was dark. It took his eyes a moment to adjust. He saw doors on the far walls, and tools hanging from pegs all around. Stairs led to observation decks.

20

The pilot pressed a few buttons, pulled off her headset, and then turned. 'Get away from the window.' Her voice was sharp, as if she couldn't believe that he had failed to do it. 'And stay down.'

Diate unbelted himself. He crawled into the back between the boxes. They were stamped in a language he couldn't read. Through small holes in the box sides, he could see wine bottles, their contents sloshing. The pilot eased the doors open, and voices, speaking in a guttural language he had never heard, echoed in what sounded like a large chamber. Footsteps rang on metal. The pilot stepped down, speaking the guttural language as fluently as she had spoken Lillish.

If they were going to remove the boxes, he had to get out quickly.

A door clanged open behind him, then he felt the shuttle shake as boxes were removed through the rear doors. He was trembling. It was only a matter of time before they found him.

The pilot had left the front door open. He crawled to it, and peered out.

The shuttle bay lacked the sparkle of the bay on the cruise ship. Odors of grease and spent fuel tickled his nose. The metal walls were rippled and tarnished. Stains and streak marks marked the gray metal floor. Iron stairs on the far wall led to a row of windows near the ceiling, The windows were too far away to give him a view of their interior. Somone could be watching him from above.

That was a risk he had to take. The voices sounded far away, and he only had a few minutes. He stepped out, staying close to the shuttle, then rounded in front of it.

A group of people, including the pilot, huddled in a corner, arguing over a pile of boxes. The rest of the bay looked empty. Behind the shuttle stood the big bay doors, and to the front, a series of smaller doors that probably led outside. He had to choose, and quickly. If he ran to the bay doors, he would have to pass the knot of people. If he ran around front, he would be in better view of the windows.

For all he knew, no one stood behind those windows. And people were on his path to the bay doors. He took a deep breath, and pushed off the shuttle, running with large dancing leaps, landing as quietly as he could, so that no one would hear him on the metal floor.

Two guards came down the iron stairs near the double doors, their boots clanging on the metal. Diate's heart jumped into his throat. He turned to run the other way, but more guards poured out of side doors. The sound of their marching feet echoed in the large room, and the group in the back corner turned to see what was going on.

Diate had nowhere to go.

But that wasn't going to stop him.

He turned back to the front, and ran as fast as he could. He could get past two guards. He was quick and agile and young. They weren't as young or as well trained. He could get around them and onto the street. Once on the street, he would be safe.

A blaze of heat seared across his right foot, and he jumped, breaking stride. The guard in front of him held a weapon in his right hand. He fired another shot that seared the floor next to Diate's other foot.

Diate stopped. He couldn't go around. They would kill him.

He was breathing heavily, even though he hadn't run that far. His pulse pounded through his body. This was it, then. There was nothing he could do. Maybe he could talk his way out of this. Maybe he could get the pilot to take him back.

The two main guards walked over to him, still holding their weapons on him. He didn't move. Their uniforms were black with silver trim, their faces pasty from lack of light. They were both young, but not as young as he was. Already their faces had deep lines etching their frowns in place. They smelled faintly of sweat and fear.

He didn't like the scent of fear.

The shorter guard reached Diate first. With one gloved hand, he pushed Diate's hair away from his face. Diate refused to flinch at the feel of warm leather against his skin.

'Talent,' the guard said with surprise. His Lillish was heavily accented.

'Stowing away?' the other asked.

The pilot walked over, surrounded by other guards. They kept grabbing her arms, and she kept shaking them off. She spoke sharply in the guttural language Diate had heard earlier.

The first guard answered in the same language.

She looked at Diate, eyes widening as if she were seeing him for the first time. She spoke again, and then said in Lillish, 'You are a Talent.'

'Yes, ma'am.'

She shook her head as she addressed the guard.

The guard shrugged. He pointed to the main door of the cabin, his words clipped.

The pilot's voice rose as she spoke. She kept glancing at Diate as if she couldn't believe he was there.

The guard took a step closer. He spoke so sharply that spittle flew from his mouth. The pilot turned away. Her face had gone white. She kept gesturing at the shuttle and shaking her head.

The guard took her arm. She wrenched free and walked over to her shuttle. She peered inside, and whistled.

Diate hadn't moved. Myla had taught him that the ability to remain still was as important as the ability to move. He barely breathed.

The pilot pointed to the back of the cabin. Her voice had become strident. She turned to Diate. In Lillish, she said, 'Who do you think you are? This is my ship. You had no right to be on it. I will see to it that you are turned over to the Vorgellians. They will make a slaver out of you!'

A tremble ran through him. If he hadn't heard her plan his escape, he too would have been fooled by her act.

The guard gave an order in a language Diate had never heard before. Other guards grabbed the pilot by the arms. She tried to shake free, but they held her too tightly. They led her toward the stairs. She struggled the entire way.

She wouldn't be able to help him. He was on his own.

The guard turned to Diate and said in Lillish, 'What does a Talent want on Golga?'

Diate met that gaze, and saw no sympathy in it. He couldn't run, and he couldn't go back. He had only one choice. 'Asylum.'

'Asylum?' The word managed to shake through the guard's calmness. Never in the history of the two countries had a member of the Kingdom sought asylum from Golga.

'I want to defect.' Diate made sure his words were loud enough for everyone in the room to hear. He wanted witnesses. He wanted as many witnesses as he could get.

'Let's take him to Scio,' the second guard said.

'We can't.' The first's frown had grown deeper. 'Cases of asylum have to go before the Golgoth.'

The cell stank of urine. Diate didn't want to touch the floor or walls for fear that something would contaminate him. A mattress, tossed in the corner, was the source of the smell. He stood near the bars, staring at the window cut into the wall high above his reach. The window was one square foot, and sent in pale yellow light that bathed everything in soft grays.

The guards had brought him here in a protected car on the electric rail system. The system was old and gave off sparks. The seats were worn and the floor scuffed. Diate had sat at the edge of his chair. Outside, the sky was overcast, and the buildings looked even darker than they had from the air. He had never been to such a dismal place.

The train had stopped behind the palace, and the guards had brought him into one of those buildings around the park. They had led him down a flight of stairs and into a cell without even telling anyone he was there.

He could rot here, and no one would know.

But, before they slammed the heavy oak door, they had promised him a meeting with the Golgoth. They said to prepare, that the Golgoth would see him in the next few hours.

Diate paced. All of the hope, all of the chances, had come to this. A meeting with the Golgoth, with the ruler of this godforsaken country. The self-declared enemy of Diate's place of birth. No Kingdom member had ever requested asylum here because every Kingdom member knew the Golgoth would never grant it.

Although they had surprised him already. The pilot, whom he had expected them to kill, had left the island. They had taken away her license – she could never return to Golga and they had fined her – but she still had her life and her career.

Diate leaned his head against the cold metal. Had Sehan known this was going to happen? Was that why he was willing to entrust Diate's life to one of his main shuttle pilots, because Golga would not kill her if they caught her? Was Golga less rigid than the Kingdom? He didn't believe it.

They hadn't fed him, and the hunger was back, gnawing at him. One bland meal was not enough to sustain him. Maybe he should raise a fuss, demand water, demand gruel, demand anything. They were going to kill him anyway. Why did he have to sit still for this?

Footsteps sounded in the outside hall, then he heard a key turn in the lock. The door swung open, and four guards faced Diate.

These were not the men who had captured him. These men had no expressions on their faces. They were slender and lean, and each movement spoke of their great physical strength.

'The Golgoth will see you now.'

Diate nodded. So it began – or ended. Either way, he would go down fighting. He would make his requests, and he would not be meek. He had nothing left to lose.

One guard held him while the other used a thin rope to tie Diate's hands behind his back. The rope was so tight it cut off the circulation to Diate's hands. Two guards gripped Diate tightly, while two others trained their weapons on him. All the precautions against escape. As if Diate had somewhere to escape to.

They led him out of his cell and through the oak door. In the corridor, the lighting was bright. Diate blinked, nearly blinded by the change. The smells faded, leaving an echo in his nostrils and on his clothes. He wondered how he looked, and thought he could guess: a thin, dirty boy with a young man's growth, blood still caked on his arms and shoes, clothes tattered from a week on the run. Certainly not the kind of person the Golgoth was used to meeting.

They turned and went down a narrow corridor tiled in white. At the end of the corridor, an open door revealed another, twistier corridor with stairs at the end. They climbed the stairs, Diate's legs shaking beneath him. The dizziness hadn't returned, but a weakness that felt like reluctance made each step difficult. The guard yanked Diate forward as if he were an animal, and he stumbled. The other guard grabbed his elbow and propelled him up the remaining steps.

At the top, another door swung open, sending in the scents of perfumed candle wax. Each tile in this corridor had been painted in an alternating black or white pattern. Ceramic skulls, spaced about two feet apart and shoulder high, lined the corridor. Inside each skull a candle burned.

Even though the corridor was hot, a chill ran down Diate's back. The guards pulled him forward until they reached double doors painted black. Two more guards with ceremonial spears stood outside.

'The Talent to see the Golgoth,' one of Diate's guards said.

One of the ceremonial guards pulled on an ornate red rope that hung beside the doors. The doors swung inward, revealing a large black room with more skull candles and guards standing along the walls. On the dais in the back of the room, under a pool of light, stood a white throne. Skulls decorated the handrests and the feet, as well as the posts at the top, and as Diate walked closer, he could see more skulls carved into the throne itself.

A guard kicked Diate's feet from under him, and he sprawled forward, skinning his arms and legs. He remained on his stomach, gasping for air, shuddering at the pain that ran through him.

A voice, deep and commanding, spoke first in a guttural language he had heard in the port, and then in Lillish. 'Let him stand.'

Diate didn't look up. Hands gripped him, but he shook them off. He waited until his breath was even before he struggled to his knees. A bald man wearing a black robe stood in front of the throne. White skulls decorated the robe in almost a checked pattern. The man's bony face looked like a skull itself.

The man was staring at him. Diate stared back.

A guard hit Diate's shoulder hard enough to make him lean forward. 'Show the Golgoth some respect.'

The man – the Golgoth – continued to watch Diate. Diate ignored the guard and rocked back on his toes, then in a fluid motion, stood up.

'A Kingdom member has never come before me seeking asylum. What do you really want, boy?'

'I don't want to speak in front of them.' Diate indicated his jailers with a shrug of the shoulder.

'I won't dismiss all of my guards.'

'You don't have to. Just dismiss these four.'

The Golgoth looked over Diate and nodded at the men. Diate didn't turn as they walked out. Instead, he watched a side door open, and a boy younger than he came in. The boy had bright red hair that curled around his ears, and a robe that matched the Golgoth's. The boy's face had the same bony potential, the same fierce, almost skull-like appearance. The boy stopped just behind the Golgoth.

The boy spoke in the guttural language.

The Golgoth nodded.

The boy walked around Diate, wrinkling his nose in distaste, then asked a question.

The Golgoth responded, then took one step closer to Diate.

26

'My son wants to know what you want,' the Golgoth said in Lillish.

Diate couldn't look at the boy. He could only look at the man, the one with the power to decide his fate.

'I want asylum.' He made sure that his voice was strong.

'I don't grant asylum to Kingdom members, especially not Talents.'

'I am no longer a Talent.'

A slight smile played across the Golgoth's lips, adding to his skull-like appearance. 'Then what do you bring us?'

Bring them? Diate had arrived with nothing. If he had had anything, he would have tried to bribe his way free hours ago. 'I can dance,' he said.

The Golgoth's smile grew wider. 'Dancing is a frivolity that we do not allow here. I only grant asylum to people who provide me some kind of exchange.'

Exchange. Diate understood the currency of exchange. But all he had was himself. Himself, and his knowledge. He swallowed heavily. All those conversations. All the times the Queen and her people had sworn the Talents to secrecy. All the dinners that Talents attended while no other Kingdom members could.

'I was a Talent,' he said, 'and a friend of the Queen's. I can tell you everything I know about her, and her parties, and the way that the Kingdom works.'

The Golgoth's smile faded. Some of the candles flickered. But no one moved. 'How do I know that she didn't send you herself to feed me information, the wrong kind of information?'

'Because she murdered my family!' The words left him before he could stop them. His voice cracked on the third word and he had to blink hard to prevent tears from following. He would not break down in front of this man. He would not.

'Really?' The Golgoth took a step back up and sat on the throne, hands clasped in his lap. 'What is your name, boy?'

'Diate. Emilio Diate.'

'The rebel poet's son?'

Diate couldn't hide the surprise on his face.

'Not all of the Kingdom is a mystery,' the Golgoth said. 'We hear things from time to time.' He leaned back and gripped the skulls between his huge hands. 'And so you come here, to continue your father's rebellion.'

'No,' Diate said. 'I came here because I have nowhere else to go.

And I haven't thought about my father's rebellion. I've just been trying to stay alive.'

'They're trying to kill you too? A Talent?'

'There has been some talk of that, sir, among the Vorgellians. It seems that they all received information from the Kingdom about a renegade Talent who was to be returned to the Kingdom for assassination.' A man Diate had not noticed before stepped out of the shadows behind the throne. He was small and wiry with tonsured hair covering a rounded scalp. He spoke Lillish like a native.

The Golgoth replied in the harsh, guttural language he had used before. Then the boy spoke up in a piping voice, and the other man laughed. The Golgoth shook his head and turned his attention back to Diate.

'You want asylum from us, Emilio Diate?'

'Yes.' Diate swallowed the hope rising within him. They could be toying with him, just before they killed him.

'Then you must renounce the Kingdom. You must abandon your Talent, grow your hair over the caste mark, and never dance again. You must publicly decry them, and declare yourself a member of Golga. You will learn our language and train in whatever profession I choose for you. You will tell me everything you know about your former homeland. And you must never have any contact with any member of the Kingdom again. Will you do those things?'

Diate thought of his home, his father's body scattered along the path, his sister sprawled on the porch. The stink of blood. The Queen's painted teeth as she laughed. He had never lived without the dance.

The Golgoth's son spoke, then laughed. He peered in Diate's face and shook his head. Diate got the message. The boy expected him to say no.

'Why can't I dance?' Diate asked.

'Because it is frivolous,' the Golgoth said. 'We don't believe in frivolity here.'

'But dance is all I know how to do.'

'Then you will learn something else.'

Diate took a deep breath. Dance was part of the world he had left behind. Dance had no place here. Whenever he danced, he would think of the Kingdom, of the blood, of the Queen's empty laughter. 'I'll learn anything you teach me.'

The Golgoth smiled. Then he clapped his hands. 'Now, get him out of here, clean him up, and take him to my palace.'

Two new guards flanked Diate.

The Golgoth's son stopped laughing. He gaped at his father, then spoke rapidly. The man with the tonsured hair added his voice to the boy's. They didn't like the Golgoth's plan. Diate waited, not even daring to swallow.

The Golgoth smiled and shrugged. He glanced at Diate. 'They don't think I know what I'm doing. But I do. You must trust me, Scio.'

Scio, the man with the tonsure, frowned. He backed into his place in the shadows. The Golgoth stared at Diate. 'You will be my protégé, Emilio Diate?'

A wild, kind of crazy joy filled Diate. He was alive. He would remain alive. The Kingdom would never threaten him again. 'For you, Sire,' he said, 'I will be anything.'

PART TWO

Fifteen Years Later

Chapter 3

Step, lift, step, step. Diate watched himself in the mirror. Sweat poured down his chest and back, coating his thin cotton shirt and shorts. Step, lift, step, step. His bare feet were cold on the wood floor. The muscles rippled along his biceps as his arms moved in time to the imaginary music playing in his head. Step, lift, step, step.

The small exercise room was quiet, except for the whisper of his movements. Mirrors reflected him on three sides, with a wooden barre running at waist height. A closed door led to the hallway, and another to the larger gymnasium.

He finished the cool-down and walked over to the barre, placing his left foot on it and stretching. After all these years, his form was still perfect. But his body had matured from a fifteen-year-old boy's grace to a thirty-year-old's precision. Some of the movements had grown more difficult, and he pulled more muscles now. But he was the strongest man on the force, and others had asked to learn his exercise routine. He would smile at them and ask them to join him for a week. They usually made it through a session and a half before begging out.

When he finished with the left leg, he put it down and rested a moment. Then he brought the right leg up on the barre and leaned into it. He could feel the stretch in his achilles tendon, and along the back of the leg. The muscles in his sides and back bulged as he twisted to reach for his toes.

They had not seen dance on Golga in three generations. The Golgoth had never guessed that Diate's strange exercise routine was the dance he had once performed before the Kingdom's Queen.

The exercise room door banged open. Strega entered. He was a slim and muscular young detective, with a continual perplexed look. When Strega saw Diate, he stopped.

'I'm sorry, Sir,' he said. 'I didn't mean to interrupt you.'

33

'You haven't.' Diate finished his last stretch, then grabbed his towel off the barre. His exercise routine so intimidated the other detectives that they usually avoided him while he did it. They also avoided the exercise room because of the mirrors and barre he had added. Few people liked to watch themselves while they exercised, although he knew it would be good for their form.

'I, uh, hope you don't mind if I use the room.' Strega's hand played nervously with his towel.

Diate wiped the sweat off his face. 'It's not private.'

'No, sir, that's right.'

Diate stopped drying himself off and leaned back against the barre. Strega was acting too guilty. 'What are you doing here, Strega?'

'I, uh, I've been watching you work out, sir. I thought I would practice on my own before I tried working with you.'

Diate smiled. 'If you can learn this routine on your own, you're a better man than I am.'

'Sir?'

'I had years of assisted training.'

Strega nodded. 'I have found that I can't do most of the fluid motions, and even the stretches hurt.'

'They're supposed to, in the beginning.' Diate slung the towel over his arm. 'I'll work with you, if you like. But you'll have to do it soon before you get into bad habits.'

'Yes, sir.' Strega said. 'At your convenience, sir.'

Diate ran his gaze the length of the man. Boy, actually. He hadn't yet reached twenty. Diate could work with Strega, if Strega had the right mental attitude. Of all the detectives who had approached him, Strega was the only one who had not approached it like he was making a challenge to Diate's authority. He had approached it like a challenge to himself.

'Tomorrow,' Diate said. 'Before early breakfast. We'll start you with a half an hour. I don't think you can do the full hour right away.'

'Thank you, sir.' Strega's confused expression intensified. He was probably wondering what Diate was doing in the room in the hour before late dinner if he usually exercised in the morning. Diate didn't have the heart to tell him that he usually worked out at least twice a day.

'Just do a lot of stretching today, and familiarize yourself with the barre and the mirror. We'll worry about form tomorrow.'

'Yes, sir.'

Diate smiled at Strega, and received a nervous smile back. Then Diate grabbed his bag and his shoes, and headed for the showers.

The hallway smelled more of stale sweat than the exercise room did. But he rarely went into the main gym, didn't know if the hallway smelled like the large open area where most of the Port City's two hundred detectives worked out. It probably did. He pushed open the shower room door and peeled off his clothes. Then he crossed the sloping concrete floor, past the rusted drains, and took his usual stall in the back.

He turned the hand-adjusted controls, listening to the ancient metal squeak. They had never had the luxury of showers in the Kingdom, although he had heard of the devices as a boy. When he finished his dance, he usually took a dip in the pond near his home, and once a week, used his mother's homemade soap and heated water for a real cleaning. The soaps provided here, milled by a factory miles away, lacked the fresh scent his mother had found.

Water leaked out the nozzle, then followed full force. He stepped under the stream, ignoring the usual temperature shifts from cool to scalding, and back to cool again. Something had made him reflective. He usually didn't think about his boyhood that much. Probably the look on Strega's face when he told Diate he wanted to try the routine – and the memory it brought of the fear Diate had once had of the Golgoth. He believed that the Golgoth would kill him if he found him dancing. But the dancing had given him strength, and the strength had made him a detective. It had taken two years before they found something for Diate to do. He had learned Golgan quickly, although not well enough to take a scholarly profession. The Golgoth had quizzed him extensively about the Kingdom until they had finally exhausted his store of knowledge. But he remained strong, and that strength had helped him get into the detectives and to rise through the ranks. He had become head of the detectives at the age of twenty-three, four years older than the boy who used his exercise room.

Being head of the detectives wasn't enough, though. He wanted to help Scio with the secret police. He had appointed himself as head of the Golgoth's local security, and Scio had complained. Scio believed that Diate would never belong in Golga.

Scio was wrong.

Diate dipped his head under the water, letting it flow into his mouth. Then he spat the water out, lathered his body, and rinsed off. The water had turned cold by the time he shut off the faucets. Off duty at last. The day had been long, and unusually dull. Sometimes, after weeks of this, he would find himself wishing for action, and he would stifle the feeling. That attitude had gotten too many detectives in trouble.

Water dripped behind him. He shook himself off. He felt braced after the brisk shower. He loved the hours before meals here. The gym was nearly empty, and he didn't have to deal with constant questions or the nervous looks from the cadets, who could not understand how a man who walked with the Kingdom's grace and spoke Golgan with a lilting accent could be loyal to the Golgoth.

They would never know what true loyalty felt like, unless someone had given them a second chance at life.

He dried off and slipped into street clothes. His clothing was stark – an odd contrast with his gray uniforms – a form-fitting white shirt gathered at the neck and wrists, and black pants with cuffs that hugged his ankles. Off duty he wore sandals. Shoes hurt his feet even worse than going barefoot did. The bane of a dancer. Constant sore and aching feet.

Laughter in the hallway made him stop. For a moment, he debated leaving – his appearance always halted the free flow of emotions around him – but Beltar and dinner were waiting. He placed his uniform and towel on the wash pile and pushed the door open.

Four cadets were standing in the hall, their light blue uniforms unbuttoned and in a state of disarray. They stood at attention when they saw him, and their hands fluttered as if they could straighten their uniforms before he noticed. 'At ease, gentlemen,' he said, and pushed past them. His footsteps echoed in the hallway. He knew the boys wouldn't move until they could no longer see him. He had never shared that kind of camaraderie. As a cadet, he had not spoken the language well, and by the time he became a first-year detective, he was known of as the Golgoth's boy. No one had wanted to approach him.

A cool breeze, smelling of salt and storms, greeted him as he opened the door. The city grew quiet at twilight. It had taken years, but he had finally learned to see the beauty in this place. The mountains added shadow and mystery, the ocean promised wealth. Storms often paralyzed the city and caused brown-outs, but he had grown to love the wild whipping wind and the pounding rain. The streets emptied during a storm, and the entire city hibernated.

He paused for a moment, surveying the street. Most people had already gone home, and were relaxing after early dinner. A few stragglers hurried out of the government buildings across the park. The gymnasium was attached to the detectives' offices, across the park from the palace.

The concrete was wet and the grass looked marshy. The storm he smelled had already passed. He hadn't even heard it while he was working out. He sighed, and turned his back on the park, heading toward the merchant's district, and dinner.

Most nights, he dined with his closest friend – his only friend besides the Golgoth – a wine merchant named Beltar. They had met during a smuggling case five years back. Beltar had been finding inferior wine among his stock, and had asked the detectives to locate the source of the problem. It had taken them nearly a week to discover that one of the pilots on the shuttle route had taken to switching cases and selling Beltar's more expensive wine for even higher prices on Rulanda.

Twilight had shaded the buildings a deep gray. The building facades changed as Diate moved from the government district to the merchant district. Here the buildings had more individuality – some with wide signs and glass fronts; others with small doors and no windows at all. The streets were paved with a red brick made on a small island just off-shore. Expensive enough to let shoppers know they had moved into an exclusive area.

A group of teenagers huddled in the alley across the street. They were speaking in low tones. Diate glanced at them, and couldn't see around their hunched backs. Teenagers didn't belong here. They lacked the wealth needed to shop in this area. That, and their posture, made him suspicious.

If he went over there, he would interrupt something. It would take time, and he would miss dinner with Beltar. Diate looked away. He was becoming as bad as the citizenry he complained about.

He crossed the street, feet wobbling on the uneven brick, and turned at the corner. He stopped in front of a wooden storefront. A sign displaying a goblet and a bottle of wine hung above the door.

No windows graced the front of the building – Beltar claimed too much light was bad for his wine. The wood facade was polished and gleaming. The brick sidewalk in front of the door was swept clean. Beltar did not advertise – he didn't need to – but everything about his store suggested class.

Diate turned the knob and stepped inside.

The tangy scent of Beltar's spiced reds mixed with the smell of onions sautéed in olive oil. Diate's stomach grumbled. He hadn't eaten lunch. He locked the deadbolt above the knob and wandered toward the back.

The shop occupied the front part of the building. Wine racks were built into the walls, with wine bottles resting in them. Along the back wall, the more expensive wines were locked in cases. Free-standing tables carried crystal goblets and ornate carafes, and a large red chair dominated the center of the room. Beltar's chair. He entertained customers there when he was working.

Diate weaved his way through the displays. He opened a door half hidden behind the expensive wine cabinets.

Beltar sat on a tall thin stool, one arm resting on the counter. His robe was pulled tight across his bulk, and he had discarded most of the jewelry he usually wore to impress customers. Rings still flashed on his fingers. On the stovetop, a white sauce bubbled. Fresh baked bread graced two plates, and an open bottle of Chianti breathed on the small wooden table in the corner. Two crystal wine goblets stood beside the bottle.

'Have you ever heard the old saw about the ancient colonists?' he said without greeting.

'Which part?' Diate sat on the stool across from Beltar.

'I was explaining to a customer this afternoon that names of wine varieties are ancient, dating before the first colonists ever discovered this planet, and he claimed that no ship ever discovered us, that we were all descended from the Vorgellians, and that most of us regressed. Only the Vorgellians maintained their technological superiority.'

'Where did he get that information?' Diate took a breadcrumb and slid it into his mouth.

'He said he had evidence. He claimed that the colony-ship business was all a lie.'

'How did he explain the sister ships flashing in the horizon on dark winter nights?'

'He couldn't. He said it's a Vorgellian hoax.'

'This bothers you?'

Beltar shrugged. 'I'm not fond of Vorgellians.'

Diate smiled a little. They had had that discussion before. Diate didn't like the Vorgellian trade practices, but he had never forgotten Sehan's kindness. Beltar knew that, and was taunting Diate instead of berating him for being late.

'What is this stuff?' Diate asked.

'Vorgellian stew. You'll like it.' Beltar slid off the stool and padded to the stove. He picked up a wooden spoon and stirred, then ladled the sauce onto the bread.

'It is not Vorgellian stew.' Diate got up and stood near the stove. He loved the small apartment at the back of the store even though the color scheme was deep red. The apartment only had a kitchen, a bath, and a living/sleeping room, but the layout was pleasant and felt roomy. Beltar had covered the walls with wine labels from his travels. They added a necessary break to all the red.

Beltar could afford a huge apartment at the top of any of the buildings along the hills, buildings with a view of the entire valley, but he preferred ostentation on his person, not in his surroundings.

'You're right,' Beltar said. 'It's not Vorgellian stew. It's better than anything they would whip up.'

He pulled forks out of a drawer and handed Diate a plate. Diate carried the plate to the table, sat down, and immediately started to eat. The white sauce had a garlicky taste mixed with the gamey flavor of rhoden.

Beltar poured the wine. The rings on his fingers clinked against the glass. 'You look tired, my friend.'

'Long day,' Diate said.

Beltar shook his head. 'Not that kind of tired. The kind of tired a person has when he's been alone too long.'

Diate did not want to discuss his personal life with a man whose life was no better. 'Good meal.'

Beltar shrugged. 'Passable meal. I could take you somewhere with good food. You could have a rest, a vacation, for the first time in your life.'

'I don't need a vacation.'

Beltar smiled. 'And I don't need to eat.'

Diate finished the sauce-covered bread, surprised at how fast he had eaten. As he leaned back, he discovered that he was full. He took the wine goblet, and felt the delicate glass shiver between his fingers. 'What kind?'

'I told you. Chianti.'

Diate shook his head. 'The spices.'

Beltar laughed, a deep throaty chuckle that resounded through his massive chest. 'The one secret you will never get out of me, detective.'

Diate took a sip, marveling at the dry bitterness mixed with a subtle flavor he found in no other wine. He would never get the secret out of Beltar, and he wasn't sure he wanted to. Beltar lived for his wines. He spent hours in the tiny kitchen after his shop closed, experimenting with flavorings, seasonings, and spices. Every other week, he traveled into the valley to check on his vineyards, and spent at least one week in four visiting new vineyards and sampling their wares. His trips usually took him off the island, and one of those buying sprees had put him in touch with the smugglers, and Diate, years ago.

'You know, you come here, eat my dinners, and stare at me three times a week when I'm home, detective,' Beltar said. 'And you never tell me what you are thinking and what you are feeling. Do you tell anyone?'

Diate took another sip of the wine. He suppressed a sigh. Beltar usually wanted something when he started discussions like this. 'What brings the question tonight?'

Beltar shrugged, and finished the last bite on his plate. 'I have been thinking about you a lot lately. I walk down the streets, and I see the other detectives in groups of two and three, but you are always alone. And the more I realized it, the more I realized you are always alone. Even when you're with me.'

'We talk,' Diate said. The wine tickled the back of his throat. He savored the smoothness. Once every few weeks, Beltar pushed Diate for information about himself. But Diate didn't talk. He preferred to remain private, to keep his memories to himself.

'About me. About my wines. About my trips. I know that you live in a hotel not far from the palace, that you came from the most entrancing island on the planet, that you were raised by the Golgoth, and that you will not discuss your past. You also will not discuss cases, unless they center around travel or wine, and you are a very good listener.'

Diate took another sip of wine. Beltar's place was usually a refuge from others who made demands on him. The Golgoth always wanted to know what was happening in his life, and Kreske, the Golgoth's son, made the same demands – out of jealousy, though, instead of curiosity. The few women he had dated always wanted to know everything about him, and when he refused to speak, they made him into their project. He hated being a project.

He felt as if he had always been someone's project.

'What do you want from me?' His tone had more anger in it than he wanted.

Beltar didn't flinch. He studied Diate, fingers gripped tightly on the glass, cherubic mouth pursed. He waited a long time before he responded. 'I am getting old, and lonely. I know a lot of people, but I like very few of them. I like you, detective.'

Diate set his wine glass down. 'What do you want, Beltar?'

'I want company.' Beltar smiled. 'I am planning a vacation, and I would like a friend to travel with me.'

'No women this time?'

'A *friend*,' Beltar said. 'Not a lover. But I don't even know if you can leave Golga. I know that you're still wanted in the Kingdom – for what, I don't know – but I don't know if it's safe for you to leave here.'

Diate picked up his glass. The spices had settled in the bottom. He swirled them around. 'I don't know either,' he said.

'Then let's find out,' Beltar said. 'I would like to make plans –'

'No.'

The word stopped Beltar as effectively as a slap. The force startled even Diate. He didn't move. His muscles felt as if they had frozen. He knew that he should speak, should reassure Beltar that he had not made a serious gaffe, but he couldn't find the words.

Beltar set his glass down. He smiled as if he understood. Diate found that even more infuriating. 'Let's walk,' Beltar said. 'I haven't been out of this place all day.'

Diate drained his glass, thankful for the excuse to move. He made himself take a few deep breaths, to calm himself. Beltar's offer was nice. But Diate couldn't explain the fear that the offer raised in him. He slid his chair back and stood up, at the door before Beltar had gotten up.

'Looks like you need the exercise too,' Beltar said with a low chuckle.

Diate never needed exercise. In fact, the Golgoth worried that he got too much. *You use that gymnasium like some men use strong wine,* he often said. Diate privately agreed. When he danced, he felt nothing, thought nothing. Not even sleep gave him such a respite. When he slept, his dreams were full of blood.

'A walk would be good,' he said, and his voice sounded as if he hadn't used it for days.

He opened the door and stepped into Beltar's back alley. The air smelled of rain and the gravel shone wetly in the thin light that slipped through the curtained window. They had maybe two hours until curfew.

Beltar stepped beside him and closed the door. 'Sometimes I walk to the ports at night. They remind me that my city, and my little room, are not the world.'

He was still trying to convince Diate to travel with him. 'You're preaching tonight?'

'No,' Beltar said, his voice a low rumble behind Diate. 'I have been feeling alone, lately.' He looked away, silhouetted in the light coming from his kitchen window. 'Maybe it's just age.'

Diate said nothing. If Beltar wanted a deeper friendship, it was more than Diate could give. 'I haven't been to the ports in a long time.'

Beltar nodded, and clapped his hand on Diate's back. 'Then let's go.'

The rain had left everything with a slightly damp smell. As they walked down the alley, the faint reek of garbage rose from the curb. Voices echoed from an open window: a man and a woman fighting; a child crying, with deep heavy hiccups. Diate wanted the sounds to stop. He always felt as if he should knock on a door, tell the couple to stop fighting, to pay attention to their child. But he was off duty, and even when he was on duty these things were none of his business. Not unless they spilled outside or had something to do with the Golgoth's security.

Beltar turned toward the port, and Diate followed, half a step behind. The streets were deserted now. The red brick had become concrete again, and the buildings dilapidated. People who lived near the ports were transient, or poor. New visitors to Golga, no matter what part of the inlet they docked at, always saw the worst part of the city first.

Their footsteps rang against the concrete. Beltar meandered, hands behind his back, staring at the ports. These ports were built by Golgans, not Vorgellians. Most were large wood buildings noted for size and storage rather than beauty. The ports were designed to process hundreds of ships and most of the trade on the planet. In the last four hundred years, Golga had worked itself into an interesting financial position. It was the breadbasket to the other inhabited islands. Most grew only specialized crops. The temperate climate on Golga allowed for both a long growing season and the ability to grow a wide variety of products. What Golga didn't grow or produce, it traded. Golga acted as the middle man for most of the islands. It bought at good prices and sold at even higher ones. Hence the large Vorgellian shuttle bay on the eastern side of the inlet. Fresh products arrived by air, and were shipped by air only a day later. Textiles and durables went by ship. The amount of money, people, and products that came through this area kept the detectives very busy.

No ships were coming in; the docking side was dark, making the nearby streets darker still. Diate liked the docking lights. Their reflection gave the ocean a prettiness that it usually lacked. On those nights, when he saw the lights sparkling like captured stars in the water, he knew that the Port City could as beautiful as the Kingdom if it tried.

Beltar slowed down so that he walked next to Diate. 'It's quiet,' Beltar said.

Diate nodded. He wasn't used to the silence. A chill ran down his back. Even the voices from the open windows had disappeared.

'Ever heard it this quiet?' Diate asked.

'Holidays,' Beltar said. 'I suppose the same in the middle of the night. But not at this time.'

Diate took Beltar's arm. The man's warmth through his soft robe felt reassuring. 'Let's go back.'

Beltar turned into an alley. Diate followed. The garbage scent was stronger here. Up ahead, an animal rustled in the piles of discarded waste. A rat, probably. Diate would have to report the presence to sanitation.

As if they would do anything.

The noise didn't quit as they got closer. Beltar glanced at Diate, and Diate felt more than saw his friend's nervousness. Diate moved a little ahead. At least he was trained to react quickly to any threat. Even prepared, Beltar was at a disadvantage.

The garbage mound was in complete darkness. The creature made small whimpering noises as it rummaged. Diate was going to walk by, when he recognized the sound.

Someone was crying for help.

In Lillish.

Only a handful of people on Golga spoke Lillish, and only Scio and the Golgoth spoke it fluently. Why would anyone call for help in Lillish here?

'Beltar,' he said. 'Someone's down here.'

Diate crouched, and stuck his hands in the garbage mound. Something sticky latched to his fingers. He winced, but forced himself to move the refuse. The cries grew more frantic. Beltar knelt beside him, and once Diate encountered Beltar's hands moving against his own. Then he plunged deeper, the smell of shit and rotted food nearly overwhelming him. His arms brushed against something warm and soft. It moved, and he nearly cried out, in spite of his training.

He grabbed the limb, and the person – a woman – yelped in pain.

'It's all right,' he said in Lillish. 'We're here to help you.' Beltar didn't have to be told that Diate had found something. He came closer, moving debris aside like a shovel. Diate slid his hands gently up the woman's skin. The refuse had covered it in goo. She was tiny. He moved his hands along her backbone to her neck.

'I'm going to pick you up,' he said in Lillish. 'It may hurt, and I'm sorry, but we can't help you here.'

She murmured a quiet assent. Diate drew his knees under him, braced himself, and lifted.

A moan, as involuntary as a breath, escaped her.

'Let's get her to the light,' Beltar said.

Diate walked out of the alley. The body he carried was limp against his. The woman they had found had fainted.

He wished the ports were active tonight. They needed help, and none was close. They needed light.

He hurried into the street, and the thin light falling from shuttered windows gave him just enough illumination.

Beltar took a step back. Diate was so startled, he almost dropped the woman. She was naked and covered with garbage, but worse than that, the smell he had noticed was coming from her. Her skin was swollen, pussed, red, and cracked. He had only seen damage like that once before, when one of his detectives had caught on fire during a fire-fighting effort.

But there had been no reports of fire in or near the ports, and she had been in that garbage for some time – since sundown at least. Whoever had done this to her had done it deliberately.

Chapter 4

Diate slipped between the garden walls. The pine trees gave off a heady fragrance that mixed with the blooming roses. Some beauty was allowed here, beauty of a natural kind, but only in places that were supposed to soothe people, places like the convalescence wing of the Golgoth's private care center.

A bird chirped in one of the branches, a high, throaty sound. Another answered, then another, and Diate looked at the sky. The blackness had given way to a light gray, touched by reddish clouds. Dawn.

He had spent the night in his office, investigating missing-person reports, examining the detective reports from the night before. Scio's people were supposed to guard the ports, but Diate had men on it too, not quite trusting Scio, as Scio didn't quite trust him. The secret police ran fine, but Diate believed he was the best one to protect both the Port City and the Golgoth.

The reports had turned up nothing. No one knew the woman was missing, and no one had reported a disturbance.

He didn't like that. That and the fact that she called for help in Lillish.

He had contacted the secret police and asked them to check on the ships and air shuttles into Golga for the past two days. Just a worry, but one he wanted to eliminate immediately.

He let himself in the wing, and suppressed a sneeze as the smell of decay and medicine washed over him. He hated this place. He had spent the first few days of his life on Golga here, and each time he had returned, it had been to watch someone die.

This wing had wood-paneled walls, and a cushioned floor to keep even the footsteps silent. The walls were bare except for wooden plaques bearing the patients' names. Some of the over-sized doors were open, revealing large rooms filled with a single bed, four chairs and a table. The windows were covered with plants. Most of the people here were elderly – former government assistants, now too old to care for themselves – who deserved the gratitude of the state. They would die in luxury, as Golga understood it.

He turned down a corridor and found himself in the stark halls of the recovery wing. The paneled walls had been replaced by a rough white wash, and the rooms were small without much more than beds and a few uncomfortable chairs. Patients did not stay here long. Once the trauma had passed, they went to another wing or another hospital.

Diate followed the corridor to the waiting room, and stopped when he saw Beltar.

Beltar lay on his side on one of the couches. His robe hung over him, keeping him warm. In sleep, he looked like an indulged baby, his rounded cheeks flushed, his lips pursed. Only the deep shadows under his eyes told of the night he had had.

Diate had urged Beltar to go back to his apartment, but Beltar had insisted upon staying. He had never seen someone so badly injured, and it had shocked him. He felt responsible for her, although he had never exchanged a word with her.

Diate felt the same, but the sensation was new to him. He rarely felt compassion for the people he found, always assuming they had done something to cause the trouble they were in. Perhaps Beltar's innocent viewpoint had rubbed off on Diate, or perhaps it was the shock of finding someone so near death who asked for help in his native language.

He sat on a straight-backed chair beside Beltar's couch. Beltar opened his eyes. 'She should be out of surgery by now,' he said. 'I was waiting for you.'

Diate understood. Beltar was waiting for him to deal with the staff. The Golgoth's private hospital rarely handled people like Beltar. They went to the city facility near the ports. Here, the government, prisoners, and foreign dignitaries had their illnesses tended. Secrets were as much a part of the air as the medicinal smell.

'I'll check,' he said, and stood up. Beltar wiped a bejeweled hand over his face. His normally immaculate fingers were stained, and a bit of garbage clung to one of his rings.

Diate walked back into the corridor and pushed a summons button. A young man came out of one of the doors, his coat flying behind him. He was not a doctor. The Golgoth imported his

47

doctors from Oleon, and even though they dressed like Golgans, their long thin frames and additional fingers identified their Olean origin immediately. The city hospital had Golgan doctors who usually trained with the Oleans here.

'I bought in a badly burned woman several hours ago,' Diate said.

The young man nodded. He dipped his hands into his pockets, toying with the material. 'They'll be bringing her into recovery in half an hour, and then waking her. Would you like to see her then, detective?'

'Any prognosis?'

'Not good,' the young man said. His face had gone pale. He was new, then, and unused to these kinds of horrors. 'She'll never be the same, even if we send her to the reconstructionists on Rulanda. They might be able to help her hands, though.'

'Hands?'

'You didn't notice?' A shudder ran through the young man. 'Before they set her on fire, they broke every bone in her hand. We'll be able to give her partial use, but she won't recover fully – at least not here.'

Diate froze. 'They broke every bone in her hand?'

'Yes, sir. They didn't miss one. And crushed is a better word. If the bones were broken, we would have a better chance at reconstruction.'

Bile rose in Diate's throat. The worry he had been nurturing had just become a full-fledged suspicion. He recognized that punishment. It was the Kingdom method for dealing with failed Talents. Had the Kingdom caught him, they would have cut his Achilles tendons and shattered his knees before killing him. That way, if he survived, he would never dance again. This woman had been a Talent, and her Talent had rested in her hands.

'I would like to see her,' Diate said.

The man nodded. 'Please wait,' he said, and disappeared through the door he had entered. Diate returned to the waiting room.

Beltar was sitting up, his eyes half open. Exhaustion added weight to him, and the night's events had left him disheveled. Diate wanted Beltar to go home, to return to being the man Diate was familiar with, a man who liked fine clothes and beautiful jewelry, a man whose sleep was never disturbed by someone else's problems.

48

'Well?' Beltar asked.

Diate shook his head. 'Partial recovery. I'm going to see her as soon as they wake her up.'

'Good,' Beltar said.

'I want you to go home, get what sleep you can. I'll come by tonight and tell you what's going on.'

'I'd like to come in with you,' Beltar said.

'No.' Diate sat on the straight-backed chair. His entire body was stiff. He didn't want to fight Beltar over his. He had to go in alone. He had to be able to talk to the woman freely. It might be his only chance. 'I need to talk to her.'

'You think she's going to die.'

Diate shrugged. 'They're optimistic.'

'But you're not.'

'If I relied on the optimism of doctors, I would only interview half of the crime victims in this city.'

Beltar sighed. 'I want to stay here.'

'There's nothing to do here. I want you to get some rest. You can come back tonight if you want to, after your shop closes.'

Beltar ran a hand over his face. He didn't wear exhaustion well. His eyes were puffy and the reek of garbage clung to him. Diate wondered if he smelled as bad.

'I would like to get cleaned up,' Beltar said. 'You'll stay with her?'

'As best I can,' Diate said. 'I also want to catch the people who did this to her.'

Beltar stood. 'This isn't us,' he said. 'I have only heard of things like this on other islands. The doctor said her hands were shattered. It was the Kingdom, wasn't it?'

Diate started. Most Golgans didn't know much about the Kingdom's practices. Beltar had learned a lot in his travels.

'We don't know who did it,' Diate said.

Beltar clasped his hands together. 'But you're frightened, my friend. I have never seen anything frighten you before.'

Diate didn't move. He couldn't. If he did, the name Beltar had given to the emotions churning inside him would become reality. 'I was startled,' he said.

Beltar studied him for a moment, then shrugged as if he knew he would get nothing from Diate. 'I will be back tonight,' Beltar said. 'Take good care of her.'

'I will.'

Beltar walked out of the waiting room. His red robe was stained and mottled, the fabric multicolored where something wet had spattered it. His slippers were ruined. He would send his clothing to the cleaners, who would discard it if they couldn't remove the stains. The city would clean Diate's clothes, and if the stains remained, so be it.

Beltar had only been gone a moment when the intern appeared in the waiting room. 'She's awake,' the intern said, 'but not very coherent. I don't know what she can tell you.'

Anticipation shot through Diate. 'I need to clean up,' he said.

The intern nodded. 'I was going to suggest it. There's a doctors' lounge off the waiting room. You'll find a scrub shower. I put out a coat and pants for you.'

Diate followed the intern's directions. The room was small, and smelled of stinkweed, something he found odd for a doctors' retreat. He tagged his clothes and dumped them in the recycler, then got into the small shower and wiped the grime off his body. He didn't take extra time, even though the hot water felt good. Water didn't get this hot in the gym, but then, they didn't need to sterilize themselves.

He got out, hurriedly dried himself off, and put on the pale blue coat and pants. They were made of an open weave, and were looser than the clothes he normally wore. He felt like a boy, able to move easily in clothing designed for flow. But he wasn't a boy. He was a man who had an unpleasant job ahead.

Within a few minutes, he was back in the hall. The intern was leaning against the wall, waiting. 'Stinkweed?' Diate asked.

The intern shrugged. 'They know it's not good for them, but they figure, hey, they've conquered medicine, they're immune.'

'They? Or we?'

'I don't smoke it. I don't even like smelling it.' The intern led him through a maze of hallways, each more narrow than the last. Through open doors, Diate heard an occasional moan and low-pitched screams. He braced himself.

'Here,' the intern said, and pushed open one of the smaller doors.

'I need to see her alone,' Diate said.

The intern nodded. 'You don't have a lot of time.'

Diate stepped into the room and let the door close behind him.

50

The scents of liniment and burned flesh mingled, and he made himself breathe through his mouth. The bed sat in the center of the room. A small table stood nearby, and a chair rested beside it. The woman was elevated above the bed on a small air cushion specifically designed for burn patients. She wore no clothing, and the parts of her skin left uncovered by bandages were red and cracked. Thick casts covered her hands, and even though her eyes were open, she stared at nothing.

'Hello,' Diate said in Lillish.

She turned her head so sharply that she gasped in pain. Her eyes were deep brown, the pupils dilated. He walked to the side of the bed, and pulled over a chair so that he wouldn't tower above her.

'My name is Diate,' he said. 'I'm a detective. I would like to talk to you.'

'Diate?' she whispered. 'The Rogue Talent?'

Those four words locked it all into place. The Kingdom had been billing him as the Rogue Talent for years. She was not from Golga. People here only knew him as head of the detectives and the Golgoth's favorite. 'I was a Talent a long time ago,' he said. 'Probably before you were born. Do they tell scare stories about me?'

'I was ten when it happened.' She wasn't whispering. Her voice was so hoarse she could barely speak. 'But they do tell scare stories about you. How can you walk?'

For a moment, he didn't understand the question. Then, involuntarily, his gaze went to her hands. He jerked it away, hoping she hadn't noticed. 'I ran too fast,' he said. 'They never caught me.'

She made a small sound and closed her eyes. He leaned forward, afraid she had fallen back into sleep. Too soon. He needed information from her.

'What's your name?' he asked.

'Martina.' She spoke with a sigh. The name was a Kingdom name. When they split off from Golga two centuries before, the Kingdom had forbidden Golgan names and the Golgan language. They had adopted a long dead language from the early colonists, made it their own, and called it Lillish.

The hairs were standing up on his arms. 'Who did this?'

She gave a half-laugh. 'The Rogue Talent.' She sounded as if she hadn't believed him.

His stomach was twisting. He had never expected to find another Kingdom member here – especially one who had nearly died from Kingdom torture. 'You need to tell me. I can do nothing unless you tell me what happened.'

'Where am I?' She glanced around the room, and he knew what she saw. The bare walls, the dull colors, the medicinal smell. So different from the world they had both grown up in.

'Golga.' The word sounded as harsh as the country's language. She jumped, visibly. 'They're going to kill me.'

'Who?'

'For being on Golga. They kill Kingdom members on Golga.'

He remembered that feeling. So many Kingdom stories about Golga were lies. But it wasn't the feeling that caught him now. It was the fact that she hadn't known, that until he spoke, she thought she was in the Kingdom. 'If they killed Kingdom members here,' he said. 'I wouldn't be here talking to you. I am a detective. I have lived on Golga for fifteen years.'

'A Talent on Golga?'

'I'm not a Talent any more.'

She raised one hand, just a little. 'Neither am I. Any more.'

Her flat tone and lack of tears sent a shudder through him. 'Tell me what happened. Who did this?'

She closed her eyes again. 'They took my little finger, and twisted it, and then yanked –'

'You don't have to describe it. Just tell me who did it, and how you got here.'

'Golga.' She shook her head a little, then opened her eyes. They were the only familiar thing on her ravaged face. 'After they started on my right hand, I passed out. I don't remember anything else. Until now.'

'Who did this?'

'I didn't go along with them. I didn't do anything they wanted.'

'Who? The Kingdom? The government?'

'They think they are,' she said.

The door opened. Diate didn't turn. 'Sir,' the intern said in Golgan.

She was watching him, watching the intern. Her pupils grew wider. He could smell the terror on her, as thick as the scent of burned flesh.

'I'll be back,' he said. 'And we'll talk. No one will hurt you here. Golga's a much kinder place than the Kingdom makes it out to be.'

He stood, wishing he could touch her, could give her some comfort. But her body looked so raw that even the slightest touch would probably make her scream.

He passed the intern on the way out the door. 'Do you have anyone on staff who speaks Lillish?' Diate asked in Golgan.

'I believe one of the doctors does, sir.'

'Then have that doctor tend her. She's frightened enough as it is.'

'Yes, sir.' The intern nodded and left, taking Diate's statement for the dismissal it was. Diate stood in the hallway for a moment, making himself breathe. Fear was contagious. And even though he had talked with her, he didn't know how she had gotten here. The Golgoth would want to know. The Golgoth would want to know everything. And Diate had no answers. Yet.

Diate stopped in his office to change clothes before he went to see the Golgoth. Then he hurried to the office of the secret police.

The headquarters of the secret police were housed in an oval-shaped building behind the palace. The lower floor, done in marble, with large fluted columns, looked impressive and forbidding. The upper floors, where the offices were housed, had the same functional utility that much of the Port City had.

It was just before early breakfast, and the lights were dim in all offices but Scio's. A guard stood at the door. Diate sent him to the gym to inform Strega that their workout session had to be postponed. He didn't want the guard to hear what he had to discuss with Scio.

Scio had added rugs to the floor of his office, good, solid, hand-woven rugs made in the northern tip of Golga. Books lined the walls – all non-fiction studies of various island cultures. Golgans considered fiction a frivolity. Diate still missed it.

Scio sat at his desk, tonsured head bent over scraps of paper. He scrawled something, then set the paper aside.

'Find anything?' Diate asked.

Scio shook his head. 'Four possibles landed in the Port City yesterday. We've recalled two, and I'll interview the pilots of the other two later today. The problem is that I know them all, and none have a history of smuggling. In fact, one of the pilots helped us the last time we had international problems. You sure this was Kingdom?'

'I wasn't when I sent you the message, but I am now. The girl said it was.' Diate sat on an overstuffed chair in front of Scio's desk. His exhaustion was catching up with him. 'She was a Talent. She didn't remember how she got here, but she was frightened when she found out where she was.'

'How convenient.' Scio tapped his pen against his teeth. 'What's her name?'

'Martina.' Diate folded his hands in his lap. 'I don't know more about her. She really wasn't up for talking.'

'The Kingdom.' Scio pushed his papers aside. He leaned back and put his hands behind his head. 'I don't think you should be working on this one.'

A flash of very old anger flared. Scio had never trusted him with the Kingdom. For years, Scio wouldn't even let Diate see the communication reports or keep Diate abreast of Kingdom changes. Diate finally had to set up his own network to keep track of the Kingdom. When it became clear that Diate's was better, Scio would occasionally send a man over for advice. 'You want me to stay away because of the Kingdom involvement?'

'I think it's better left to those of us with no ties.'

Diate's entire body was tense. 'I have no ties there. This is not a normal case. You need me.'

'You have more than the usual amount of involvement in Kingdom matters. You're obsessed, and obsession gets in the way of work. I don't want you on this.'

Diate smiled and leaned back in the chair. 'You have no say in this matter. I'm staying on the case. I understand these people. No one else here does.'

'You also have a vendetta.' Scio set his pen down. He frowned at Diate. Scio hated it when Diate mentioned his knowledge of the Kingdom. Until Diate arrived, Scio had been the resident expert. 'A vendetta will make you careless.'

Diate shrugged. 'That vendetta is fifteen years old. I have worked on other Kingdom cases. You worry too much, Scio.'

'And you don't worry enough.'

Diate stood. 'I'm going to see the Golgoth. You have nothing else?'

'Not yet,' Scio said.

Diate started out of the room, and then stopped. 'This is Kingdom,' he said. 'If they didn't come in from the shuttle ports, that doesn't leave us many other options.'

'Some kind of infiltration.'

'Maybe,' Diate said. 'But Kingdom members are easy to spot. No. I was thinking that we might have to check out their embassy.'

'But that's neutral ground,' Scio said.

'Only if they choose to keep it that way. Dumping their bodies on our soil doesn't bode well for the neutrality of an embassy.'

Scio frowned, his round eyes narrowing. 'I don't think you should say anything to the Golgoth about the embassy yet. I think we have to find more information before we can come to any conclusions.'

Diate nodded. He would give Scio that point. But the Golgoth had to be informed. The Golgoth was Diate's defender. He would keep Diate on the case. He turned around and left the room.

The hallway was still empty, although he did pass two other guards on his way out. He hurried out the door and across the palace lawn, noting that heat was rising, making the flower scent even headier. He went to a back entrance, where a guard opened a door without acknowledging him, and went inside.

The palace always made him feel small and lost, even though he knew the corridors as well now as he knew the alleys of the city. The black-and-white design tile pattern made the rooms look endless, the walls taller than they were. If he stayed in the palace too long, he got a headache which one of the doctors once described as an odd kind of eyestrain. It seemed his eyes tried to find the real corners, the breaks in the patterns, and when they couldn't they overcompensated.

Two more security guards passed him. He took the twisty back steps that led to a tiny dark corridor only a handful of people knew about. No light filtered in here, no windows broke the expanse of black wall. Candles substituted for incandescent lights on the walls, and wax grew in little piles at the base of each candelabra. Dust tickled his nostrils. The Golgoth was getting even more paranoid as the years went on. Now he wasn't letting anyone clean the corridor leading to his quarters.

Diate stopped in front of an oval-shaped door and knocked, then glanced at the walls. Tiny flickerings on the ceilings assured him that the hidden surveillance equipment was still in place. When he got back, he would have one of his people update a report on it. He didn't like the isolation the corridor invited.

He knocked again, and heard a muffled curse from inside.

Footsteps approached the door and stopped. After a moment, the bolt slid back and the door swung open.

The Golgoth stood in front of him, eyes blurry from sleep, looking too pale in a plain white robe. 'Yes?'

Diate pushed inside as the Golgoth closed the door. One small lamp beside an interior door shone against the gloom. No skulls decorated this room like they did the rest of the palace. The furniture had clean lines, the walls were painted white, and everything looked as simple as an impoverished merchant's cottage. The Golgoth tolerated artifice only in his work.

'Something serious?' the Golgoth asked. All trace of sleep had disappeared from his face. He lit another lamp and sat down on a pile of pillows on the hard wood floor.

'Serious enough for me to disturb you,' Diate said. He chose not to sit, not wanting to get into a comfortable position with the man who helped raise him. He paced along the floor, his soft shoes whispering against the wood. 'I found a woman last night. She had been beaten and burned and left to die in a pile of garbage near one of the ports.'

The Golgoth made a disgusted sound, but his expression remained neutral. His gaze moved as he followed Diate's path across the floor, but nothing else did.

'She spoke Lillish.'

The Golgoth let out a small sigh and tilted his head downward. 'She is still alive?'

'Barely. She's a Talent.'

The Golgoth shook his head. 'It seems too careless. We have never had anything like this happen before.'

'That we know of. I want to get someone looking at the bizarre and unsolved deaths we've had over the past several years. If I hadn't found her, if she hadn't been alive, if she hadn't spoke Lillish, we probably would have assumed that she was one of ours. No one is going to look twice at a burned body lying in a pile of garbage.'

'Do you believe that this is the Kingdom?'

Diate stopped pacing and stood with his back to the Golgoth. 'She is a Talent. They set her on fire, which is more than enough to teach the average person some kind of lesson. But before they did that, they broke every bone in her hands. When we talked, I told her I was no longer a Talent. She said she wasn't either, and she held up her hands.'

56

'If she is from the Kingdom, and they did dump her here, then we are in a serious diplomatic crisis.' The Golgoth spoke slowly.

'I know,' Diate said. Relations between Golga and the Kingdom were formal at best, volatile most often. The Kingdom had been founded by a group of artists who had fled what they considered persecution on Golga, and settled on a nearby island. Years of warfare had solidified their position as a separate country. Not until the reign of the Golgoth's father did the fighting between Golga and the Kingdom stop. Small pockets of isolated fighting still flared up now and then, but fast-acting diplomacy usually put the conflagrations out. 'Let's see if I can get more information from her, and we'll see what else we can turn up. This could be a set-up, and she could be some kind of pawn.'

'You think they know you'd be investigating this?'

'I hope not,' Diate said. 'But we can't rule out any possibility.'

The Golgoth remained silent. Diate turned around. The Golgoth's head was bowed, his hands clasped in his lap. Diate tensed.

The Golgoth finally brought his head up. His gaze was level. 'And you, Emilio. How do you feel about this?'

Not Diate, not detective. Emilio. The family name. Diate took a deep breath. A small tremor ran through his right hand.

He touched her head, his hand lost in matted blood. Her eyes were open and he knew the look. Terror. Terror he had missed. He wanted to apologize, but she wouldn't hear him. She would never hear him again.

'It startled me when she spoke Lillish,' he said.

The Golgoth waited, motionless.

Diate shrugged. His throat had gone dry. She had spoken Lillish, and he became protective. He heard his sister's voice, saw his sister's face. Part of him wanted to run, to run as far away as he could.

'And that's all?' the Golgoth said.

'I don't know yet.' Diate's hands clenched into fists. 'I don't know.'

The medicinal smell had grown stronger, and the hospital walls seemed brighter in the artificial light. Diate walked down the corridor. He would check on Martina, and then go back to his apartment and get some sleep. He had managed to grab a bite of food after he saw the Golgoth. Then he had worked with Scio for several hours, did one quick workout, and come here. The Golgoth's words haunted him. He wasn't sure how he felt.

When he reached the corridor outside Martina's room, he stopped. Beltar sat in a chair, arms crossed over his broad chest. His red robe was neatly pressed and the garbage that had covered his hands was gone. His rings sparkled in the fake light. When he saw Diate, he smiled. 'They tried to kick me out, detective, but I told them I was waiting for you.'

Diate swallowed back his annoyance. 'You were supposed to go home.'

'I did, and I opened my shop, and did an amazing business. I managed to get here before early supper.' Beltar lowered his voice. 'She's a real mess. What did she do to make someone treat her like that?'

'I don't know.' The question had been floating around in Diate's brain as well. If he found the answer to that, he might have the answer to his life, his trauma. 'She was awake then?'

Beltar shook his head. 'They don't expect her to wake up again until some time tomorrow.'

'Let me check on her,' Diate said, 'and then I'll walk you home.' He pushed past Beltar and opened the room door. The smell of burned flesh had grown overpowering. He stifled an urge to cover his nose.

She looked smaller somehow, her bandaged hands large on the blankets covering her chest. The air cushion was lower, and her position had shifted slightly. They would keep rotating her so that every part of her body had a chance to heal.

And you, Emilio. How do you feel?

They had come too close. Part of him always believed he had gone too far for the Kingdom to find him. He used the Golgoth's precious and expensive communications system to keep track of the Kingdom, to know when they got too close to Golga. He had always thought he would be protected.

He had become a creature of myth. The Rogue Talent. To kill him would vindicate the myth. But he was a man now, not a boy. A strong man with an entire force of strong people behind him. So why did two words, whispered in Lillish, scare him so?

Help me.

'I'll try,' he promised the sleeping woman. 'I'll try.'

He pulled the door closed behind him. Beltar had moved his

chair across the hall and stood beside it. 'I've been talking to her doctors,' he said. Diate shook his head. With the repair of his clothes, Beltar had become himself again. He would get past any obstacle put in front of him. 'They say she'll be disfigured for the rest of her life. She'll probably never have full use of her hands again.'

'I know,' Diate said.

'There are some doctors on Rulanda who specialize in reconstruction. It's kind of an upper-class resort where they do all sorts of rehabilitation. Her doctors think it would be good for her.'

'I suspect she has no money.' Diate started down the hall.

Beltar kept pace with him. 'She doesn't need any. I'll pay for it.'

'Do you know how much it will cost?'

'Do you know how much money I have?'

Diate looked at Beltar. The robe was fine, the jewelry expensive. He knew that Beltar's wine shop did excellent business, but he always thought that if Beltar were truly rich, he would have one of the oversized houses at the end of town, not live in the tiny apartment attached to the shop.

Beltar met his gaze. 'I have more money than I could spend in three lifetimes. Let me help her.'

Everyone acted as if Diate were responsible for her. She had her own life, her own responsibilities. 'Do what you can,' Diate said.

Beltar smiled. 'Good. As soon as she's ready, we'll book passage. Be sure to bring summer clothes. Rulanda is warm.'

'I'm not going,' Diate said.

'You have never taken a vacation, as long as I've known you,' Beltar said. 'I think you're entitled to one.'

'I can't leave here.'

Beltar smiled. 'But we need you. You speak her language. You have the credentials to protect her, to explain how a Port City wine merchant is traveling with a Kingdom member.'

Diate's skin had gone cold. If he left Golga, he left safety. But Beltar had a point. Scio had complained that Diate's exhaustion was making him careless. The Golgoth had been offering a vacation for years. And Diate didn't want to leave Martina unprotected.

Because this time, they might kill her.

Chapter 5

He had never expected Rulanda to be so beautiful. Or so isolated. Tiny towns stood near large lakes. The town they visited was the largest, because of the clinic. Three deep warm lakes surrounded the small town near the clinic. Each lake had a white sand beach protected from the streets by a mile of forest. The trees were large and ropy, with pale green moss hanging down the sides, like ripped fabric. In those forests lived the Hoste, one of the few species not imported to this planet. One of the few native species that had survived. They were protected, and only certified observers could see them.

Diate wandered down the town's narrow street. The air was thick. It smelled of loam and fresh water, and the deep humidity encouraged slow, easy movement.

He wore top-sider shoes made of leather thin as gloves. Through them, he could feel the curve of each rock, each pile of dirt. His pants were casual leggings, bought at one of Rulanda's portside stores, and his shirt was a thin cotton weave. He looked no different from most of the tourists gracing the small street. Beltar had insisted on that. He wanted Diate to feel everything about his vacation, including the difference in clothing.

They had arrived on a shuttle a few days before. The entire trip had made Diate nervous. He hadn't been on an air shuttle since he arrived in Golga. He had wanted to take a ship, but Martina's doctor had overruled him. This shuttle had been full of passengers, and he hadn't been allowed to sit near the pilot. Instead, he had glued himself to the window, and stared as island after island raced past.

When they went over the Kingdom, he had stared, hoping to see a difference in the layout, something that was visible from the air. But he had seen nothing. It had looked the same as it had on the night he left.

The street was quiet in the noonday heat. Only a handful of

tourists wandered about. Those residents who weren't working were napping. Diate liked the pace, but knew he would never be able to bring it home.

Another thing he would never bring home was the item he was in search of now. In the short week they had been on Rulanda, he had become addicted to iced coffee, a local drink grown on the island. Diate had thought the beverage too bitter at first, until Beltar showed him how to sweeten it with sugared milk. While the rest of the town slept, Diate was searching for an open cafe.

The town had only a handful of stores, most of which contained handmade items and overpriced local merchandise. Four restaurants surrounded the massive hospital complex, and tiny beachfront stands sold iced candy and cool drinks. The town had one large hotel, which had rooms for guests on short budgets, cabins for guests with unlimited funds. Beltar had rented two cabins, and placed Diate in the nicer of the two.

Between visits to the hospital, Diate had slept for the first two days. He hadn't realized how exhausted he was, even though he had no real cause to be. Beltar said it was the accumulated stress of all the years. Diate thought it might be the change in climate.

The exhaustion had eased the day before. He had spent it exploring the town and swimming in its lakes. He hadn't swum since he was a boy. The warm lake water had soothed him, and stretched his muscles in an unfamiliar way.

This morning, though, he had found he didn't want exercise. He had spent the hours observing people. Now that they were all napping, he had some time to himself.

The small coffee shop at the end of the main street was open. Two couples sat under large umbrellas overlooking the street. Diate never understood why anyone would sit streetside when the cafe also had chairs overlooking the area's largest lake.

He touched his forehead, making sure his hair covered his caste mark. He wished the mark could be removed. Perhaps the reconstructions here could do it, but Diate did not have the wealth to pay for such surgery. Besides, the mark had not been a problem on Golga. Here, however, he had already been mistaken for a Kingdom member. He hated the deference the people had shown him, the assumed love of beauty. There were other Kingdom members here – he had seen two magicians the day before buying coffee at the cafe – and he didn't want to be mistaken for someone in their party.

He nodded at the couples outside and slipped inside the door. A lazy fan circled overhead, making a ticking sound that soothed rather than grated. The tables inside were empty. The proprietor, a middle-aged man, slouched on a chair behind the counter, hat pulled over his eyes. The place smelled of coffee and fresh baked goods. Beltar came here every morning for sweets before heading to the hospital. Diate visited the hospital at night. Martina had come through her surgeries nicely, but hadn't yet awakened.

Diate stood against the glass counter and cleared his throat. The proprietor pushed his hat back against his forehead and grinned. Without asking what Diate wanted, the proprietor got up, filled a tall thin glass with ice, and poured coffee over it, adding milk almost as an afterthought. He put the glass and a small spoon on the counter, and returned to his chair as Diate counted out the money and stuffed it in a jar on the other side of the glass. The proprietor's hat was back over his eyes before Diate could even say thank you.

The glass was cold against his fingers. Diate took it to the back, where he sat at one of the tables overlooking the lake. No umbrellas shaded patrons on this side, and his normally dark skin had taken an even darker hue in the few short days he had been coming to the cafe.

He sighed. The Golgoth had been right. Diate had needed a vacation, even a working vacation like this one. He had little to do except reflect and rest.

A breeze came off the lake, ruffling his hair and tugging at his thin shirt. He braced one foot on the chair across from him, taking a sip of the cool drink. Its bitter sweetness combined on his tongue and sent a shiver of delight through him. Beltar had promised that they would bring the ingredients home, but Diate knew that the coffee would never taste the same as it did here, overlooking a quiet lake on a sunny afternoon.

Voices inside the cafe made him look up. A slender woman with a mane of blonde hair stood at the counter. She wore the same clothing he did. The leggings clung to her thighs, and a bit of fringe on the sides added height to her frame. She was delicately made and well proportioned, and when she turned, he realized that her face was as delicate as the rest of her. He recognized her. He had been watching her from a distance since he arrived.

She was buying iced coffee and a pastry.

A wistfulness filled him. Martina would never have that delicate beauty, even after the surgeries. The Rulandan doctors promised partial use of her hands – most of the bones had been crushed and the ligaments had been cut – and they could hide some of the scarring on her face and body. Her skin would never have the elasticity of normal human skin, but it would at least be comfortable to look at.

Which was more than she was now. Diate had only been able to talk to her briefly before the surgeries, eliciting little more than her desire to come to Rulanda. The doctors here wanted her to concentrate on healing. They promised him many chances to visit with her during her long convalescence period.

The woman inside the shop came to the back door and gazed out. The breeze blew her hair away from her face. Bright blue eyes, a button nose, and a thin bow-shaped mouth. The ancient space travelers' idea of beauty. No caste marks. He couldn't explain why that made him feel such relief.

She saw him and smiled. He flushed. The smile felt as intimate as a caress. She walked over to his table. 'Mind if I join you?' She spoke Rulandan like a native. She was as uncertain of his background as he was of hers.

'Please,' he said in the same language, and pulled back a chair, surprised at how smooth his voice sounded. His command of Rulandan wasn't as good as hers. He used the language rarely on Golga. The Kingdom's habit of teaching the children to speak at least eight languages had paid off more times than he could count.

She set her coffee on the table and sat beside him, facing the lake. 'I love it here,' she said. 'I try to come here once a year.'

'It's beautiful,' Diate said.

Again the smile, and the feeling of warmth. She gazed at him sideways, a slight twinkle in her eye. 'Vacation?'

He didn't understand what she was doing. No one had ever just sat and made conversation with him before – at least not for a reason he couldn't discern. 'Yes,' he said, 'I'm on vacation,' and wondered why he lied. Maybe because it felt like a vacation, sitting in this hot air on this deck overlooking a lake.

She took a sip of her iced coffee. 'I've seen you around.'

He started. He had seen her, several times, but each time he had looked, she had been doing something else. He thought she hadn't noticed him. Even though he didn't move, he felt a tension build inside.

'You're not comfortable here.' She was good, better than he wanted her to be. He wasn't used to being observed.

He sipped his coffee and looked away from her, hoping she couldn't see how much she had unnerved him. 'I like it here.'

'Then you don't know how to relax. You're constantly on alert, watching everyone.'

'You must watch everyone too,' he said. 'You seem to have me down.'

'Actually, I don't. You interest me. You move with a grace I've seen among Kingdom members, and yet you're traveling with a Port City wine merchant.'

'I'm afraid I didn't notice you.' The lie slipped out before he could stop it. Old habits, old *protective* habits, died hard. He longed to reach over and touch her, to feel her hair, the curve of her cheek.

'I wasn't sure I wanted you to see me.' She pushed her hair away from her face with her left hand. Then she tore off a bit of pastry and took a bite.

He frowned. She knew who he was. She had to. 'Why not?'

She shrugged, and looked over her coffee glass at the lake. 'Because you see things so clearly, you might not like what you see.'

He followed her gaze. Two teenaged boys scampered into the water while a girl stretched out on the sand. 'You don't know me. What I think shouldn't matter.'

'It shouldn't, should it? But it does, somehow.' She took another sip of her coffee and stood. 'The hotel has a lovely formal dining hall with some first-rate entertainment. I would love it if you joined me for dinner tonight.'

The breeze carried her scent to him: musky woman mingling with the faint hint of flowers. The urge to touch her almost overpowered him. 'At twilight?'

She nodded. 'I'll have a table waiting.' And then she walked away, leaving her glass, the pastry, and that tantalizing scent. He watched her walk down the side stairs to the beach, and didn't look away until she had disappeared in the ropy trees.

A wood sprite. Or a sea nymph. All those stories his mother had told him as a child. Fairy stories about magical creatures that ensorceled with a mere glance. He wouldn't miss that dinner. He hadn't been with a woman in a very long time.

Foolish man. She probably knew who he was, and was teasing him. How many Kingdom members could travel with someone from the Port City? But she might not be from the Kingdom. People from all over the galaxy vacationed here.

Maybe he was relaxing. A woman hadn't ever appealed to him like this. To be fair, most women weren't interested in him when they learned who he was, and what he did. But the handful who were, well, he had never let them into his private life, nor had he visited theirs. The relationships ended as quickly as they started.

Odd thing to think about when he had just received an invitation to dinner from a woman he barely knew. A woman he could never have a relationship with because he didn't know who she was or where she was from. He didn't want to know. This freedom was a luxury he had never had before, and probably would never have again. He didn't know what he would do until twilight.

Soft laughter mingled with music greeted Diate as he stood in the hall outside the dining room. The smell of fish, greens, and light spices greeted him. His palms were damp, and he stifled the urge to rub them on his new slacks. He adjusted his dress tunic – light cotton, like most of the clothes manufactured for this part of Rulanda – and stepped inside.

It took a moment for his eyes to adjust to the dining room's darkness. As he blinked, items came into focus: large plants spilling out of man-sized plant holders; big white cane chairs surrounding white cane tables, the large backs giving the illusion of privacy. The hand-sculpted candles illuminating each table, and the wall candles in their wrought-iron holders, added softness not light to the room around it. Off to the right, a flight of stairs led down to patio dining on the edge of the lake. Glasses clinked together. The soft conversation and laughter continued, but the music had stopped.

'May I help you, sir?' A slender woman with dark hair flowing down to her shoulders had appeared beside him. She spoke to him in Lillish, her accent excellent. He resisted the urge to wipe his hands again. He often came to places like this in an official capacity, but rarely as a patron.

'I'm meeting someone here,' he replied in Golgan, annoyed that she had mistaken him for a Kingdom member. 'A woman. But I don't see her.'

The woman smiled. 'Miss Sheba. She warned us that you would be here. She said she is running late, but if you like, you can wait for her.'

The woman's Golgan was not as fluent as her Lillish. Sheba. A Kingdom name, but a popular one that had spread through the southern islands because of a famous singer nearly a century before. He decided not to worry about it. He hadn't seen any suspicious behavior from her.

He glanced around the dining room. He recognized no one else. He could go back to his room and try again later, but that seemed awkward. He would sit and wait, and if she didn't show within a short time, he would chalk it all up to an odd experience.

'Have you a table?' he asked.

'Certainly, sir. Miss Sheba reserves her table for each night that she is here.'

'She sounds like one of your regulars.'

The woman smiled. 'She does not miss a season.'

The woman led him off to the right, down the flight of stairs and past the small stage. A sitka rested across a chair, and a small flute lay on the floor. The stage had an air of recent abandonment, and imminent return.

She stopped at a small corner table on the patio, but in a corner to shelter it from the wind. It wasn't until Diate sat down that he realized the table had a spectacular view of the lake.

'May I get you anything?' the woman asked.

'Have you a wine list?'

She handed him a leather-bound booklet she had been carrying under her arm. He studied the selections, written in six different languages, before finding Beltar's prize wines. 'The two-year-old lightly spiced Riesling,' he said.

'Very good choice.' The voice was huskier, richer than he expected. He looked up to find Sheba standing beside the woman. The woman nodded as she completed his order, and as quickly as she had appeared, she vanished.

Sheba left him breathless. Her blonde hair floated like sunbeams around her face. She wore a diaphanous gown made of a see-through material. He hadn't seen a dress like that since he left the Kingdom. Golgan women were less forward, more retiring. He had always missed the ease of Kingdom clothing. It meant nothing – women often wore seductive dress without planning a seduction

– but he couldn't stop his gaze from traveling the length of her body.

She had a slender neck that tapered into strong, well-shaped shoulders. Her breasts were large and firm, the nipples painted red in Vorgellian fashion. She had a narrow waist that flowed into wide hips. Her pubic hair was the same startling blonde as the mane that surrounded her head. She had combined a Kingdom dress with Vorgellian make-up, and made the look wholly her own. He made himself stop staring, and returned his gaze to her face.

'You speak Golgan,' he said, and mentally kicked himself for letting his surprise show.

She shrugged. 'It's the language of commerce. Only fools fail to learn the language that supports our economy.'

He smiled. Discussing trade with a woman dressed with such abandon seemed odd, even to him.

'Will you join me?' he asked. His voice sounded deeper, alien to his own ears.

'Only if you let me share the Riesling.' She pulled back one of the cane-backed chairs and sat close to him, the table hiding her lower body from his view. 'I don't even know your name.'

'Emilio.' His personal name. The one only a handful of friends knew. The word had slipped out of him like a sigh.

Inside, music had started, but not the sitka and flute music he had expected. The full-stringed sound of a pre-colonization orchestra. They played an ancient waltz.

Sheba smiled at him. 'I'd love to dance.'

Instantly he froze. 'I don't –'

'You do.' Her tone was confident. 'And if you don't, you should. You move so beautifully.' Without letting go of his hand, she stood, the thin folds of the dress swirling around her. He stood too, letting her lead him to the tiny dance floor. Four other couples were dancing – poorly, their movements inexperienced and awkward. Sheba stopped, and Diate swept her into his arms, suppressing a groan as the warmth of her body ignited his.

He was all sensation and motion again, his limbs following ingrained commands. Sheba flowed with him, as if her body were part of his, and they let the music dictate the rhythm of their connection. He buried his face in her hair and lost himself in the flowered scent of her. Only the music existed, and her soft skin, and the way their bodies moved in unison.

67

Then the music stopped, and he came to himself, realizing with a flush of embarrassment that the other couples had fled the floor. Applause scattered around them, and people murmured their approval. Diate's flush grew deeper, and a thin thread of terror worked its way through his body. Sheba kept her arm around his waist.

'You're spectacular,' she said softly. 'I knew you could dance.'

He didn't reply, and instead led her back to the table. The spiced wine waited for them, the bottle open, the cork in front of his place, awaiting his approval.

He sat down and let the terror work its way through him. He didn't know anyone here except Beltar, and Beltar would never tell the Golgoth that Diate had danced. His position was safe; his future was safe. He had nothing to fear.

Except the odd emotions coursing through him. He couldn't remember ever being this attracted to anyone.

'Is something wrong?' Sheba asked.

Diate picked up the cork and sniffed it. The spices tickled his nose. He grabbed the bottle and poured, the clear white wine splashing against the sides of her glass. 'I haven't been that close to a woman in a long time.'

She cupped her glass, held it close to her face, and leaned toward him, a smile touching her lips. 'Was this for aesthetic reasons?'

'It certainly wasn't planned.' He sipped his wine, letting the sweet spices trip over his tongue before the alcoholic bitterness bit him. The interior shivering was fading. 'You have an advantage over me, you know.'

'I do?' She rubbed the glass against her cheek, her gaze intent on him.

'You've been watching me for days. All I know is what I've found out this afternoon.'

She smiled and leaned back, taking a sip from her wine. He could see the tops of her breasts, and remembered the feel of them against his chest. 'And what have you found out?' she asked.

He had to be cautious, revealing only what he had learned that day, and not what he had seen observing her. Observing her, he had noted that she spent most of her time alone, watching the performances and exploring the town. 'I have found out that you're a regular visitor to this place, that you always have this table when you're here. You seem interested in me, for reasons I haven't yet discerned.'

She looked away. A slight flush touched her cheeks. 'I find you attractive.'

She was not Golgan. She didn't look Vorgellian. There was a chance that she was a native of Rulanda. But she could also be Kingdom. Kingdom women always expressed what they wanted.

He put his hand on hers. 'You are the most beautiful woman I've ever seen.'

Her eyes widened just a little. Then her smile grew. A waiter appeared, as if summoned. He bowed to them then waited. Sheba looked as annoyed at the interruption as Diate felt. 'Two trout,' she said, 'with a side of etofin and rice.'

The waiter bobbed again and stepped away from the table.

'I hope you don't mind,' Sheba said. 'The trout isn't really trout, by Vorgellian standards. It's a local equivalent, but very very good. Etofin is a leafy vegetable that's only grown in this area of Rulanda. I figured you should try the native cuisine.'

Diate didn't mind that she ordered for them, although he did feel uncomfortable about her aggressiveness. Only a handful of people had ever taken control of his life. The last was the Golgoth, all those years before. 'You assume I've never had it before,' he said.

She laughed, a high fluted sound that drew the attention of other diners. 'Methinks I do assume too much.'

He couldn't resist any longer. He cupped her face with his left hand and brought it close to his. With a smoothness he didn't know he had, he bridged the gap between them and tasted the spices on her lips, before delving inside to find the wine mingling with the sweet taste of her. The kiss went on too long, flushing him, making him hard.

In it, he allowed himself to forget that she had misquoted literature, an ancient poet that his father had made him study all those years ago.

Finally their lips separated. 'I bet you make love as well as you dance,' she said, her words puffs of air against his skin.

'There's only one way to find out.'

Her eyes glittered in the candlelight. He could feel the heat on her skin. They stood together, as if they were already lovers, their movements synchronized by intimate knowledge. As they walked past the desk, Sheba stopped and spoke to the woman.

'We just ordered. Please, leave it as a late dinner outside my door.'

The woman nodded and smiled. Diate barely registered the motion. He walked with Sheba out the door and across the lawn. She stopped on the wide expanse of grass and put a hand on his arm. 'I don't do this on first acquaintance,' she said. 'It's been years –'

He put his finger under her chin and pulled her mouth toward him. He kissed her upper lip, then her lower. He didn't care if she was Kingdom or Rulandan. All he wanted to do was lose himself in her. 'Then let's enjoy the night,' he said. 'You can teach me how to relax.'

She laughed, and led him to a cabin not far from his own.

She used a passkey to open the door. She stepped in before him, and picked up the throw rug in front of the door, covering glass that leaned against the wall, protecting it, probably, in case they were careless. Inside, candles were already burning. Pillows sprawled across the floor over a thick rug, soft as a pillow itself. A fire burned in the small fireplace, touching the air with the pungent odor of woodsmoke.

The door clicked shut behind her, and she was in Diate's arms. He ran his hands over the curves, made silken by the thin gown she wore. He brought his palms down across her breasts, tweaked her nipples with thumbs, then gripped her narrow waist.

She didn't move, but her breathing quickened. He knelt, took one breast in his mouth, staining the fabric. The Vorgellian rouge tasted of sugar and dye. His hands explored her hips, her thighs, and the narrow V between her legs. Desire coursed through him like good wine. He wanted to drink her all at once, but knew he would enjoy her more if he sipped.

He grabbed the hem of the dress and brought it up, peeling it off her like a second skin. Her skin was golden in the candlelight, the same tawny shade as her eyes and hair. He stood and pulled her against him. Her back was as soft as the material that had encased it. He kissed her neck and shoulders before she tugged off his clothes and pulled him down to the pillows.

The satin fabric against his bare skin aroused him further. He had to use all of his training for control. She kissed him back now, explored his body with her hands, repeating his gestures, palms sliding down his chest, thumbs teasing nipples. Her tongue followed until it found its way down his body, encasing his hardness in warmth.

70

He shuddered, the control slipping. He grabbed her arms and brought her up, tasting himself on her tongue. Gently he eased inside her, and all control fled. He was his body: the hard leanness absorbing her warmth, buried in wet, the throbbing in his groin, the sheer pleasure of touch. He slid his hands in her hair, spilling it over his face, breathing the floral scent of it. She moaned and grabbed him, her body shuddering, her legs wrapped around him, holding him close, forcing him deeper. He moved without music to a rhythm he had never heard before, and all the while the pleasure in his body grew, until it erupted in a burst of sensation so fierce he cried aloud.

Then the energy left him. Sheba's arms tightened around him and she buried her face in his shoulder. He had had a woman once, a brief interlude marked with moments of passion, but those moments had been nothing compared to this. He and Sheba were joined – he couldn't tell where he ended and she began. And he never wanted to find out.

Sleep overtook him, and he didn't fight it, safe and secure in her warmth.

When he awoke, the fire had burned itself to embers. He pulled a coverlet over Sheba, who stirred but did not wake, then put on his clothes. The terror that had found him on the dance floor had found him again. His heart pounded in his throat. He hadn't danced this time, but he had lost himself. He had never done that before, and couldn't again. If he lost himself, he lost everything he had.

As he opened the door, he saw the untouched dinner tray. Delights untasted. He walked across the quiet lawn. The lake shimmered in the moonlight, as magical as the woman who had held him. He unlocked the door to his cabin, went inside, stripped, and slipped into bed. The covers were cold and uninviting, and he knew he had been crazy to leave.

He awoke to a pounding on his door. He climbed out of bed, feet resisting the cold wood floor, and slipped on his leggings. In his imagination, he saw Sheba out there, angry because he had left her, but when he pulled open the door, he was surprised to find Beltar, looking wide awake and pleased with himself.

'She's awake,' Beltar said.

71

Diate blinked, wondering how Beltar knew. Then he realized Beltar was talking about Martina. 'The surgeries are over?'

'She's wrapped up like a Jovasian in too much sunlight, but she's alert and ready to talk.' Beltar peered around him. 'You going to invite me in while you get dressed, or are you in need of privacy?'

Odd question. Diate stepped out of the way of the door. 'Come on in.'

Beltar stepped inside and closed the door. Diate's cabin lacked the lush rug and ornate pillows of Sheba's, but the front room had been designed for comfort. Large cushions bolstered the chairs and sofas, placed strategically to create intimate groupings. His fireplace was made of stone – and he hadn't used it so far. A large oak table graced the dining area, and a small kitchen provided any meal he wanted, if he didn't care to go to a restaurant.

He went into the kitchen now and pulled the remains of the ice coffee he had brought in bulk out of the freezer unit built into the wall. 'Want something to drink?'

'Please.' Beltar reached into the oversized pockets on his robe and brought out two carefully wrapped rolls. He unwrapped them and put them on a plate, their faint doughy scent making Diate's mouth water.

Diate set both glasses of coffee down. Beltar took one.

'Looks like you had an interesting evening,' he said.

Diate felt himself flush before he could turn away. 'What do you see?'

'A man doesn't get bruises like that on his shoulders from sleeping alone.'

Diate's flush grew deeper. Beltar laughed, and took a sip of his coffee. 'Don't be embarrassed, detective. We all have personal lives.'

Diate glanced up sharply at Beltar. He thought he knew all about Beltar's personal life – at least his life in the Port City. But Beltar never said anything about the trips he took, except to report whether or not they were successful. Did he meet women on them? Did he have nights of incredible passion like that one?

'I just hope I get a chance to meet her,' Beltar said.

'She's around. People like that are hard to miss in this tiny place.'

Beltar smiled. 'I think I like her already. She takes the edges off you, detective. Makes me think you don't do this very often.'

Not at all, Diate almost said, and stopped himself. He made

himself take a sip of the coffee and rip off a bit of the roll. The roll tasted of sugar and a bitter spice he couldn't identify. 'I've never been on vacation before.'

'This isn't vacation now. Get dressed. You've got another woman to visit.'

Diate smiled, took another bite of the roll, and disappeared into the bathroom. On his first day here, he had studied this room. The large tub in the center doubled as a whirlpool, and the shower had a steam feature. The water temperature for each device could be set and stored in a simple memory system built on the side. The plumbing fixtures were made of gold, and the water that flowed from them was clearer than any water he had ever seen. It had a clean wintry taste he associated with his childhood. Even now when he walked in the room, it made him feel as if he were in the center of luxury. As it was supposed to.

He set the shower on short wash, hit the on switch, adjusted the water pressure to hard, and jumped in, scrubbing himself quickly. Somehow he couldn't see Martina with the memory of Sheba still on his skin. He examined his upper arms and shoulders as he washed. A string of bright red bruises ran along the skin like a poorly designed paisley. He touched one, surprised it didn't hurt. When the water shut off, he stepped out, using a towel as thick as Sheba's rug to dry himself off.

For the hundredth time, he wondered how much the cabins were costing Beltar. But he knew that if he asked, Beltar would brush him off as he had each time before.

Diate slipped on a new pair of leggings and a tailored tunic, then put a pair of clear sandals on his feet. He combed his hair and stepped out, to find Beltar eating the last bit of roll off Diate's plate.

'Couldn't let it go to waste,' Beltar said with a smile.

'Good thing I wasn't that hungry,' Diate replied. He finished the last of his iced coffee, set the dishes in the sink, and set the plumbing for a hot cleaning. Then he led Beltar out the door and into the early morning sunshine.

The grass sparkled with dew. Diate had never seen dew before, and had thought, during his first few days, that it had rained each night. The lake had a faint fishy odor, and the breeze was cool. He glanced once at Sheba's cabin, and saw no signs of life. Then he followed Beltar to the hospital.

The hospital – or the Recovery Center, as it was euphemistically known – was in the center of the small town. The hospital came first; the town appeared around it. Two Olean doctors had bought land near the small lake with the thought to building a resort. An accident had happened requiring their different skills, and that led them to realize that combining the resort with one of the best surgical facilities outside of Oleon would give them double the number of clients. Or in this case, triple.

Beltar pulled open the wide glass doors. The inside of the Recovery Center had a faint floral odor. No medicinal or sick smell at all. The staff had told him when they first brought Martina in that each part of the facility had its own air recycling unit. That way the germs in the viral diseases area did not transmit into intensive care. Diate found the concept novel and forced himself to remember it so that he could tell the Golgoth.

Plants of various sizes and from various parts of the world graced the waiting area. Each plant had one thing in common: it was able to survive in artificial light at a relatively consistent temperature. Still, it startled him to see the blue figs of Ziklag mixed with bright green ferns found south of the Port City. He recognized no Kingdom plants there, and tried to remember what kind of Kingdom plants existed at all.

He and Beltar took the glass steps branching off to the right, leading to the reconstruction wing. Martina had a light, airy room overlooking the lake. Even though Beltar had probably paid extra for the view, she hadn't been able to enjoy it until now.

Beltar pushed her door open, and they stepped inside. Two white chairs sat bedside, and a couch with matching ottoman faced the window. If it weren't for the bed and the equipment surrounding it, the room would look like it was part of a small apartment.

Diate took a step forward. The smell of burned flesh no longer clung to Martina. But Beltar was right. Bandages covered her entire body. Her hands were in casts hanging from small wires, keeping the palms flat a few inches above her torso.

'Martina?'

'Detective.' Her voice was stronger, not the wispy, tremulous voice of a victim, but something that almost had power.

'Diate,' he reminded her, and wondered why he hadn't given her his first name, as he had done with Sheba. 'How're you feeling?'

'Like a piece of fish about to go to market.'

He laughed. He had seen fish wrapped the way she was. He took one of the chairs. Beltar sat beside him. 'Beltar says you want to talk.'

'I told Emilio that you had some concerns.'

She inclined her head toward Beltar's voice. Her eyes were bandaged this time. Diate hadn't noticed that before. 'Emilio,' she said. 'Like your father.'

Diate started. He had forgotten how famous his father had been.

'Yes,' she continued, 'I do have concerns. I don't know if you know that Rulanda is a prime Kingdom work and leisure spot. Beltar assures me that no one knows that I'm here, but I think if they find me, they'll kill me.'

'I'm here to prevent that,' Diate said.

'But you're not going to sit beside me all day,' she said. 'I want to know what other plans you have for my protection.'

Diate glanced at Beltar. Beltar shrugged, but his eyes twinkled. He was pleased that Martina was a fighter.

'We have registered you as a member of the Golgoth's family. I told the hospital that should any harm come to you it will cause an international incident. Unless you tell someone who you are, the hospital has no reason to disbelieve me. Your caste marks were destroyed when you were hurt. The security here is first-rate. They have had many delicate patients before, and handled many difficult incidents.'

She didn't move for the longest time. He wondered if she had fallen asleep. Then she stirred, a little. 'You think that's enough to protect me?'

'I think that's more than enough to protect you.'

She nodded a little. Diate leaned toward her. The bandages took away her fragility, and made her seem more mysterious. He wanted to touch her, to comfort her – he, a man who rarely touched anyone – and because of her injuries, he couldn't touch her at all.

'What happened to you?' he asked.

A small shudder ran through her. 'Is Beltar still here?'

'Yes,' he said, 'I am. Do you want me to leave?'

'No.' Her voice was soft. 'I just wanted you close by.'

Beltar reddened. Diate didn't move. He wished he could see through her bandages, watch the expression on her face. He didn't realize, until they were gone, how much he relied on visual cues.

'What happened,' she repeated, and turned away, as if she

75

didn't want to face them even though she couldn't see them. 'I was a Talent, Diate. A pianist, top of my form. I got sent on B concerts, while they groomed me for A.'

Diate tensed. He remembered the competition, the undercutting that went along with A and B assignments. Those assignments brought the most revenue into the Kingdom, and the performers were watched more closely than any others.

'I met a man on a ship heading out to the Derad Fiefdom, and we spent all our time together. He went with me to Derad, and then wanted to come home with me. Some of the guard met me one night and warned me away from him. When I didn't listen, they sent me home.'

Diate nodded. He knew that the Kingdom was very strict with its performers. They had to follow the rules, or be banned from performance altogether.

'They questioned me about him, and when it turned out I didn't know anything, they sent me to my parents' house.'

'Who was the man?' Diate asked.

'His name was Itzak.' Her voice softened. 'He was tall and slender, much like you, detective, and he spoke with an accent I didn't recognize.'

'Itzak Linconi?' Linconi was a free-range assassin who worked for any country that hired him. He specialized in Talent assassination.

'He never told me his last name.'

'And he found you.'

'Yes, detective.' Her voice had a wry patience. 'Is that odd?'

'Where did you serve before you met him?'

'Do you know him?'

'Yes, I do,' Diate said. 'He kills Talents, for a price. Where did you serve?'

Beltar stiffened beside him. Martina took in a deep breath.

'I – hadn't served with anyone. I had been recommissioned. They tested my music Talent late.'

'Whom did you work with before?' Diate asked.

'A man named Santiago.' She said the name with a heaviness that implied that Diate should know Santiago's name as well. It struck a distant memory, but one he couldn't grasp. 'I wouldn't do the jobs he asked. So I left, and retrained. My family had an aptitude for music. The Queen said I could retest, and I did.'

Diate frowned. Something was missing here. 'You were attacked after you left Itzak?'

'At home,' she whispered. 'They came for me when my mother was gone, and they said nothing. They tied me up and broke my fingers. I passed out, and that's the last thing I remember until I saw you.'

Diate suppressed a shudder. Beltar had gone white. Martina hadn't moved while she spoke. Her voice remained flat and dispassionate, as if the events had occurred to someone else.

'They said nothing?' Diate asked.

She shifted in the bed. 'Not a word.'

Beltar gripped his chair as if to hold himself in place. Diate closed his eyes. *His mother, reaching out toward the baby* . . . He opened them again. 'You're sure it was the guard?'

'They dressed like the guard.' Her voice became stronger.

'But you did nothing to warrant this treatment?'

'If I did,' she said, 'I don't know what it could have been.'

'You took part in no rebellion? Did you speak against the government?'

'They retrained me. Would they have done that to someone they were going to kill?'

He took a deep breath. 'I don't know any more,' he said.

She turned her face toward him, the bandages etching the hollows of her eyes. 'Don't you believe me, detective?'

'It's an odd series of events.' He stood up. He couldn't sit still any longer. 'Do you understand what happened to you?'

'I was nearly killed for failing to tell them any more about Itzak.'

'No.' He paced behind his chair, squeezed Beltar's shoulder, and walked over to the window. Five small boats clustered on the lake. On the far beach, a group of children played. 'No,' Diate repeated. 'You received the worst punishment the Kingdom can give out. You were tried – and almost executed – for treason.'

Silence followed his words. Diate didn't turn away from the window. He couldn't see Martina's reaction, and he didn't want to see Beltar's. The children splashed in the water, and he wished he could hear their laughter.

'I did not commit treason.' Martina's voice was small. 'I would not.'

Diate turned. She still faced his empty chair. 'They think you did.'

77

'By sleeping with Itzak?'

'Something must have happened before that. Who was Santiago?'

She shook her head. 'He had nothing to do with this.'

'Then who did?'

'I don't know.' She had moved her legs up, squinching the blanket beneath her knees. Beltar stood, his mouth open slightly, his forehead creased. New wrinkles Diate had never seen before lined Beltar's face.

'Something must have happened,' Diate said. 'They don't do this to people on a whim. If you remember, I'll be able to protect you better. Treason is not something the Kingdom takes lightly.'

She pushed herself back into the pillows, as if she could hide by burying herself in the bed. 'Are you saying they'll try to kill me again?'

'If they know you're alive. And this time, they'll do what they can to make the experience even worse than the one that came before.'

'Emilio.' Beltar reached out to him, as if begging him to stop. Diate shook his head at his friend. He approached the bed.

'Some of us survive the nightmare, Martina. I did. But you'll have to trust me. And the more information I have, the better I can help you.'

She sighed, and kicked at her blankets. 'I'm tired,' she said.

Diate nodded. 'We'll leave you for now. But I would like to talk, later.'

'Okay.' She buried her face in the pillow and made herself as small as she could, even though her hands remained elevated. Diate took one more glance at her, then let himself out of the room. Beltar stayed inside.

Diate walked down the corridor to the small sitting area in an alcove underneath wide glass windows. The children had left the lake, and the boats had scattered. He sat in one of the chairs and sank in its softness, amazed that the very plushness of the town urged him to relax. But he didn't want to relax. Martina's story bothered him. She presented herself as ignorant and blameless, and yet the woman who demanded protection seemed neither. Had she learned from her experience, or was she hiding something?

A door clicked softly down the hall, and Diate looked up. Beltar was walking toward him, head down. When he reached the alcove, he sat down and rubbed his eyes. His skin was still pasty and sickly-looking.

'How badly did I upset her?'

'How much did you want to?' Beltar's mouth maintained a thin line. He kept his hands gripped tightly together as if he were holding them back from Diate's throat.

'I want her to tell me the truth, Beltar. She's afraid right now, and afraid of me. If she lies to me, I may not be able to help her. She will have better luck with us and with the Golgoth if she did commit treason.'

Beltar leaned back a little. 'That makes no sense.'

'It makes a lot of sense,' Diate said. 'If she committed treason against the state, that means she has no feelings for the Kingdom. She might actually be able to help us out, to give us information on the Kingdom or be willing to work against them.'

Beltar swallowed. 'Sounds crass. I thought you helped her because she was injured.'

'I did.' Diate gripped the arms of the plush chair. 'Eventually, though, she'll need a way to live. She'll need a home, and a job, if she can work. The state is more willing to help her if she helps it.'

'I'll provide for her,' Beltar said.

Diate shrugged. 'Then she's lucky. Most people who live in the Port City have no one at all.'

Beltar expelled a bit of air, and his entire body relaxed. 'You had no one.'

Diate watched as understanding worked through Beltar's face. 'Except myself.'

He stood. The window glass felt cool against his back. 'It's almost midday. I have some iced coffee waiting for me.'

Beltar nodded. 'I think I'm going to sit here for a moment. The glimpses I get into your world, detective, always take the breath out of me.'

'Is that bad?' Diate asked. The answer mattered to him. One of the things that most mattered to him was Beltar's respect.

Beltar looked at his hands, at the marks his own fingers had left when he squeezed his palms together. 'No, it's not bad. It's just different. I look at the world as a place full of clients, people I want to introduce to my wines, my style of life. You look at the world as a place that could kill you when your back is turned.'

'It could,' Diate said.

'I suppose.' Beltar ran his palms along his robe. 'But wouldn't you rather live like I do? If you die, you die.'

Diate glanced out the window at the empty lake. If he could, he would stay here forever, living in a small town with nothing to do, a place where people took naps in the middle of the day. But he had no way to survive in a place like this.

'I would love to live like you do,' he said softly. 'But if I turn my back now, someone will put a knife in it.'

He sighed, and slipped his hands in the pockets of his tailored tunic. Then he turned his back on the window and walked away.

The mid-afternoon sun had reached its zenith. Diate walked across the heat-baked street, feeling the hot cracked dirt against his sandals. The town was quiet. Even the tourists remained indoors. No one sat on the streetside porch of the coffee shop.

A hand touched his arm. He jumped, heart pounding. A woman stood beside him, a silver circle over her nose. Talent. Magic Talent. He bit back his anger. No one had snuck up on him like that in a long, long time.

'So the woman in the Recovery Center is not your wife.' The Talent spoke Lillish.

Diate did not reply. Any answer he would give would be defensive.

'You do not love her. That's good.'

'What do you want?' Diate asked.

'You don't remember me, do you?'

Diate stared at her. A face swam across his memory, a face with fewer lines, with skin untouched by the sun. 'You're Torrie. You're the one who found me on the Vorgellian ship.'

She reached up and tucked a strand of hair behind his ear. He didn't move. 'The Diates have always been tied up in the fate of the Kingdom,' she said. 'You know that, don't you?'

Her fingers moved along his cheek up to his temple and caressed his caste mark. 'It's a shame to waste a Talent. I'm glad you're coming back.'

He wrenched away from her. 'You turned me in on that ship. You set these wheels in motion.'

She smiled. 'We couldn't let another Diate die, now could we?' She touched her own caste mark in salute, and then walked away.

The breeze made her gown flow behind her. She almost looked as if she were floating. He made himself breathe. She couldn't hurt him now.

But she could hurt Martina. How had she known? He shook his head. He had never understood Magic Talents.

The Recovery Center was under strict orders to keep all visitors away from Martina except for Diate and Beltar. When he went back this afternoon, he would make sure that the rule was obeyed – even though he was convinced that the woman who headed the Center's security would never allow any breach.

Torrie was gone. The street was empty again, the breeze blowing dust across the wooden sidewalks. He bounded up the stairs to the coffee shop. He wanted his iced coffee, and he wanted it in private. He would find out what Torrie was doing here later. And he would make sure she never got near Martina.

We couldn't let another Diate die, now could we?

He had always though his escape miraculous, always thought that Sehan had helped him out of the goodness of his heart. Sehan and Torrie's conversation returned to him.

I thought you admired his father.

His father is dead.

Ideals live on.

With coaxing.

Coaxing. Did coaxing mean using a round-about way to save Diate's life? He shuddered once. Had someone really controlled him all this time?

Chapter 6

Diate closed his eyes and rested his feet on the chair across from him. He clutched an iced coffee in his right hand. A breeze off the lake ruffled the hair on his forehead, easing the midday heat. In the distance, a train whistled. Trains and a handful of private electric cars were the only transportation into and out of the town. The hospital had a communications net, but people who were not on the hospital staff couldn't use it, not even if there was an emergency. When Beltar had told Diate that, Diate had thought he would feel claustrophobic there. Instead he felt protected.

A finger caressed his collar bone, followed by the scent of flowers. A thrill of excitement ran through him. He opened his eyes. Sheba was bending over him, her lips close to his.

He kissed her. She was more potent than any wine, richer than any iced coffee. He reached up, cupped her cheeks, then ran his hands down her neck and onto her shoulders. Her fingers encircled his wrists.

'You're a lot more eager than I thought you would be when I woke up alone this morning,' he said.

Eager? He wanted to take her across one of the tables, with the lake breeze blowing on them, in full view of the coffee shop customers. But she held him fast, her grip tight on his wrists, and her mouth just a tad too far from his.

'Sorry,' he said.

'Sorry isn't good enough.' She let him go, circled behind him, and pulled over a chair. The wind toyed with the split seams of her blouse and teased her short skirt. She was barefoot. As she straddled the chair, he noticed that she wore nothing under the skirt. He took a deep breath and made himself relax. 'If I had wanted a night of great sex, but nothing more, I'm sure most men here would have obliged me.'

'You want more?' The ache in his body occupied his brain; he had trouble concentrating on what she said.

'I thought we shared something very special.' She took his iced coffee, and sipped from it.

'We did.' He watched as her lips caressed the edge of the glass. With a skip of the imagination, he could remember how those lips felt caressing him.

'Really?' She set the coffee down. 'Then don't abandon me again in the middle of the night.'

He took the glass, his hand shaking badly. He drank from the same place she had, and he could taste her on the rim of the glass. He leaned back and studied the lake. It was empty, but the breeze made little ripples in the surface. 'I have lived most of my life alone,' he said, uncertain about whether he should reveal this much of himself. 'And it's been a long time since I have been that intimate with another person.'

Out of the corner of his eye, he could see her. She was staring at him as if his words made her re-evaluate him. Slowly she reached out a hand and took his. He squeezed, the physical connection a lifeline he had never known he needed.

'I'm sorry,' she said. 'I'm too demanding, aren't I? We've only known each other twenty-four hours. It feels longer.'

He didn't answer. Instead, he pushed his glass aside and pulled her closer. He clung to her hand, slipped his other hand into her soft, fragrant hair, and pulled her head forward, catching her lips with his own. This kiss lacked the gentleness of the first – it was rough, insistent, as if she felt the desire as deeply as he did. He hooked his feet around the legs of the chair and slid forward so that their bodies touched.

A flame exploded between them. He forgot the breeze, the coffee shop, the lake. All that mattered was her, and the way she felt.

A hand on his shoulder made him start. He pulled away like a man climbing out of a deep sleep, and looked up. Beltar stood behind him, a smile on his face.

'I take it this is the lady.'

Diate shoved aside the irritation he felt at being interrupted. He took a deep breath. 'Beltar, this is Sheba. Sheba, Beltar.'

She ran a hand through her hair, messing it worse, adding to her windswept look. Her lips were bruised and her eyes half-closed, as if she too had difficulty recovering. 'Pleasure.'

'Yes.' The smile had left Beltar's eyes. He had taken a small step backwards.

'I adore your wines,' she said. 'I drink almost nothing else when I'm here. Why don't you market them on all the islands?'

The question startled Diate. He thought Beltar's wines sold everywhere.

'Each island has its own regulations. Some dislike the spices I use. Others object to the alcoholic content. Still others want to charge a huge surcharge that I oppose.'

'Hmm.' She folded her arms on top of the chair, resting her chin on them. 'I hadn't realized it was so complicated.'

'Direct marketing always is.' There was something subtle in Beltar's tone. A hint of sarcasm? A bit of judgment? Diate couldn't tell.

Sheba stood and swung her well-formed leg over the chair. Diate felt her physical withdrawal like a blow.

'We missed dinner last night.' Her voice was husky, as it had been before she spoke with Beltar. 'Should we try again tonight?'

'It would be my pleasure.'

'Same place, same time.' Her smile was for him. 'I promise to be a bit less revealing.'

Then she walked into the coffee shop and disappeared from his view. Diate's heart slowed to its regular rate. 'I swear, Beltar,' he said, 'it's like I'm drowning and she's air.'

'I knew a woman like that once,' Beltar said, easing his bulk into Sheba's chair. 'Girl, actually. I was sixteen and a bundle of nerve endings. One touch from her, and I lost myself.'

Diate sipped his coffee. The liquid had warmed and gained a flavor he hadn't noticed before. 'At sixteen, I was running for my life. I have never felt like this before.'

Beltar laughed. 'And you never will again. Welcome to first love, detective. Better late than never.'

'I don't know if I'm in love.'

'It doesn't matter. Your body is. Enjoy it. It only happens once. I wish I could feel it again.'

Diate glanced back over his shoulder, but he couldn't see Sheba. 'You didn't like her.'

Beltar shook his head. 'She wasn't what I expected. I thought she'd be as rigid as you. But she flows. Makes sense, I guess. It takes the sensual ones to draw out the reserved ones.'

Diate glanced at Beltar, feeling a bit perplexed. He had never thought of himself as reserved. He rarely thought of himself in relation to other people at all. 'She says I'm the first in a long time.'

Beltar frowned, then leaned back on the chair. 'Perhaps,' he said. 'I've never seen her with anyone.'

'You know her?'

Beltar shrugged. 'Not really. We are often at the resort at the same time. Come to think of it, I always noticed her because she was alone, and looking so serious. Perhaps you do share things in common.'

Diate finished the last of his coffee and stood. The sexual energy he had felt around Sheba had become restlessness. 'I need to walk.'

'That's not what you need.' Beltar grinned. 'Sorry I interrupted you, detective.'

Diate flushed. Beltar caught Diate's sleeve as he stood. 'Look, I was looking for you for a reason.'

'I'm not going to apologize to Martina. I need her candor.'

The breeze scattered Beltar's sparse hair around his scalp. 'No,' he said. 'I understand what you did, even if I didn't like it. I was wondering if you were willing to do a little sleuthing.'

'Sleuthing?' Diate slid his chair in and picked up his glass.

Beltar shrugged. 'I've been coming here for a long time. And for the last several visits, the resort has been having a curious problem.'

Diate glanced at Beltar. Beltar looked almost guilty for asking – he who had nagged Diate so hard to take a vacation. 'My brain is the only part of my anatomy not getting any exercise this trip.'

Beltar's hangdog look disappeared. 'Let me take you to my friend. He'll explain the problem better than I can.'

'All right.' Diate brought his glass inside and set it on the counter. The proprietor didn't look up from his slouch against the wall. Beltar trailed behind him. Diate turned. 'I don't know where we're going.'

'Oh.' Beltar pushed open the outside door. Still no one had taken a table streetside. 'We're going back to the resort.'

They walked down the empty streets, past small dust devils blowing across the hot dirt. It wasn't as hard-packed as Diate thought. He saw no sign of the train that had gone by earlier. The resort's oversized handcarts hadn't even gone by.

The resort looked as sleepy as the town. Tall trees with wavy fronds decorated the doorways. Ferns and other leafy plants covered the brown dirt. Every morning, gardeners with watering cans tended to the plants, making sure each had its requisite share of moisture. One morning, Diate had watched the entire ritual from his bedroom window. He had never seen such attention to detail.

The path leading to the double doors was made of flat, oblong-shaped rocks. The rocks came from the other side of the island and were brought in by train. Tourists could buy some if they wanted, but the prices were incredibly high for something that could be picked up off the ground.

The double doors stood open, and from inside a few bars of a musical composition echoed. Then the music stopped and he heard voices, the tones tense. Someone was rehearsing, and it wasn't going very well.

The air inside was cooler, the movement of overhead fans adding a comfort the lake breeze didn't hold, and it smelled of mint. Beltar took the lead, walking quickly down a small corridor marked for private use.

They passed several plants spilling off stands. The plants were the source of the mint smell. These plants appeared to be native to Rulanda. They had the same rich forest green color as the undergrowth near the lake had. The leaves were wide and ribbed, and trailed to the floor. The plants looked even lusher because of mirrors placed behind them. The mirrors revealed a Diate who looked more haggard than he felt. The results of his broken night's sleep? Or did he look like that all the time? He didn't know.

The corridor ended in a formidable oak door. Beltar knocked once, then pushed it open and stepped inside. Diate folllowed.

A tiny man sat behind a wide desk. More plants graced his walls, and an oversized picture window revealed an enclosed courtyard Diate hadn't seen. The man didn't look up as the two entered. Behind them, the door clicked shut.

'Tellen,' Beltar said. 'This is the detective I was talking about.'

Tellen finally seemed to notice them. He stopped studying the papers on his desk and studied his guests instead. His features were small also, except for his eyes, which were large and wide. They grew wider as they focused on Diate. 'I didn't know Talents were detectives.'

Diate's hand went instinctively to his forehead. His hair was blown back, away from the caste mark. He should have made sure that the hair covered it, but he had forgotten. Odd that he hadn't noticed it in the mirror. The mark was such a part of him that he no longer considered it special.

'I think I'm probably the only one,' he said. 'I'm Diate.'

Tellen stood and left two fingers braced on the desk. 'Enjoying your stay?'

Diate couldn't stop a smile. 'Very much.'

Tellen nodded, as if he had barely heard the answer. 'I normally don't ask things of our guests, but Beltar has become a friend over the years, and he insisted.' He swept a hand to indicate the chairs ringing his desk. 'Please.'

Diate and Beltar sat. Tellen leaned against the desk, thin fingers tapping. 'I don't know how familiar you are with the area.'

'Only what I've seen,' Diate said. 'Although I must admit I have discovered a passion for iced coffee.'

'Coffee beans were planted all over this side of Rulanda by early settlers. They considered the drink essential to their way of life. On other islands, the custom died out because the beans did not thrive.' Tellen's fingers continued their drumming. The sound was even and rhythmical. 'I trust you haven't seen any natives. Are you familiar with the Hoste?'

Diate rested his hands on his thighs. 'I've never seen them. I only knew they were on Rulanda because Beltar told me. I thought they had their own islands farther south.'

'Most of the Hoste have died off in the islands.' Tellen licked his lower lip. 'Here they've been protected. Since the climate is favorable, they prefer to live in the woods and continue their natural existence. They have a small shelter in the clearing. They are interesting craftspeople with many talents. They maintain the plants in this building and do much of the gardening on the cabins. If you had come with Beltar a few years ago, you would have seen another native skill, something this resort was once quite proud of.'

'Etched glass,' Beltar said. 'It was stunning, Emilio, and very delicate.'

'All of our good crystal, our light fixtures, mirrors and windows were made of Hoste glass. The Hoste spend months on a single piece, so the resort represented decades of work and negotiation. About three years ago, the Hoste glass started to disappear.'

'Breakage?' Diate asked.

Tellen shook his head. 'Theft.'

'It's illegal to export Hoste glass,' Beltar said. 'I wanted a few decanters made out of it for my special customers, and I had to go through almost a year of red tape to be denied.'

'It's an important collectable to art dealers all over the world, and none may transport or work with it. Yet it finds its way to outside markets.'

'I haven't seen any of the glass,' Diate said. 'All of it was stolen?'

'No,' Tellen said. 'Just enough pieces that we recognized the pattern as theft. Because this resort has no internal security – we never thought we needed any since we could screen our guests – we did not solve the crimes, and thought the best thing we could do was to store the glass for a few years until the interest died away.'

'Seems sensible,' Diate said.

'We thought so.' Tellen stopped drumming. He clasped both hands together. His right thumb moved across his skin to the same rhythm as his fingers had tapped. 'Until a few weeks ago, when I had occasion to check the storage room for the first time in nearly a year. Half the pieces we stored are gone. And in the last week, another has disappeared.'

'Do you think the perpetrator is still here?' Diate asked. 'I saw a train arrive during mid-afternoon quiet. Surely it takes passengers when it leaves.'

'Sometimes,' Tellen said. 'But in slow months like this, the train arrives once a week and leaves about a week later. The electric cars are stored in our lot outside of town, and we must be contacted before one is removed.'

'No one has left since last week?'

'That's right. And I noticed the room was fine after last week's train arrived, so the theft occurred within a marked period of time. Also, this has been going on for a number of years. I think some of the engineers might be involved.'

'Vorgellians?' Diate asked. 'They rarely do this kind of thing alone.'

Tellen shrugged, thumb still nervously rubbing.

Diate leaned back in his chair. 'This suggests regular customers are at fault. Why haven't you blamed Beltar? He wanted etched glass and was unable to get it.'

Beltar choked and turned red.

'Beltar is an ethical man,' Tellen said.

'Yes,' Diate replied. 'Beltar is. But an ethical man, beyond reproach, is a wonderful pose for a smuggler.'

Beltar glanced at Diate as if Diate were betraying him. Tellen's thumb stopped moving. 'I don't like you impugning the honor of my friends.'

'Most of your regular clients are friends, aren't they?' Diate hadn't moved, although his relaxed posture was now a pose. 'If it turns out to be one of them, I will have to impugn that person's honor.'

Tellen got up and walked to the window. He gazed out at the enclosed courtyard. His slight frame had gone rigid. Beltar glanced at Diate, a silent plea on his face. For what, Diate couldn't tell, and he didn't want to find out.

'If this gets out, it could ruin my resort,' Tellen said.

'If it continues, you will lose a great deal of money in investments. If you're known as an easy mark, the glass will be the first target. Others will follow.' Diate kept his tone conversational.

With the door closed, the room had grown stuffy. A bead of sweat trickled down Diate's back.

'What will you do if it is one of my loyal customers?'

Loyal. Intersting phrasing. The man looked at his clients as personal friends. 'I will come to you,' Diate said. 'We'll discuss the actions to take.'

Tellen turned, the light from the window surrounding him like a halo. 'Unless,' Diate said, 'my work puts me in personal jeopardy. If that happens, I will take whatever measures necessary to protect myself.'

'We've never had a death at this resort,' Tellen said.

'Nonsense,' Diate replied. 'The owner of the coffee shop was telling me of a man who drowned in the lake not two weeks ago. It happens, Tellen, and you cover it up. If something happened in this case, you would cover it up too. I'll be as discreet as I can.'

Tellen looked down.

'You need to be honest with me,' Diate said. 'About everything.'

Tellen nodded, without meeting Diate's gaze.

'First we're going to look at that glass,' Diate said, 'and then we're going to investigate that drowning death a bit more closely. The answers might be right there.' He stood. 'And one more thing: Beltar's not guilty. He and I have worked together before on smuggling cases. He knows that I get results. He wouldn't bring me in at risk to himself. He's too smart.'

'Thanks,' Beltar murmured. 'I think.'

Tellen smiled at the joke, but his gaze remained unfocused. Despite Diate's request to see the glass, Tellen hadn't moved. 'Forgive me,' he said, 'but I have seen no proof of credentials, and I know nothing of you but Beltar's recommendation.'

'You didn't check my registration forms?'

Tellen flushed slightly.

'You still find it odd that a Talent would be a detective.'

Tellen nodded. 'I am sorry, but your papers say you're from Golga.'

Diate shrugged. 'I never expected you to trust me immediately. In fact, your willingness to talk with me as frankly as you did had me a bit worried. I wondered how many others you had told.'

'None,' Tellen said.

Diate held up his hand to keep Tellen from continuing. 'How long have you been in business?'

'I helped my father run the resort when I was a boy,' Tellen said.

'Have you always allowed the Kingdom here?'

Beltar put a hand on Diate's arm. Tellen noticed it, and frowned before he spoke. 'They have always performed for us, and over time our resort gained enough of a reputation to bring in the upper-level bureaucrats and assistants to the Queen. Is that a problem?'

Diate shook his head. 'If you have been doing this for a long time, you should remember the Rogue Talent.'

'The dancing boy. I saw him perform once, at a special gathering for honored guests of the Queen. I thought it a shame that he disappeared.'

Diate had forgotten that engagement. Fragments of a memory rose: the crowd, dressed in silks and linens; the hall, close and stuffy; the routine that stretched his muscles and made him pant; the sweat running down his cheeks, staining his costume; the Queen, smiling at him. He stared at Tellen for a moment, wondering where his loyalties lay, and then realized: Tellen's loyalties lay with Tellen's town and Tellen's resort. 'I am that boy,' Diate said. 'The Queen murdered my family and I was the only one to escape.'

Tellen's flush grew until he was completely red. Diate's tone must have been harsher than he thought. 'I never meant any disrespect.'

'You never gave me any.' Diate stood. This was not a story to tell sitting down. 'I smuggled myself on a cruise liner heading here. I never made it. They found me and sent me to Golga, thinking the Golgoth would execute me. But he didn't. And now I head the detectives in the Port City.'

Tellen was watching him, eyes wide. Beltar was the one who spoke up. 'But those still aren't credentials,' he said. 'If you would like those, we have travel papers in my room. They carry his place of birth as well as his place of employment.'

Tellen was staring at Diate as if the man in front of him had become an entirely different person. 'No,' Tellen said without looking at Beltar. 'We saw your travel papers when you checked in. We simply do not make note of place of birth.'

Diate did not like the intense scrutiny. He walked to the back of the chair, looked at the plants thriving against the wall, and peered into the mirror. Tellen was watching his every move. 'I think,' Diate said, 'it's time to see the glass.'

Tellen finally looked away. Diate turned around, glad the gaze was off of him. Beltar stood. Tellen ran his finger along the side of one mirror and the wall slid back. 'Follow me, gentlemen,' he said.

Diate glanced around the room again, wondering what other surprises were hidden behind the plants and mirrors. He hadn't inspected the resort with the thought of hidden rooms in mind. Odd that, since the Port City was a warren of hidden tunnels.

Beltar followed Tellen through the darkened doorway. Diate stepped in behind them. The air had a musty odor, and the passageway had a chill dampness no other place in Rulanda had. Diate resisted the urge to wipe the dank air off his bare skin.

A thin illumination from the door was all the light they had, until Tellen reached up and turned on an overhead beam. He used a key to unlock a small door, which all three men had to duck to get through. This room had its own internal glow, which came from the ceiling.

Diate glanced up. For a moment, he thought the entire ceiling was made of lights. Then he realized that they were underneath the pool he had seen in the small courtyard, and the pool had a glass bottom. The water refracted the light, making it thinner inside the room itself.

A child sat on the rim of the pool, looking down at them. A little girl with a serious face. If Diate looked hard enough, he thought he could see tears. 'Is she watching us?' he asked.

Tellen glanced up. 'The pool is artificial. We put a one-way mirror on the bottom. We can see her, but she can't see us.'

Diate nodded, and turned his attention to the rest of the room. The air was even colder here than it was in the hallway, but the damp feel was gone. Like the ceiling, the walls were made of glass that reflected light. Against the walls, pieces of glass leaned. Diate crouched in front of one of them.

The etchings were faint, almost figments of the imagination, until the light caught them just right. Then he was transported into a world he had never seen before. Naked women with flowing hair sat astride four-legged creatures with long muzzles and flowing tails. Small men, the size of Tellen, danced around the creatures, holding hands. A bonfire burned in the center. Diate could almost smell the smoke and hear the men singing. The sound of hooves pounding earth caught his ears and he wished he could join them.

'Beautiful, aren't they?' Tellen asked.

Diate made himself look away from the magical world. 'I've never seen anything like it.'

'And you never will again. The Hoste have a touch that makes these pieces live. We have had guests who have stared at the glass for hours. Some even accused us of fostering an addiction.' Tellen ran his hands along the top of the piece that Diate had been looking at. 'Still, I hate hiding these away. It's almost as if the spirit has left the resort. I can remember walking the halls alone and feeling as if someone was with me. The etchings on the light fixtures made patterns on the walls, and I sometimes thought those patterns reflected differently, as if the figures were really with me.'

Diate glanced back at the women and the dancing men. The piece next to it portrayed another naked woman. She sat alone on a stump, a lake behind her. The scent of loam filled his nostrils and her soft voice rang in his ears. He could see how Tellen would miss the company of these pieces. Anyone who owned one of these etchings would not be alone.

'That's why they're so highly desired,' Diate murmured.

'No,' Beltar said. 'That's only part of it. The international trade society determined that Hoste glass was a rare product with

92

unknown properties. They planned to study it, to see what kinds of addictions, if any, it caused. They also were trying to determine how the glass fits into Hoste society. Some rumors claim that the figures on the glass house the spirits of the dead. The study is proceeding, but Hoste glass cannot be removed from Rulanda legally. Yet, it is a desirable commodity, and collectors consider it an important part of what they do.'

'I have another theory,' Tellen said. Diate stood to turn his attention to the conversation and away from the delicate figures carved in the glass. 'I think most collectors are very lonely people. They collect things and give them value because those things helped the collector survive a difficult period or because they give the collector worth. I think some collector found Hoste glass and discovered that in addition to the satisfaction a beautiful collectible brings, this one also brought its own ghosts along – actual creatures to keep the collector company.'

'How much would Hoste glass bring on the market?' Diate asked.

'The pieces are priceless,' Tellen said.

Diate glanced around at the room filled with glass pieces of all shapes and sizes. This area, as big as his apartment, contained more wealth than he had seen in his lifetime. 'You know about the Kingdom, don't you?'

'Everyone knows that a certain segment of the Kingdom uses theft for survival. I screen my customers,' Tellen said. 'I have never had any trouble with them.'

Diate permitted himself a small smile.

Tellen caught it. 'Until now, perhaps.'

'And the performers?'

'You know how the performers are chosen,' Tellen said. 'I have nothing to do with who is hired here.'

'A, B, or C list?'

'B.'

Diate nodded, and sighed.

'That's the second time today I have heard you refer to the A or B list,' Beltar said. 'What exactly does it mean?'

Diate ran a finger along the edge of the glass pieces, as Tellen had done. The glass was rounded and smooth beneath his fingers. 'Exactly what you would assume. It refers to level of Talent. I was an A list performer. I had only to perform. Martina was a B level.

She had to perform and scout – most of the time. Only occasionally would she have to resort to level C tactics.'

'Tactics?' Tellen asked.

'Stealing. Hustling. Planning missions. A level C performer can't bring in the revenue a level A performer can. So the C performer must make money in other ways. The Kingdom was founded on Talent, but it's funded on organized piracy. Someone found this room, Tellen, and they've been robbing you ever since.'

Tellen ran a hand over his face. Then he glanced up. Diate followed his gaze. The young girl was gone. Through the distortion of the water, he could see the branch of a tree.

'How much of this do you know and how much is bitterness?' Tellen asked.

'Good question,' Diate replied. 'I know how the Kingdom functions. I had a very political father and a number of siblings of varying degrees of Talent. I was an A level, spared from most of this, and I heard about it quite often from the others I was training with. I had to learn only the most minimal pirating skills. As an A, all I had to do was report back on the potential wealth of an area I visited. As for bitterness, I feel it. I feel it every day of my life. In cases like this, I always suspect the Kingdom first, and I have never been wrong.'

'But he does consider other possibilities,' Beltar said. He stood near the glass as if it drew him close.

'I hope so,' Tellen said. 'I rely on them for the entertainment here, and I have had a good relationship with everyone who has come to Rulanda.'

'Some of them have taken advantage of it,' Diate said.

Tellen's gaze was appraising. 'I appreciate your help, detective, but I can't agree with your way of viewing the world. Most of my clients are my friends.'

'What if you discover that your friends have been stealing priceless glass from you at a profit?'

Tellen looked at the piece Diate was touching. His expression was wistful. 'I'll talk to them, see why they've been doing this and what they need.'

'They need money,' Diate said.

'Not that much,' Tellen said. 'I can't believe that logic, simple reason, and friendship wouldn't count for me.'

'I guess we are different,' Diate said. 'Because I have no trouble believing someone would pretend friendship in order to make a profit.'

'Your past has warped you, detective.'

'Funny,' Diate said, 'I would argue that your past has warped you.'

Chapter 7

The files on the hotel guests were kept in a room behind the oversized front desk. The room had no windows and smelled of moldy paper. Dust motes rose each time something disturbed the air. Diate had sneezed when he entered the room, and then sneezed again each time he opened a file.

Some guest files, like Beltar's, were kept in large books bound with ribbon. Others, like his, contained a single sheet of paper and were kept loose in a box the size of a small desk, marked by year. This year's box was already half full.

Tellen had come into the room long enough to show Diate where everything was, and to pull the file on the dead man. Diate waited until Tellen left before investigating the files. He wished he had more time. Tellen only wanted him in the room long enough to read the dead man's files. Diate wanted to see what other patterns of guest behavior he could find in the resort.

He figured he had until early dinner before Tellen would kick him out. So he started with his file and Beltar's. He wanted to get a sense of the kind of information Tellen put into his files. Diate's merely noted the items he had told the registration clerk. Beltar's contained everything from wine labels to bits of personal history written in a scrawl Diate later figured to be Tellen's. Tellen was a gossip. He loved finding out personal information about his guests and recording it in their files. It didn't appear to be in any particular order. It was as if the files were large personal scrapbooks instead of blackmail material.

From Beltar's file, Diate learned that his old friend had been mated once, and that the woman had disappeared under what Beltar thought mysterious circumstances. Tellan's scrawl added a supposition that the woman had left Beltar – *no matter how wealthy and good-natured a man is*, Tellen had written, *a woman still wants him to look attractive.*

A flash of anger flared through Diate. Beltar had always looked attractive. His clothing was expensive, he was well-groomed, and he cared for himself with a fastidiousness Diate had seen in no one else. Tellen was a man with interesting prejudices, and not the host he thought himself to be.

A single notation was added later in the file. Beltar's mate had left him to return home on a trip, and had died along the way. Poor Beltar. No wonder he understood sadness so well. No wonder he worked so hard at fighting loneliness. The notation made Diate wonder about Tellen's original impression. Maybe Beltar hadn't felt that his mate had left under mysterious circumstances at all.

Reluctantly, Diate set aside Beltar's file and pulled over the dead man's. A cloud of dust so thick that Diate felt it as well as saw it rose from the stacks. He coughed, wondering how much dust could form in so little time. Probably because the room had almost no ventilation, and documents had been stored here since the resort opened.

He opened the file. The dead man's name was Marcus Feledon, and he had been coming to the resort before Diate was born. Originally a travel scout for a small company in Golga, Feledon had moved to the Vorgel to learn the secrets behind their engineering prowess. Vorgellians were notoriously tight-lipped about such things, preferring to maintain the technology themselves. Feledon had to have another way to earn a living on Vorgel, or he was remarkably well accepted. He spent every holiday at the resort, and only missed one, after his mate had died.

Diate wiped a finger over his nose and then sneezed again. His hands were covered with dirt. He might have to break off so that he could clean up before he met Sheba for dinner.

He sighed, and thumbed through the file, noting nothing unusual. Feledon was an exemplary guest who left his room spotless and supported the resort financially as well as by word of mouth. Only on the last visit did anything odd happen.

Since his mate died, Feledon had traveled alone, except for his last visit. He arrived with a woman half his age whom Tellen had originally thought was Feledon's daughter. It became clear, midway through their early supper, that Feledon did not treat the woman like a daughter at all.

Two nights into the visit the neighboring cabin reported shouts and poundings coming from Feledon's cabin. Tellen investigated personally. The cabin was quiet when he walked up, but all the lights were on. When he knocked on the door, he waited quite a while before it opened. Feledon stood there, looking flushed. He asked what he could do for Tellen. Tellen said he had heard reports of a disturbance. The young woman peeked her head around Feledon's shoulder. She was naked. She assured Tellen that everything was all right. Her face was as flushed as Feledon's.

Four days later, Feledon drowned. The young woman found him, her distress so great that she could barely hiccup the words. Tellen examined the body, saw no unusual marks or bruises, and assumed that Feledon had gotten caught in the undertow, as too many other guests had previously.

The file ended just after that. Feledon had no family, so no outside investigation occurred. The young woman accompanied the body home on the next air shuttle off the island. Tellen had the cabin cleaned carefully, but found nothing unusual.

Diate closed the file and held his hand on the cover for a moment. The cursory investigation made him uncomfortable. If he were planning a murder, this small corner of Rulanda would be the place to do it. Numerous murders could have occurred here, and no one would have conducted a real investigation. Nothing in the file made him think that this case was connected to the smuggling. Just an odd gut feeling, and a sense of timing.

He put the file back in the box, and dug through the pile until he found another thick one. He hadn't known until he pulled the file out that he was looking for Sheba's.

Hers was nearly as thick as Beltar's. He coughed as another cloud of dust rose around him. For a moment, Diate clasped the file to his chest. What right did he have knowing things she was unwilling to tell him? Every right. She probably had as many secrets as he did.

He opened the cover and settled back to read.

A sound at the door startled him. He slammed the file shut and tossed it back in the box. Then he leaned over and piled more papers on top of it. He was still bending over when the door opened.

'Find what you were looking for?' Tellen asked.

Diate stood up and wiped his hands. He found he liked towering over Tellen. 'I found Feledon's file, but the information in it was so slight as to be almost non-existent. You need some kind of security or special investigative team from somewhere else in Rulanda for these kinds of things.'

Tellen shut the door and leaned on it, looking up at Diate. 'We don't have security teams anywhere on Rulanda. Resorts don't require them.'

'Every place requires protection,' Diate said.

Tellen smiled. 'Again we're at that mysterious crossroads in our backgrounds. In all my years here, I have never felt the need for "protection." '

'Until your glass starts disappearing.'

'Even then. Your friend Beltar recommended you. I listened with some reluctance. I am feeling the same reluctance now.'

Diate crossed his arms in front of his chest. 'Things are not as tranquil here as they seem. I suspect I could go through all of those files and find a number of cases as mysterious and questionable as Feledon's.'

'I don't like your insinuations, detective.'

'You hired me to investigate the disappearance of some priceless objects. You're paying me to insinuate.'

'Which reminds me.' Tellan's hands clutched the doorknob. Diate could see them hunched behind him. 'We have not discussed fees.'

Diate pushed the box back into its corner. 'We will discuss my fee if I can help you. Until then, this is merely exercise for my mind.'

'I pay for services,' Tellen said.

'You will,' Diate said, 'when I have results.' He smiled a little. 'Nice change of subject, but I'm not done yet. Feledon dies two weeks ago, about the time that you discover the glass is missing. If this place weren't so small, I would think it a coincidence. But it isn't, is it, Tellen?'

Tellan's mouth tightened. 'Feledon drowned.'

'Yes he did,' Diate said. 'The question is, who helped him drown? The woman he was with? Or someone else?'

'Are you accusing me?'

Diate wiped the sweat off his forehead with the back of his hand. 'I'm accusing no one and suspecting everyone right now. And I don't like the way you're withholding information from me. Now, tell me about the back entrance to the storage room.'

Color suffused Tellan's face. 'Who told you about that?'

'No one,' Diate said. 'But I did figure that since the only entrance was through your office, and I presumed you owned the only key, no one could get in that way. Therefore there was another entrance. And it isn't through the pond. No water has touched that room in a long time.'

Tellen ran a hand over his face. The dirt on his fingers smudged his skin. 'There is an entrance off the kitchen that we sealed nearly a dozen years ago. I checked it after this whole thing began, and found it still sealed.'

'I would like to see it tomorrow,' Diate said.

Tellen nodded, and wouldn't meet Diate's gaze. Tellen wasn't used to this kind of close scrutiny. He had owned the resort since his father died, and had never answered to anyone. No wonder he bristled when Diate questioned him.

'It is early supper,' Tellen said. 'I'm going to have to lock the room. Will you need to see this again as well?'

Diate glanced at the box with Sheba's file in it. The box nestled against a stack of others, half buried in dust. 'No,' he said. 'I'm done here for now.'

Tellen opened the door and backed out, then held it for Diate. Diate followed. A guest standing on the other side of the counter glared at him, as if his dirt-stained clothes and sweat-covered face disgraced the hotel. Tellen locked the door behind him. Diate made his way out of the back.

'I will contact you late morning,' he said.

'Fine.' Tellen's fingers brushed at his hair, and Diate didn't have the heart to tell him about the smudge running across his face.

Diate stepped out of the building and into the thin evening light. He sneezed twice. A breeze licked the sweat off his arms, and cooled him. If Golga kept records like that, the entire nation would be a fire hazard. He shook his head, and walked to his cabin.

The woods on the far side of resort land were silent. Two sailboats graced the lake. Somewhere out there, small creatures with amazing vision etched glass so precious it could not travel off this spot. If he had more time, he would make Tellen or someone take him to the Hoste, and see if they were having problems. But dealing with natives would be difficult, and if he could wrap up the case without dealing with them, he would.

He unlocked the door to his cabin and stepped inside. Immediately the hair on the back of his neck rose. He closed the door quietly and eased into the room. A faint scent of flowers reached him, and he relaxed a little. The smell had alerted him. Someone – Sheba? – had been here.

He scouted the living room, then walked down the tunnel-like hallway. Sheba was sprawled across his bed, sound asleep, one hand tucked under her chin, the other across her belly. She was naked.

For a moment, he studied her, examined the play of light and shadow across her golden skin. She was slender and well-muscled. Her breasts fit easily into his palms. The curves of her buttocks were tight where they slid into her well-formed legs. The chill air had made her nipples hard. Her lips were parted slightly. She looked radiant.

He went into the bathroom, took off his clothes, and scrubbed the dirt from his body. Then he crawled in bed and pulled her against him. She stirred, wrapping one leg around him, leaning against his torso for warmth. He ran a hand along her back, warming her skin. With his other hand, he tilted her face toward his and tasted her mouth.

She sighed and moved against him, as sensual in sleep as she was awake. He kissed her slowly, gently, the hand on her back was working its way between her legs. He waited until she was wet, then slipped inside her. She didn't open her eyes until her first orgasm, and then only to cry his name. Her passion increased as her consciousness did, and together they rode the wave to the most delicious, shuddering climax he had ever felt.

When they were done, she stretched. 'I could be awakened like that every day of my life.'

He cradled her head against his chest. 'I didn't expect to see you until late dinner.'

'I couldn't wait,' she said.

'I'm glad you didn't.' He kissed the crown of her head, feeling desire war with the tiredness he felt.

'I ordered dinner to be brought here,' she said. 'It should be waiting outside.'

It was. She had ordered the same food they had missed the night before. They ate together on the bed, sitting crosslegged, naked, knees touching. The food had an odd, bitter-sweet taste to it that Diate associated with the iced coffee. When they were finished, he set the plates on the floor, and kissed Sheba. He found that he liked the bitter-sweet taste best on her.

They made slow, passionate love long into the evening, neither of them wanting to give up sensation for sleep.

101

*

The second floor of the Recovery Center was quiet. Diate slipped past the plants and up the stairs, flashing his identification four times before he was free to go into Martina's room.

The heavy security pleased him.

As he pushed open the heavy door, she stirred. Her hands were still elevated, but she wore thinner bandages on her face. He couldn't tell if she was awake or not.

'Martina?'

She turned her head toward his voice. Her eyes were no longer bandaged. They were the only signs of life on her body. 'Emilio?'

The name sounded strange coming from her. He let the door close, then took a chair beside her bed. 'How're you feeling?'

'Is Beltar with you?'

'No.' He had wanted to come alone that morning. He didn't want to see Beltar's disapproving gaze as he spoke with Martina. He also didn't want the distraction so soon after he had left Sheba. He had never experienced a night like that in his entire life. His body still tingled with the memory of it.

'You think I'm lying to you,' she said.

He glanced at his hands, then at her bandaged ones. A piano player. With the damage the Kingdom had done to her fingers, she might never play again. 'Your story makes no sense,' he said. 'They had you in custody, and then they let you go. A few days after you're home, they try to kill you. Why do it in the open? Why not do it when you're in custody, when there will be no witnesses and no reason to justify it?'

Her body stiffened. 'You can believe what you want to, but that's what happened.'

He sighed. 'I'm not your enemy, Martina. I'm really not. I think we have more of a kinship than you're willing to acknowledge. I survived the label of traitor, and you will too.'

'You weren't captured. You weren't burned.'

'That's right. I wasn't injured much, physically. By the time I got to Golga I was starving, and my feet were covered with sores upon sores, but I never had to go through the kind of physical pain that you did.'

She closed her eyes and turned away, her movements sending the sharp scent of liniment through the room. 'Then you can't understand.'

'Do you have family?' The question came out before he could stop it.

She didn't open her eyes, but tilted her head to catch his words better. 'They weren't home when the guard came.'

'I grew up in a family of five,' Diate said. 'We were close. My sister and I even danced together, until they determined that she was barely a C and would have to prove herself. She got assigned to a cruise ship, but never got to serve.'

'I know the story. They were murdered.' Martina's voice was vaguely mocking, as if a dead family couldn't compare to her physical wounds. And it probably couldn't, but Diate didn't want to abandon the topic – not yet.

'No.' The words eased out of him like an involuntary breath. 'They were slaughtered. I found them when I came home from my lesson. My instructor wanted to send me to the Queen that day. I would never have seen all that blood if I had stayed. I would never have gone home. I would still be dancing somewhere, making money for them –'

His voice broke and he stopped, a flush creeping up his cheeks. He rarely spoke of that, and never spoke of it in such detail. He took a deep breath and steadied himself.

Somewhere during his speech, Martina had started watching him. Her eyes glittered through her bandages. 'Surgery doesn't remove those scars,' she said. The sarcasm was gone.

'Any more than it will touch the memory of the abuse you suffered.' He made himself meet her gaze, his face hot.

'It's not the same,' she said.

'No, it's not.'

She pushed back in the bed, the movement making her hands swing. She closed her eyes, tears forming around the lids. Tears of pain. Diate wondered how badly she hurt.

'I refused,' she whispered, as if saying the words would bring someone into her room, someone who wanted to kill her. 'I knew about you years ago, detective. It's odd that you're the one who is protecting me.'

Diate leaned forward. He frowned. 'What did you refuse?'

She blinked a few times, then turned toward him. 'I was a Diate Rebel.'

The term made Diate start. He had never heard it spoken before.

'People who follow the teachings of your father. They're called

103

Diate Rebels. The state tries to control them – and sometimes it kills them. Many of the rebels have moved away from the island, but some stay and study underground. I stayed.'

Diate felt giddy. He had trouble drawing breath. He had known about the rebels, but all the reports he had gotten dismissed them as a rag-tag, disorganized band of kooks. He hadn't realized the extent or the seriousness of their organization.

The Golgoth's voice echoed down the years. *And so you come here, to continue your father's rebellion?* The Golgoth had suspected, even then. Odd that during the years, they had never discussed the rebels.

'What did you refuse?' Diate asked.

He could sense rather than see the tension in her body. She didn't want to discuss this. 'I refused to play along with their plans for rebellion,' she said. 'I left. That's when I applied for my Talent position. The Minister of Culture was kind enough to give me an off-season audience with the Queen.'

'They didn't know of your rebellion?'

'No.' Martina's voice was small. 'I've been lying here thinking that they discovered it after I went home. And that's why they sent someone out . . .'

Diate frowned. It still didn't make complete sense They did checks on Talents. They would have known before. Unless the rebels were very good at remaining secret. And they weren't. Diate had known about them on Golga. He would have to think, to figure out what other scenario might fit. Until then, he would take this one at face value.

'That would explain why they used the punishment for a traitor,' Diate said. 'But the burning, Martina. I don't understand that. It's the punishment for a magician Talent.'

'They didn't explain why they were doing it,' she said. Her voice hitched halfway through. She made a small, bitter sound. 'I guess I deserved it, for being so stupid.'

'No one,' Diate said, 'deserves to be treated the way they treated you.'

The mid-morning heat felt like mid-afternoon stickiness. The locals in the Recovery Center were talking about a bad heat wave. One of them warned him out of the sun.

He stood for a moment just outside the Recovery Center doors, breathing the thick air. Sweat appeared on his skin the minute the door closed behind him. They didn't have to worry about him overexerting. Even walking in the heat felt like work. By mid-day, the heat would be overpowering.

He meandered across the lawn. The air had lost its fresh scent. The fishy smell of the lakes became cloying. No wonder people had said there was a definite season to Rulanda.

He pushed the hair off his face. In staff cabins behind the resort, some of the air shuttle pilots who did resort runs made their twice-monthly homes. The pilot who had brought Diate in had pointed out the cabins from the air. Beltar had confirmed their presence later. The pilots' cabins were slightly smaller than the rest, since the pilots weren't there all the time.

Sweat dripped down his forehead. The frustration he had felt back in Golga had returned. It gnawed at him from the inside. Diate Rebels. Slaughter still occurring on the Kingdom in his father's name. Affecting people like Martina, who had repudiated the teachings. Nothing changed. Everything remained the same.

He wished he could look beneath the bandages, see what the surgeons had done to her face. He wanted to touch her, to hold her, to show her that he understood how she felt.

But maybe he didn't understand. Maybe he had been wrong when he spoke to her. Maybe the losses he suffered were nothing compared to hers. The internal scars he had were healing. She would look at hers forever.

Sweat dripped off his forehead into his eyes. When he stopped at the cabin, he would ask for a drink. He felt a bit woozy. The heat was a living thing, as vibrant as the lake or the grass beneath his feet.

The staff cabins were sprawled in a vague pattern with the largest (and, he presumed, the most important) nearest to the resort. The others drifted back in an angle, with the views getting smaller, until the cabins at the very end had only a view of other cabins and could not see the forest or any of the lakes.

He wandered down the stone path, catching only an occasional odd glance from the staff members who watched from their windows. When he saw someone watching him, he would nod and smile, as if walking down this path was as normal to him as breathing.

The last two cabins were the tiniest, looking big enough for little more than a room and a bath. A Vorgellian woman sat on the stone path just outside one cabin. The shade covered her, darkening her skin. She wore a thin shift. Her oversized feet rested in a bucket filled with water.

'Excuse me,' Diate said in Golgan, 'but are you one of the air shuttle pilots?'

Her eyes opened. She stared at him for a moment, their odd color reflecting his concern. 'Yes,' she said in Lillish. 'I am a regular on the Kingdom circuit.'

Meaning he had insulted her by addressing her in Golgan. She was above ferrying merchants and merchandise. She carried Talents of all stripe – famous and infamous. For a moment, he didn't know if he should tell her he was a Talent or a detective. He decided to tell her his official position only if she asked.

He switched to Lillish. 'Did you know a human by the name of Feledon?'

She didn't move, but her expression shifted enough to let him know that she had known Feledon and had cared about him. 'What are you doing, writing about him?'

She had seen his tattoo, and was going to treat him as a Talent, then. Diate shook his head. 'No. Actually I hadn't heard he was dead until yesterday.'

She relaxed. Amazing what a non-directed response could do. 'How well did you know him?'

'Well enough to be surprised by his death.' The misleading remarks came as easy in Lillish – easier perhaps – than they did in Golgan.

She nodded then. 'Me, too. Feledon was afraid of the water. He would never go in it.'

'Do you know what happened?'

Her smile was cold. 'I have my suspicions.' She leaned up on one elbow, facing him. Her long frame had the muscle of some-one accustomed to using her body. 'I suppose you do too. But you can't do anything to me. We're on neutral soil, and besides I don't work for the Kingdom. I work for the resort.'

It took Diate a minute to understand what she meant. She thought he was a lower-level Talent, someone working with the smuggling ring or the guards. He shook his head. 'I'm not anyone with the Kingdom. I'm not here to discover anything about you.'

'Just a friend of Feledon's. What's a Talent doing befriending a man like that?'

'Our paths crossed,' Diate said. 'He intrigued me.'

The Vorgellian nodded. 'Me, too. I can't help thinking it's my fault. On the last flight in, he commented on the way the shuttles were built for extra storage, and asked if they brought more than the weight-required luggage. I said no, and wouldn't answer more questions. You know how he was when someone refused to talk to him.'

Diate looked away. His suspicions made sense. The Hoste glass was smuggled one piece at a time via air shuttle. The ships were heavily inspected, but the shuttles weren't because they were so small. Feledon had stumbled onto the smuggling ring, and had paid for it in traditional Kingdom fashion. But because the resort was neutral ground, and because Feledon was well known, the death had to look accidental. 'Were you here when he died?'

'No. I had flown out the day before. Maybe if I had known –' She shook her head. 'I'm getting off this circuit, you know. Four more rounds and I have enough to retire somewhere where the humidity isn't so high and people actually do things at night.'

Diate stared at her for a moment. He never thought about the future in those terms. He rarely thought about the future at all. What would he be if he wasn't a detective? He had no real family, a few friends, nothing he cared about outside his work. Retirement held terrors for him he didn't want to examine.

'Do you know the woman he was with?' he asked.

'Wheleaan?' She looked away. 'Poor kid. She really loved him. She was hysterical when I saw her, almost a week after they found him.'

'I never met her. How did she know him?'

The pilot stretched again and sat up, pulling her feet out of the bucket. 'I don't know. And I never cared. From the moment I met her, I knew they were right for each other. It just worked, you know?'

An image of Sheba asleep on his bed rose in his mind. His cheeks grew hot. 'I know.'

'I bet you do.' She smiled. 'I wouldn't mind a piece myself, but when a man blushes like that, I don't think it matters what another lady wants. It's one woman and one woman only, isn't it?'

He couldn't answer that. He had always refused invitations, acting only when the woman had been forward. Like Sheba. Like the pilot now. Only he wasn't acting.

She sighed and drew her knees up to her chest. 'What's your interest in Feledon?'

'I don't know,' he said. 'His death seems so out of place here.'

She looked at him sideways, assessing him. 'You don't come here often, do you? I would have seen you before.'

'You would have.'

She stared at him for a moment, then sighed. 'It's not always peaceful here.'

'What do you mean?'

She shook her head, stood up, and brushed herself off. 'I could get fired for disparaging the resort. I have four rounds left before I'm done.'

'I won't tell on you.' He was looking up at her, neck straining.

A small smile froze on her lips. 'No, you probably won't. But even so, there are some risks I'm not ready to take.' She touched her forehead in mock salute. 'I liked talking with you. Sorry we didn't meet before your lady showed up.'

'Me, too.' He smiled at her. Then he paused, as if the question he was about to ask were a casual one. 'Do your passengers often exceed the weight-required luggage?'

'No,' she said, 'but they only bring luggage one way. To Rulanda. Check the shuttle schedules. Passengers usually trade their luggage after late lunch on the day before a flight.' She didn't wait for his response. She turned, and disappeared inside her small cabin.

Diate sat outside for a moment, feeling the oppressive heat on his skin. A bead of sweat ran down his back. She had given him a time table, which was probably more than she had given Feledon.

Yet Feledon had died because he had discovered the smuggling operation, and had probably decided to do something about it. He would have reported to Tellen. Then Tellen would have checked the storeroom, and next thing, Feledon was dead. Diate wondered if the resort owner would leave those details out if asked directly, and he wondered if asking was worth the struggle of getting an honest answer.

He would decide later. Right now, he had a storeroom to visit.

Tellen was in his office, door open. The heat of the day hadn't reached inside yet. Ceiling fans kept the air circulating and Tellen looked cool.

'When does the next air shuttle leave?' Diate asked.

'Tomorrow,' Tellen said. He frowned slightly. 'Why?'

Diate felt a chill run down his back. He had only a few hours before he had to position himself near the pond. 'You showed Feledon the storeroom.'

Tellen looked tiny behind his desk. His thin lips were pursed. 'I did not,' he said.

'But he knew of it.'

'I said nothing.' Tellen clasped his hands together so tightly the knuckles showed white.

'No,' Diate said. 'I don't suppose you did. But he came to you, questioning the extra space in the Kingdom shuttles because he had seen that kind of thing before, hadn't he? And then you went and checked the room, and that's when you noticed how much stuff had been taken, and how serious the problem was.'

'Are you saying I killed Feledon?'

'No,' Diate said. 'I think your panic about the missing glass might have caused someone else to realize that Feledon knew more than he should, and that other person killed him.'

Tellen hid his face in his hands. 'How do you know I spoke with Feledon?'

Diate smiled, closed the door, and slid into a chair. 'You're asking me to discover things for you. I'm merely following a trail.'

Tellen shook his head, then sighed. He brought his hands down, revealing features so white that he looked bloodless. 'We fought,' he said. 'He kept blaming the Kingdom, like you did, and I claimed that they could do nothing.'

Diate leaned back in the chair. The upholstery stuck to his hot skin.

'I have thought, ever since, that the conversation had something to do with Feledon's death.'

'Who overheard you?'

'Everyone. The door was open. I wasn't paying attention to who was nearby. I was trying to get Feledon out of my office.'

Tellen's eyes had grown bigger, his voice softer.

'And what is it about the Kingdom that makes you feel so protective toward it?'

Tellen stood, and turned toward the window. He clasped his hands behind his back and stared into the small garden, as he had done during Diate's first visit.

Clearly, this presaged an important part of the discussion. But whether it meant that Tellen was going to fabricate a story, or whether he was going to tell the truth, Diate couldn't yet tell.

'The resort wouldn't survive without them,' Tellen said. 'The Recovery Center helps, but so many patients would go directly to Oleon if the resort weren't here. Here patients can recover and their families can enjoy all the amenities of luxury living, without a high price tag. After the center was built, this resort thrived, and it thrived on the meals we made, the comfort and privacy we gave our guests, the natural wonders, and the Talent we were able to bring in from the Kingdom itself. We get A-level performers here, often before they make A status. To some people, knowing the A Talent before it becomes famous is a plus. For others it's an affordable way to see art and performances they would ordinarily miss.'

'Is Torrie part of this?'

Tellen's hands remained clasped behind his back as he turned to face Diate. 'Torrie?'

'The magician Talent I have seen on the grounds.'

Tellen pursed his lips. 'I don't believe she has any association with the Kingdom. I have seen her hide people from Kingdom officials.'

Diate frowned. 'You're saying she's a rebel?'

Tellen shook his head. 'I don't know what she is. All I know is that she doesn't disrupt life here to give me an excuse not to take her money.'

'What kind of excuse would you need?'

'Something violent. Something that frightens the guests. She has been quiet in all the years that she has come here.'

Diate didn't say anything. The fact that his path had crossed with Torrie's again made him nervous. He suppressed a sigh. He would get no more information out of Tellen. Whatever Tellen's relationship with the Kingdom – even if he was telling the truth – was too important and too longstanding for him to risk, even on this kind of accusation.

Diate stood. 'I need to see the storeroom again.'

Tellen stared at Diate for a moment, as if he didn't understand what had just transpired. Then he went over to the mirror and opened the door behind it.

The passageway had the same damp feel it had had the day

110

before. As they ducked into the storeroom, the dampness eased into a coolness that felt refreshing. The glass shimmered around him. The shadows changed as water moved in the pool above. This time, as he stepped into the chamber, he didn't look at the Hoste glass. Still, he heard rustles and giggles, as if the figures in the glass were watching him.

He walked to the far wall. 'This is where the kitchen is?'

Tellen nodded. 'But the door has been sealed. I checked.'

Diate ignored him. The outline of the door was hidden in the stone blocks that made up that corner of room. A clear, thin seal did cover the doorway, but as Diate got closer, he noted that in several places the seal had slipped, as if it had stretched over time. The seal was cool against his fingers, pliant, but not sticky. The floor and the area under the door itself had a polished cleanness that suggested regular use.

'How closely did you check the seal?' he asked, 'Did you touch it?'

'No.' Tellen's voice echoed in the cavernous room.

Diate backed away from the door and wiped his hands on his pants. The sticky feeling lingered, although there was no residue on his fingers. The seal had been broken. It had just been replaced to look like it hadn't been touched.

'Well?' Tellen asked.

Diate stared at him for a long moment. Tellen looked genuinely perplexed. Some people did not deserve the things they were given. 'You're a fool,' Diate said, and walked back along the passageway alone.

The door to Sheba's cabin was open. Diate hadn't been there since the night they made love. He wanted to see her, just for a moment, before he became a detective again.

The inside of the cabin smelled faintly of candle wax. The shades were drawn against the morning light, but the day's heat had yet to seep inside.

Sheba came out of the bathroom, toweling her hair. When she saw him, her face registered surprise for a brief moment. 'Hello.'

The surprise didn't show in her voice. She had been expecting someone else. He glanced behind him, but saw no one. 'Bad time?'

'No.' She finished rubbing her hair and let the towel fall to her shoulders. She wore a skimpy shift made of a thin shiny material.

He crossed the room, feet brushing against the scattered pillows, and slid his arms around her silky softness. She leaned into him.

'Missed you,' he said.

She murmured in his ear, one hand stroking his back. 'I don't like being away from you either.'

Her wet hair smelled of flowers. A cool drop of water ran down his shoulder, sending a shiver through him. 'Ever been this way for you before?'

Her hand cupped his buttocks. 'What way?'

He was glad she couldn't see his face. 'This quick.'

She pulled back from him. Her wet curls framed her face. Water dripped on her bare skin, trickling onto the shift, staining the fabric dark. 'No.'

That single word resounded between them. Diate reached for her, then Sheba's posture became stiffer. He followed her gaze over his shoulder. Torrie stood at the door, her white gown flowing to a breeze Diate couldn't feel.

'I've been looking for you, Talent,' she said. 'Your woman is dying.'

Diate's heart stopped. 'Martina?'

'Is she your woman?'

He had crossed the room before he realized it. He grabbed Torrie's shoulders. 'I won't play these games. Has something happened?'

'Death happens to all of us, Talent,' Torrie said.

Diate pushed her away from him. She took a step back, nearly losing her balance. He started out the door, then stopped and turned.

Sheba's face had drained of color. She clutched her shift with one hand, the material bunching over her breasts.

'I'll be back.' He didn't wait for her answer. He ran down the path, through the thick, damp air. His lungs heaved, and he nearly choked. Sweat poured down his body. After he had gone a few feet, his entire body ached.

She had done it. She had found some way to escape, to end it all. He could see her still form, and he wanted to shake it, to bring life back into it. Beltar would never forgive him if she died.

He would never forgive himself.

He yanked open the door to the Recovery Center, and felt a blast of cool air hit him. One of the attendants shouted something at him as he ran to the stairs. He ignored it.

Diate took the stairs three at a time. He was breathing through his mouth, a dizziness he had never felt before pounding his head. When he reached Martina's door at the top of the stairs, he pushed it open.

And stopped.

Beltar was there, talking quietly. He stood when he saw Diate. 'You don't look good, detective.'

Diate let the air out of his lungs, then staggered under a wave of dizziness. He grabbed a chair for support. 'Martina?'

'Did all the trains stop? Are we trapped here forever?'

Even though her tone was dry, it took a moment before Diate caught both the fear and humor behind her words.

I've been looking for you, Talent. Your woman is dying.

But Martina was fine. And so was Sheba. He had no other women.

Talent.

So maybe, just maybe, she wasn't talking to him.

But Sheba couldn't be a Talent.

I don't know what she is.

A shiver went through him. Beltar handed him a glass of water and he drank it quickly, rubbing his hand over his mouth when he had finished.

Martina. He had mentioned Martina's name. He had been so disoriented by Torrie's comment that he had given away Martina's identity.

'Something happen, Emilio?'

Diate pulled the chair behind him and sank into it. The cool wood felt good against his skin. 'I had a feeling something was wrong. I didn't mean to scare you.'

'Didn't I tell you that you shouldn't exercise in this heat? Do you know what it can do to you?'

'I think it's already done,' Martina said.

'I just need a moment,' Diate said. A moment to think. Sheba couldn't be a Talent. She had no mark. He had touched every inch of her body. He knew.

Government officials did not have caste marks. But they were not called Talents, either.

'Sorry,' he said. 'Didn't mean to scare you.'

'That's all right,' Martina said. 'Barge in any time.'

He couldn't resist a smile. He hadn't expected her dry humor, but it suited her, made her more real, gave her a face, even though she was still hidden by bandages.

'Where have you been all day?' Beltar asked.

'Working on that problem you found for me.' Diate wiped the last of the sweat from his forehead.

'And?'

'Close.'

'Is this a male secret, or something I should know about?' Martina asked.

'Know anything about Kingdom smuggling on Rulanda?'

She let out a small snort. 'Only that this is one of the most profitable places in the world for them. That's what I was trying to tell you the other day, detective.'

'I can understand why,' Diate said. 'Your friend does not believe in security.'

'He doesn't need it.' Beltar sat in the chair beside Diate. 'The transportation system ensures he knows about his clientele.'

'He doesn't know much about me, and he's been losing priceless glass. Clearly the system doesn't work.' The dizziness had come back. Diate rested his head on his arms.

'What are you finding, Emilio?'

His skin felt sticky against his arms. He needed a good night's sleep. He needed a true vacation. 'I know when, but not who.' He sighed. It was probably late lunch now. 'I need to go.'

'You're not well,' Beltar said.

'Well enough,' Diate said. 'Martina, I'm going to have them place a guard on this room. I'll make sure only Center staff enter. Beltar will stay now, won't you, Beltar?'

'Only if you tell me what this is about.'

'The security isn't as tight in this town as I had hoped. I am going to take some extra measures. I'll be back tonight, Martina, to watch over you.'

'Why not this afternoon?' she asked.

'This afternoon, I have a date with some Hoste glass.'

Chapter 8

Diate stepped out of the doors at the Recovery Center. The warm air hit him like a blow. He took a deep breath to ease his dizziness. Beltar had offered to stay with Martina for the early part of the evening. Diate would take the first night shift. He had promised to sleep a bit, to get rid of the dizziness before he returned. He also had to talk to Sheba, to clear things up between them.

He stopped for a moment and wiped the sweat off his face. As he did, he saw a familiar figure heading up the path.

Torrie.

Her long robes flowed around her. She walked with her head down, her hair braided around her ears. He crossed a small expanse of cut grass.

'Torrie!'

She looked up, and smiled when she saw him. 'Your Martina is all right?'

'What were you doing back there?'

'I was merely telling you what I felt.'

He grabbed her shoulders and shook her. 'You felt nothing. You came to find out information from me.'

Torrie smiled. She put her hands on his, like a lover would. 'Someday, you will kill someone like this.'

He made a disgusted sound and pushed her away.

Her smile grew. 'What makes you think I need to find out information from you? I know things you do not.'

'Magic Talents are not all-knowing.'

'No, they are not.' Torrie tucked a loose strand of hair back into her braid. 'But we have greater knowledge of the future than most. Sometimes we lose track of now. I had a friend named Martina who disappeared. I would like to see this woman of yours.'

Diate stiffened. He had made a mistake. He only hoped Martina wouldn't have to pay for it. 'She is not a woman of mine. She's part of the Golgoth's family, and she's under guard.'

'The Golgoth's family? A woman? With a Kingdom name?'

'Our nations were once part of the same culture,' Diate said. He clenched his fists tightly.

Torrie inclined her head slightly. 'Which is why the Kingdom has always been careful to use Old Colony names instead of Golgan names when children are born.'

'She can't have any visitors,' Diate said. 'Doctor's orders.'

'A doctor will let friends visit. You have visited.'

Diate took a step toward her. Torrie did not take a step back. 'If you or any Kingdom member gets close to her, I will personally see you executed.'

Torrie studied him for a moment, her eyes glittering. Then she laughed. 'I do believe you will. You have death in you, Emilio Diate.'

'Your people put it there,' he said.

She nodded. 'Truer than you think.' She shrugged, a little. 'I do not have to see her. Tell her that we know who she is. Tell her that we are happy she is safe, and is finally doing her job.'

'Her job?' Diate asked.

Torrie's smile grew mysterious. 'She will understand. You don't have to, Talent.'

She whirled, sending a slight breeze through the oppressive air. She started back down the path, then stopped and looked at him over her shoulder. 'I promise that none of us will touch her.'

Promises did no good. He waited until Torrie was out of his sight before going back into the Recovery Center. He hurried into the main offices downstairs, and ordered a double guard on Martina. No Kingdom members could go in at all, not even himself. He would come to the security office and ask for a guard, using the code phrase they had devised before going upstairs. That prevented magic Talents with illusionist tendencies masquerading as him. He also made the guards promise to touch anyone who passed them. Touch would make an illusion shatter like an image spun of glass.

He paused at the steps and looked up, wondering if he should warn Beltar. Then he decided against it. Torrie had given her word, and would probably live up to it. The Kingdom had a curious code of honor. Even if she didn't, the extra measures he had just employed would help. And Beltar would block anything suspicious. That would take care of things until Diate got back.

116

The air outside felt more oppressive than ever. Before he slept, he had to see Sheba.

But Sheba would have to wait. He needed to position himself near the kitchen. The glass would come out the back entrance, not through Tellen's office.

In the shade, the dirt on the path was fine-shifted sand. It seeped into his sandals and stuck to his hot feet. As he walked, the dirt grew harder, baked into dry cakes by the unrelenting sun.

Trees covered the resort, hiding it from this side of the path. As he rounded a corner, a fence came into view. Vines hung over thin clay walls, looking hand-painted green against the brown surface. He had never entered the resort from this direction, but he knew if he slipped through the gate, he would find himself near Tellen's pond.

The sound of a door slamming against a wall echoed in the silence. A man cursed, and another voice shushed him. Diate stopped and leaned against the wall. The clay was cool against his skin. Vines brushed his cheeks, his hair. He longed to push them away, but didn't.

Instead, he peered over the edge of the wall, using the vines as cover. Two men were coming out of the kitchen, each carrying a small piece of glass. Another man held the door, while another stood guard at Tellen's window.

They were early. Perhaps they had kitchen help.

'Hurry!' one of the men whispered in Lillish.

The whispering continued even after the man finished speaking. Soft voices, conversing in a language Diate didn't understand. He recognized the tone, though. Fear. The creatures in the glass understood, and they felt fear.

Through the open door to the kitchen, Diate could see no one. Tellen was probably resting, which made sense, given the heat of the day. The chefs would be having early dinner before they had to prepare food for the resort. The men carrying the glass were red-faced and sweating. Apparently Hoste glass was heavier than it looked.

He had several options. He could watch and follow, see where they brought the glass. But he knew the ultimate answer to that. They would take it to the port, probably by electric car, where a sympathetic air shuttle pilot would ferry them off the island. He could sneak around front and report to Tellen. But that would do no good, since Tellen had no security force to assist him. Or he could try direct confrontation himself.

Diate swung his body forward, blocking the gate opening. He placed his hands on his hips and smiled.

'Hello, gentlemen,' he said in Lillish. 'Beautiful glass.'

The whispering stopped. The images in the glass shifted, as if they were watching him.

'Heavy too,' the first man replied. Diate recognized him as one of the band members from the previous night.

'Then you might want to set it down, since we need to talk.'

'We haven't got time,' said the man at the door. His hair was as dark, black, and curly as Diate's father's had been.

'It's killer carrying something this heavy in this heat.' The man holding the kitchen door crossed his arms, biceps bulging from the simple movement.

'I'm sure.' Diate checked their positions. Only four, as he had thought. And only the man holding the kitchen door had any real strength. 'My name is Diate. I'm the new security officer at the resort. I assume you gentlemen work here?'

They glanced at each other. A trickle of sweat ran down the first man's face. 'We're taking this to one of the cabins.'

'You don't expect me to believe that, since the Hoste glass is kept in storage, never to be removed.'

'You accusing us of something?' The man next to Tellen's window had moved closer to the pond.

'I suppose I am. Four men who speak Lillish, one of whom plays every night with the band. What are the rest of you? Class C Talents?'

Curly, at the kitchen door, flushed. Talents were very conscious of rank.

'I would suggest that you set the glass down.' Diate took a step inside the courtyard. Leaves crunched under his feet. Small gravel rolled along the cobblestone path. This area lacked the care the rest of the resort had.

'We are in a hurry,' the man near Tellen's window said. The leader. His eyes had a brightness the others lacked.

'Yes. The chefs will be back for early supper soon. And Tellen will be done with his rest.'

The leader frowned, then glanced at Diate. 'There are four of us, and no one to help you. You're wasting your time.'

118

'We'll see,' Diate said. 'Have them set down the glass. I hate breaking priceless art.' He wouldn't, but they didn't know that. He had to make them think he would.

The men didn't move, but the images in the glass did. They swivelled, as if trying to watch Diate. Sweat dripped on the second man's piece of glass.

'Such a pity,' Diate said. He whirled, the bottom of his feet kicking gravel toward the first man's glass, careful to miss. Soft cries filled the courtyard. The man twisted, protecting the glass with his body. The other glass holder turned too, afraid that Diate would go for his piece next. The leader ran toward Diate. Curly let the kitchen door swing shut as he hurried across the cobblestone path.

Diate scooped up more stones and lobbed them at the glass, again making sure he would miss. The stones thumped off the men's backs. The leader lunged for Diate. Diate's right foot shot forward, catching the leader in the groin. The leader gasped and fell backward, landing in the pond with a splash. Water flew in all directions, coating Diate and the other men, rippling against the glass. The images cried out again. Some raised hands as if to protect themselves from the wetness.

Curly reached for Diate and Diate ducked under him, hooking Curly's legs with one foot and yanking him backwards, slipping by as Curly fell with a thud to his back.

The leader was dragging himself out of the pond. The first man saw Diate approach, and pulled a knife from his boot. Diate ignored the weapon. Instead his fingers found the fragile end of the square piece of glass. The glass rippled beneath his fingertips.

'Take another step toward me, and I'll shatter it,' Diate said. The cries from the glass almost sounded like sobbing.

The first man hesitated. Curly sat up, gasping for air. The leader had risen to a half-crouch, and the second glass holder clutched his piece of glass to his legs like a long-lost child.

'That wouldn't do the resort any good,' the leader said.

Diate shrugged. 'What's one piece of glass when they've been losing hundreds?'

'Still priceless.' Another voice. Tellen's. His Lillish had a rough lilt. He stood at the gate, with three chefs beside him, blocking the way. 'What's the procedure, detective? Do we tie them up?'

Diate looked at the four men, their eyes wide, their bodies tense.

'You might send for a little more assistance. And prepare a room where we can talk with them as well as hold them until a security shuttle can arrive.'

One of the chefs ran off as another opened the kitchen door. Two more chefs stood behind that.

'You were supposed to be sleeping,' the leader said.

Tellen's smile was cold. 'I hate it when someone falls into the pond. I always check to make sure that no children are chasing my fish. Imagine my surprise when I saw sunlight reflecting off two of my favorite pieces of Hoste glass.'

A collective sigh rose from the glass. The images returned to their original positions.

The first man still hadn't moved from his crouch, the knife extended before him. Diate walked forward and ripped the knife from his hand. Then he brought the blade up and pressed it against the soft skin under the man's chin. 'Never take out a weapon,' Diate said, 'unless you mean to use it.'

The man tried to move his head away, but Diate pressed the tip into the skin hard enough to draw blood. 'I'm pleased to see that you all value the art you're stealing, but at what price? How many people have died to maintain this little operation? Or was Feledon the only one?'

The man's jaw trembled. A drop of warm blood fell on Diate's thumb.

Footsteps echoed in the kitchen, and the men guarding the door stepped back. The chef who had gone for help had returned with five other men, some of whom Diate recognized as grounds-keepers. They grabbed the leader, Curly, and the second man, but waited for Diate before touching the man before him.

Diate's entire body was tense. Another drop of blood ran down his hand. The man's lower lip trembled. 'People like you,' Diate said, 'do not understand the kind of destruction they cause.' He ran the tip of the knife from the edge of the man's chin to his Adam's apple, leaving a cut deep enough and wide enough to scar. 'Get rid of him.' Diate brought the knife down, felt the blood drip off his fingers onto the ground.

The chef and groundskeepers kept their gaze averted as they grabbed the man's arms and yanked him away.

'That wasn't necessary,' Tellen said. He had come up beside Diate, his small frame barely reaching Diate's shoulder. Diate glanced down. Tellen's skin had turned white with two red splotches on his cheeks.

'You have no concept of what's necessary and what isn't,' Diate said. 'Follow them. Make sure they're secure in the room. Have someone pick up the pilots on the resort and bring them too. I'll be there in a few minutes. I have some business to take care of.'

Diate handed Tellen the knife, smearing Tellen's skin with blood. Then Diate bent over and plunged his hands in the cool water of the pond. The water had a scummy feel. The blood floated across the surface, tingeing everything red.

He stood, wiped his hands against his leggings, and walked out of the courtyard. His dizziness returned, and he noted for the first time since he had encountered the men that his throat was dry. He would find Sheba, take her to the coffee shop, and they would talk. He needed something to get the memory of blood and knives from his mind.

His clothes stuck to his body, and he wiped a damp strand of hair from his forehead. He loped across the lawn, ignoring the exhaustion and the dizziness. When he found her, he could relax. She would hold him, and murmur to him, and together they would make all the blood, all the pain, go away.

The shadows looked wrong as he approached Sheba's cabin. Her windows were open, shades up. She had never had her shades up, not in the entire time they had been at the resort. He frowned, a shiver of unease running along his spine. Someone sat on the porch, but the shape looked too lumpy and long for Sheba. He made himself walk.

As he stepped into the shade of the gnarled rope tree that stood to the side of Sheba's cabin, the figure stood. Torrie. She had been waiting for him.

The adrenaline from the fight still flowed through him. He suppressed the urge to lunge at her. 'Why can't you leave me alone?'

Torrie wiped her hands on her robe. 'You are impulsive. Your impulsiveness will harm you someday.'

He stopped close enough to touch her. She smelled of sandalwood. 'What gives you the right to meddle in my life?'

She smiled, sending a cascade of wrinkles across her face. She was older than he had thought. The smile made her eyes twinkle. 'I am a Talent, just like you. What gives you the right to dance?'

'I don't dance.'

'You do. In the privacy of your rooms, you dance. In your heart, you dance.'

All of his muscles went tense. He had told no one about his dance. Even the detectives thought it merely some kind of odd routine he went through. 'So because you're a Talent, you have the right to make these pronouncements.'

'I am not just a Talent. I am class A. I am one of the stars of my generation. We have much in common, you and I.'

'We have nothing in common.'

She shrugged, the smile fading from her lips but remaining in the laugh lines around her eyes. 'Someday, you will come to me and beg for my help. You will apologize for the ways you treated me, and you will tell me that I am the only person in the world who will be able to understand what you're living through.'

He knew better than to deny her. Kingdom magicians, the truly talented ones, had a knack for seeing things no one else did. 'My life will change that much?'

'It already has.' She reached out with trembling fingers and brushed the hair from his sweat-covered forehead. Her forefinger rested on his tattoo, tracing the fading blue design. 'You cannot deny this heritage. You are not of Golga. Your soul dances even though you try to suppress it. Look beneath, Talent, and you will find your heart.'

Her touch sent an odd tingle through him. He pulled away. 'I'm here to find Sheba.'

She let her hand drop to her side. 'I know. I will leave you.'

She brushed past him, leaving the scent of sandalwood in her wake. A short distance down the path, she stopped.

'The woman you love is dying, Talent. Remember that.'

'What do you mean?' he shouted, but she had turned her back on him, and he knew she would give him no more answers than she already had. The words filled him with a different kind of dread – a less immediate dread. A dread of something in the future.

The original colonists brought myths of their homeland, his father once told him. *Worlds filled with multiple, jealous gods, odd monsters, and mystical creatures. One tale told of an oracle that spoke in riddles both complex and simple. The man who deciphered them became king over all. Our magicians are like that, and we have no true kings. No one understands until it is too late.*

Too late.

Diate took a deep breath and walked up the stairs. The cabin was quiet. The throw rug was back in its place before the door. Pillows were stacked against the wall, and the thick, comfortable rug rolled into a corner, revealing a hardwood floor as polished as his own. Even the ashes in the grate had been swept out. Dirty towels cluttered the floor in the bathroom, and a single cup sat in the kitchen sink. But the bedroom was as neat as the front room. No personal items covered the tables; no clothes hid in the drawers. It looked as if Sheba had cleaned everything out since the last time he saw her.

'I've been looking for you, Talent,' she said. 'Your woman is dying.'

'Martina?'

'Is she your woman?'

And Sheba's face, drained of color. Her hand, clutching her shift, the material bunching over her breasts. She thought he had lied to her. She must have thought he had another woman, one he really cared about. *Your woman.*

The woman you love.

He had said nothing. He had explained nothing. And he had left her with Torrie. Who had probably told Sheba who he was. She thought he was from the Kingdom when he was from Golga. Somehow, she must have thought that he was using her, betraying her, when he truly cared for someone else.

But how could he use her? He didn't even know who she was.

Finally, his heart started beating again. 'Sheba! Sheba!'

He ran through the cabin, pulling open cabinets, searching through drawers. She was gone. She had left him.

And no trains had arrived in the last day.

He hurried out the front door, leaving it ajar, feet slapping against the steps. The cars were so far away, and it was so hot. But he had to find her. He had to explain.

He would tell her everything. And she would hold him.

She would understand.

His run was frantic, out of control, limbs flying across pavement. The doors to the cabins were closed, and no one stood on the street as he approached town. Even the coffee shop looked closed and uninviting.

A sound overhead caught his attention. He looked up. An air shuttle skimmed above the trees, sunlight glinting off its metal surface. Sometimes people hired shuttles.

Beltar had, to get them to the resort.

If she was on that shuttle, she had to have left just after Diate. It took two hours to get to the port by car. And that was assuming she could get her pass from the desk.

He stared at the shuttle as it zoomed by. Could she see him there, standing alone among the closed and dusty buildings?

Could she see?

Did she care?

'Sheba,' he whispered.

He had other places to check, but already he knew that he had lost.

PART THREE

One Year Later

Chapter 9

The Pavilion glowed white against the starry sky. A gentle breeze blew the ornate, tentlike curtains, and even from two blocks' distance, Diate could hear laughter echoing across the water. The ocean reflected the sky and the Pavilion's light. The cargo boats and the merchant ships on the far side of Embassy Row looked almost beautiful when touched by the Kingdom's light. It was hard to believe that this patch of beauty existed in Golga.

On some nights, Diate stood outside the electrified clear fence sealing off the Kingdom's embassy and listened to the music. His feet would ache and his legs twitch as if they could force him to dance. He would stare at the light, and part of him would want to join the merriment, while another part reminded him of the horrors it masked.

His palm was wet. He wiped it against the right leg of his gray detective's uniform. The fact that the Kingdom had asked for him made him nervous. The fact that Sheba had asked for him made him very nervous.

When he had left Rulanda, he had spent days in the Golgoth's communications room, using his contacts and sending messages on the network. What he discovered made him feel like a lovesick fool. Sheba was Sheba Carbete, Minister of Culture, and sister to one of the most notorious assassins in the business. His contacts claimed there was no way Diate could have known because she didn't allow likenesses of her to leave the island.

But he had known. He had ignored it. She spoke too many languages, dressed like a Kingdom woman (with Vorgellian make-up), and had danced too easily. Even her lack of tattoo marked her as a government No-Talent. She had given him the signs, but he had been unwilling to see.

The question he hadn't been able to answer was whether or not she had known who he was.

Probably. How many Kingdom Talents traveled with Golgan wine merchants?

Yet, if she had known, why had she been so pale when she found out about Martina? Or had something else happened? For the last year, he had seen Sheba pick up the throw rug as she entered the cabin, and cover a piece of glass.

Tricky memory. He wanted it to be wrong.

He typed in the night's entry code and slipped through the gate. The land felt different here, as if the soil had been imported from the Kingdom itself. It hadn't. An embassy was merely a patch of land granted as a courtesy by the Golgoth. But Diate couldn't shake the feeling that magic had touched this part of the city, a magic the world of merchants and business could never touch.

The laughter grew stronger, mixed with conversation. People in flowing clothes stood just outside the curtains. They all seemed to be smiling. Their joy pulled him forward. He couldn't remember the last time he felt joy.

Her hand touched his face. He slid his head back on the pillow and she kissed his neck. Warmth ran through him. She spoke, words feather-soft against his skin: You never smile, Emilio.

He shook the memory from his mind and made himself walk forward. No music yet. That disappointed him. Of all the things he had onced loved about the Kingdom, he had loved the music the most.

'Look what this sorry city dredged up.' A man, half-hidden in shadows, raised a glass to Diate. 'Did you come to live a little, detective?'

A shiver ran down Diate's back. The man's tone was lilting and beautiful, even though he spoke Golgan.

'I was invited,' Diate said, wondering why he had to justify himself to a young man he had never met.

'Ooo. Someone wanted to bring a bit of reality to the festivities.'

Diate kept walking, his solid shoes sinking into the marshy ground. The man's hostility added to his nervousness. Diate should never have come. Whenever he faced the flowing clothes, heard the fluid tones of the language, saw the art, he felt like a child again. A helpless, angry child.

But he wasn't a child. He was one of the most hated and feared men in the city. And he would be safe. He had made sure of that. His men were all over the embassy. Scio had people there as well.

Sheba wouldn't be stupid enough to attack him in Golga, but he wanted protection in case he was wrong.

He made himself walk straighter, carrying the power on the outside, even if he didn't feel it on the inside. No mistakes. The Golgoth was counting on him. The Kingdom's invitation had spooked them both.

Perfumes reached him, mixed with the moist decay of the river. People parted as they saw him. They moved to other conversations, other stations around the outside of the building. The breeze carried the burning scent of a mild hallucinogen, but he ignored it. Drugs were not illegal in the Kingdom, and technically, the embassy was bound by Kingdom laws, not the city's.

He slipped in through one of the curtains. Dozens of lights illuminated the crowd. Candles mixed with artificial light mixed with soft pastel screens to create a multi-colored glow across the wide chamber. The people around him moved, except for one man who grabbed his arm.

'No slipping in, detective,' the man said in Golgan. 'Use the front door.'

Diate shook his arm free and gave the man a harsh look. The man smiled, then plucked a jeweled goblet off a passing tray. He raised the drink in silent toast to Diate.

Diate went back out of the way he came. He didn't like the way they all knew him. Of course, the clothes helped. The Golgoth had wanted him to dress for a Kingdom function, but Diate couldn't. He had to wear his Golgan clothes to remind himself who he was. Who he would always be.

It was cooler outside than inside – the candles created a lot of heat – but the night was as bright. Diate pushed his way through the crowd until he reached the front of the Pavilion, and stopped when he saw the paved path leading to the front door.

Formal entrance. He would be announced. They wanted all the guests to know he was here.

He sighed. So be it. He would play their way until he found out what they wanted.

The crowd thinned near the entrance. Muscular women in matching gowns kept people back, pointing to side doors and keeping the entrance clear. Diate crossed from the marshy grass to the pavement, his footsteps adding a counterpoint to the hum of conversation.

129

One of the women stopped him. She was slight, but through the cut of her gown he could see the muscles ripple on her arms and back. The red caste mark on her right temple marked her a Trader, although it was probably a ruse to hide her governmental rank.

'How did you get in, detective?' Her tone was not friendly, even though her Golgan was fluent.

He answered her in Lillish. 'I was invited.' He pulled the ornate invitation from his breast pocket and handed it to her.

She studied the invitation, then returned it to him without looking at him, keeping her head down as a sign of respect. Sheba's position as Minister of Culture was the second most important in the Kingdom. Only the Queen was first.

That was the odd thing. The thing he couldn't figure out. His sources told him the Queen would be here as well.

'Up the stairs, sir,' the guard said. 'The herald will announce you.'

Diate tucked the invitation back in his breast pocket and walked alone down the paved path. A few people looked at him curiously, but most were intent on their conversations. He would tell the Golgoth that the embassy had a cursory guard during official functions, a fact that they might someday be able to use.

He walked up the wide marble steps and through the front doors of the pavilion. The doors were made of stained glass. He didn't have time to study the pattern, although he knew it would probably be anti-Golgan.

He clenched his fists. They could do what they wanted. This was Kingdom soil. At least, as long as the Golgoth wanted to give them this small measure of protection.

Diate had fought the embassy. Ever since its proposal and its quick appearance, he had argued that it did not belong in the Port City. Relations between the Kingdom and Golga were too harsh, and could erupt too easily. He didn't want to deal with the inevitable tensions the embassy would cause.

And here he was at the first official function.

As a guest.

Of Sheba.

From this angle, the crowd appeared stationary. An orchestra, composed of twenty players, was setting up on a raised platform in the center of the room. To the side, a curved staircase was roped off. The tentlike curtains on the outside hid the building's solid foundation. The walls were made of a shiny wood.

The orchestra hadn't started playing yet. For a moment, he wondered if he was early, but if he were, then so were most of the others. No. Something else caused the festivities to start late.

A herald, dressed in red robes and wearing a large gold hat which left the gender indeterminate, extended a hand to Diate. Diate placed his invitation in it. The herald banged a large gold staff twice. The conversation stopped.

'Emilio Diate, head of the Port City detectives,' the herald said.

The joy leached out of the room. A few partygoers moved closer together, as if by huddling, they would protect each other from Diate's presence.

Diate stared at the crowd. A few faces reflected puzzlement. He could feel the curiosity: how did the son of a famous rebel leader become the head of detectives on another island, in a repressive city, with the enemies of the Kingdom itself? But then, he supposed most of them knew about the Rogue Talent.

They all wanted to see him in the flesh.

He stepped down two stairs onto the polished wooden floor. The conversations began again in the back of the room and moved slowly forward. His presence wasn't forgotten, but it was no longer important.

No one approached him. No one even smiled at him. He felt odd. Once he had been the center of attention at these functions. He grabbed a glass of spiced wine, and went to an empty chair near the orchestra. Sheba would find him when the time came.

The orchestra warmed up. Occasional notes honked and bleated through the room as the players tuned their instruments. The players took their seats, and the conductor, a little man with fringed white hair, raised his baton.

Diate extended his legs and leaned back, ready for a small treat. He sipped the spiced wine, feeling it cool and bitter against his throat.

The conducter brought the baton down and the strings sang the first bars of a piece Diate hadn't heard since he was a boy. He resisted the urge to close his eyes, to let the music sweep him away. He had to remain here, had to watch, had to pay attention.

Around him, couples took to the floor and eased into a dance. He noted the small blue stripe of a Talent on many foreheads. If he had remained in the Kingdom, he would have led the dancing too.

He hadn't danced since Rulanda. He had practiced, but not danced.

He tried not to think about it: the warmth of her body against his, the musk of her skin. She had been so delicate beneath his hands, so warm, so alive . . .

So treacherous.

Tellen had handed Diate her file after they realized she had not checked out or paid for her stay. For almost a decade, she had been Tellen's Kingdom Talent contact. She booked the events. She found the acts.

The Hoste glass smuggling on Rulanda had been her baby.

The men never mentioned her. They had all denied her involvement. But the fact remained: she had left at the very moment the others had been caught. She booked the Talent. She must have cased the resort for decades.

She had led the smuggling.

And she had escaped.

Outsmarted by a woman he thought he loved.

She still visited him, in his dreams. She would stand beside his bed, wearing the see-through gown from their first night. He would open his mouth to yell at her, to scream his anger and frustration at her –

Then her hand would touch his cheek, and he would pull her down beside him, and lose himself in her, and make her promise to never leave him again –

'More wine, detective?'

He opened his eyes. He didn't remember closing them. A woman in a dress that revealed the rosy aureoles around her nipples leaned over him, balancing a tray in her left hand. He shook his head and she smiled, leaving her breasts in his face a moment too long.

Careless. Too careless. He needed to be alert here, and yet the Kingdom lulled him, with the flowing music, the candlelight, the soft conversation. Ever since he got back from Rulanda, he had been diligent, brutal even, but one step into this place and all the fight was gone.

He scanned the crowd, seeing no faces he recognized. When he was a boy, he would have recognized them all, would have known them all. Now he only knew the ones wanted in Golga, or the notorious ones, the ones legends were made of.

The dancers weaved and bobbed to the soft rhythms of the strings. No daring dancing here tonight. No individual moments of showmanship. This was not a performance put on for a special guest. This was an official function, where everyone blended into everyone else, and whatever happened, happened off-stage.

His father had hated such functions.

Diate had never understood them. In those days, he had understood nothing but the dance.

Silver hair caught candlelight across the dance floor. Diate watched as a tall, reedy man made his way through the crowd. The man wore a thin black material that absorbed the light. His movements were harsh and quick. They stood out among the flowing frivolity of the other guests.

He stopped beneath a candelabrum, and the flickering light illuminated his features. Tonio Carbete, Sheba's brother. A class D Talent known for bawdy beerhall songs, and a class A assassin, wanted in Golga for three separate murders.

Had he been the one to crush each of Martina's fingers?

Diate didn't move. He could do nothing. He had known Carbete would be here, but he had hoped that they would never see each other. Diate didn't want added complications on this night.

With an unmusical squeal, the strings stopped playing mid-bar. Support instruments, reeds, and the piano continued for another stanza before stopping too. Conversation ended with the music. A small rustle filled the hall as people turned to see the source of the disturbance.

Diate strained, his height giving him slight advantage over most people in the room. Carbete watched too, arms crossed in front of his chest.

Nine women had entered through the side doorway Diate had been barred from. Eight flanked a taller woman who walked in the center. Her hair was rich and black, her skin even darker. She looked nothing like the woman Diate remembered, but he recognized her clothes, her jewelry, and her stance.

The Queen of Tersis, ruler of the Kingdom.

Bows flowed like a wave as she made her way to the orchestra. She climbed up beside the conductor, smiled at her people, and clapped her hands.

'Let the celebration continue!' Her voice had the husky warmth of a torch singer.

Diate remembered when she ascended. The Queen who had murdered his family had died in an aborted coup, and another took her place. That Queen lasted eight days before this one, a child of eighteen, had brought a small group of assassins into the palace.

No coups, no assassination attempts, no internal violence in the ten years since.

She didn't belong in Golga.

Diate forced himself to unclench his fists. His palms were damp.

She got off the stage and made her way through the crowd to the rooms in the back. Four of her women surrounded her. The others stayed in the crowd. She was not going to join the festivities, but she had announced her presence. She wanted the Golgoth to know she was here.

Thanks to Diate's sources, the Golgoth already knew.

A shiver ran down Diate's back despite the hall's warmth. He had argued against this for weeks. The last time a Queen of Tersis had set foot in Golga, the Golgoth had died. The Kingdom had nearly taken over the Port City. Only the Golgoth's son – the current Golgoth's father – managed to stop the takeover by pitting himself against Kingdom assassins. The secret police had started a year later to monitor all ships and outsiders who entered Golga.

The conductor tapped his baton against his hands, then raised his arms. The orchestra brought up their instruments and, as he nodded, launched into a festive tune. Dancers flooded the floor, bodies straining in time to the music.

Carbete had threaded his way through the crowd, stopping just outside the door the Queen had disappeared into. Diate set down his wine and pushed his way past clusters of people, swaying to the orchestra's beat. His footsteps fell on the off beats, his walk almost a dance in itself.

Although he was aware of it, he couldn't stop it.

A woman approached Carbete. She wore the blue of the Queen's attendants. Her long tawny hair and her easy gestures made her look like Sheba.

She had her back to him. Diate made his way through the last knot of people, trying to watch Carbete instead of the woman. Up close, Carbete's features had the thinness of an aristocrat – a granite handsomeness made all the more intriguing by his nearly colorless eyes. He usually killed women by becoming their lovers and then slitting their throats during the act of love. He killed men during lovemaking too, but not by cutting their throats.

Carbete noted Diate as he moved around the last person. Recognition brought a half-smile to Carbete's face. They had never met, but it was as much Carbete's business to know his enemies as it was Diate's.

'Our guest.' His voice was smoother, deeper than the bass in the orchestra. The man had a sensuality Diate usually noted only in women.

The woman turned, and Diate froze. It was Sheba. Somehow he had expected their first meeting to be more formal. He had expected to be across the table from her. But he wasn't. He was right beside her.

Her eyes were as wide as they had been the last time he saw her and spots of color rose in her cheeks. Her floor-length gown was ribboned, revealing her legs as she moved. Her breasts protruded through well-designed holes in the garment, and a triangle farther down revealed part of her flat stomach and her pubic hair.

Sheba.

All the emotions of his dream pushed at him and he grabbed her shoulder so that he could pull her close to yell at her, to tell her how badly she had hurt him. Torrie's voice echoed in his mind: *You will kill someone like this.*

His hand clamped around the delicate skin of her neck and a shudder of desire ran through him. She tilted her head up and her flowery scent engulfed him. He leaned forward, and suddenly his lips were on hers, his body pressing against hers, her hands pulling him against her, her warmth driving him crazy.

'Sheba.' Her name escaped him as the kiss grew more passionate. His hand slipped from her neck to her breast and his mouth would have followed if someone hadn't grabbed him and pulled him back.

'Even among our people, sex in public is considered too risqué,' Carbete said, eyes crinkling with amusement.

Here. In public. The Pavilion. Diate took a step back, away from Sheba. He needed to regain control.

Sheba took a step away from him as well. She patted at her hair, adjusted her dress, her gaze never leaving him.

'What are you doing here, dressed like that?' she asked.

135

'You invited me,' he said, taking the invitation from his pocket and handing it to her. 'And these are work clothes.'

She studied the invitation, turning it over and holding it up to the light. 'Diate,' she breathed.

'It's real enough,' Carbete said.

'You know something about this?'

Carbete shrugged. 'Only that a representative of the Golgoth would be here.'

'I knew that too. But no one told me who the representative would be,' she said.

Diate listened, keeping his hands away from her. He didn't know why she was playing this game. She had known he would be here, just as he had known. After what had happened on Rulanda, she probably assumed he was stupid enough to believe the small ruse.

She frowned, tucked the invitation in the sleeve of her dress, and took a step forward. Diate didn't move as she brushed the hair off his forehead. 'You're a Talent. How–?'

'Haven't you heard of the Rogue Talent?' Carbete's voice held laughter. 'Really, Sheba, the Minister of Culture should be better informed about the famous criminals of her country.'

'Shut up!'

Diate's heart was pounding against his chest. Two spots of color had risen in her cheeks and he longed to caress them away. But the hall had grown quiet and everyone was watching them.

Sheba noticed the silence at the same time he did. She glanced at the people around her, then took a deep breath, struggling for composure much as he had. 'I need a room, Tonio. A *private* room.'

He bowed slightly. 'Your wish, Sheba. Follow me.'

She turned her back on Diate and followed Tonio through the silent people. Diate trailed behind. Women stared at him, their mouths partially open. The men stood rigidly, hands clasped behind their backs. A few – men and women – wore cutaway garments like Sheba, the clothes revealing rather than hiding the genitals. Odd that he hadn't noticed it before. The revealing garments were a sign of both wealth and power. Most of these people had arrived after he did.

He followed Carbete and Sheba through a curtain beaded with gems and into a small dark room. Carbete lit a candle and led them down a flight of curving stairs. He opened a door at the base of the stairs, and entered, lighting wall candles with his.

The walls were covered with tapestries, and so was the marbled floor. The air was cooler down here, and the music, as it started up again, sounded faint and muffled. Pillows were stacked against the far wall. Carbete pulled down two thick ones and set them a few feet apart.

'Thank you, Tonio.' Sheba had her back to him. 'See that no one bothers us.'

'Your wish,' he said, bowing again. As he passed Diate, he leered. Diate kept his face expressionless. Carbete had every right to assume Diate and Sheba were going to make love.

Diate was going to stay as far away from her as he could. Just as he had planned. He would not touch her again.

They waited until the door snicked closed before moving. Diate checked behind the tapestries, finding only white walls. Sheba whirled, crossing her arms and hiding her breasts. 'You never told me who you were.'

The playacting continued. He figured her information sources were as good as his. He would go along, and find out what she wanted. 'You never asked. You saw my tattoo and made an assumption. Beltar should have made you wonder.'

She snorted, and wiped a strand of hair from her face. 'Unlike Golgans, we travel with people from different nationalities all the time.'

'Beltar is a Golgan.'

'You know what I mean!'

'You mean I surprised you.' He wiped his hands on his gray slacks. As long as he stayed this far away from her, he would be all right. He sighed. 'I'm here now. What was so important that the Kingdom was willing to break a diplomatic silence of nearly six decades?'

'We built the Pavilion,' she said.

'I assume that event was related to this one.'

Her eyes reflected the candlelight. 'I'm not ready to negotiate with you. You're merely the head of the city's detectives. You hold no national office at all.'

'If you weren't ready to negotiate with me,' he said, 'then you should have invited someone else.'

'I didn't invite you.'

Diate let a smile play at his lips. 'The invitation came from the Minister of Culture. Think this through, Sheba. Do you really want the Golgoth to think that you can't even control your office?'

She put a hand to her face and pushed her hair back. The gesture was a nervous one. 'This caught me by surprise. I'm not used to it.'

'Stop the games.' Diate clasped his hands behind his back, holding himself rigid. 'We can negotiate like two adults.'

She shook her head. 'You're not capable of negotiation. I sent for the Golgoth.'

'He would never have come here on his own. I can relay information to him.'

'He didn't get any such invitation?'

'No,' Diate said, still playing along. 'Your people probably switched it, thinking I'm a better choice. At least I know Kingdom custom.'

'Someone knew about Rulanda and wanted to embarrass me.' She smoothed her hands over her dress, then tugged at it, as if she didn't want it to reveal as much of her body as it did.

She was a good actress, but not good enough. He knew too much about the systems within their government to believe that she could be so easily fooled. She knew too much, had too many sources. But obviously, her fingers weren't into Golga. If they were, she would never have believed this to be a way to gain his confidence.

'You left Rulanda in a hurry.'

'I didn't want to stay,' she said. 'You made a fool out of me.'

'You left because we caught the smuggling team.'

She froze. 'I know. I should have realized. I didn't find out about that until I got home. You're very good, Emilio. I actually thought you cared. How is your woman now?'

He couldn't answer that. Martina was fine, but she had never been his woman. 'I have no woman.'

'That's not what Torrie said.'

'Torrie helped me escape to Golga. Did you know that?'

Sheba stiffened. 'So?'

'So? So perhaps she isn't what she seems.' He didn't want this conversation to continue. He wanted to do business and then leave. He didn't like being this close to her. 'Look, I'm not very comfortable here. I would like to return to my office. You said we had something to discuss.'

The music wove its way through the walls, its baseline adding a counterpoint to their discussion. The candles flickered, making the shadows deeper.

She turned her back to him, and clasped her hands behind her head. 'You represent the Golgoth in all things?'

'No. I'm merely here to find out what you want.'

'But you can't negotiate for him.'

'That's right. I am, after all, just a detective.' He couldn't keep the sarcasm from his voice.

'All right.' She sighed and turned around, her movement sending a slight breeze into the tapestry behind her. It depicted a banquet with a dozen officials and royalty around a curved table. Some of the threads gleamed silver. 'Tell the Golgoth we would like to be invited to the Peace Festival.'

Her eyes sparkled in the candlelight. Diate kept his hands clasped behind his back so that he would not touch her. 'The Peace Festival is only for nations with which Golga has diplomatic relations.'

'Then it's not really a peace festival, is it?'

'The last time we let your people on our soil, you tried to assassinate the Golgoth.'

She took a step closer to him. He had to work at not taking a step back. 'In those days we had dreams of taking over Golga,' she said. 'Its heritage is ours, after all.'

'What's to stop you now?'

'You, detective.' The words sounded like a caress, not like the words of an enemy. For a moment, he felt trapped between his mind and his desire: he had no clue how to respond to her. He had no idea about the way she truly felt about him.

Yet, that kiss had caught them both by surprise.

When did he not respond to her comment, she shook her head. 'We're a nation, Emilio, with our own strengths. We no longer have any need for Golga. There will always be a faction that believes we do – the back-to-the-homeland group. But they live in the past. Those of us who live in the future know that Golga will always be our rich neighbor, one desperately in need of art and music and –'

'And theft? We're ripe for the plucking. You've never been able to infiltrate our ports. That's why all the other nations trade through us. They know their goods are protected on our ships.'

She had stopped moving forward. 'I thought you had no say on whether or not we could attend the festival.'

'That doesn't stop me from having an opinion.'

She brushed her hair off her shoulders. Her nipples were hard in the room's chill. 'If you hate us so much, how could you have made love to me?'

Back to the personal. The set-up had been good, from the very beginning. This meeting confirmed his suspicion. She had known who he was on Rulanda. 'I let myself believe you were something else.' But that didn't solve the problem. He knew who she was now, and he still wanted to touch her. 'Why do you want to attend the Peace Festival? To normalize diplomatic relations with us?'

The eager expression faded from her face. She took a step back, as if business made her uneasy. 'There are those of us who believe that normalizing diplomatic relations with you would lead us out of smuggling. We would be able to pursue performance and government and learn how to function as a true nation in this galactic confederation of nations.'

'That would mean changing the Kingdom's entire economic base as well as its governmental philosophy. We're not fools here, Sheba. I doubt the Golgoth will go for that.'

'If we normalize relations, Golga will have a new market for its goods. You won't have to like us, but that shouldn't stop us from benefiting economically from each other. And we're not talking about doing this immediately. We're talking about the Peace Festival as a first step. The Queen would like to meet with the Golgoth, to discuss these things.'

The Kingdom wanted more than normalizing relations. The economic benefit to them would be too painful for the gains. 'I told the Golgoth I would bring this to him. I want you to know that I will advise him to refuse your request. Your people aren't trustworthy, and because of the position you hold, neither are you.'

He turned. The door was in front of him. He put his hand on the knob.

'You never did tell me, Emilio, how you became one of our country's greatest criminals.'

She knew the story. Everyone on the Kingdom did. But she wanted to call up his pain. He refused to let himself feel it. 'I am a class A Talent who chooses not to dance for the nation he was born to. Your world – which tolerates theft and murder – considers this a crime. I came here, where crimes are things that harm other people rather than things the state decrees.'

He opened the door and stepped into the hall, not waiting for her reply. Carbete sat at the base of the stairs, holding an unlit stem of stinkweed. He smiled and stood.

'You surprise me, detective. I thought I would have heard her cry out.'

Diate pushed past him. 'I don't beat women.'

'No,' Carbete said, voice floating up the stairs. 'But from the way you acted upstairs, I thought you fucked them.'

Diate shoved aside the beaded curtain and stepped into the light. The music throbbed and plucked at his ears. The dancing had grown frenzied. Women smiled at him and thrust their uncovered breasts in his face. The air smelled of spiced wine.

He made himself walk through, even though he wanted to run. The beauty was only superficial. It had no depth. He slipped through a side door and took a breath of fresh air. Through the gate, he could see the towers of the port. Through the gate, Golga waited. Golga, where there was no beauty, so he expected no warmth.

Chapter 10

Sweat poured down Diate's back. The gym, although it had been cold when he arrived, was too warm now. He took a deep breath then spun into the last of the routine. Step, step, spin, leap. His feet landed with a soft thud on the hardwood floor.

Memories from the night before seeped into his head. He took a deep breath and executed another leap, banishing thought entirely.

He was about to begin again when he noticed Strega leaning against the barre, hair matted to his head, breathing so hard he could barely move.

'We're not done,' Diate said.

'We've missed early breakfast.' Strega paused between each word, gasping for air. 'And we've done the routine five times. I can't do it again, sir. I'm sorry.'

Dancers do what they have to.

Diate stopped himself before he repeated Myla's words. Strega wasn't a dancer. He was merely an ambitious young detective who worked hard at staying in shape.

'You're right.' Diate pulled his towel off the barre. 'We're done. I'll meet you in the showers.'

Strega struggled for air for a few more minutes before walking out the side door. Diate toweled off his face. He had arrived before Strega, unable to sleep. Every time he had closed his eyes, he saw Sheba's face. Finally, he got up and came to the gym in the darkness just before dawn. He had performed the routine two times more than Strega had, and the tension he had felt from the night before still hadn't left his body.

He didn't like the game she had been playing with him. Either she was insulting his intelligence, or she wanted something.

Or both.

Either way, it wouldn't be good for Golga.

The Golgoth would want to know how it went. Diate would

recommend that not only should they keep the Kingdom from attending the Peace Festival, but they close the embassy as well.

How is your woman now?

She had been smart, though. If he hadn't had the communication system, if he hadn't known who she was, he would have been easily suckered. For the last year, he had vacillated between assuming she had left when she found out about Martina or that she had left upon notification that Diate had arrested the smugglers. After last night, he found himself believing more and more that Sheba had left because she thought he was about to arrest her, than because she thought he had another lover.

He slung his towel over his shoulder and went through the open door. The sound of shower spray hitting tile floor resounded in the cavernous rooms. Diate tossed his towel over a bench and stripped, hoping warm water would calm him.

Strega stood, hands against the wall, spray beating on the back of his head. The muscles in his back and arms had thickened and grown more powerful in the last year. Diate turned on the shower next to Strega. Strega didn't move.

'You okay, sir?' Strega's words burbled as water trailed into his mouth.

Diate stepped into the hot spray, letting water needles dig into his back. 'Concerned because I worked you too hard, detective?'

'I don't think you even knew I was there.'

Diate closed his eyes. He *had* forgotten. When he was thinking, he was worrying about how to talk with the Golgoth. For the most part, though, the morning workout was the first time since the night before that he had not thought of Sheba.

Diate soaped down, rinsed off, and shut off the shower. Now the air was cold. 'You did well this morning, detective. I promise I won't work you so hard tomorrow.'

'I won't hold my breath,' Strega said.

Diate grabbed a clean towel off the stack outside the shower room door, dried off, and dressed. His eyes burned from lack of sleep. He stretched, feeling the pull in his muscles. He had not done a proper cool down, and he would feel it for the rest of the day.

Outside, the dry heat of the morning had just begun to conquer the night's coolness. The light brown road was cracked and caked. No rain for months. The Port City would feel the effects of a drought soon. No more long showers. Water rationing. It had happened twice since Diate had come to Golga. He didn't want it to happen again.

He slipped inside the ornate oval building housing the secret police. Between the fluted columns to the left, a large table stood with snacks for late breakfast. Diate insisted that someone maintain a constant supply of food for both the detectives and the police, since sometimes their work prevented them from getting a good meal. He took a soft apple from the spread and played catch with it as he walked up the marble staircase.

He avoided Scio's office, and merely nodded at the other members of the police. They would talk with him later. He needed to speak to the Golgoth first.

He glided behind a fluted column and pressed a hidden button. A doorway slid, revealing a back passageway into the palace. Diate slipped inside. He took a bite of the apple, savoring the tartness. He was hungrier than he had thought. The last time he ate was sometime before he went to the Pavilion.

The passageway was dark, but familiar to him. He finished the apple just as he arrived at the palace door. He pushed the button and the door eased open. In the thin light, he saw a garbage bin inside the passageway and tossed the apple core in it.

The passageway opened into the Golgoth's hallway. Diate had wanted that door sealed, worrying for the Golgoth's safety, but the Golgoth wouldn't hear of it. He wanted Scio to have quick access in case of emergency, although Scio rarely used the passageways. Diate used them more than anyone, preferring the shortcuts, and trying to keep his mind fresh. He would be the one to save the Golgoth should anything go wrong.

All of the candles in the hallway were lit, the skulls grinning crazily at him. Because he was expected, a page stood outside the Golgoth's door and swung it open as Diate stopped.

'The Golgoth waits,' the page said.

The words no longer sent a shiver through Diate, although once they had had the power to paralyze him. When he first arrived, he had worried that one wrong move would jeopardize his position with the Golgoth. Even something as simple as making the Golgoth wait might make the Golgoth send Diate back to the Kingdom. To his death.

Diate stepped inside. The Golgoth's apartment was hot, almost stifling. Diate wished he could stop the page from closing the door. But with a quiet snick, the door shut behind him.

The Golgoth stood in front of the fireplace, his black and white robes flowing around him. Embers glowed, still giving off heat, despite the day's warmth. The Golgoth had been getting cold at night then, and had brought in someone to keep the fire burning while he slept.

The Golgoth did not turn to face Diate. 'You kissed her. I thought your feelings ended when you discovered who she was.'

Diate took a deep breath and expelled it. No secrets. He knew there were no secrets in this place, but still he wished that no one had reported on his meeting with Sheba. The ironic thing was, the reporter had to have been one of his own people. He had had several stationed near the Pavilion ever since the Kingdom arrived.

'I can't keep my hands off her.' Diate flushed as if he were still a boy. Diate could not lie to the Golgoth. They had discussed his meeting with Sheba before he went to the Pavilion. He was supposed to act businesslike. The kiss had caught him by surprise too.

The Golgoth shoved his hands in the pockets of his robes. The larger skulls on the material rippled as if with laughter. 'Are you bewitched?'

Diate opened his mouth to deny the accusation then thought for a moment. Torrie had been around the entire time. But bewitchings of the kind the Golgoth mentioned were the stuff of myth. 'A bewitching wouldn't make me feel like this. A bewitching affects the eyes, not the body.' Diate grabbed the railing above the stairs. 'A potion would make me lust for her like this. But a potion only lasts a few hours, not a year.'

'Yet you drank before you saw her.'

'Spiced wine. Not enough.'

The Golgoth whirled, his robes flying out, revealing his small, bare feet. 'Emilio, I thought you knew control, better than any of my people.'

'So did I,' Diate said.

'I wanted you to tell me that moment was planned.'

Diate swallowed. 'I wish I could. It – it was embarrassing. The whole thing. She was the first – the first–'

'The first lover you have had for longer than a night. I know, Emilio.'

145

Diate brought his head up. He knew that Scio kept tabs on him, but not tabs that good. 'What does Scio have, people watching my bedroom?'

'You're close to me.' The Golgoth's lips turned up in a slight smile. 'If anyone gets close to you, that person must be checked out. You swore to me it was over.'

'I thought it was,' Diate said. 'I didn't touch her again.'

The Golgoth smiled. 'You didn't have to.'

Diate took a deep breath. 'Let me brief you. Then Scio can handle this from now on. You can confine me to my quarters. I don't plan to see her again.'

'What you plan doesn't matter,' the Golgoth said. 'What you have told her matters more.'

Diate was frozen in position. Even though he looked down on the Golgoth, he felt like a prisoner being interrogated. 'I do not speak about business to anyone, except you. I have been loyal to you ever since I set foot in this place.'

'Your loyalty's not in question. Your judgment is.' The Golgoth sat cross-legged on a low-slung couch near the fire. He patted the cushion across from him. 'Join me.'

Diate's fingers ached from the pressure he put on the rail. He released it and walked down the three steps, his shoulders tense and braced for another accusation. He approached the Golgoth, but did not sit.

'What does she want?' the Golgoth asked.

The heat from the embers shimmered across the wood floor. Diate longed to open a window. 'The Kingdom wants to attend the Peace Festival. The Queen wants to meet with you.'

'What do you advise?'

'That you say no.'

'Which is what you advised when they asked to build the Pavilion. But they have done nothing.'

'Yet.'

'Yet . . . you sleep with a woman who comes from a nation you claim to hate.'

'That was a year ago.'

'The signs were there.'

Diate couldn't deny it. He had had this discussion with the Golgoth before. 'I do not plan to see her again.'

'But you will.'

Diate looked at the Golgoth. His bald head was shining in the faint light. 'This is the first time in our relationship,' Diate said, 'that you haven't trusted me.'

The Golgoth smiled and shook his head. 'You misunderstand me. I want you to see her again.'

Diate froze. His skin turned cold despite the heat. 'Why?'

'Because I think you're right. I think they are up to something, although I don't think they'll do anything at the Peace Festival. I think the Festival is merely a first step toward something larger. You can find out what that something larger is.'

'No one will trust me. They know how long I've lived here.'

'They're egotistical enough to believe you would want to go back. She would believe it, if you did it for love, wouldn't she?'

'I doubt it,' Diate said. 'She was playing some kind of game with me. She wanted me to believe that she didn't know I was coming. She wanted to use that as a way to discuss our relationship.'

'Have you any idea why?'

Diate let out a sigh. 'I think she wanted me to believe that she still cared for me. That she left because of my actions, not because of the smuggling.'

'It sounds as if she wasn't very convincing.'

'I know who she is. She could never convince me.'

'But what if she thought she did?'

'You want me to fool her? Like she was trying to fool me?'

'Yes,' the Golgoth said.

Diate took a deep breath to steady himself. Trick her? Use her the way she might have used him? 'I can't,' he said.

'Can't? Or won't?'

'Can't.' The word was little more than a whisper. 'I have no control around her. Last night proved that. I forget myself when I'm with her.'

'Yet you told her nothing about yourself or about us, even in Rulanda.' The Golgoth smiled. 'That sounds like control to me.'

'It had nothing to do with control. Such things didn't matter there.'

'They won't matter now.' The Golgoth stood, and moved beside Diate. A faint odor of incense enveloped him.

Diate shook his head. 'You don't know the magnitude. The Queen is here –'

'I know.'

'– and Tonio Carbete, the assassin. If he's here, so are others.'

The Golgoth frowned. 'Carbete?'

Diate clasped his hands behind his back. He couldn't stop pacing. 'He's their best. He favors a contact poison, activated by saliva or body fluids. He uses it often during sex. The victim dies within minutes, usually suffocating to death.'

The Golgoth laughed. 'I promise not to make love to any men.'

Diate sighed. 'He has other methods. He's good. If he's here, they're planning something.'

'Good,' the Golgoth said. 'Then talk to Scio. Let him worry about it.'

'Scio doesn't understand –'

'Scio has protected me for decades. I want you working with the woman. During the Peace Festival, you must convince her to trust you. Convince her that you will go home with her. And go, if you have to. Learn everything you can about their politics, about their plans. Then tell me.'

'I can't go back there.' Diate didn't move away from the Golgoth, although he wanted to.

'You can on the arm of their second in command. No one will try to brand you a traitor then.'

'And if I betray you?'

The Golgoth chuckled. 'You won't.'

'I lose myself in her,' Diate said. 'If I do that now, you could die.'

'Scio will protect me,' the Golgoth repeated. He put his arm around Diate's shoulder. 'What you're feeling is lust, Emilio. Lust commands only a physical loyalty. You owe me your life. And nothing – not even a woman – will change that.'

Chapter 11

The bags were heavy in his arms. The hot bread burned through the canvas sack, scorching his skin and sending a wonderful odor through the air. The downstairs door to the apartment building was open – so much for the security the landlord had promised – but this time Diate didn't complain.

The front hall smelled of cooking grease. The walls were covered with dirt and the floor boards creaked under his feet. He took the narrow steps two at a time. The pain in his arm grew, and he shifted the canvas bag, but it didn't seem to help.

At the top of the stairs, he pushed at the only door, but it didn't budge. He cursed silently. His entire day had gone like this.

'Martina. It's me. Open up.'

He shifted the bags, wondering if he was actually burning his arm. Her steady footsteps marked her progress to the door. A slight scratching told him that she was working to unlock the bolts.

It would take her a minute. He set the canvas bags down. A red splotch on his right forearm marked the place where the bread had rested. He pushed on it, watching the skin color change from red to white. Not serious. But painful.

The door swung open, and Martina stood in the doorway, her face flushed. 'Sorry,' she said. 'I couldn't get the top bolt.'

'It's all right.' He picked up the bags and pushed his way past her through the narrow hallway into the kitchen. He set them on the counter, then opened the cupboard and pulled out some burn lotion, rubbing it on his forearm.

'You okay?'

'Bread's warm,' he said. He put the lotion away and wiped off his hands.

The kitchen was spotless. Light shone through the small window over the sink. The white walls were unmarked and the white furniture matched perfectly. Cups hung within easy reach and so did most of the pots and pans. The drawers were slightly open so that Martina could hook a finger against the lip and pull.

He and Beltar had worked for weeks making this space usable for her, since she wouldn't move in with either of them. *I don't want to be a charity case*, she had said, although she let Beltar pay for her apartment and Diate provide most of her food. She just wanted privacy and dignity – something every human being deserved.

She pried at the bags, moving the hems apart to reveal the food. Her claw-like hands were almost useless. The webbed scars running up the back of her skin shone in the odd light.

He gently eased her aside. 'I promised I would cook tonight.'

He reached inside one of the bags and brought out a small green clipping one of the street vendors had given him. The street vendors called Martina the Detective's Lady. They knew nothing about her except that Diate cooked for her regularly and always brought her plants.

She took the clipping and cradled it in her hands. Her fingers weren't entirely useless – they could close down into open fists – but any other range of movement was almost impossible. 'Great,' she said, and kissed him behind the ear. 'Thank you.'

She took it into the living room, where she would do something mystical with it. He only brought the clippings. He didn't understand how to make them grow.

He took out the bread, the beef, and five different kinds of green herbs, then lit the stove. The apartment was an old one, and the stove was not Vorgellian-made. Diate checked the pilot light and lit each burner, then put a skillet on top of each and cooked the herbs separately.

For nearly a year, he had been bringing Martina dinner. Usually Beltar joined them, but Beltar was on a buying trip until the next day. At first, Diate had cooked dinner because Martina could barely get around her apartment. Now, the three of them had become a kind of family. The bonds were unspoken, but true.

He combined the herbs into a single skillet and added the meat. Then he broke up pieces of bread and cooked them in butter. He added wine to the meat herb mixture, making a thin sauce, then scooped everything into plates. He poured two glasses of Beltar's best red and carried them into the living room.

The living room smelled of mint and greenery. Plants hung from the ceiling, trailed off tables, and crowded the oversized picture window. A few sturdier plants hung off the fireplace's mantel. The lush greenery gave the room a richness it hadn't had when Beltar and Martina had chosen the place.

The hardwood floor was covered in plain rugs, and she decorated Kingdom style with large pillows instead of chairs. Her only concession to Golgan style was the heavy wood table that sat below the window, with three matching chairs pulled up to it. Beltar always sat in a chair. Diate preferred the pillows when he wasn't eating.

Martina had just placed the clipping in a small tube of water that hung from a peg near the window. Her black hair had grown to her shoulders – something she was proud of since the doctors weren't sure it would ever grow back. Her slender form had a grace that appealed to him. But when she turned –

When she turned, his gaze always went to the scars striping her face, to her mismatched and crooked lips, to the eyes half hidden under folds of skin. In the right light, her features fit together, and the beauty she had once held reappeared. And he thought that one of the biggest tragedies of all: that she had to wear the ghost of her former beauty like another scar.

He wished he had been able to find out more about what happened to her, but his sources had known nothing, and Martina rarely spoke of it.

'One of these evenings, do you think you could build me a window box?' She braced a hand against the window and stepped down from the chair. 'These clippings you've been bringing me lately would do better growing outside.'

'Sure.' He set the glasses down. The crystal clinked against the table. Her request pleased him. He didn't mind the extra work. She hadn't been outside in months, and then only to doctor's appointments. Perhaps working at the window, getting her arms and upper body used to the outdoor air, would slowly change her isolation. 'Have a seat. Dinner's done.'

She pulled back a chair to the left of the table, her usual spot. 'Sometime I'll cook for you,' she said.

He smiled, as he always did when she said that, and didn't respond. He didn't want her anywhere near the stove, near any fire at all. During the cold season, he had stopped or sent one of his men every few hours to make sure her fire remained lit. He knew she hadn't been burned because of her own carelessness, and yet he had nightmares filled with Martina in flames.

151

He went back into the kitchen, grabbed plates and spoons, and brought them to the table. She was sipping the wine, her hand shaking as she brought it to her lips. In the first few weeks, she had broken several wine glasses just trying that simple maneuver. Sometimes he wondered how she handled the delicate work of tending plants.

She set the glass down and brought her plate over, stirring the contents with her spoon. The sharp spices of dinner mingled with the green smell of the room. 'Something's bothering you,' she said.

He took a bite. The herbs gave the beef a spicy flavor, and the wine added the right touch of smoothness. 'I was at the Pavilion last night.'

Her spoon clattered against the table. Flecks of food spurted into the air and landed on her face, his arm. She hadn't dropped anything in months. She reached with a shaking, claw-like hand, but couldn't pick up the spoon. He had to hand it to her.

She nodded, then rested her head against the back of her other hand.

He hated the feeling of distress coming from her. He longed to touch her, but knew she would move away. 'I was there working,' he said. 'I was invited. They want to attend the Peace Festival.'

'They'll be in town,' she whispered. He still couldn't see her face.

'They've been in town for over a year, just not allowed outside their small patch of land. They won't find you, Martina, and even if they did, they couldn't –'

'Recognize me?' Her tone was bitter. 'They wouldn't know who I was because I'm so ugly now?'

He didn't know how to respond to her. They had argued about her appearance before and he wasn't able to convince her that she was attractive, probably because he lied. Beltar did a better job. Beltar thought Martina was beautiful.

'I was going to say,' he said slowly, 'that they couldn't extradite you even if they found you. You have my protection, and by extension, the Golgoth's.'

'They wouldn't try to extradite me.' Her voice was muffled. 'They would try to kill me.'

He sighed and took another bite of food. It didn't taste as good as it did just a moment before. 'They won't find you, Martina. You never leave the building, and only Beltar and I know about you.'

'And the Golgoth.'

'And a few of his people, yes. But they certainly won't tell anyone from the Kingdom.'

She wiped the back of her hand over her face, pulling at the skin and making the scars turn white. The surgeons wanted to do more grafts, but her body kept rejecting them. Finally they had to leave her as scarred as she was. 'Magic Talents could find me without me leaving.'

Tell her we know who she is. Tell her we're happy she's safe and that she's finally doing her job.

Diate had never told her. He hadn't wanted to frighten her. He shook away the memory. 'Yes. They can. But they need a reason to look. Do they have a reason?'

She brought her head up. Her eyes were red-rimmed. 'You believe I'm being silly.'

'No,' he said. 'I just wish you weren't always so frightened. Your whole world has become these few rooms.'

'And you and Beltar. And the plants.'

'That's not enough,' Diate said. He took a deep breath. 'The Golgoth wants the Kingdom to come to the Festival. And I have to work on the planning. Because of that, I have to get involved with them, work with them, and I won't be able to come up here during that period.'

Martina chewed on her lower lip. 'Why?'

He took another bite of stew, made himself chew and swallow. 'I'm sure they'll follow me. I'm sure that they'll check me out as much as they can. They don't need to know about you. It's just a precaution, Martina. You're very precious to me.'

She blinked rapidly, looking away from him and pretending to stare out the window. 'What about dinners? What about the plants?'

'I'll talk to Beltar. He's a better cook than I am. He can help you with dinner. It's not forever. It's just for a week or two.'

Martina sat rigidly, her right hand still clutching the spoon. 'Who's the woman? The one with the golden hair and the pretty eyes? The one who wears the see-through clothes of the rich?'

The food turned to a lump in Diate's stomach. His heart pounded against his chest. 'What are you talking about?'

Martina didn't move. 'I see her in dreams sometimes. She makes you smile.'

A chill ran down Diate's spine. 'I thought you were a musical Talent.'

She blinked again, then faced him. 'I was. They don't destroy the hands of magical Talents.'

'No,' he said, that chill raising hairs on his arms. 'They burn them.'

They stared at each other for a moment. Martina finally looked away. 'Are you saying my dreams are true?'

'The woman I met in the Pavilion had golden hair and wore a dress that revealed more of her body than it hid. She is the Minister of Culture –'

'Sheba,' Martina breathed.

'– and she does not make me smile.' He stood up and wished he could begin his stretches right there. More things had knocked him off balance in one day than they had in years. He had argued with the Golgoth, tried to prevent the entire plan, but the Golgoth wouldn't hear of it. And now Martina confessed to prophetic dreams like a magician.

'Do you love her?'

'I would be very happy if I never saw her again.' He picked up his dish and carried it into the kitchen. Some parts fit. The burning. The uncanny way she had at times of knowing how he felt. But her fear seemed unjustified. A magician who got burned had to have had a lot of power, enough that the entire Kingdom feared her. If she had had a lot of power, they never would have let her out of the Kingdom.

Providing they knew.

Providing she had been telling him the truth.

He leaned on the counter and rested his head against the half-open cabinets, feeling the edge of the wood dig into his skin. Martina shuffled into the room behind him and slid her hands around his waist.

'If I were a magical Talent, I would not look like this,' she said. 'I would call up something pretty and wrap myself in it.'

'There are different kinds of magic Talents,' he said. 'Just like each musical Talent has a different instrument, each dancer has a preferred style.'

'Would you hate me if I were magic?'

He turned in her arms and brushed the hair away from her face. The fire had burned away all tattoos, giving him no clue who she was. 'I don't hate you,' he said.

She leaned her head against his chest, and he moved his hand away from her skin to stroke her hair. Whenever he touched her leathery, scarred skin, the memory of the night he found her returned: the pungent smell of burned flesh, the melted way her body had felt.

'Then why does my being magic scare you?'

I believe you owe me a favor. You would never have found the boy without me.

He didn't answer her. 'Why haven't you told me?'

She pulled back a little and raised her face toward his. 'My mother had magic Talent. I have dreams sometimes. Dreams so unpredictable that I rarely trust them. Look at my hands. They only do that for Talents who use their hands. Magic Talents use their minds.'

'All Talents use their minds,' Diate said.

'Yes,' she said. 'They do. What would be so different if I were a magician?'

I believe you owe me a favor.

'Nothing.' He kissed the leathery skin of her forehead, and pulled away from her. Nothing would be different. Except that she would have knowledge that he did not. Except that he could never trust her again.

'You once told me your father was a minor poet. Do you have a way with language?'

'We all did,' Diate said, his back to her. 'Not enough to call a Talent. Are you saying that's what your dreams are?'

'You're important to me,' she said. 'Sometimes I dream about what's important.'

The tension eased out of his shoulders. He feared magic Talents, at a time when he thought he no longer feared anything. Torrie had made that fear stronger on Rulanda. At least she had never touched Martina. Even though Torrie knew about her, she had never touched her.

'You said, a moment ago, when I was describing her, you said you knew Sheba.' He ran a hand over his face. Information. Everything boiled down to information.

'We met. She is the one who recertified me as a music Talent. She introduced me to the Queen.'

'What do you know of her?'

'Sheba or the Queen?'

'Both.' He turned and leaned against the door frame. The kitchen window was the only one without plants. The room looked as empty as it had when he and Beltar prepared it for Martina. It was the only room she spent no time in.

Martina brushed a strand of hair from her face with the back of her hand. 'Let's go back in the other room. I haven't finished that wonderful dinner you made me.'

Diate led the way. He returned to his chair and rocked it back on two legs, using a corner of the wall for support. With one hand, he held his wine glass. The other he kept at rest on his leg. He didn't want Martina to know how nervous he suddenly felt.

'You know a lot of this,' Martina said. 'I know you must.'

'Tell me anyway.' He wanted a different perspective, an inside perspective, instead of his hate-filled one.

'The Queen killed the last Queen almost a decade ago in a short but very bloody coup. The coup seemed almost unplanned. It happened so fast that the new Queen had no one she trusted around her. She brought in people from the provinces and others who had been traveling. She brought in my aunt from the north and made her Minister of Culture.'

Diate nodded. He had checked all of this after he had returned from Rulanda. So far nothing was different.

'My aunt worked until she died – natural causes. Believe me, I checked – a few years ago. She kept the records, and made sure the Talents remained in line.'

Diate leaned back in his chair. 'But Sheba recertified you?'

'Families can't do that. They might be biased.' Martina smiled. 'And I wasn't ready until a few years ago.'

Martina took a bite of her stew and chewed it carefully. All of her movements were deliberate, as if moving still hurt her. The stiffness would probably never go away. Sometimes he woke up in the middle of the night and wondered if he had done her any favors by helping her survive.

'For a long time, the Queen had no second. Then she heard about a woman who was making the Kingdom more money on resort islands like Rulanda than anyone else had. Tonio Carbete introduced the Queen to his sister, Sheba, and they became friends.'

Diate swallowed. The wine left a sour taste in his moth. Finally he had a question he didn't know the answer to. 'No one seemed worried that an assassin's sister was so close to the Queen?'

156

'Sheba seems to be different to her brother.' Martina paused and brushed a strand of hair off her face with the back of her hand. 'Sheba saved the Queen's life more than once, and as a reward, the Queen made her Minister of Culture.'

'Quite a reward,' Diate said. 'She had to have other reasons.' And she did. Diate knew of the trust, and the money, as well as Sheba's complete control of the Talents.

Martina shrugged and took another bite. 'I only know the gossip. The relationship worked well for a few years, but a year or so ago, they had a falling out. When I – left, no one expected Sheba to last for more than a few days.'

Diate nodded. He had not heard of the falling out. Sometimes the inner workings of Kingdom government did not get passed to his sources. Perhaps the falling out was the reason Sheba was at Rulanda. To prove herself again. The timing would have been right. But she hadn't proved herself at all. The mission had failed. 'And you don't know what changed.'

Martina's smile was bitter. 'I'm out of the loop, now, detective.'

Diate sipped his wine. The spices tickled the back of his throat. 'Odd that she would still be in power if the Queen disliked her that much.'

'Kingdom politics are like the wind. Sometimes they blow strong, sometimes they blow cold, and sometimes they don't seem to be blowing at all. But they always have a mind of their own.'

That he remembered. The favorites who suddenly turned up dead. The silence that certain comments engendered. The whispered shushings whenever someone brought up his father.

The bodies on the steps – his sister, arms extended . . .

'Things are so much more stable here.' Martina ate the last bit of her stew and pushed the plate away. She set the spoon down carefully so that it didn't clatter.

'Hereditary monarchies usually are.' Diate brought his chair back to rest on all four of its legs. A cautious hereditary monarchy, with a standing army that hadn't gone to battle in over a decade. If it weren't for his vocal urgings, the secret police force would have become more of an information-gathering organization than a force that maintained any physical power. But Diate made sure the Golgoth understood the necessity to maintain a forceful defense even during his battle for peace. Until this week, the Kingdom had indicated no desire to join any peace talks, and Golga would always have remained at risk from them. The Kingdom's army was strong and cunning. Diate was glad Golga had not battled the Kingdom since his arrival.

Martina shook her head. 'It's more. I know so many minor Talents who think nothing of killing someone who gets in their way. There's an attitude here that life is precious, an attitude that isn't there in the Kingdom.'

Diate set his glass down. 'You haven't been out enough to know that. The Kingdom was founded by people from Golga. The patterns are the same. Golgans value things above all else. They want to become rich. As a rich country, Golga looks at anything that smacks of violence as something that threatens property. If Golga were a poor country, I think it would use any means it could to get the riches it desires.'

'You're justifying the Kingdom?'

'No,' Diate said. 'I've just spent years trying to understand it.' Trying to understand the memory, the coppery scent of blood filling the place he had once called home.

'When I met Sheba, she seemed nice,' Martina said, 'but the Queen's people always thought she was dangerous.'

Diate laughed. 'Of course she's dangerous. Anyone who reaches that level of power in that country has to be.' And that was where his fear came from. He had had few challengers on Golga. The last major challenge came when he ran away from the Kingdom, when he had saved his own life. Sure, he had been in dangerous situations. He had been knifed in the ports; he had subdued famous assassins. But he had only struggled for his very existence once.

Once was more than enough.

'Do you understand why I won't see you until after the Festival?'

Martina sighed. She rubbed her curved fingers against the wine glass. 'I wish you didn't have to get involved with those people at all.'

Diate finished his wine with one gulp. 'Me too,' he said. 'But the Golgoth has asked me to do it. I can't refuse him.'

'Even at the price of your own life?'

He stood and kissed her on the forehead. 'It won't cost me my life. If they were going to do something about the Rogue Talent, they would have tried last night. And we were ready for them, just as we will be during the Festival. I'm safe enough. I just wish I could find out what they really want.'

'They want whatever's the most precious,' she said. 'And if they can't own it, they'll destroy it.'

Chapter 12

The offices of the Port City detectives were darker and dingier than secret police headquarters. Housed in a small building a block from the palace, the offices were tiny rooms – many without windows – bundled together like books on a shelf. Large meeting rooms covered the second floor, and desks stood side by side in the far ends. Most of the detectives used their lockers at the gymnasium to store personal items since fewer people had access to the locker rooms.

Diate's body tingled from his morning workout. For the second night in a row, he hadn't slept well. His dreams were filled with Martina and Sheba, talking to him, fighting with him. Touching him.

He unlocked the door to his own office. He had the largest office in the building, stuck in the far back corner of the third floor with windows on both outside walls. The faint scent of old coffee reached him. Beltar managed to bring Diate some after each trip, something Diate appreciated. He stepped inside. A large mahogany desk sat in the center of the room with a matching straight-backed chair behind it. Bookshelves lined the inner walls, and a single hand-woven Kingdom tapestry hung behind the door. Beltar had brought him the tapestry. It depicted his brothers wrestling on the floor of their house. An aunt had woven it during happier times.

Diate flicked on a light and took a seat behind the desk. In the last few days, someone had stacked reams of paper on the polished surface. Reports to approve, decisions to make. He could spend his entire life in this room, reading papers and never going out on the street.

He leaned back in his chair and stared for a moment at the sculpture which sat atop the file cabinet. A boy and a girl, backs arched in opposite directions, hands flung over heads, one foot up in complete abandon, gave the piece a fluidity most sculpture lacked. He had found it a few years ago during a raid on smugglers in the harbor. Golgan policy allowed people to take Kingdom items, since they could not be returned. All other smuggling loot went back to its own country.

He had taken the sculpture with him, refused to let anyone else carry it, and placed it on top of the cabinets. Sometimes he ran his hand across it, hoping for life in the metal. But there was none. There had been none for decades.

Still, he thought it a miracle that he had found it. He had believed that all of his mother's sculptures had disappeared in the raid on the house. Instead, the most precious one survived: the one that depicted him and his sister before she got downgraded, before his father started on that final campaign. The sculpture captured joy – the unbounded joy of two children who loved to dance.

'You can't get any work done when you stare into space.'

Diate blinked and sat foward. The Golgoth's son, Kreske, stood at the door. His thatch of red hair was mussed and deep shadows made his round eyes seem even rounder. His blouse and leggings were wrinkled, as if he had put on dirty clothes before coming to Diate's offices.

Diate stood. 'Kreske. It's been a while.'

Kreske stepped into the room and surveyed it. 'Amazing we live within a block of each other. I don't believe I have ever seen your office.'

'What reason would you have?' Diate went around Kreske and gently shut the door. The tapestry swung against the glass pane, then stopped, blocking the view.

'I never expected Kingdom trappings.'

Diate stiffened. 'Family trappings actually. Most of the books were published here, but those that weren't were written by my father. I got all the Kingdom stuff from raids and occasional sales. I have a friend who looks out for anything that came from my family.'

'I thought you hated those people too much to have any reminders around.'

'Not the family,' Diate said. 'The family is the reason I'm here.'

'Me too.' Kreske went over to the window and placed his hands on the sill. 'You aren't going through with this stupidity with my father, are you?'

Diate returned to his desk and leaned on it, crossing his hands in front of his chest. 'Which stupidity is that?'

161

'Letting the Kingdom go into the Peace Festival. Having him meet with the Queen.'

'I argued against it. But your father makes the final decisions, not me.'

'And Scio?'

'Scio thinks times have changed.'

'Well, I don't.' Kreske turned. He ran a hand through his hair, messing it more. 'Look. I don't know how well you know the history of this place, but every time those people come into the city someone dies. They think Golga is theirs by some ancient birthright.'

'Kreske.' Diate placed his hands on the desk, bracing himself against the strength in Kreske's words. 'Your father knows all of this. I've argued with him, but he's convinced this is the right decision to make.'

'Well, unconvince him. You're his favorite. He'll do what you ask.'

In the middle of the night, he awakens to a sound outside his room. A little red-haired boy stands at the door, shaking his fist at Diate: 'He hates you. He will never love you. He will only love me!'

'I've already asked,' Diate said softly. 'You're his son. You convince him.'

Kreske ran a hand over his face, then looked away. 'He says I don't know what I'm talking about. He says someday he will let me know all the things he was thinking, but not now. I'm not ready.'

Diate shook his head. Protecting Kreske from vital information would certainly not help Golga. Kreske had to learn how decisions were made, so that when he became Golgoth, he could make them himself without thinking twice. 'You need to talk to him again, and have him explain this to you. It's time you understand what your father is doing, Kreske.'

'I know that.' Kreske sighed and slumped into the padded chair beside the far bookcase. 'Why is he allowing those people here when you oppose it? You know them better than anyone.'

Diate walked over to the sculpture and turned it over in his hands. Then he handed it to Kreske. 'My mother made it,' he said. 'That's my sister. And me.'

Kreske ran a finger along the ridges in the metal. He brought it closer to his face and stared at the young Diate.

'Maybe,' Diate said, 'your father thinks it's time to heal the breach between the two nations. Maybe I'm too bitter to agree.'

Kreske traced the young Diate's face. 'I don't remember you looking like this.'

'I barely remember what it felt like.'

Kreske handed the sculpture back to Diate. Diate set it carefully on top of the file cabinets, the metal making a soft thunk against the wood. 'Are you saying my father might be right about this?'

'I don't know,' Diate said. 'I don't know if I'm a judge of it. You might be, if he gives you all the facts. But I can tell you this: I'm going to be working with Scio and we'll do everything possible to make sure the entire city is safe.'·

'Arm patches?'

Diate looked up. Arm patches had been out of use for so long that he had forgotten they existed. The Vorgellians devised the system so that spies undercover had a non-visible communications device. 'I don't know.'

'There's only a few of you competent enough to deal with the Kingdom on a one-to-one level. If there's trouble, you need to know where the trouble is.'

Diate stared down at Kreske. His skin was paler than its usually ghostly shade of ivory, his features lined with fatigue. He had been giving this a lot of thought, and he wasn't a child any longer. He was a man who would someday run a country, and he was doing his best to protect that country's interests now.

'I'll talk to Scio,' Diate said. 'Arm patches were an option neither of us thought of.'

'Let me in on some of the planning,' Kreske said. 'I want to make sure it's done right.'

Diate nodded. Kreske had the same feeling about this meeting that Diate did. 'Talk to your father. If he won't let you help, I will. We'll work together on this one.'

Kreske stood and clasped Diate's hand. They held each other for a moment, and Diate felt a small shiver of pleasure. They had never worked together before. How wonderful if that was about to change.

'I'll talk to my father,' Kreske said.

'Good.' Diate let go of Kreske's hand. 'And let me know if you need my help.'

Kreske smiled. His teeth were even, white, and perfect. The skull-like grin of a Golgoth. 'I will, Emilio. Thank you.'

He opened the door and let himself out. Diate remained by the sculpture for a moment, his heart pounding heavily. The pleasure he felt at working with Kreske was overshadowed by the worry. He couldn't shake the feeling that something would go wrong.

The Pavilion looked different in the daylight. The white building reflected the sun's glare, and the ornate tapestries covering the side doors had a dirty tattered look. The gate was battered, and the grounds, which had seemed beautiful in the candlelight, were trampled and mud-covered.

The silence disappointed him. Somehow he always expected this area to have music.

Diate palmed his security code into the gate and waited as the door swung open. A guard appeared at the main double doors, her arms crossed in front of her chest. She wore a sheer garment that clung to her body, revealing the curve of every muscle.

He stepped inside. Even though he was still on Golga, the land felt different here. His shoes clipped on the paved walk. Sunlight glittered on the ocean, magnifying the whiteness of the Pavilion itself. He couldn't look directly on it. Instead he concentrated on the guard.

Her face had no expression at all. It was as smooth as the building's facade. Since she had come outside, she had not moved. An occasional blink of the eye was the only thing that clued him to the fact that she wasn't a statue herself.

As he started up the steps, he nodded. She nodded back.

'I'm here to see the Minister of Culture,' he said in Lillish. 'My name is Diate. I believe she's expecting me.'

'I know who you are,' the guard said. Her voice was low and rumbling. 'She expected you last night.'

Diate ignored the tremor that ran through him. 'I didn't have her answer until this morning.'

'She is in a meeting. I'll send someone to see if she can be disturbed. You wait here.' The guard disappeared inside the door.

Diate stood outside, staring at the images in the stained glass. Each pane told a story in itself, but taken together, they showed the history of the revolt against Golga. In the first pane, a slender woman danced before the palace. The Golgoth's guards were emerging from the door, set to arrest her. In the second pane, she reclined in prison, her beautiful dancer's body broken and crushed. Rescuers were sneaking in the window, carrying a robe to

164

hide her as they made their escape. The third depicted the woman and her rescuers on a Vorgellian ship, huddled in the corner as they flew to the nearby island of Tersis. And in the fourth, they stood on the dry dusty surface, one of the rescuers in tears at the barrenness of the place. The woman had her back to the rest of them. She shook her fist defiantly at Golga, a blue and white city off in the distance.

Diate shuddered. Not the kind of art diplomats should place in an embassy. The view was not even representative. The Kingdom and Golga couldn't see each other across the waters.

The guard emerged. 'I have sent someone to speak to the Minister,' she said. She returned to her stance, feet shoulder length apart, arms crossed in front of her chest.

'Thank you.' Diate knew he would get no more conversation out of her. He glanced to the side, and noted that even the rough plaster surface of the Pavilion carried artwork. Small figurines singing, making pottery, and writing. Each art form practiced in the Kingdom appeared within one meter on the wall and was repeated in the next meter. So much detail. None of Golga's buildings, even the ones assembled over long periods of time, had that much detail.

The door opened. The guard leaned her head in and nodded. 'The Minister will see you now.'

She held the door open all the way and Diate stepped inside.

The wide hall looked barren and empty, and smaller than he expected. The hardwood floors gleamed and the tapestries were pulled back, giving the room an airy outdoorsy feel. A woman just inside the door took Diate's arm and led him to the side, where the wide staircase opened to the second story.

Their footsteps echoed in the silence. Dust motes floated in beams of sunlight. If he hadn't been there two nights before, he would have thought the place had been deserted for a long time.

At the top of the stairs, a railing carved with the faces of animals overlooked the floor below. Diate grabbed the railing, felt the rough wood beneath his skin. Up here the floor was made of marble tile, and murals covered the wall. Each mural told another chapter in Kingdom history, and in each outdoor scene, Golga floated in the corner, a silent menacing face upon the proceedings.

The woman stopped at two wide double doors made of the same carved wood as the railing. She knocked, then stepped away.

165

The door swung open, revealing a ballroom flooded in sunlight. Tonio Carbete bowed to Diate, then stepped out of the way. Sheba stood in the center of the room. The long windows cast her shadow out before her, and the sun kissed her hair as white as Carbete's. She held out a hand to Diate.

'Shall we dance?'

With the sun at her back, he couldn't see what she was wearing, only the shape of her body. The expression on her face was also cast in darkness.

He put his hands behind his back. 'I have a response to your question.'

She sighed. 'All business, Emilio?'

He didn't move. Her flirting made him nervous. He probably should respond to it, act as if he welcomed it, so that he could help with the Golgoth's plan, but he wasn't an actor. He didn't want to touch her. He didn't want to lose himself again.

'Very well.' She took a step forward, out of the sunlight. Diate had to blink to clear the glare from his eyes. 'Leave us, Tonio.'

Carbete bowed again, and pulled the doors closed behind him.

Sheba looked smaller out of the sun. Her clothes were form fitting, but revealed nothing. She extended a hand, showing him the paneled walls of the rest of the room. 'Would you like to see if we're alone?'

'It doesn't matter if we are or not,' he said. 'The message I have is not secret.'

She came closer. He had to stifle an urge to step back, to keep distance between them. 'We are alone,' she said. When he did not answer, she frowned. 'All right. Tell me what your message is.'

'The Golgoth welcomes you to the Peace Festival, and would like to see the Queen. You must contact his appointments secretary to arrange a time.'

She nodded, her posture mimicking his. 'We are free to walk through Golga?'

'You are free to travel in the Port City with the appropriate documentation during the Peace Festival itself. Until then, I have three passes so that some of your people might prepare for the meeting and your participation in the Festival.'

'Three?' She raised her eyebrows. 'We'll have performers in every event, more than any other country. We need more than three.'

166

'You get three. You already have an advantage in the competitions.'

She shrugged, and smiled a little. 'If you allowed performance in this dismal place, you would do well at the competitions yourselves.'

'We allow the Festival,' Diate said. 'It is enough.'

'Because,' she said, 'it is a trade festival, and you make a lot of money.'

'Because,' he said, finally taking that step back, 'it promotes peace.'

She sighed again, and looked away from him. 'Is this how it is going to be between us, Emilio? This coolness?'

He longed to touch her, to tuck a loose strand of hair behind her ear, to caress her cheek. 'I don't see how it can be any other way.'

She brought her face close to his. 'You don't belong here, on Golga. This place ties you up and makes you stiff. You have none of that dancer's grace, none of that fluidity –'

'I have a life here,' he said. 'I would be dead if I remained in the Kingdom.'

'Not any more.' She spoke softly. 'Things have changed, Emilio. You can come home.'

She reached for him, but he ducked out of her grasp. He hadn't expected her to be so warm. The surprise from two nights before seemed to have faded. She seemed to be trying a new tactic.

'I am home,' he said. He pulled the passes from his pocket and handed them to her. Their fingers brushed and he longed to catch her small hand with his own. 'Be careful with these. My people are trained to capture Kingdom members, using any means possible. They will continue that practice until the festival starts.'

'And what happens if someone gets captured?'

'It depends on what they've done. And who captures them.' He permitted himself a small smile he didn't feel. 'Some of my people can be rough.'

'Is that a threat, Emilio?'

'No.' This time he did reach a hand up and cup her cheek. 'It's a warning. Be safe, Sheba.'

Her skin was warm against his palm, warm and soft. She leaned into his touch and made the gesture more of a caress. He smiled a little, then removed his hand. In Kingdom style he bowed and backed away.

She watched him go, not moving. Finally he stopped at the door, turned around, and let himself out.

The wide hallway was empty. Carbete had disappeared. Diate made himself walk to the stairs without looking at the murals. They made him uneasy. The entire place made him uneasy.

Sheba made him uneasy.

He couldn't play the game the Golgoth wanted him to play. He couldn't pretend to go away with her, pretend to love her. Either he had to let go and be with her, or he had to stay away.

Yet touching her had felt so good. He had missed her each day since his return from Rulanda.

And he owed the Golgoth his life. The Kingdom held nothing for him at all.

Except Sheba.

Chapter 13

The surgery room was all white. Even the table on which Diate sat was white. His legs were crossed beneath him, the gray of his uniform looking bright and out of place in this testimony to cleanliness. His shirt was off and hanging from a peg behind the door. In the other room, the Olean surgeon hummed as she prepared.

Diate sighed and looked at the thin red scar in the center of his left forearm. He hadn't worn a patch in over a decade and even then it had only been used in practice drills. Scio had memories of its use in the Port City, but he said that patches weren't always reliable.

The patches had a simple use. They sent a one-time message, agreed upon before the bearer went undercover. In this case, the patch would go off if the Golgoth was in trouble from the Kingdom. Diate would then hurry to the Golgoth's side, if possible. If not, Diate would take the necessary action in his current location.

Scio wasn't supposed to use the patch until Golgoth met with the Queen. Even then, he would only use it in case of emergency.

The table's surface was cold. Goose bumps had risen on his bare skin. They kept the surgery rooms cool for the surgeons, so they wouldn't get too hot working under the lights, but Diate wished that they had some consideration for the patients as well.

Scio hadn't wanted to reinstate the patches. Diate wanted the extra measure of protection. He wanted to be as close to the Golgoth during the Queen's visit as possible. Scio wanted Diate to concentrate on Sheba, but in this instance, the Golgoth had agreed with Diate.

'We need all the protection we can get,' the Golgoth had said to Scio. Diate believed that Kreske had probably talked with his father.

The surgeon came in the room. She was small for an Olean, her willowy form half Diate's height. Her hands, with their extra fingers and delicate bone structure, had an agility that suited them to delicate tasks. Her white uniform carried the ghosts of ancient blood stains.

'Your record says you've worn a patch before. Any trouble?' Her voice was as tiny as the rest of her. Still, it echoed in the near empty room.

'No.' He extended his arm. She bowed over it. Her silver hair caught the light and glinted it back to him. Her touched was gentle as she probed the scar.

'Small incision, good penetration, no excess scarring. I am amazed, with the dense muscle and the lack of fat on your body. I would think that the patch rubbed and did some damage.'

'We only used it a few times, and it was nearly a decade ago.'

She nodded and turned away, opening a small drawer under the table. 'You were younger. The body is more elastic when it's younger.'

He smiled. That was a fact he faced every morning. He had twice the skill he had had as a boy and half the elasticity.

She took a small vial out of the drawer. Then she put a cloth over the end of the vial and tipped it. 'This is a local anaesthetic,' she said. 'It will numb you. I need your right arm, please.'

He glanced at the arm, unlined and unmarked. 'I prefer to do the left, over the old scar.'

'No,' she said. 'There could be damage that I can't see.'

'You just told me that area was clean.'

'But not clean enough to risk further trauma. Right arm.'

Diate crossed his arms in front of his chest. 'I have a lot of work this week, some of it with a woman familiar with my body. She'll ask too many questions if I have a new wound on my right arm. If the scar is on the left, I can tell her that we had to reopen the area and do a little extra surgery.'

The Olean sighed. 'Detective, I would prefer to perform the surgery on the right. I don't want to risk damage to the left.'

'I would rather risk damage to the left than have too many questions raised at the wrong time. Even the smallest question might cost my life.'

She didn't move, as if his words had given her pause for thought. 'The risk is minimal in either case, isn't it?' he asked. 'We're only talking about fractions of degrees' difference.'

170

'Yes,' she said.

'And I'll have use of the arm.'

'Minimal for a day. Complete within two.'

'Then I see no reason not to.'

'I do. But this is a special case.' She set the vial down, and sighed. 'All right. If you don't mind two incisions. They might be harder to explain . . .'

'You won't need two.' He extended his left arm. She picked up the vial again and coated the cloth. Then she ran the anaesthetic across the skin. The liquid was cool. It tingled as it was absorbed through the pores, then his arm grew numb. He could still feel his hand and elbow. It was as if his wrist had fallen asleep without the rest of his arm.

She took his wrist and strapped it on a small metal cup. Then she pulled a tiny scalpel from the drawer. 'I recommend that you don't watch,' she said.

'I'm sure I've seen worse.'

'I'm sure you have. But not being done to you. Look away, detective. You have nothing to prove to me.'

He averted his gaze. The white walls were stark after the ornate decoration of the Pavilion. He hadn't thought about it before – the lack of artwork in Golga. The Kingdom had artwork on every surface. Even the clothes were decorative. But Golga favoured plainness. Since so many of Golga's older buildings were gone, Diate couldn't tell which country had responded to the other – if they had had an effect on each other at all.

Something warm landed on his palm. He turned. His skin was open and peeled back. Blood spattered his wrist and palm – unnumbed areas – that was the warmth he had felt. She had made a nick in a vein, and she brought a small clear machine the size of his thumb to cover it. The machine connected the vein and made sure the blood continued to flow properly.

He felt lightheaded. She was right: he had nothing to prove. He gazed at the door. 'Find any damage?'

'No.' Her voice held a smile. 'There isn't even much of a scar.' He didn't look again. Something cool brushed his thumb, and metal clinked on a metal tray. After a few minutes, he felt something tugging at his skin.

'Done,' she said.

The machine was gone. The skin was closed and a bit bruised.

The scar looked angrier and redder, but not much different. In a few days, Sheba wouldn't notice anything at all.

'You'll be sore when the anaesthetic wears off,' the Olean said. 'Don't stress the arm for the next two days. Any problems, see me at once.'

'Yes ma'am.'

She unhooked his wrist from the metal cup. Then she used her cloth to wipe his hand clean. With one hand, she opened a clear bandage and taped it on the wound. 'I'm sure I don't have to tell you, detective, that these things are only for emergencies.'

'But you told me anyway.'

She nodded. 'I've seen too many people with damaged arms from too much testing and use of the patch in routine. Use some other way of communicating for the routine work.'

He wanted to smile at her, but couldn't. 'This week will be anything but routine.'

By the time he had walked the few blocks to Beltar's store, he felt as if he had been stabbed. His arm throbbed. The surgeon hadn't given him anything to block the pain, and at the time he had been glad, but now he wasn't so certain. He could endure this kind of pain when it happened during his dance. He wasn't sure he wanted to tolerate it in the line of duty.

He resisted the urge to clamp the arm protectively against his side. The pain would ebb. Until then, he would act normally.

Despite the early twilight, a lot of people remained on the street. Most hurried, huddled against the growing darkness, but some ambled like Diate. A young man carrying a toolbox ducked into one of the nearby buildings. A woman, wearing the heavy garments of a Jovasian, kept referring to a piece of paper as she walked. The week before the Festival. The city would change.

The sign on Beltar's door read 'closed,' but Diate turned the knob anyway. The door opened, sending out stale air and incense. It had been a long time since he had come to the store. If he ate with Beltar these days, it was in Martina's apartment.

He let the door click closed behind him. The shelves were empty – particularly the wine shelves toward the back. Diate recognized the chaos that hit the store during one of Beltar's trips. Beltar always took wine with him, and brought other kinds back. The store suffered during Beltar's absence. 'Beltar?'

172

Diate's voice echoed. Dust rose from neighboring surfaces. The assistant Beltar hired didn't appear to have done a good job in Beltar's absence. Had the store been unlocked during Beltar's entire trip? Diate walked toward the back. 'Beltar!'

A muffled response came from the apartment, followed by a small crash and a curse. 'Emilio?'

Diate turned the corner into the kitchen. Beltar was crouching, his robe splayed behind him, picking up glass shards off the floor. 'Don't startle me like that,' he said.

'You left the door open.'

Beltar cupped the glass in his left hand and opened a cabinet. He tossed the glass inside, and it tinkled as it fell. 'I always do as I finish up. You know that.'

'I thought you had quit when we started eating at Martina's.'

Beltar shrugged. 'Some habits die hard.'

Diate took a deep breath to ease his pounding heart. He hadn't realized he was so on edge. But with the surgery, and the stress of the Festival, he shouldn't have been surprised. 'I need to talk to you.'

'I didn't think this was a social visit.' Beltar pulled out one of the kitchen chairs and sat down. 'You look too serious.'

Diate grinned. 'So how was the trip?'

'Tiring. But I found an entire new variety of wine on Tacen. They've been cross breeding grapes and using some genetic engineering techniques with the help of a renegade Olean. Looks like neither Oleon nor Vorgel are doing well at hanging onto their technology secrets these days. The wine's not quite white and not quite red, but with qualities of both, and it doesn't take as long to ferment. Best of all, it takes to the spices like something I've never seen. They don't separate out, so there are no bad batches.'

Diate pulled a chair closer to the table. 'You didn't expect this?'

Beltar grinned and leaned back. The chair groaned. 'They said they were using experimental techniques. The last place that used experimental techniques had developed a non-alcoholic wine. What they didn't seem to realize was that it had been around for a millennium – grape juice.'

Diate laughed. He missed Beltar when he wasn't in town. 'It sounds as if your already profitable business is getting better.'

'There's always room for improvement.' Beltar stood. 'Some wine?'

Diate paused for a moment. He probably shouldn't, with the ache in his arm, but he had no more work to do that night. Maybe the alcohol would dull the pain. 'Is it the new stuff?'

'I have some without the spices. They haven't had time to blend.'

'Will it be any good?'

Beltar walked into the small kitchen. 'Not as good as it will be, of course. But good enough.' He opened the cupboard and pulled down a bottle. The bottle was thin and clear except for the label. The wine inside wasn't a blush as Beltar had led him to believe, but a light pale green.

Beltar acted as Diate's steward, opening the bottle and giving Diate the cork to sniff. He had never smelled a wine so green and fruity. 'You sure this is aged?'

Beltar pretended indignation. 'I know wines, Emilio.'

Diate smiled and set the cork down. 'Just checking.'

Beltar pulled two glasses off the rack above the sink and poured the wine. It filled the room with the green, fruity smell. He handed a glass to Diate, who sniffed, swished the glass to see if the wine had any sediment, and then took a small sip.

The wine had a fresh minty flavor and a soft bite on the back of the palate. It went down smoothly. 'A man could get used to this,' he said. 'It's dangerous.'

'High alcohol content,' Beltar said. 'So be careful.'

'When am I not careful?' Diate asked.

Beltar grinned. He brought his wine to the table. 'Quite a find, eh? Imagine with a touch of 'simmon, a dash of florenz –'

Diate couldn't but he said nothing. He took another sip and let the flavor wash through him, a flavor that made him think of days when he was a little boy, before the dance was everything, before –

'So,' Beltar said. 'What is this serious thing you need to discuss with me?'

Diate sighed. His arm didn't throb as badly when he kept it still. 'Festival week. It's going to be worse than usual.'

'Is that why you're so pale?'

Diate shook his head. 'Exhaustion.' The fewer people who knew about the patch, the better.

'I noticed Fauvinians flocking out of a huge ship when the air shuttle banked for landing. I had forgotten about the Festival.'

Diate set his wine glass down. He wanted to remain fresh while they discussed this. 'It will be worse this year. The Golgoth has decided to let the Kingdom participate.'

Beltar froze, arm raised for another sip. 'Was he in his right mind?'

'He says it's time to make peace with them.'

'No wonder you're pale. Have you told Martina?'

Diate nodded. 'She's frightened, afraid they'll find her. I told her that they wouldn't. But she's still afraid.'

'I can't blame her. She ever find out about that trouble on Rulanda?' Beltar completed the sip, then took another, finishing off the glass.

Diate shook his head. 'I never told her. I never thought they could get here. I didn't expect the Festival. I think she'll be fine, though, as long as I stay away from her.'

Beltar frowned and drummed his bejeweled fingers on the wooden tabletop.

Diate anticipated the question before Beltar asked it. 'I have to make sure nothing goes wrong during the Festival, and I'm Golga's liaison to the Kingdom because of my past. I'm afraid they'll keep a close watch on me, and get what secrets they have.'

Beltar gripped the edge of the table. 'You're afraid you'll lead them to Martina?'

Diate nodded. 'They'll wonder who she is, if she's someone they can use against me. Or Torrie could have tipped someone. If I stay away from Martina, they won't find her. I don't want them to see her. She's just beginning to get better.'

'Have you seen her since the Kingdom has arrived?'

'Once,' Diate said. 'But they had no way of traveling freely through the Port City at that time. They do now.'

'Have you no way out of this assignment?'

Diate picked up the wine glass and swirled the wine around. The Golgoth wouldn't meet with him anymore. *No more protests, Emilio,* he had said. *I have noted them and made my decision.* 'I'm the only candidate,' he said. 'And I'm stuck.'

Beltar nodded. He got up and poured himself another glass of wine, then downed it. 'Awful waste of a good year,' he murmured. He poured another glass, then brought it back to the table. 'I'll watch her. I won't let her out of my sight.'

'Thank you,' Diate said.

Beltar swished his new glass of wine. He stared down into the liquid as if it had answers to questions he hadn't asked. 'I do worry about her not having your protection.'

Diate took another sip of wine. 'Right now my protection is no good, and I can't spare any detectives. If you're really worried that someone will snatch her away from you, pay someone to watch over her. I can guarantee that anyone you hire will do a better job than I will. I'm only there a few hours a day. And some days I can't come at all. If you hired someone, that person would be there all the time.'

'But Martina would never allow it. She only trusts us.'

'If she had no choice, she would allow it. She has us under her thumb, Beltar. We don't make her do anything she doesn't want to do. And we can't take care of her forever. Someday we might want to go on with our own lives. What if you mate?'

Beltar blushed. He sipped his wine, then brought the glass to the table. 'No woman has wanted me for a long time, Emilio. Not even Martina wants me. As soon as the bandages came off her eyes, she wanted you.'

Diate shook his head. 'She doesn't know what she wants. She likes you better than me.'

'I guess that really doesn't matter.' Beltar rolled his wine glass between his fingers and gazed out the windows at the alley. 'I wouldn't mind taking care of her for the rest of my life. I wouldn't mind at all.'

Diate was quiet. He had always known Beltar felt that way, but he also knew that Martina didn't want a real relationship. Not yet, and maybe not ever, as wounded as she was. 'Maybe I'm just speaking for myself then,' he said. 'Maybe I can't imagine eating dinner in that small apartment for the rest of my life.'

Beltar studied him for a moment. 'Maybe you feel like you need a change.'

Diate smiled. 'Maybe I do.'

Beltar drew the curtain and reached back to lock the door. 'I've been thinking about this for a while. I've been watching you. You're not a happy man. You never have been. You work, but you haven't found your place here.'

The back of Diate's throat had gone dry. He wanted to stop the conversation right there. 'The Golgoth gave me my place.'

'And he's making you pay for it. You don't want to be with the Kingdom.'

Diate made himself swallow. He wasn't sure what he wanted anymore. 'No,' he said. 'I don't.'

'Yet as a condition of staying here, the Golgoth is forcing you into a dangerous position. And if he decides that the Kingdom is welcome in this city, you'll be in that position again. And the position is one you ran away from.'

Diate shifted in his chair. 'What's your point, Beltar?'

'I need an assistant. You like wine, and you like me. We travel well together, and now that the Kingdom has invaded Golga, one place is the same as the next to you. I could make you a rich man. You still may not be happy, but you at least would have the kind of home you like. You could afford the kind of life you like.'

Diate didn't move. He had lived so long without possibilities that he didn't know how to face them.

Beltar saw the confusion on Diate's face. 'You don't have to decide now. Just think about it. Think about it while you're working with the Kingdom this week, while you can't visit your friends because it might endanger them, when you go home to that hole of an apartment of yours. And then talk to me.'

Diate looked down at his hands. 'Sounds as if you already know what I'm going to decide.'

Beltar shook his head. 'I don't pretend to understand you, friend. I just know the choice I would make.'

'You've already made it,' Diate said. 'You made it a long time ago. I've never done anything else –'

'You danced,' Beltar said. 'You were famous once.'

'I was a boy.'

'But that doesn't matter. You've lived more lives than most of us. And if this job doesn't kill you, then you could live even more. And I would love to work with you.'

Diate was silent for a moment. A woman's voice rose from an apartment opposite, and something thumped next door. Beltar was quiet.

'You're a good friend,' Diate said. 'I promise. I'll think about this. I'll see if it's right for me.'

Beltar smiled. 'You have to make choices eventually, Emilio. You can't be a detective forever. Someday your body will give out, and someone will kill you, or the Kingdom will decide they want you back home after all and the Golgoth – who'll be Kreske at that point – won't defend you. Then what will you do? Run again? It's better for you to choose something now than wait for them to force you to choose something you don't want.'

Diate nodded. He wished it were as simple as Beltar made it sound. He pushed away from the table. 'I didn't just come to talk with you about Martina.'

The smile faded from Beltar's face.

Diate stood. He couldn't discuss this sitting down. He paced across the small kitchen. 'Sheba is here. I have already met with her twice.'

'Emilio, you can't —'

Diate held up his hand to silence Beltar. Beltar already knew Sheba's position in the Kingdom. They had discussed it over many bottles of wine when they returned from Rulanda. 'The Golgoth wants me to. He wants me to convince her that I love her and will go back to the Kingdom with her.'

Beltar seemed to have shrunk into himself. 'For the gods' sake,' he said. 'Why?'

'To learn the secrets we don't know about their government. To send me in as deep a cover as we can, both for the sake of the Festival, and for the future.'

'Would you leave with her?'

Diate stopped at the window. The alley was dark. 'I don't know,' he said. 'I saw her the second time, and wasn't sure I could pull this off. I wasn't ready to start the deception yet, and we only have a few days.'

'What if something goes wrong? If you're seen with a Kingdom woman, you could lose your position here, and your respect.'

'I know,' Diate said. 'But the Golgoth has ordered it. I guess that's one of the reasons I'm telling you. I want someone else to know, someone outside of the government. I also want Martina to know. If something goes wrong, I'll take you up on that job offer. I may have no other choice.'

Beltar grabbed the bottle of wine and refilled their glasses. 'I don't like this,' he said. 'I don't like that woman. I never have. What if she was planning on something like this?'

'I think she's planning on something else, Beltar,' Diate said. 'And I'm not sure what it is. But I have to be ready for all contingencies. I need you, my friend, should something go wrong.'

Beltar got up and brought Diate's wine glass to him. He stood behind him, not quite touching him, but close enough to offer support. 'You know that I will help you,' he said. 'Through anything.'

Chapter 14

The stairway was dark. Diate reached up, fingers finding the sharp edges of broken glass instead of the light case. He sighed. Glass shards crunched under his shoes. He mounted the stairs, duffel swinging heavily against his back.

The conversation with Beltar had left him discouraged. Beltar was right. Diate had no real future in the Port City. More years at the same job, doing the same things. The very real threat of losing his position once Kreske became Golgoth. Night after night of returning to this darkened hallway until some night the darkness wouldn't be caused by vandals but by someone seeking revenge.

The wooden stairs creaked under his feet. Normally, he had enough courtesy for his neighbors that he walked up the side of the stairs, avoiding the creaks so that they wouldn't be awakened by his late night hours. This night, he didn't care. Let them wake up. Let them complain. They had no recourse against him.

Light filtered through the window at the top of the stairs. Moonlight mixed with the streetlight just to the left illuminated the number on his apartment door. He punched in the code and the door swung open. He palmed a switch near the door and blinked as brightness flooded the room.

Home. Handmade tapestries covered the floors and walls. Oversized pillows were propped in all four corners. An expensive mahogany table – a gift from Beltar, found in his many travels – lay beneath the room's only window. A book sat open on the table's surface, one of his father's which Diate was rereading. A small, rarely used kitchen went off to the left, and to the right, his bedroom with a mattress raised a few centimeters off the floor. Statues stood on mantels, and books hid behind the tapestries. The colors were rich and vibrant, the designs bold. A bit of the Kingdom inside Golga's drabness.

He never let anyone in here. His apartment gave him away even more than his office. He was afraid of what they would think.

He was afraid of what they would do.

He kicked the door shut and leaned against it. Sometimes he didn't understand his own mind. When he had first moved out of the palace, he had tried to live like a Golgan – the drab, functional furniture, the unpainted walls. But with the help of Beltar, Diate acquired pieces of the Kingdom and brought them home. The others he pulled from government warehouses where confiscated property of an enemy state were stored. With each bright item, he gained a little more peace.

He would think about Beltar's offer – no matter what happened – once the Festival was over.

Diate walked into the bedroom and set his duffel in the closet across from the bed. The duffel brushed against a small tattered piece of leather in the far back corner. Diate crouched and touched it. The leather felt soft against his fingers, and for a moment, he was trapped inside the cargo seats of the cruise ship again. The goatskin bags holding his water had long since disintegrated, but the larger leather bag, battered and rotting, remained. The Vorgellian captain had left it with the Golgoth on a pass through the Port City. When Diate saw it, nearly a year after he had run from the Kingdom, he wasn't sure if he wanted it.

But he had kept it, unopened, all those years.

He peeled off his clothes and washed down in the tiny, closet-sized bathroom off the bedroom. Then he sprawled on the mattress, leaving the lights on all over the apartment.

The mattress felt soft against his back. He draped one arm over his eyes and stepped out of himself for a moment. He had no right to complain. The Golgoth had saved his life. If Diate had remained on that cruise ship, he would have died. If he had remained in the Kingdom, he would have died. The life he had here was better than no life at all.

A knock on the door startled him. He sat up, listening. Someone had to be at one of the neighbor's doors, past curfew, trying to get in. The knock sounded again, louder than he had ever heard one. He got up, slid on a pair of pants, and was tying them at the waist as he made his way across the living room.

When he reached the door, he stopped. 'Who is it?'

'Sheba.'

Surprise made him open the door before he had a chance to

think. She wore a blousy shirt, tight leggings, and boots. When she saw him, she smiled.

'I didn't expect you to be asleep, Emilio.'

'It's after curfew,' he said. The words sent a shiver down his back. 'You'd better come inside.'

She stepped in, glancing at the tapestries and the pillows. As she walked into the room, her fingers traced a statue sitting on a pedestal.

He didn't want her to touch anything. He didn't want her to know his secrets. 'You shouldn't be out after curfew,' he said. 'It's not safe, especially for you.'

'I can take care of myself.' She still hadn't looked at him. She was peering at a tapestry that hung beside the kitchen door. 'Do all Golgans make themselves rich off illegal merchandise? Or is this part of your heritage showing?'

His face grew warm. 'These things were brought into Golga illegally and were confiscated. They would have gone into some warehouse. I couldn't bear that.'

'No,' she said. 'I suppose you couldn't.'

He didn't respond. He hadn't moved from his post near the door. When he first returned from Rulanda, he had imagined her here, sitting on a pillow, eating grapes from his fingers and sipping Beltar's wines. Later, he had pretended she would come, and he would slam the door in her face, forcing her to leave him forever. But now, as she stood in the room, he could do nothing.

She turned, her eyes wide. 'I didn't expect this,' she said. 'I thought you were the prim and proper policeman who'd long forgotten his ancestral home.'

'If I had forgotten it, I never would have touched you.' The words came out before he had a chance to think about them and their truth.

She smiled, a soft smile that made her look like a young girl. 'My mother brought me up with the story of the soul mates. Do you know it, Emilio?'

'Yes,' he said. His mother had told the story too, always in the presence of his father, always holding hands. Each soul had a mate, and Kingdom members should not join with others until they found the person with whom they could discuss anything, could do anything, and, his mother would say slyly, because of whom they could love no one else.

182

'I wonder about us,' she said. 'I can't put you out of my mind.'

He couldn't forget her either, no matter how hard he tried. 'It doesn't matter –'

'It does,' she said. She wandered over to the table and rested her fingers on his father's book. 'We come from the same place. We might have been destined.'

'I can't go back there, and you can't stay here. Destiny counts for nothing now, Sheba.'

She picked up the book and studied it, careful to keep one finger in the center to hold his place. 'There are people back home who believe in your father's teachings,' she said. 'His poems are back in print and so are his pamphlets. Even people in the government believe what he said about the Talent system. It is wrong. It does discriminate, and it divides us instead of drawing us together.'

Diate's body had gone rigid. 'You people killed him because of those beliefs.'

'I was a child when he died,' she said. 'So were most of the others who agree with him. We all saw the destruction the Talent system brings, how many lives get shunted away from the dreams. How much poverty and unhappiness the regimentation brings. No one can silence a man who spoke the truth.'

Diate crossed his arms over his stomach. The gesture felt protective. 'If that's true, then why don't I see any change?'

She caressed the book with the palm of her hand. 'What changes could you realistically see, Emilio?'

'When we were on Rulanda, the Talents opened the door for smuggling, just as they have during the past. I see you, with no caste mark, working in government, as most people with brains and no Talent do. I see hundreds of your people each year, and none of the differences that you talk about have shown up through them.'

Sheba set the book down, leaving it open to the place that he had marked. She looked at the table, not at him. 'You make the same mistake your father did. Change doesn't happen overnight. That kind of change is revolution, and in revolution, people get killed.'

'I know,' Diate said softly.

'Real change happens over time, little bit by little bit. We have made changes within the country, Emilio. You just haven't seen them yet.'

'Is that why there is a group that calls itself the Diate Rebels?'

She brought her head up sharply. 'They're a bunch of fanatics.'

'That's what people used to say about my father.'

'The rebels want to remake the government in their own image. They don't want to follow your father's teachings. They want to create their own government, any way they can.'

'You still kill people associated with the Rebels.'

A frown touched her forehead. 'No, we don't. Who told you that, Emilio?'

His body was shaking. 'I've seen the evidence of it.'

Her frown grew deeper. She looked at him, then looked away, as if she didn't know how to respond. Finally, she said, 'I'm not lying to you. We are making changes.'

Strands of hair curled around her neck. If he brushed them away and kissed the skin, she would arch into his arms. He didn't move. 'While you wait for change, people continue to get hurt.'

She snorted and pushed the curtain back from his one small window. 'Hurt. What kind of hurt are we talking about, Emilio? Lack of affluence? I had a chance to sing as a child and was ruled No-Talent. Do I look hurt by that? Many of the people who get branded B and C Talents have choices to do other things. They still prefer to perform. Others make their own way. Your sister didn't complain when she was assigned to a cruise ship, did she?'

'My father did.'

'Your father did. Because he saw it as a step down. The Talent system is a way into a system of privilege and stardom. It's not for everyone. If it were, it wouldn't be so spectacular. No one gets hurt. Some people don't become famous, that's all.'

'That's not all, and you know it.' He crossed the room and stood on the other side of the table. He had left his father's book open to the military sonnets. 'There aren't enough legitimate jobs for everyone. Some people have to go into smuggling. And then you get people like your brother, Carbete –'

'Who is talented at his profession.' Sheba pressed her face against the glass. 'And who is a lot better off than most of the people here, who must bootstrap themselves up each generation, whose talents count for nothing unless they leave this place, who have no way of improving themselves. The rich stay rich here, and the poor die in misery. You have no right to preach to me about hurts, Emilio. Just because you've been hurt by the Kingdom doesn't mean that the rest of us have.'

He froze in place. She faced him, her cheeks red, eyes sparkling. 'I think you could come home,' she said. 'Your father is a folk hero now. You may have recognized me on Rulanda as a member of the Kingdom, but I felt shock when I saw you here and learned who your parents were. I own all of your father's writings. I teach his words to my colleagues. I *believe* in what he's done. All you do is run away from it.'

'They would have killed me too.' The words were a whisper.

She shook her head. 'You know that isn't true. People still talk about you – the most talented dancer our country has ever produced. No one can execute some of the moves you could do. We're not a stupid people. The state may have considered your father a traitor twenty years ago, but it always considered you an asset. No one destroys its own asset.'

He leaned on the table. Its solidness gave him support. 'Is that why you're courting me now?'

Sheba smiled and shook her head. 'You were a dancer, Emilio. Twenty years is too long. You're too old. Dancers decay, unlike painters or writers. Your father makes you more of an asset now than your dancing ability.'

'Bodies decay,' he said, 'but the mind grows. I'm a better dancer now than I ever was.'

'I have no way of judging that,' she said.

He wasn't sure what he was doing. Trying to prove that he could dance? Trying to make himself into an asset so that she would want him more? Trying to recapture something he thought he had lost a long time ago?

Trying to see what she really wanted?

He nodded. 'That's right. I guess you don't. The Golgoth forbids dancing in the Port City.'

'Except during the Festival.'

He looked up. She was watching him, her eyes darker than usual. Her intensity made him nervous. 'Don't you know that if you got caught after curfew, it would cause a major incident?' he said.

She smiled, a slow sensual smile that sent a tingle through him. 'If I got caught here, it would cause a major incident, too.' She reached across the table and caressed his cheek. He leaned into her touch, suddenly so aroused his body shook. 'You could dance for me at the Festival, you know. As a member of the Kingdom.'

He made himself pull away. 'I live in the Port City. I'm Golgan now.'

'You'll never be Golgan. Until you face yourself, you'll always be that scared little boy hiding away in a place where he doesn't belong.' She tapped the book. 'Maybe you need to read this again. Your father had wisdom.'

'My father,' Diate said, 'had a blind selfishness that got him killed.'

She walked toward the door. He wanted to reach for her. He wanted to touch her, but he didn't let himself move. She had lied to him before. She could be lying to him now. 'You shouldn't go out after curfew,' he said.

She shrugged. 'I would love to stay, but I don't want to fight all night. And you're not ready to listen to me.' She put her hand on the knob and paused. 'Believe in me, Emilio. I believe in you.' Then she opened the door and let herself out.

He didn't go after her. He didn't try to stop her. If his men found her on the street, they would bring her to him anyway. Despite his warnings, he knew that she would be safe enough. She knew it too.

With one finger, he closed his father's book. The slam echoed in the silent apartment. Then he carried the book to its place on the shelf. He had most of his father's poems, but few of the pamphlets. Over the years, he had forgotten what his father had preached, remembering only the gist of it – that the Talent system had to be changed, that it destroyed too many lives.

But Diate had never believed that. And that was what he couldn't say to Sheba. He had never agreed with his father. Diate had loved being a Talent. He had loved the attention and focus. He had loved it to the day he came home to find his family murdered, and even then he had still loved it.

And he thought that love had killed them.

If he hadn't been Talented, his sister might have been chosen as a B or C level Talent. Some families had two or three C levels. But an A level required special handling, special concentration. And often, the family with an A level had no one else because no other sibling could compare. His sister had danced with him. If she had danced with someone a bit less Talented, her Talent would have shone through. But she hadn't and now she was dead.

And he couldn't even remember what she had looked like. What she had sounded like. He could barely remember what kind of person she had been.

His father had wanted his sister to have as many opportunities as Diate did. Perhaps his father's plan wasn't that radical after all. Perhaps the Kingdom could follow those precepts without much change.

But it didn't matter what could happen in the Kingdom. He had to concentrate on now. Sheba wanted him to go back to the Kingdom with her. The task the Golgoth had set before him looked easier than ever.

She was wooing him for a reason, a reason he needed to discover.

And the only way he could discover it was at her side.

Chapter 15

Diate sat at his mahogany table. His arm throbbed and his head ached. He had made himself an herbal tea that Martina guaranteed as a painkiller, but the drink had yet to make a difference. He was tempted to break into a bottle of Beltar's wine, but that would do him no good. He had to make it through the day.

The surgeon hadn't warned him about the pain. He had expected something mild, like the headache he carried, instead his arm had swollen and was tender to the touch. When she removed the patch, he would ask her what side effects he would feel then.

He sighed and sipped more tea. The draught was bitter, and burned against his nostrils. Maybe he had misunderstood Martina. Maybe if he poured it on his sore arm, the pain would ease.

He wrapped his fingers around the cup. The surgeon had asked him not to exercise for a day or so, but the lack of movement was driving him crazy. At this time of the morning, he was usually in the gym, working with Strega. The exercise, the dance, kept him sane. He hadn't realized how important it was until he wasn't allowed to do it.

Dancers decay.

Bodies decay, but the mind grows. I'm a better dancer now than I ever was.

Perhaps. But this morning, he felt as if his entire body had betrayed him.

He got up, grabbed an old shirt from his bedroom, and ripped it into a triangle. Then he tied the shirt into a makeshift sling and put his arm in it. He made a quick twirl around the room, wincing as his arm bumped his torso. He took another piece of the shirt and tied the arm to his chest.

It would work. It would have to. Damn the surgeon. He had a routine to follow.

He took the sling off and placed it inside his duffel. Then he slung the duffel over his shoulder and let himself out of the apartment.

The street was full of people, even though most had yet to have early breakfast. Some were carrying pieces of wood, others carried makeshift signs. A number came empty-handed from the center of town. Diate stood and watched for a moment, recognizing a number of faces from the chronically unemployed. Someone, probably Scio, had put the poor to work this year, making the Festival something for everyone.

Maybe they were even getting paid.

But knowing Scio, many of these people worked for free as a way of staying out of prison or repaying charity. Scio believed in making up for past debts before working toward the future.

Diate shifted his duffel on his shoulder and walked through the crowd. The workers were amazingly quiet. No one spoke to anyone else. Perhaps they would start speaking when curfew officially ended. Or maybe they had nothing to say to each other.

The air smelled of dust and overheated bodies. Some people buckled under the weight they carried. Diate twisted to avoid getting hit with oversized packages. No one paid attention to him.

When he reached a cross street, he peered down it. The center of the city was a few blocks away, but he could still see the focus of the activity.

Hammers rang against nails as Golgans built booths. Two Vorgellians worked on a new booth at the corner, assembling it with light and silent tools. Four Erani huddled around a newly planted tree. They were nearly hidden in their long white robes. Only their thin voices made them seem alive. A small, hunched person wearing protective clothing stood in the shade and watched one of the booths going up. Diate stared for a moment, and realized he was looking at a Jovasian. He had never seen one in the daylight before.

He continued his walk to the gym. The Festival preparations made him nervous. He hated the influx of new people, the delicacy of dealing with different cultures. Fortunately, much of this fell into Scio's purview, but every year some group had a clash with the detectives. This year, Diate wasn't going to be around enough to stop it.

The crowd thinned as he got closer to the gym. Most of the

189

activity centered on the Festival. As he walked past the two-story gray buildings surrounding the palace, he saw only a handful of guards and a few detectives making early morning rounds. Odd that he hadn't seen any closer to the Festival itself. He would check on that as the morning progressed.

He let himself in a side door, and breathed the familiar scents of ancient sweat and dry heat. He changed clothes, put on the sling, and let himself into his favorite workout room.

Strega was already there, going through the latter half of the routine. 'Thought you weren't going to come,' he said.

'Me too.' Diate hung a towel next to Strega's on the far side of the barre. 'Doctor says I'm supposed to go easy for a few days.'

Strega laughed. 'It's clear how well you listen.'

Diate shrugged. 'Go easy means something different to me than it does to other people.'

'Obviously.' Strega arched and stretched, his body glistening with sweat.

Diate eased into his routine, leaving off the arm work for the day. He stretched as best he could, occasionally losing balance as he failed to adjust for the lost arm. Twice he bumped the arm against his torso, the second time wincing with so much pain that he nearly cried out.

Strega began his routine over again, his bare feet thudding against the wooden floor. From time to time, he would glance at Diate in the mirror as if he were trying to keep track of him. Diate said nothing. Instead he let the pain in his body absorb him, take him down into its depths, and he worked with it. He had danced with sprained ankles, with broken toes, and with injured knees. He could dance with a swollen arm as well.

He finished with a whirl, feeling the sweat fly from his face. He staggered for a step, then reached for his towel. Strega was already drying off.

He nodded toward Diate's arm. 'Looks painful.'

'Yeah.' Diate glanced at it. A large purple bruise had formed over the scar. 'If the swelling doesn't go down in a few hours, I'm back to the surgeon.'

'Patch?'

Diate nodded.

Strega sighed. 'This Festival has everyone on edge. I've got port detail. I was hoping for more interesting duty.'

Diate nodded. Someone competent handling ports was good. If any trouble occurred, it would happen there or near the embassies. Especially near the Pavilion. Diate smiled and slung the towel over his shoulder. 'It'll come with time, and then you probably won't want it.'

'Oh, I'll want it.'

Diate glanced at Strega. Sometimes he forgot how young Strega really was. Diate opened the door to the hallway and let cool air into the gym. Strega's papers had crossed his desk years ago for approval, and Diate remembered the athletic tests and the high intelligence scores. But all the other details escaped him.

'You volunteered?'

Strega glanced at Diate. 'For port duty?'

Diate shook his head. He stepped into the hallway. No one else was in sight. 'For the detectives.'

'Yes, sir.' Strega's voice remained quiet. Most volunteers did not become detectives. They usually wanted the job for the wrong reason – the ability to use force, a desire for power, an excuse to kill. The most successful cadets were usually drafted and promised that with an excellent service record, they could retire early. 'It just looked like one of the more interesting jobs to me. I was strong and healthy and I like order.'

Strega's affection for order was obvious. Diate pushed open the locker room door, stripped, and got into the shower. Too bad Diate didn't like order that much. Sometimes, he believed that chaos served a purpose too.

'And why do you train with me?'

'I think I told you, sir, when I first asked. I wanted to submit myself to the most vigorous ritual possible. You're the strongest man on the force and you're not the biggest. I want that.'

'Still?' Diate turned on the water and held his hand beneath the needle spray until the water grew warm. Then he got under it.

Strega turned on the shower beside him. 'You have something I can't achieve. And it's not just practice. You have a way of moving that I've never seen in anyone else. It disarms people. That's part of your secret, I think, that talent for movement. And I don't think it's something I can learn.'

Lumps move like that, Emilio. You must fly with each step. Soar with each movement. A dancer dances even when he is standing still.

The water beat on Diate's head. He guarded his arm from the

191

intensity of the spray. 'Movement is a learned skill. You began learning when you were much older than I was.'

Strega didn't reply. Diate lathered his body, then rinsed off and stepped out of the stream before shutting off the water. Strega finished a moment later and toweled himself vigorously.

He followed Diate into the locker room, leaving bare footprints on the floor. 'What was it like?' Strega asked, the question sounding hesitant and almost frightened. 'Growing up in the Kingdom. What was it like?'

The old woman smelled of spices and apples. She touched his head. He ducked. His sister giggled. 'Guard him,' the woman said. 'He is blessed.'

'Very different from here,' Diate said. 'When I think of it, I think of it in color. It's as if Golga has no color at all.'

Strega stared at him, clearly not understanding. Diate shrugged. 'I was a child,' Diate said. 'Everything seemed normal to me then. Nothing seems normal now.'

'Yeah,' Strega said. 'I know how that feels.' He opened his locker and pulled out a jar of ointment. 'Look, this works for me whenever I've been injured. It might work for you.'

Diate took it and opened it. The ointment smelled faintly sweet, almost flowery. He rubbed some on his sore arm, and the places he touched stung and then turned cool. 'Thanks,' he said.

They finished dressing and went their separate ways without speaking. As Diate walked to the palace, he noted that the swelling in his arm had started to go down. He was glad that Strega had given him the ointment. It might make the healing go quicker.

The guards outside the palace cradled heat weapons to their chests. They wore their dress uniforms – black with white skulls – and each man had shaved his head. Diate had never seen so many uniformed people in one place. Instead of putting his mind at ease, he found the sight frightening. For all its problems, the Port City had been a safe place to him, and these men in uniform, with weapons, seemed to be the dawning of something dangerous.

Diate nodded at them as he went in. Only one man nodded back. Diate didn't recognize him. But that meant nothing. More people in the Port City recognized Diate than the other way around.

He let himself inside. The palace was cold this morning and dark, the windows shrouded by curtains. Candles flickered in the skull-shaped holders at the base of the stairs. No one had bothered with the brighter artificial lights.

More guards lined the stairs. These guards also wore dress black, and had heat weapons. They wore high boots, which, according to regulations, hid knives. They faced each other like statues and, like statues, did not blink as Diate passed.

He took the steps two at a time, his feet sinking in the well-worn depressions in the marble. A slight smell had invaded with the chill air. The guards didn't represent protection. They represented fear.

He had never expected the Golgoth to be frightened of the Kingdom. He had always thought the Golgoth would protect him from them.

Diate reached the top of the stairs and followed the winding hallway. Before each public room, the guards were doubled. He didn't look inside to see if extra guards had been placed there as well. Finally, he saw one of the Golgoth's staff.

'I'm looking for the Golgoth,' Diate said.

The man nodded. 'He's in the audience chamber.'

'With someone?'

'No,' the man said. 'He is determing the best place for his meeting.'

The chill had finally seeped into Diate's bones. He thanked the man and hurried down the hallway, past the rows of guards leaning like corpses against the too-white walls.

The door to the audience chamber stood open. Half a dozen extra guards milled outside the door. Diate stepped inside. The Golgoth and Scio stood in a far corner, one of the secret panels pulled back to reveal a chamber filled with cobwebs and dust.

'Emilio.' The Golgoth held out his hand. Diate took it, letting his fingers get lost in the Golgoth's great palm. 'Scio and I were thinking of holding the meeting here.'

Scio closed the panel and stood in front of it protectively. Diate saw the body language and wondered at it.

'It's protected,' Diate said, 'as long as someone is in the listening booths. But it can also be a trap, down here at the end of the hall.'

'I'm sure she'll want her own people to examine the room,' the Golgoth said. He touched another panel, and as it started to open, Scio pushed it closed.

Scio leaned against the panel, hands behind his back. 'I'm sorry, Diate. But as long as you're working directly with the Kingdom, I don't want you to know our specific plans.'

Diate stared at Scio. Scio had never trusted him, but he had always shared his plans. They had agreed a long time ago that the Golgoth needed both of them for protection.

Diate kept his voice calm, even though his throat had gone dry. 'I know where the listening booths are in this room.'

'Yes, but you don't know which we plan to have filled and which we don't.'

The Golgoth was staring at Diate. The guards looked away. Scio's mouth formed a small line. They weren't going to tell him anything. The most important meeting the Golgoth had since Diate had become head of the detectives, and no one was going to let Diate help. They needed him. The Golgoth would be in danger without him.

'I spent sixteen years here with you people,' Diate said. He made himself take measured breaths as he spoke. 'Half of my life. The adult half. And now, because the Kingdom is in the Port City – something I recommended against – I am no longer trustworthy.'

'Your emotions cloud you.' Scio spoke softly. 'It's procedure. You're working with the enemy. If they turn against you, then you have no information to give.'

' "The enemy." ' Diate turned to the Golgoth. 'You didn't use that word with me.'

The Golgoth bobbed his head once, not taking his gaze from Diate. 'Because I'm not sure I believe it. They've asked to attend a Peace Festival. And you are wrong, Scio. His emotions do not cloud him. He knows as much about this type of security as you do.'

'But,' Scio said, 'it's my job to protect us, just in case.'

The Golgoth shook his head. The odd light in the room hid his eyes in shadow, making him look as if he had none at all. 'And to do that well, you must listen to Emilio. Come. We should not have this discussion here.'

He looked at one of the guards. 'Send for my son. Have him meet us in my chambers.'

Diate frowned. 'You're bringing Kreske in?'

'It was your idea,' the Golgoth said. 'And you were right. He needs to know more about this place, especially now.'

The guard had disappeared down the corridor. Scio shut the listening booth, and then led the way out of the audience chamber.

The Golgoth clasped Diate on the shoulder. 'Let's go.'

Diate let the Golgoth hold him as they walked. Diate was a tall man, but the Golgoth was taller. He had always seemed like a giant, and as Diate had grown, he realized that the Golgoth was exceptional. His son, Kreske, was tall as well, and shared the bony, skull-like features that made the Golgoth seem more than human.

Scio's small form swayed as he walked. He had a sense of purpose, a commanding way of moving that belied his stature. People moved out of his way or nodded as he passed.

Guards continued to line the hallway all the way to the Golgoth's personal chambers. There, the guards thinned, as if the chambers did not exist. Probably Scio's method of decoy – an ineffective one should the Golgoth get in trouble alone in his rooms. Diate would have to speak to him about that.

Scio paused in front of the door, waiting for the Golgoth to open it. The Golgoth tried the lock, and looked surprised when it turned. 'Kreske must already be inside.'

Diate pushed the Golgoth out of the way and went in first. Nothing looked out of place. Kreske stood in the middle of the floor, by the fireplace. 'You're right,' Diate said. 'Kreske's here.'

The Golgoth passed him and went inside. Diate followed, Scio trailing. 'You can't do that,' Diate said to the Golgoth. 'You need to let us check if something is out of the ordinary.'

The Golgoth smiled. 'I know. I'm sorry.'

Scio glanced at Diate, sharing a 'see-what-we-must-put-up-with?' frown.

The chambers were humid and smelled of wood smoke. Clothing hung over a chair and the pillows on the couch were fluffed. Diate had never seen the chambers so messy. The Golgoth was not sleeping well.

'What is this all about?' Kreske asked.

The Golgoth closed the door. 'I want us all to know what is going to happen this week. But I don't want anything to leave this room.'

Scio nodded. Diate did as well. Kreske's eyes widened as he realized he was going to be included. 'Yes, Father,' he said, sounding young and eager.

Diate walked to the fireplace. Embers still burned among the ash. He didn't look at the Golgoth. Diate knew that this meeting was going to focus on him.

'Emilio, you've seen the woman. What have you learned?' the Golgoth asked. He went down the steps as he spoke, and circled behind Kreske. Springs squeaked in the couch as the Golgoth sat down.

'I haven't learned anything.' Diate put his hand on the marble. It was cool to the touch.

'Nothing professional.' The Golgoth's voice had a power even when it was soft. 'But something personal.'

Diate turned, not relinquishing his hold on the smooth mantel. He didn't want to discuss personal things in front of Kreske and Scio.

The Golgoth smiled. 'You hunch, Emilio. Shoulders move up to your ears, and round forward as if you're trying to protect your heart. You stood like that the first day I met you and gradually it went away, except when you're afraid of something.'

Diate made his shoulders relax. As they straightened, something cracked in his back. He hadn't known that the Golgoth could read him so clearly. He hadn't known that he gave himself away that easily.

Scio remained on the stairs. Kreske had moved to the other side of the room. He was staring at the floor.

The discussion would happen no matter what. Diate couldn't say no to the Golgoth. 'She says my father's work has been rediscovered and I could live in the Kingdom now. She says she wants me to go there with her.'

'Do you want to?' Scio asked.

Of course he wanted to. He wanted to see the land his father had dreamed of. He wanted nights like he had spent on Rulanda, nights cradled in Sheba's arms. 'No,' he said.

Kreske looked up. 'Does she think you do?' The question was astute for Kreske.

Diate shrugged. 'I don't know what she thinks.'

The Golgoth leaned back on the couch. 'I meet with the Queen in two days. The Festival will continue after that. If you can hook up with Sheba within that short period of time, and remain with her throughout the Festival, it would help us all.'

Diate's grip on the mantel tightened. 'My detectives are afraid of the Kingdom, and my second in command feels the same. We have people in this town from all over the world. The wealth that the city has is at risk, and Scio is concentrating on keeping you alive, so his men are focused on the palace here, not in the Port City itself. I would be of better use doing my job.'

196

The Golgoth smiled. 'Nice argument. But I would rather know what the Kingdom plans from all of this, and how they feel after the Queen and I meet.'

'And I can handle this,' Scio said.

'It takes two of us to run this city,' Diate said. He met Scio's gaze. Scio knew the difficulties. Denying wouldn't help.

'We will be working together,' Scio said. 'Just in a different capacity, for once.'

The heat from the fireplace warmed Diate's legs. He stepped away, into the room itself. 'The Kingdom is not going to tell me anything. Even if I do manage to convince Sheba, there's Carbete and all the others. They won't trust me. I've been working here, in the government here, for too long.'

The Golgoth nodded. 'Point taken. But lovers are different. Lovers share secrets. And she's close enough to the Queen to know information we want. Convince her, Emilio. Convince her that she can trust you.'

Diate felt suddenly light and dizzy. He eased himself into a chair across from the Golgoth. 'To do that,' Diate said, 'I would have to renounce my ties to Golga.'

'Then do so.'

The lightness had turned into a trembling. 'You don't understand. I would have to do it publicly. I would have to renounce my entire life for the past sixteen years. I would have to turn my back on you.'

'I do understand,' the Golgoth said. 'I've known that from the beginning of this plan. As long as we care about each other, Emilio, as long as we both know the truth, it doesn't matter.'

'Yes it does,' Diate said. 'I live here now. I have people who rely on me. I don't want them to think I'm someone else. I want to stay here. To do what you ask, I would have to lose everything.'

The Golgoth shook his head. 'You lose nothing. If they're trying to harm us, we catch them and you become a hero. If they're not, you become our ambassador, and people will understand that you were gaining their trust.'

He leaned forward, his elbows resting on his knees. 'If I'm wrong, Emilio, and they're not here in peace as they say, then you will save us all.' He turned to Kreske. 'Forgive me, son, but you're not ready to rule. That's my fault and something I'm trying to change. Emilio, you're the only one I can trust, and in this case, trusting you means letting you go.'

'And what happens if the Kingdom seduces him back?' Scio asked.

Diate froze. Sometimes Scio knew him too well.

'It won't,' the Golgoth said. He continued to speak directly to Diate. 'Part of you loves the Kingdom, but there's too much hatred mixed up in that love.'

Diate looked down at his hands. They were not as smooth as they had been when he first arrived in Golga. Lines had formed around the knuckles. Scars covered the backs of his fingers. He had spent years in the Golgoth's service, and he didn't regret one of them.

'You have no passion for Golga,' the Golgoth said. 'So life is safe here for you. In the Kingdom, passion would overwhelm you.'

'What if I want passion?' Diate didn't look up.

The Golgoth laughed. 'Then we find you a woman.'

Diate didn't smile. He had a woman. She was mercurial and beautiful and second in command in the Kingdom. 'Sometimes I think you give me too much credit.'

'Sometimes,' the Golgoth said, 'I don't think you give yourself enough.'

Diate didn't move. His entire body had gone rigid. His shoulders had hunched forward. He couldn't seem to get them to move back.

'Emilio, I know you don't want to do this. I am sorry for the choices that I give you. But you're the only one, and we have an opportunity now. You can help us.'

Diate looked up. The Golgoth hadn't moved, but his skull-like face had an expression Diate had never seen before.

'If we can finally make peace with the Kingdom, real peace, we'll go a long way toward changing Golga. We can relax some of the laws here, and open trade to parts of the world that don't welcome us. Your actions could make a difference for an entire generation of people.'

Diate licked his lips. 'What happens if I don't succeed?'

'Then we lose nothing. If you succeed, we gain everything.'

'You make it sound easy.'

'That's because it is easy.'

Diate sighed. He would not change the Golgoth's mind. Even if Diate stayed away from Sheba, he would be shut out of the process, forced to remain on the sidelines. The Golgoth thought this would do some good. Diate had to try. He stood and looked at them all. 'I'm sorry for the things I have to do to prove myself to her.'

The Golgoth stood too. A bead of sweat ran down the side of his cheek. 'I know.'

'I would never betray you,' Diate said to the Golgoth.

The Golgoth nodded. 'I know that too.'

Diate almost reached for the Golgoth, but in all the years they had known each other, they had never hugged. Here was the man who had saved him, who had trained him in the art of survival. Here was the man who had believed in him – still believed in him – and Diate had no words, no way to show the Golgoth how much he had meant.

The Golgoth seemed to sense Diate's discomfort. 'It's all right, Emilio. We will go with this. When it's over, we'll make sure everything gets put to rights with the people around us. Between us, things will never need repair.'

'Thank you, sir.' Diate's voice sounded stiff. He felt like the boy who had first stood in that audience chamber, expecting death. It had taken him weeks to realize that no one would hurt him. Perhaps this experience would be the same.

He nodded once to Kreske, to Scio, and to the Golgoth. Then he walked past them all, went up the stairs and let himself out of the room. The air in the hallway was cool. Diate stopped, leaned against the wall, and took a deep breath.

The Golgoth met with the Queen in two days. Two days to win over Sheba. Two days to gain her trust.

He only knew one way.

He had to become one of them again.

He had to dance.

Chapter 16

Diate didn't stop at detective headquarters. Now that he had made his decision, he had to live it. He left his duffel in the gym, tucked in the back corner of his locker. His arm wasn't swollen any longer, but a painful purplish bruise ran along the scar. He felt lighter than he had for a long time.

After he left the gym, he walked down the center streets, not meeting anyone's eyes. Now that the sun had been up for a few hours, the day was hot. Three times as many people were on the streets as before, all of them looking purposeful. Many wore the heavy clothing of cooler climates. Some wore headdresses around their hair, leaving only their faces visible. Children ran between people's legs, laughing and shouting.

The usual smells disappeared under the scents of overheated skin and strange perfumes. The heat shimmered off the pavement. Diate loosened his collar, anxious to be out of his uniform. Detectives hurried past him. Sometimes they nodded a greeting. He ignored them.

The kiosk in the center of the city bore the blue and white flags of the Festival. Since the early morning dozens of booths had gone up – most made of the pine that grew like weeds on the mountain slopes, but some were made of strange lacquered material brought by the Vorgellians. One booth was all silver and reflected the sun like a mirror. A woman wearing a thin gown disappeared through a curtain in front of the booth. Inside, images flickered on a screen, bringing back a lost memory. Taped images. Video. Moving theater. An art form so expensive only the Vorgellians could afford it. He hadn't seen taped imagery since he was a boy.

His mother had paid to have a tape made of his father speaking. She had kept it in one of the special cupboards, stored neatly in a cardboard box. Diate had always wondered at it. The equipment to replay the tape existed only in Vorgel. Perhaps his mother had been saving to buy the equipment herself.

He turned away from the booth and followed the signs to registration. A Vorgellian sat there, long fingers on the keyboard of a small computer. Diate had seen computers. The Golgoth had a few, linked into other systems on other islands. The technology was old and expensive, and again in the hands of the Vorgellians. Over the years, the Golgoth had sent delegation after delegation to Vorgel to discuss training others in their technological expertise. The Vorgel had always refused, citing the scarcity of component parts and the difficulties in absorbing these ancient arts. But no one was fooled as to the real reason. The Vorgel made a fortune from selling their technology and their expertise. They weren't going to lose their corner of the market just because someone else wanted to learn how to maintain equipment.

He found himself staring at the computer. He had never seen one that operated in the open. The others were attached to walls, in carefully maintained rooms. He wondered if it worked along the same principle.

The line was small. Most of the groups had already registered.

'I need information on the dance contest,' he said.

The Vorgellian did not glance at him. 'Yes, detective. In Golgan?'

'Whatever is more convenient.' He had no worry that he wouldn't understand the language. He spoke most of the languages represented here fluently.

She pressed two buttons and a long slip of paper slid out from beneath the thin white base. The paper curled on the end. She grabbed the curl and handed it to him, her attention already on the person behind him.

He stepped out of the line and glanced at the paper. The information was in Lillish, which meant that many more people had asked for it in that language than in Golgan.

Then he smiled. Of course, no one had asked for it in Golgan. Dancing was forbidden here.

The dance contest would start after early breakfast and run until early lunch. If the contest had too many entries, it would set up a separate trial area for dancers to qualify for the contest. He had nothing to do until the morning, when he had to show up before early breakfast to register.

His hands had started shaking. He folded the paper and put it in his breast pocket. Not even a day to prepare. That was probably for the best. He didn't really want to think about it.

But he had to let Sheba know. It would do him no good to dance before the Festival and not have her there.

Before he left, though, he wanted to check out the dance space. He wandered through the booths, following the map the Vorgellian had provided. The booths centered around seven stages, which surrounded the kiosk. The stages already bore their signs, written in several languages.

Three men still worked on the dance stage. They huddled over the wooden floor, sanding it smooth. The floor gleamed like marble. Diate didn't want to be the first to dance on it. The first dancer risked falling and hurting himself.

The dance stage was also the biggest. Thin white ropes defined its edges, narrowing the performance area so that a meter of floor remained on all sides. That way, a dancer wouldn't fall off the stage and disqualify himself.

Diate paced around the stage. The scritch-scritch-scritch of the hands sanding rose above the pounding and the sounds of conversation. The stage was smaller than the gym floor, but roughly equivalent to the space he used when he danced.

He stopped and stared for a moment, picturing himself in the space where the three men huddled. His body would float as he leapt, his feet making soft thuds on the wood when he landed. The air was thin and would be hot by the time he started. Sweat would cover his body, but it would feel good as he moved. He would fly free and dance unfettered, in the sun, for the first time in years.

He was holding his breath. He let it out slowly, his heart pumping as if he had danced. Without realizing it, he had slipped into the old ritual. The pre-performance preparations. He could give a mediocre performance tomorrow, but he saw no point. He wanted to prove to Sheba that he could still dance.

Despite his age, he still wanted to be the best.

He turned his back on the stage and made himself walk away. Two women huddled under a booth, holding it in place while a third balanced a wooden table top above them. A slender man in long black robes worked alone to set up a small tent-like structure. Two Vorgellians huddled next to a woman half hidden by blankets. The Vorgellians gestured as they spoke, their voices soft but demanding.

Diate flowed through the crowd, his steps growing lighter. He wanted to shed his detective's clothing, wear his own clothes for the first time in decades. His feet barely touched the ground, and already he could hear soft music in his head. Music that was never very far away.

'Emilio!'

He froze, body rigid and prepared for flight. He took two deep breaths and made himself turn. He was still a detective, still in charge. He had to remember that.

Beltar stood in one of the booths. Wine bottles glistened on the shelves behind him, and he held another in his hand. His booth was built for maximum shade, with an excellent view of the stages.

Diate didn't want to be here. He wanted to be invisible.

Beltar held out a hand. 'Would you like a bottle of wine, my friend?'

Diate made himself walk to the booth. Already he had put Beltar behind him. He had put the Port City behind him. On this day, he had returned to the Kingdom and he didn't want anyone to bring him back.

'I have quite a bit of your wine,' he said, conscious of the people around them. He stopped in front of the booth's wooden facade, smelling the richness of pine mixed with Beltar's spices.

'You okay?' Beltar asked under his breath. He held a bottle out. Diate pretended to inspect it. 'You don't look so good.'

Diate ran his finger on the bottle's surface. The glass was cool. 'I'm working, Beltar,' he said. 'And things are going to be more difficult than I thought.'

'Martina?' Beltar's voice rose a notch in panic.

Diate shook his head. 'No. Me. Please, as you watch tomorrow, remember what we discussed.' He took a bottle from Beltar and turned it over. 'I thank you, friend,' he said in a louder tone, 'but I'm not ready to buy yet. Besides, I don't think I should take advantage of my status to purchase goods before the booths actually open.'

'A man with a conscience.' Beltar laughed, but the joy didn't reach his eyes. 'I should warn you that only my most expensive wines are left.'

'All the better for me,' Diate said. 'I can't afford them on a detective's salary.'

He nodded once and escaped the booth. He couldn't be around Beltar now. Beltar didn't belong in the Kingdom. Beltar was part of the Port City, part of his immediate past. Beltar would take care of Martina, and Diate would worry only about himself.

And Sheba.

And the Golgoth.

Once Diate was out of Beltar's view, he broke into a small jog. He had to be away from the crowd, away from the hustle and bustle of the Festival. He found a side street and stopped, breathing harder than he had thought he would. He must have run farther than he planned.

The street was empty. Even the windows of the apartments looked as if nothing but emptiness lived behind them. He glanced around once to get his bearings, and remembered.

This was the street where he had found the musician.

The smell came back first: rich and ripe, the overpowering odor of a body days dead. He had put a kerchief to his nose and broken open the door to the apartment. The smell wafted out first, so strong he could almost see it. Then a silence followed.

The first room of the apartment looked like any other in Golga. Functional furniture, few decorations. But the smell came from the second room, the one in the back. As he slipped inside, he noted musical instruments – violins, violas, guitars, sitars, wykasis, and cellos – hanging from the wall. A harpsichord sat beneath the window, and pieces of a piano were scattered on the floor. A large pool of dried blood covered the piano and the flooring. Diate glanced up.

A man hung from the ceiling, hands and feet nailed in place, a piece of piano wire wrapped tightly around his neck. His skin was gray and putrefied. Diate didn't need a pathologist to tell him that the man had lost all the blood in his body.

He had stayed in the room long enough to gather evidence, not that he needed it. Obvious Kingdom killing of a Talent hiding out. Then he had sent his men in to cut the body down.

Diate stared at the window, shaking himself out of the memory. Even if he danced well, even if he left with Sheba, he wouldn't be safe. Kingdom politics changed with the wind. One day, she might be Minister of Culture. The next, she might be dead.

The buoyancy he had felt near the stage had left him. His body felt heavy and tired.

Part of you loves the Kingdom, but there's too much hatred mixed up in that love.

Too much history. If he had stayed in the Kingdom, he would

have had to pay a price for his Talent and he wasn't sure anyone should have to pay.

No wonder the windows above him were empty. Someone else had paid the price too.

He sighed and hurried along the street, anxious to put the memories behind him. The sounds of the Festival faded, replaced by the clanging of the docks. He was still a few blocks away, but he knew he was getting close.

The air smelled different here. The tang of metal mixed with the heavy dampness of the ocean. The ship ports weren't too far away either. The detectives guarded both the shuttle port and the water ports to make sure nothing illegal entered the city.

Too often they missed, as the dead musician could attest.

People scurried into and out of buildings at the end of the sidewalk. Offices, located near the ports, maintaining imports and exports, overseeing the arrival of goods into the city. Every few weeks, the detectives took the files and examined them for irregularities. Every few months, they raided the buildings to find the hidden books. Sometimes the methods paid off. Usually they caused a great deal of turmoil for nothing.

Diate walked past, then stopped, facing the large avenue that separated the ports from the rest of the city. To his left, and many blocks away, the ships docked. A large ship, bearing a Jovasian seal, blocked the view of all the others. The dock workers would have to wait until nightfall to process that ship because the Jovasians avoided sunlight.

Diate moved out of the way as a group of small women left the port. They were talking and laughing in Ordweian. They walked around him and disappeared into one of the office buildings, probably to get processed before they joined the festivities.

He hated the Festival.

The ports loomed above him like an ancient fortress. Their black Vorgellian walls absorbed the light and made them almost alien. The ports had no windows on this side, although the oceanside had long docks and sliding doors that rose whenever a ship needed to unload.

He crossed the avenue. The metallic, oily scent of the ports rose and made him sneeze. He hurried past the bay doors. The docks were amazingly quiet that morning. He had expected a lot more activity the day before the Festival officially started.

The ports cast a shadow over the sidewalks. Diate shivered with a sudden chill. His footsteps rang on the pavement. Just ahead, on the far side of the ports, was Embassy Row. The Pavilion was closest to the ports, not because of the heavy use, but because the land was considered the least valuable of all.

'Sir?'

Diate stopped, blinked before his eyes focused on the man in front of him. Detective uniform, serious countenance, familiar build. Strega.

'Things going all right?' Diate asked.

'Quiet today, sir. We expect more activity tomorrow.'

'Good.' Diate glanced at the unreflective black wall. He didn't care about the ports or the Festival. He didn't care whether things were going well or not. Sheba was waiting for him. He finally had his chance to be free.

He glanced down the street, saw two Erani standing on the roof of their embassy. He pointed them out to Strega, who nodded. Then Diate ceased being a detective. His legs moved him forward without his own volition. He had gone nearly a block before he realized he hadn't said good-bye to Strega.

Not that it mattered. The boy would do well on his own. He was strong and capable, someone Diate should probably train for his own job someday.

If Diate kept the job much longer.

He wasn't sure he liked the person he had become in the last few hours. Decisive and indecisive, wanting things he wasn't sure he could have. He would test his emotions on Sheba. If she wanted him – really wanted him – he might have to rethink his position with the Golgoth.

Sixteen years was a long time to give in repayment of a debt.

Finally Diate stepped out of the ports' shadow. The sunlight warmed him, eased the chill from his body. He stopped, letting the heat caress all of him.

The Pavilion rose in front of him like a piece of the Kingdom on Golgan soil. Flags waved from the top of the building, and its curtained walls swayed in the breeze. The Pavilion looked accessible, even with the fence surrounding its perimeter. As if he could open the fence, walk inside, and be welcomed, no fuss, no bother, no checking into tall office buildings just outside the ports.

The Kingdom was so good at superficial things.

He walked to the gate, keyed his code into the lock, and let the door open. He stepped inside, watching the main door for the female guard he had seen before. She didn't step out. No one approached him. He walked along the curving sidewalk. Bells whistled down the harbor, signaling the approach of another ship. He didn't look. The ports would block his view anyway.

At the moment, all he cared about was Sheba.

Sheba. If he closed his eyes, he could still feel her hand on his cheek: the deep, and sudden arousal her touch had caused. Maybe, when he told her he would dance, she would hold him. Maybe she would take him to her rooms and he could forget all the odd emotions that rode through him. Maybe –

Two guards – both male, both larger than Diate – slipped through the double stained-glass doors. They stood in front like immobile statutes, arms crossed, feet hip distance apart. A dual barrier Diate would have to cross.

He mounted the stairs and stopped in front of them. They both wore pale yellow tattoos on their right biceps – tattoos he had never seen before, but recognized. State security. The Elite Team.

'My name is Diate,' he said. 'I'm here to see the Minister of Culture. I believe she's expecting me.'

The men didn't move. They stared past him.

'Gentlemen,' he said. 'I am here on business. It's important that she see me.'

One of the men looked at Diate. 'She sees no one today.'

She had to see him. He couldn't dance if he didn't talk with her first. He swallowed back the fear. 'She will see me.'

'I am sorry,' the guard said. 'You are not welcome.'

Diate clenched his fists, but left them at his side. 'I am chief of the Port City's detectives. If you do not let me in, I will revoke your passes and ensure that the Kingdom may not participate in the Festival.'

'Big threats.'

The voice came from behind him. Diate turned. Carbete stood at the base of the stairs, long arms hanging at his side. His clothes were fluid, full sleeves, wide pants, but not transparent as they had been the night of the ball.

'I need to see Sheba.'

'She's not here,' Carbete said.

'Where is she?'

Carbete shrugged. 'I am not her keeper.'

Diate's fingers dug into his palms. 'She said I was to see her. I need to talk to her.'

'I'll give her the message.' Despite his casual stance, Carbete looked as dangerous as the men blocking the door.

'It's important,' Diate said. 'If you don't tell her –'

'If I don't tell her, I die. I've already been through this with her.' Carbete had a half smile on his face. 'It's only flesh, detective. Her skin is as soft as any woman's.'

Diate opened his mouth to deny the taunt, but forced himself to say nothing.

'In fact, she's not the best I've had. She doesn't move enough and holds back too much.'

Diate's clenched fists tightened. His nails bit into his palms. Carbete was trying to shock him. He was succeeding. Diate took a deep breath to calm himself. 'Then you must be doing something wrong. She's an animal when she's with me.'

Carbete's smile grew. 'You're not different than the rest of us, detective, despite what you think. She's my sister. I have never touched her.'

'I know your relationship,' Diate said. The muscles in Diate's back relaxed. 'I also know that accepted sexual practices on the Kingdom differ from other places.'

Carbete laughed. 'My sister will be pleased to learn you think her capable of incest.'

Diate smiled in return. He made his hands relax. 'I'm sure you will delight in telling her.' He let the smile fade. 'Now, give her my other message as well. I will be at the dance contest at the Festival before early breakfast tomorrow. I'll expect to see her there.'

'Is that the only message?'

'That's all.'

Carbete put his hands behind his back. 'Such agitation for such a little thing. I'll tell her, detective, but I won't guarantee that she'll be there.'

'If she's not,' Diate said. 'I'll come after you.'

'You don't frighten me. You've lived here too long. Golga is a soft place, and you have become a soft man.'

Diate's body trembled from holding himself in place. He would not fight with Carbete. Not now, anyway. Diate walked down the stairs. He stopped beside Carbete.

They were the same height and had roughly the same build. A rangy strength hovered about Carbete, as did that odd sensuality. No wonder he had taken so many lovers. No wonder he had killed them.

'I don't have to hurt you when I come after you,' Diate said. 'I have enough information linking you to deaths in this city that I could put you in Golga's prisons for a long time. Men die there, thin, starving, forgotten. Is that how you want to end up? The great Tonio Carbete, lying in his own piss, babbling incoherently?'

Carbete didn't move away from Diate, but the amusement left his thin face. 'This meeting means a lot to you.'

'Yes, it does,' Diate said. 'I'm glad we understand each other. I will see Sheba there tomorrow. Right?'

Carbete did not back down. His gaze met Diate's. 'Only if she wants to come.'

Chapter 17

Diate didn't sleep. He spent the night pacing his apartment, going over the routine in his mind. At times he would stop and gaze out the window at the quiet streets, wondering if Carbete had given Sheba the message, wondering if she too was unable to sleep. Probably not. If she had heard, she knew. She would be waiting for him, and then it would all begin.

The thought of holding her again made his entire body tingle.

When the first pink rays of dawn kissed the buildings, Diate went into his bedroom and sat on the undisturbed bed. The time had come. He had no more opportunity to prepare. He took several deep breaths, opened the closet door, and pulled his old tattered pack out of the back corner.

The material disintegrated in his hands. It smelled faintly of rotting leather. He should have checked before. His paints and his extra shoes were in there. He had thought that they might not fit, but he had never thought that they would be ruined.

He reached inside, fingers brushing the goatskin bag his mother had always insisted he use to protect his dance equipment. As he pulled it out, he marveled at how small it was.

The bag was fine. A little dusty, darker than he remembered, but unharmed. He reached inside and pulled out his extra pair of dancing shoes.

They were black and scuffed, the ties loose and falling around his palms. He bent the shoes twice, pleased to find them so limber. He had expected them to crack. He ran his hands along the soft surface. Calf leather, imported from Colodo. Very rare. Very expensive.

He extended his right foot and slipped a shoe on. The leather clung to his skin. His foot was broader now, scarred with time and age, but the shoe had enough give. He could wear it.

He took off the shoe and set it on the bed. Then he reached in the bag and pulled out his tights and his white ruffled shirt. The tights molded to his legs, showing each muscle, each ripple of flesh. They fit like a second skin. He pulled the shirt over his head, tied the sleeves in place, and left the front open to the navel so that the cloth wouldn't pull tight against his shoulders. He slipped on the shoes and tied them tightly around his ankles.

Then he grabbed the paints.

The plastic case, imported from Vorgel, was dusty and heavy. He opened it. The paints were dried and cracked in their small squares. He touched one and felt it flake against his fingers.

For a moment, he stared at them. This wouldn't work without the paints, and he had nowhere else to get any. Then he remembered the day of the intense heat, when he first danced for the Queen, Myla spitting on the dried-out paints and touching them to his cheek.

He carried the box to the kitchen, his feet floating across the floor. He moved differently in these clothes. He felt different in them. Lighter, freer.

He poured some water on the paints and waited for a moment. The water pooled at the top. He mixed the red with the back of the ancient brush, then washed off the brush's tip before dipping it into the next color. The paints were grainy, but they would work.

With a single movement, he closed the box and walked back to the bedroom. He caught sight of himself in the full-length mirror, and stopped, startled.

The boy was back. His face was older, a little more weathered and lined, but it had an open expression Diate hadn't seen in years. The boy moved as if someone had blessed him, as if each movement was a gift from an unknown god. He stared at himself for a moment, trying to see the detective hidden under the clothes. But no trace of that man remained.

Diate wasn't sure he wanted him back.

He dipped a finger in the blue paint and accented his caste mark. Then he added three dots of yellow along his left cheek to signify his family code. Even though he hadn't done them for decades, the movements felt familiar. Part of the ritual his body had not forgotten how to perform.

With the end of the brush, he scooped red paint. He leaned into the mirror and stopped. Red was the crucial color, for it would signal his moods, and his desires. Lines slashed under his eyes meant anger. Lines drawn along his chin meant hatred. A small oval on the cheek signified love.

He couldn't do any of those. Anger and hatred conveyed the wrong message. Love was too personal. Sheba would never see his action as a global expression of defection if he declared his love for her in the dance.

His hand trembled as he brought the paintbrush tip to the corner of his eye. With a single, practiced movement, he sketched a small red tear that trailed onto the upper end of the cheekbone.

Sorrow. Grief.

Forgiveness.

With the tear, he would let them all know he wanted to go home.

He put the brush back in the paint box and put the box in the bag. Then he tossed the bag on the bed. For a moment, he surveyed the apartment. He needed to take possessions with him, things he wanted to keep.

He pulled out his duffel and put the clothes he had bought in Rulanda in it. Then he added his favorite book of his father's poetry. If he had time, he would have gotten the sculpture from his office, but he was running late. Maybe after the Festival was over, he would be able to get it.

His hands were making the decision for him. If he took his favorite possessions, there was a good chance he was never coming back. He ran a hand across the bruise on his arm. He hoped the Golgoth would forgive him. No one else would.

He slung the duffel over his shoulder. It was lighter than usual. Odd that he would leave with so little. Or maybe not. He had arrived with nothing.

He stepped out of the apartment and pulled the door closed behind him. No one else was up in the building. Just as well. If he hadn't recognized himself in the mirror, his neighbors might not recognize him either. They might panic with a Kingdom member in their hallway. They might attack him. And what would he say in his defense? He was acting under the Golgoth's orders? The entire city knew his history. They would all think he was defecting.

For all he knew, he was.

He took the steps two at a time, avoiding the creaks by habit. He pulled open the front door. Cool morning air washed over him. The city was silent, waiting for the day to begin. He closed the door quietly behind him. New life. New chance. New beginning.

No one was on the street. The building work must have ended, and most of the contestants for the various performances were not from Golga. A few had participated the year before, and after the Festival was over, the Golgoth had them brought in for questioning. Diate had sat across a table, listening as Scio grilled them. *Where did you learn to dance? Who gave you the flute? Where did you find that play?*

Most of the performers had smuggled in their knowledge, but from Rulanda or other vacation spots. Still, fewer people would perform this year, knowing that an investigation awaited them when the Festival was finished.

He half-walked, half-ran to the Festival grounds. As he approached, he saw women in white robes hurrying out of a building. Erani. Dozens of people in Kingdom clothing huddled near the information booth. He passed them all – the Jovasians draped against the sunlight, the Rulandans in their stately dress, the Vorgellians holding tools and making finishing touches on the odd black booths – and stopped in front of the dance stage.

Another Kingdom member had arrived before him, a small woman wearing a see-through gown of the rich. She was too tiny to be Sheba. The woman turned, and Diate saw performance paints all over her body. She would dance nude.

An Erani was already checking in, small form lost in the large white robe that the Eranis wore everywhere. Diate wondered how the Erani would dance in it, but he supposed he would find out.

The judges' table sat empty. Tiny buttons linked their tabletop to the screen at the edge of the stage. When the dancer finished, a rating would go up in a dozen different languages. The dancers with the highest ratings got to perform again. The best dancer of that group won, but Diate had no idea what the prize was. He didn't really care. He wasn't there to win a prize.

The Vorgellian finished with the Erani, who went off to the sidelines to pace. The woman approached the table, giving her name softly, and stating her affiliation as Kingdom. When she finished, she followed the Erani, but kept her distance as she waited for the contest to begin.

Four more people got in line behind Diate. Two were Vorgellians, another was from the Kingdom, and the fourth looked like another Erani, but Diate couldn't tell since she wasn't wearing white.

'Sir?'

Diate looked up. The Vorgellian was speaking to him. He realized, with a start, that she was the same woman he had spoken to the day before.

'Who is minding your information booth?' he asked.

She smiled, the look softening her angular features. 'We switched. I prefer the dance.'

She didn't recognize him. Her dark eyes looked past him, as if they had never seen him before. She poised her long, graceful fingers over the keys. 'Name?'

'Emilio Diate.'

She glanced up then, hard, the shock registering in the absence of expression on her face. His name was familiar in the city, and she clearly knew who he was. She scanned his face for the detective she had seen the day before, just as he had done in the mirror.

He smiled. He didn't feel like the detective anymore.

Her hands shook as she typed his name. A thin line ran across the screen, translating his name into the official twelve languages of the Festival. Affiliation came up next, and she typed 'Golgan.'

'No,' he said. 'I'm here for the Kingdom.'

She took her fingers off the keys. 'I don't understand.'

'You're not supposed to understand. I'm here for the Kingdom.'

She clasped her hands in her lap and looked away. 'I can't type that. The Golgoth will check these. He'll know. What are you doing, detective?'

'Exactly what it looks like.' Diate leaned across her. She smelled faintly of cinnamon. He grabbed her arms and placed her fingers back on the keyboard. 'I want the Golgoth to know.'

'He'll question me. They'll take me into the palace and –'

'But no one will hurt you.' He glanced up. Half a dozen people were watching, their expressions carefully neutral. 'You have witnesses. I am here for the Kingdom. I told you that. You aren't making anything up.'

She swallowed so heavily he heard the sound. Slowly she deleted the word 'Golgan' and replaced it with 'Kingdom.' It scrolled across the screen, each language creating a new word.

'Music?' Her voice was tentative now.

'The Ler-de-Lyn.'

She froze again, then closed her eyes as she typed. The Ler-de-

Lyn was the Kingdom's national anthem. It had also been his best song as a boy, the one that had first brought him to the Queen's attention.

'You're third,' she said, without opening her eyes. 'Wait over there.'

He walked along the rim of the stage. Its wood was smooth and polished, just as he had thought it would be. He was glad that he would be third. Some of the glass-like surface would be gone; although not much because two dancers were not enough to get rid of the sheen.

The Vorgellian hadn't looked at him. She was processing the next dancer. Diate shook the nervousness from his arms and scanned the growing crowd. People walked around the booths, stopping to talk with the merchants. Most were from Golga, although some of the other nations had brought their own observers.

A slender woman worked her way toward the stage, long golden hair flowing behind her. Diate's breath caught in his throat. Sheba was going to come. He wasn't sure what he would say to her when she arrived, but at least she would be there.

Then the woman stopped at a booth. Her hair was too dark and her build too slight. She was still a girl. Not Sheba at all.

He let the air out of his lungs and paced. He didn't care if anyone knew how nervous he was. Sheba wasn't there. And this performance was for her.

'The prize isn't all that special,' the woman beside him, the dancer, said in Lillish.

He stopped pacing. She was young, young enough to have been born after he left the Kingdom. 'For me it is,' he said.

She crossed her arms in front of her chest. 'I've never seen you before. You look awful old to be here.'

Something he would have said, once, in all his ignorant arrogance. 'I am old.'

'They only want As to dance in this competition.'

'I am an A.' And probably have been longer than you've been alive. He thought the words but didn't say them. 'Is this how you get rid of your competition? Talk them to death?'

She smiled, a little. 'I just didn't want you to get in trouble. They're being really strict this year.'

'Both the Queen and the Minister of Culture know I'm here. If they didn't want me to dance, they would have said so.'

'You know them?' The girl was no longer the prima ballerina. She rubbed her slender hands together, the movement so graceful it could almost be part of her routine. 'I danced for the Queen twice this year, but never got to socialize. They said I had to wait for that.'

'It's not as wonderful as it sounds.' But the glamour had impressed him at fifteen, too. Impressed him so much that he had spent an entire night arguing with his father about the importance of the monarchy to the Kingdom itself. Diate fought for the Queen, his father for everyone else.

'Maybe it's not wonderful,' she said, her tone disbelieving. 'But it's an honor. And I'm ready for as many honors as I can get.'

The other Kingdom dancer had come to the side of the stage. He looked over Diate and crowded in close enough to hear the conversation. 'The Rogue Talent, I presume?'

Diate turned just enough to gauge the man behind him. Taller, thinner, and at least ten years younger. Old enough to be confident in his Talent, but young enough to be cocky.

The dancer smiled, quirking a dimple in his left cheek. 'We studied you in school. All your moves, and even your defection.'

The young woman was looking at him with an awe she had probably reserved for the Queen. 'You can't be the Rogue Talent.'

'Think about it,' the young man said. 'He escaped to Golga, and we're here now. He's the right age, and we've never seen him before.'

'The Rogue Talent wouldn't know this Queen.'

'He might,' the young man said. 'They're not going to let you come back. People as old as you can't dance. Especially after living in a heartless place like this.'

Diate smiled in return. He crouched, and checked the laces on his shoes. Then he stood again. A crowd had formed around the stage, most in uniforms for various Golgan jobs. Some Erani hovered near the edge, and a few Vorgellians stood at the front. No Sheba.

'How long have you been dancing?' he asked the young man.

The young man straightened. 'All my life.'

'So have I,' Diate said. 'What the body loses in agility, it gains in practice and skill.'

'I saw you dance once,' the young man said. 'I was five. My mother said there was nothing more beautiful in the world. But I knew I could be. I knew that someday I would be better than you.'

Diate had forgotten about the jealousies of the Talents, the insecurities and the fears. 'Someday you will be better than me. But today might not be that day.'

More dancers stood behind them, and the Vorgellian at the computer was checking in the last three. The contest would go on all day, and into the night, which was lucky for the Jovasian who cowered under dark clothing at the end of the line.

The crowd had grown heavier, and the sun stronger. The smell of unwashed bodies mixed with the dirt off the road. A thin layer of dust had settled on the stage. The poor young girl would have a tough time of her routine. The dust would make the stage even slicker.

The last of the dancers trooped over to the side. The judges filed into their places. The Vorgellian nodded at a thin, dark-haired man standing near the stage. He pushed up the rope and climbed on, his shoes leaving pointed prints in the dust. The Vorgellian pressed buttons on her computer and music, rich and full, played loudly enough to silence the crowd.

Diate stood stiffly. No Sheba. But two Kingdom magic Talents had moved to the right side of the crowd. He looked for Torrie, but didn't see her. At least she wasn't at this crisis point in his life. The other Talents might be there to see the younger dancers.

No one at all was there to see him.

He turned his back on the crowd and eased into a stretch, one leg in front, the other extended behind. The muscles strained and twitched a little. He was too stiff.

The man on the stage announced the dance contest in each language. His Golgan was fluent and his Lillish careful. Diate did not listen to the others. Then the music shifted into something he had never heard before: a collection of rolling sounds mixed with trills.

The Erani mounted the stage, her white robe flowing behind her. She was small and slender, her form nearly lost in the clothing. As the music swelled, she brought her arms out and began to twirl. For a moment, it almost looked as if she could fly. She executed several leaps, and the robe floated behind her like tailfeathers. She moved so quickly it seemed as if her feet never touched the ground.

He hadn't seen a routine like this one before. It was very simple, but beautiful. The music added to the birdlike flavor. The trills rose in another crescendo, as the Erani ran and leapt off the stage.

For the moment that she was airborne, she looked as if she could sail forever. The audience held its collective breath. Diate bit his lower lip. If she fell, she would ruin the entire routine.

But she didn't. She landed flat, her robe swirling around her, hiding her small feet. She glared at the audience for a moment, then bent over in a bow.

The applause was loud and long. Diate finished his stretch. A nervousness had crawled into his stomach that had nothing to do with Sheba. The old competitiveness was back. He wanted to do better than the Erani. He wanted to show them he was still the best in the world.

The man climbed on stage, complimented the Erani, and then glanced at the dancers. The young woman pulled off her dress, and took a step forward. The man held up his hand, signaling that she should wait. She shifted from foot to foot, breathing carefully. Diate stopped stretching and stood close to her, hoping that his presence would reassure.

Still no Sheba in the audience. No Carbete, no Queen. No Kingdom royalty at all.

The screen burst into twelve colors. Each language had its own – green for Golgan, and red for Lillish. The Erani's scores cast a rainbow hue on the crowd. Diate didn't read the scores, but the young woman did. She let the air out through her teeth. The Erani's scores must have been high.

'You do not compete against her,' he said. 'You compete against yourself. What was your score last competition?'

'I came in third.' She didn't look at him as she spoke.

'Not your ranking. Your scores.'

Then she did glance at him, as if she hadn't realized there was a difference.

'Tens? Twenties?'

'Tens,' she said softly.

Still young. Just starting to compete. And no one had explained to her that dance was an individual sport, a person bettering herself.

'Concentrate on yourself,' he said. 'No one else. Not me, not the Erani, not your friend here. Only concentrate on the music and the movements. Your goal is not to win, but to do the best you can.'

218

Her mouth was open slightly. She nodded, then returned her attention to the stage. The man announced a name and extended a hand to her, helping her through the ropes.

'Why did you tell her that?' The young man behind him asked.

'Because she needed to hear it.'

'She'll do better now.'

Diate glanced at him. Myla's training, so different from the other dance instructors. *They will play mind games with you, Emilio, and try to take away your belief in yourself. But if you do not care about them, they will have no power over you.* 'That's the point,' he said.

The young man frowned and glanced up at the stage. The music started: a march performed with wykasis, flute, and percussion. The effect was both airy and military. The young woman stepped into center stage and arched her back, putting her arms in the air and spreading her fingers so wide that they no longer looked human. She pirouetted and leaped, each movement making her body seem boneless. Her form was good, not great, and her dance too simple, without the flare of the Erani. She wouldn't impress the judges.

She would be brilliant when she got older.

She did a series of full turns around the stage, slipping slightly on the last one, and recovering with a flourish. Her feet thudded to the music, and small bits of dust floated in the air.

The march was building in a crescendo. Diate turned away from the stage and sat in the dirt.

'What are you doing?' the young man whispered. 'You're next.'

Diate ignored him. He untied the laces on his shoes and pulled them off his feet, placing them on top of his duffel. He moved to the edge of the stairs, spit on his hands, and rubbed his toes and heels.

The music stopped and applause swirled around him. A lump formed in his throat. Sheba wasn't here. He had to remember the advice he had given to the girl: he had to dance for himself. Alone on Golgan soil. He had never expected it to come to this.

Rainbow colors spread across the dirt, and the applause grew. Her scores must have been good. She passed him as he hurried down the steps, the scents of perfume and sweat trailing behind her. The man was talking again, praising her performance. The first strains of the Ler-de-Lyn played beneath his words.

'Now,' the man finished in Golgan, 'we have an odd treat.

Emilio Diate, who has spent the last sixteen years in exile here on Golga, has decided to return to the stage. This morning, he is dancing for the Kingdom to their national anthem, the Ler-de-Lyn.'

Diate stood, ignored the man's offered hand, and crawled through the ropes himself. His damp feet left footprints on the smooth wood. His soles stuck to the wood, but he had traction. He didn't have to worry about slipping.

He stopped center stage, bowed, and scanned the audience. No Sheba. No Carbete. But Beltar stood at his booth just inside Diate's vision, a stricken look on his rounded face.

Diate turned away. He slipped into a crouch, knees bent, head down, hands covering the face, and waited until the full orchestra joined the opening trumpet in the Ler-de-Lyn. He rose on his left foot with his right foot extended behind him, and jumped. His feet touched beneath his body, and he landed on the right foot, the left extended behind him. The music continued to build, and his dance grew wilder, pirouettes and jetés extending into full leaps. Sweat beads flew off his hair, remaining airborne for a moment before disappearing. He followed, as free and exhilarated as they seemed.

He was outside, in the air, dancing before a crowd, not trapped in a gym, staring at the mirror. He had never felt so limber, so able to fly. As the trumpet theme flourished, so did he. With a half-run and a jump, he managed a back flip, toes pointed, and landed perfectly, one foot extended behind him. He whirled like a small top, until his body became a blur even to him. The music crashed around him, and he opened into his final pose – arms extended, feet apart, head thrown back, as if he were about to welcome his lover into a hug.

Then the music stopped, and he folded in on himself, reappearing as he had started, crouched, bent, hiding. His heart pounded and his skin was flushed. Sweat ran down his back, along his sides, and dripped from his hair onto the stage.

The applause was tentative at first, then it built around him like a wave, crushing him with its strength. He stood, arms at his side, and bowed. Several people clapped with their hands above their heads, to show him their extreme pleasure. He nodded and waved, then froze.

Sheba stood in the back of the crowd, Carbete beside her. From this distance, they looked identical.

Beltar was directly behind them. He had moved to the front of his booth, one jeweled hand covering his mouth.

The announcer climbed beside Diate and urged him to bow again. He did, and then he escaped the stage, grabbing a towel from an attendant as he went down the stairs.

The young man stood there, feet bare too. 'I'm still better than you,' he said, but his voice had more bravado than truth in it now.

Diate wiped the towel over his face. He no longer cared about the dancers. 'You will be,' he said.

He grabbed his shoes and duffel and pushed through the crowd, avoiding people's gazes, ignoring the hands that patted his back. A detective stood in the center of the crowd, looking as shocked as Beltar. Strega. Diate turned his back on him and headed toward Sheba.

She was walking toward him. They met just at the fringe. She wore no makeup and her blouse was loose but not see-through. She stopped just outside of his reach.

'Sheba,' he said, and extended a hand. She grabbed it and pulled him into her arms. The feel of her warmth against him electrified him, and he pulled her closer, face buried in her hair. She pushed him back just enough so that she could kiss him.

She tasted of fresh water and sunshine. He drank like a man dying of thirst, his hands all over her. Hers were in his hair, holding his face to hers. She made small, pleased noises in her throat.

Finally, they separated.

'I didn't think you'd come,' he said.

'I didn't think you'd be here. I thought it was a ruse.' She slipped the duffel off his shoulder and tossed it at Carbete. Then she put her arm through his. 'I'm glad to see you, Emilio.'

Such understatement. He held her close, hips touching. They fit so well. 'Are you free?' he asked.

She nodded. 'I'll take you back to the Pavilion. We have the day.'

The day. He didn't want to think beyond it.

'You look better this way,' she said. 'That uniform had you trussed like a prisoner, with none of your natural grace and this freedom. You're beautiful, Emilio.'

'I'm supposed to say that to you.' He smiled.

'I don't care what you say, as long as you're here.'

'Mr Diate, sir.' The Vorgellian in charge of the contest had followed him. She touched his shoulder and stood back. He turned, holding Sheba so tightly that she had to turn too. 'You're leading, sir. Don't you want to stay, to finish this out?'

'You are dancing for us,' Carbete said. 'We don't mind receiving the prize.'

Diate studied Carbete for a minute. He couldn't see beyond the amusement in the other man's eyes. 'If I win, Mr Carbete will stand in for me. I have more important business.'

Sheba stifled a giggle, the sound almost too girlish and happy for the woman he had known.

Carbete frowned. 'I can't –'

'We don't mind receiving the prize, Tonio,' Sheba said. 'And you have nothing to do today either.'

'Except keep an eye on you.'

'Emilio will do that. He's one of us, Tonio. No one from this place can dance like that.'

So she had seen the entire performance. He hadn't been sure.

Carbete nodded, then the amusement reappeared on his face. 'They were right when they spoke of your talent, detective. You must have been brilliant in your prime.'

He bowed, just a little, and followed the Vorgellian back to the stage. Sheba laughed. 'You're brilliant now. He just doesn't want to admit it.'

'This from the woman who doubted I could still dance?'

She placed her hand on his forearm. 'I'll never doubt you again, Emilio.'

She spoke the words lightly, but they seemed to have heavier weight. Now he had two people who believed in him – believing that he would betray the other. A shiver ran down his back. He wouldn't think about it. They had the day.

And the night.

Various people in the crowd eyed him warily as they passed. He pulled Sheba closer, as if she were his shield against the world. Maybe she was. Maybe this was as good as it would get – ever.

Another performance was happening on a stage just off to the right. A woman stood with a man, arms extended, declaiming in Utani. Translations appeared on the screens behind them. The crowd surrounding the stage was silent, spellbound.

They crossed the street, taking them away from the Festival. Sheba tugged on Diate's arm. 'Wait. I need some air.'

She was breathing heavily. He glanced at her. Even though she was slender, she was not in good physical condition. She didn't exercise and her skin showed the signs of too much good food. Maybe someday he could get her to dance with him.

He brushed the damp hair of his forehead. 'I need to get cleaned up.'

'There's a wonderful place in the Pavilion,' she said. Her voice was throaty. He wondered what kind of place she meant, and thought he knew.

They joined hands and walked through the winding streets. People passed them, on the way to the Festival. No one was going in their direction.

Diate barely noticed them. His detective's eye took in their relative poverty, the lack of joy with which they moved. He had never realized how the Festival was entertainment for people who had little joy in their lives. He had always seen it as extra work, maintaining diplomatic relations with the other cultures. He had never looked at it as a participant before.

They turned onto Embassy Row, and passed the buildings for many of the other cultures already attending the Festival. The Erani building, with its open roof and opaque windows, looked deserted. The Jovasian embassy was as dark and shrouded as the Erani was open. Six hired guards stood around the building, holding pikes. At twilight, the door would open, and a single light would illuminate the yard. The Jovasians would become a presence at the Festival only then.

The Pavilion looked as empty as it had the day before. Sheba keyed her code into the lock and watched the gate open. She was bouncing on her toes, as if the excitement of the moment had taken hold of her. She took his hand, and dragged him toward the door.

Diate stared at the building. It wasn't really Kingdom, even though it had tapestries and stained glass. Perhaps that was what buildings would look like when Golgan and Kingdom met.

A single guard came out, saw Sheba, and held the door open. She smiled at him, then took Diate inside.

The great hall looked empty and unused. Their footsteps echoed in the silence. She led him to a back room and down a staircase as narrow as the one they had trod the night of the party.

A damp smell permeated the lower level. Diate hadn't noticed it the night before. The air had a chill that felt good against his overheated skin.

Sheba led him past the listening rooms, where they had talked that first night, and through a long, intricately painted corridor. The air grew warmer and more humid as they progressed, until they turned a corner and the hallway opened up into an ornate marble room.

The floor, ceiling, and walls were made of white marble tile. Two wide steps led up to a platform. A huge rectangular tub, also made of white tile, sat at the top of the platform. Steam rose from the water's surface. Plants not native to Golga sat on the corners of the tub. Thick, multi-colored towels hung from racks. Long, rose bath mats covered the platform floor. A flush heated Diate's cheeks. He remembered places like this from his youth. He had first seen a couple making love in a room much like this one. But he had never seen a public bath so empty.

Sheba turned and grabbed both of his hands. 'Everyone's at the Festival. No one will bother us.'

He gazed at the hot water, realizing for the first time how much his body ached. It would feel good to sink into that heat, to let it caress his flesh. 'I'm covered with paint.'

'We have a Vorgellian filtration system. The water recycles and always stays clean.' She leaned into him and kissed him, sticking her hands in the back of his pants and pulling him close. 'Let me wash you off.'

She slipped one hand around and untied his drawstring. The pants fell to his knees. Then she tugged off his shirt. He let his duffel and shoes clatter to the floor.

Her hands were all over him, touching, teasing. He took off her blouse and helped her out of her leggings. She pulled off her shoes and tossed them near his as he stepped out of his pants.

Her flesh was soft and warm against his. He buried his face in her hair, letting her scent fill him. She dragged him toward the tub, and they climbed in, still touching.

The water was hotter than he had expected, and scented with an odd, almost bitter chemical. She grabbed a washcloth and some soap from a side bin and lathered his face. Then she dipped the cloth in the water and brought it up, careful to scrub off the paint. The cloth came away blue, yellow, and green.

'The tear doesn't come off,' she said.

He took the cloth from her and scrubbed. No matter how much pressure he applied, the red dye did not spread to the cloth. 'It's old. Something must have happened in the storage.'

She smiled. 'I like it. You don't look like that detective anymore.'

She ran the cloth along his back, hand sliding across his skin, down the front. He pulled her onto his lap, and they kissed, slowly, leisurely, the water making their bodies slick. He slipped inside her and she moaned, tilting her head back. He kissed her throat as she gripped him with her legs, and then they moved together. The rhythm grew faster and faster until he could wait no longer. He shuddered to a climax, and at his first cry, Sheba joined him, her body tightening in orgasm.

The water was suddenly too hot. Diate climbed out, careful to remain inside her. She put her head on his shoulder. 'I missed you,' she said.

The tile felt cool against his buttocks. He stretched out his legs. The aches had left his body and he felt better than he had in months. Sheba curled against him, goose bumps rising on her bare skin.

'You're cold,' he said.

She shook her head. 'Just right.'

He stroked her hair, holding her. Her grip remained tight on him. The lack of sleep was catching up to him. He swayed, a little.

'You all right?'

'Tired,' he said.

He felt her smile against his chest. 'Wonder why.'

She let him go and got up. The separation yanked at him, made him feel suddenly empty. He wanted to get her and bring her back, so that they could remain joined like that, forever.

She took a towel off the rack and dried the water on his back and chest. He lifted a leg and she dried that too, spending too much time on his genitals. Her touch made him hard again, but she shook her head.

'Never expected the stamina, did you?' he asked.

She smiled. 'Fake stamina. We'll get to the best part and you'll fall asleep.'

'No faith,' he said.

'Practical,' she countered.

He took the towel and dried her, then stood beside her. Together they walked to a mat. Sheba pulled three more towels off the rack, using two as pillows and putting the third over them like a blanket.

Then she laid him down and settled beside him. He put his arm around her, determined to stay awake, to enjoy the moment, but sleep kept bubbling over him. Just a nap, he promised himself, and that was the last thing he remembered for a long time.

Chapter 18

He arched, already near orgasm. The woman on top of him smelled like Sheba. He slid a hand along her back, feeling the ridges of her vertebrae. She moaned in pleasure, and he came fully awake, realizing that this was not a dream.

He held her hips in place and plunged inside her, his body tingling. Each nerve ending was alive. He trembled, holding back, wanting to please her more. Her face, neck and upper chest were flushed, her eyes too bright, her tawny hair mussed and cascading about her shoulders.

She had never looked so beautiful.

Her hand gripped his shoulder, fingernails breaking the skin. Her excitement helped his build, and he pulled her closer. She called out his name, her voice echoing off the marble walls.

As he had dreamed. Better than he had dreamed.

He lost himself inside her, lost track of where he ended and she began. An orgasm ripped through her, surprising in its intensity. She called out again, head thrown back. He caught her and held her in place as he rolled them over, placing his arms beside her as he rubbed against her. In. Out. The tingles turned into small heat explosions along his skin. Another orgasm tightened her, her mouth trembling with the intensity.

'Emilio –' she breathed, and the softness, the gentleness, shattered his control. This orgasm shook him to his core, and immobilized him almost completely.

He collapsed on top of her, but couldn't move. 'Sorry,' he said.

Her hand was in his hair, stroking him, cradling him, holding him in place. 'Feels good,' she said.

'How long –'

She smiled. 'I like you when you're dreaming.'

He rolled beside her. The towel was bunched at their feet. There was no way to tell time in the room, no way to tell how long he had been asleep.

Not that it mattered.

'I'm hungry,' he said.

'I can fix that.' But she didn't move, her body curled and warm against his. She sighed, a soft little sound of contentment.

He felt content too. The restless energy that had always haunted him was gone. He found that he didn't miss it.

She rolled up, hair brushing his shoulder. She crossed the room and pressed a small button in the wall. A voice, small and tinny, responded. 'Can you bring something down for us to eat?' she asked.

The voice said something else Diate didn't catch.

Sheba laughed. 'I don't care. Something good. And wine.'

She let the button go, and faced him. Her body was perfect, long supple legs, rounded hips, small waist, and breasts that fit in the palms of his hands. The odd lighting added to his sense of disorientation. Earlier he hadn't cared where it came from. Now he searched for it, finally seeing glowing globes half-hidden under scooped marble holders. Most of the light was shielded, but what remained reflected off the water.

He stood, a little dizzy. He staggered and caught himself on a towel rack. 'Guess I need food more than I thought.'

She put her arms around him and eased him back on the mat. 'You slept like the dead.'

He leaned against her. His body ached in places where he hadn't thought he had muscles. He stretched, wishing the pleasant feeling he had had a few moments ago would return.

The door opened, and a man he had never seen before came in carrying a tray. Diate reached for a towel, but Sheba put her hand over his. The man set the tray on one of the marble steps and backed out of the room, closing the door behind him.

Diate's heart pounded and a flush ran through him.

Sheba smiled. 'If we don't acknowledge our nudity, neither will he.'

She slipped out of his grasp and got up, grabbing the tray and bringing it over. Her body had a grace that he loved. He wondered how many other people had seen it. Had shared it. He took a deep breath. Jealousy caught him in the ribs. And he wouldn't have thought of it at all except for her casual attitude a moment earlier.

He bit back the questions. He had no right to ask. He doubted her experience was as limited as his. She came from a place where morals were looser, where people lived as they wanted to. A place he had never entirely felt at home.

She set the tray on the edge of the mat. Some meats, cheeses, and fruits were arranged in small half-circles on the platter. Bread covered with butter sat on a side plate. Two goblets of wine stood beside the bread plate.

Diate took a piece of bread, pleased to feel its warmth against his fingers. He ate quickly, his body grateful for the nourishment. Sheba picked at the meat, layering it on a slice of bread, and placing a piece of cheese on top. She ate slowly, alternating bites with sips of wine.

'I wish it could always be like this,' she said.

Diate stroked her hair. He did too. Quiet, peaceful, with simple things and each other for amusement. He made himself a small sandwich and ate that too, taking only a sip of wine. It was unspiced and almost bitter, certainly not anything Beltar would touch.

Beltar. His mind settled on his friend's face for a moment, then he forced it away. He wanted this time with Sheba to last. He wanted nothing to interfere with it.

He put the wine glass down, and took Sheba's out of her hand. Then he drew her into his arms again, uncertain whether he wanted to make love or just hold her. She sighed and curled against him.

They sat there for a moment, then he leaned forward and kissed her hair.

A sharp burning pain shot through his left arm. Diate gasped and pulled back.

'Emilio?'

Another pain, this one even more blistering, traveled along his arm into his shoulder. He glanced down. The patch was glowing. Someone was trying to contact him. The Golgoth. Something had happened to the Golgoth.

'Emilio, what's wrong?'

His breath came out in small gasps. Even when the pulse faded, the pain remained. He stood, staggered back, and reached for his clothes.

'Emilio?' Sheba stood with him, touching him. He backed away. Something had happened. While he was here. While he wasn't able to protect the Golgoth.

'What time is it?' His words came out harsh.

'I don't know,' she said. 'We slept a long time.'

He grabbed her and shook her. 'What time is it?'

'I don't know.' She pulled out of his grasp and brushed her hair from her face. 'That was Stefano with the wine, so probably morning, after late breakfast. Why? What's going on?'

'Morning.' He slid into his pants. The Queen was meeting with the Golgoth. And something had gone wrong.

We have all day.

Sheba was supposed to be with him. She was guarding him so that he would stay away from the Queen.

Another pain ripped through his arm. He couldn't grip the side of the pants. He tugged with his right hand, until they were all the way up, then he tied them quickly.

'Emilio, please, tell me what's happening.'

A fury that matched the pain ran through him. He wanted to grab her and fling her away from him. He couldn't believe he had touched her. 'I think you know what's happening,' he said.

'No,' she said. 'Emilio –'

He took her arm and held her for a second. If he dealt with her, he couldn't save the Golgoth. She would have to wait until later. 'Stay here,' he said. 'We're not finished yet.'

'Emilio –'

He pushed past her and sprinted for the door, ignoring the aches that were still present in his body. He was tired, more tired than he had been in days. But he couldn't let that stop him. He had to get back. He had to see if he could save the Golgoth.

He took the stairs two at a time, pushed past the servant who had started for the stairs, and ran for the front door. Another pulse burned his arm, the pain so intense he almost cried out. Something was wrong with the Golgoth, and something was wrong with his patch. It wasn't supposed to hurt this much.

With his right hand, he tugged open the heavy glass doors and ran down the front walk. He didn't wait for the gate lock to open, but vaulted the top instead.

The sun was up. It was too high in the sky for breakfast – he guessed the time was closer to early lunch. The meeting had been going for a while.

And something had gone wrong.

Embassy Row was empty, except for a few people walking

toward the Festival. His feet slapped against the dirt as he ran. Some people glanced at him. No one tried to stop him. Everyone pretended to look away from him.

He saw a few detectives, hidden in shadow. They were watching him. They probably thought he was a Kingdom member late for a contest.

A man stepped out of the shadows near the ports. Diate recognized him before the man recognized Diate. Strega. Diate held up his arm. It was throbbing.

'The patch has gone off. I need you,' he said.

'Yes, sir.' Strega fell into a run beside him. They didn't speak as they hurried into the city. Rocks from the uneven road cut Diate's bare feet. He didn't break stride. He avoided the Festival streets, not wanting to get caught in the crowd. Strega tried to ask a few breathless questions, but Diate didn't answer them. His arm throbbed. The pulse had died or maybe it no longer worked. He didn't care. He had to get to the palace.

He ran past the detectives' offices, the secret police head-quarters, the economics building, and to the palace itself. A guard at the stairs tried to grab his arm, but Diate shook him away.

The guard at the door wouldn't let him pass.

'I'm Diate, you idiot,' he said.

The guard peered at him.

'Let me in. Something's gone wrong.'

'He's wearing an arm patch,' Strega snapped. 'Let him in.'

The guard didn't budge. Damn their training. It was too good.

Strega grabbed Diate's right arm, and flipped open his own identification. 'He's with me. Let us in or I will report you.'

The guard pulled open the door. Diate shook free of Strega and ran through the wide entrance hall. All the guards that had been posted two days before were gone. He hated the emptiness. The entire palace was set up for destruction. Scio had failed. No one was protecting the Golgoth.

Voices echoed from the upstairs corridor.

The worn stairs were cold against his feet. His legs ached so badly that he had to take these stairs one at a time. He could barely breathe. His side ached. He had arrived at the palace in record time, but it felt too late.

When he reached the top, he saw dozens of guards milling in the hallway before the audience chamber. They wouldn't let him pass.

He used his elbows and shoulders to push his way past. No one looked at him, and they should have. They should have stopped him. Strega should have been beside Diate, helping him get inside. No wonder there were problems, if a man dressed as he was could get this close to the audience chamber.

The guards were all straining to get a view of the chamber itself.

When he reached the front of the guards, he stopped. The audience chamber doors were opened wide. The Golgoth was sprawled on the floor, fetal position, hands twisted like claws, mouth open in an odd rictus. His skin was black, as if it had been crisped by fire. His eyes were open. He was dead.

Diate glanced around the room. Kreske was huddled against the wall, hands over his face. Scio clasped a small device – apparently he had called Diate. Several guards were in the room. Some stood, but a group held two men, dressed in official Kingdom garb. Another Kingdom male lay dead on the floor, a knife in his chest. Four guards held a woman whom Diate had only seen once. The Queen.

Diate ignored her. He went to the Golgoth. The Golgoth's skin had a bitter-sweet odor, and was already cooling. Diate stood. 'What were you thinking, Scio?'

Scio looked up as if he had seen Diate for the first time. 'It was going so well,' he said. 'And then, he kissed her hand. We just didn't expect –'

'Kissed her? You let him touch her? Her?' Diate whirled and walked toward the Queen.

Her dress was ripped and her hair tangled about her face. The guards held her hands at her sides. She wore gloves. The tips of her fingers were as black as the Golgoth's face.

Diate took her hands in his and examined the fingers.

Skin poison. Tonio Carbete's trademark. Sheba's brother.

When the Queen had extended her hand for a ritual greeting, the Golgoth had kissed each fingertip. The moisture activated the poison in his mouth and he was dead within minutes.

They must have been long minutes.

Her hand was shaking. 'You're Sheba's Talent,' she said. 'Please, help me. I didn't know –'

'Didn't know?' Diate yanked her from the guards' grasp. 'You didn't know that your actions would kill him? Or that you would get no help?' He grabbed her shoulders, shaking her, shoving her against the wall.

232

'I'm no one's Talent,' he said. His fingers dug into her flesh, and he pulled her forward before slamming her into the wall again.

She put her hands against his arms, trying to free herself. 'Please,' she said. 'I didn't mean –'

'You had no right,' he said. 'He trusted you.'

The yard smelled of blood. The house smelled of blood. The baby's head, turned at an odd angle –

'He trusted you,' Diate repeated. He slammed her against the wall again. More blood spattered him. She tried to twist away, but he tightened his grip.

'He believed you when you said you wanted to talk peace.' Diate's grip tightened. She twisted again, and he shoved her against the wall harder than before. Her head slammed against the skull candleholder, shattering it.

The thud of her head against the wall echoed in the large room. She didn't cry out anymore. Blood spattered his skin, his face.

'Emilio.'

He whirled. The Queen crumpled to the floor. Scio stood behind him, a solemn expression on his round face. 'She's dead, Emilio.'

Blood covered the wall. She lay at his feet, legs crushed beneath her, arms spread, the back of her head flattened and matted with blood. Her eyes were empty.

As empty as the Golgoth's.

Diate pushed past Scio and went to the Golgoth. He crouched beside him. The Golgoth's face was locked in an expression of pain, his lips curled and twisted away from his teeth, his eyes staring. Diate picked him up.

The body flopped in his arms. Diate was shaking. He hadn't hurt her badly enough. He wanted her to suffer, as he had suffered. As his family had suffered. As the Golgoth had suffered.

Diate carried the Golgoth past the guards and through the door.

The guards stared at him as if they had never seen him before. And he supposed they hadn't. He had always been calm before them, always proper, not this Kingdom rebel, barely dressed and covered with blood. Strega stood at the fringes of the crowd, face white. He reached for Diate, but Diate turned away.

His feet were made of ice. He walked alone across the floor and pulled open a door leading to a stairwell.

He climbed the circular stairs, the weight of the Golgoth slowing him, going round and round, past floors he had forgotten existed, until he reached the top windowed room. He kicked open the door with one foot and carried the Golgoth inside.

The room smelled musty. Windows let in the daylight, illuminating the black benches, the undecorated walls. Diate laid the Golgoth on the center bench, stretched out his legs, and closed his eyes. He tried to close the Golgoth's mouth, but didn't have the skill.

He went over to a cabinet, pulled it open, and took out a series of oils. His hands shook as he mixed them. The Queen's blood decorated his fingers like paint. He stopped once to check his upper arms. The poison was no longer activated. Even though she had touched him, he had been spared.

The wrong kind of miracle.

He mixed the oils with his index finger, then carried the bowl back to the Golgoth's side. He set the bowl on the floor and started to remove the Golgoth's ceremonial robe.

The door squeaked open behind him. Diate did not stop working the buttons, moving one of the Golgoth's arms so that the robe slipped off his shoulder.

'Emilio.' Kreske came up beside him and crouched. 'You have no right.'

Diate ignored him, unbuttoning another button, tugging the robe open.

Kreske put a hand on Diate's arm. Diate cried out in pain. He rocked back on his toes. His left arm was swollen and throbbing.

'He's my father,' Kreske said. 'I must do the ceremonial rites.'

Diate clutched his arm to his chest. 'I never got to do the rites for mine.'

'I know,' Kreske said. 'But he's my father. He can't substitute for yours.'

Diate touched the Golgoth's blackened face. 'I should have been here. I told him that.'

'Performing the rites won't bring him back.'

'No,' Diate said. 'I guess they won't.'

He stood, legs shaking. He had been wrong to come here. Wrong to grab the Golgoth. Wrong to touch the Queen. His emotions were out of control, running away with him, holding him in a way that they shouldn't.

It was all Sheba's fault. All of it. If he hadn't been with her, the Golgoth would still be alive.

He had told her to wait.

Diate walked out of the room, leaving Kreske to cradle his father. The stairs were cold, the walk down looking longer than the walk up had been. He was shivering, the pain in his arm so intense that he couldn't let it brush against his body. He made it back to the main floor, where the guards were still milling. He looked inside the audience room. The bodies remained, but the prisoners were gone.

'I need people,' he said. 'Come with me.'

No one moved.

He clenched his fists. 'Do I become someone else because I am wearing different clothing? You did nothing to save the Golgoth. You can at least come with me and try to recapture the people who murdered him.'

Strega came forward. 'I'm with you, sir.'

Diate glanced at them. 'One man? All these years, and I only command one man?'

More guards came forward, most wearing detectives' uniforms.

'Good,' Diate said. 'Someone get Scio and tell him to send his men to the Pavilion. We haven't got much time.'

The guards followed him down the stairs. He let himself out the front. He moved as quickly as he could, but he was too tired to run. His body felt as if it would never work right again. He avoided the Festival streets, and hurried down the back roads. People on the way to the Festival stopped as the troop walked by.

The gate to the Pavilion was open. Something like fear rose in Diate's chest. He had told her to stay. Then he made himself breathe. Maybe she had. Maybe Scio had already arrived.

Maybe she was dead too.

He ran through the gate. The stained-glass doors stood open as well. He ran in, and heard nothing. The main entrance hall was empty. The men clustered behind him, their boots making scuffing sounds on the wood.

The silence sent a fear through him as great as the one that had sent him back to the palace.

'Go upstairs,' he said to the men beside him. 'Strega, have some of these men examine the first floor.'

'Yes, sir.'

He didn't watch to make sure his orders were carried out. He went into the basement.

The rooms leading to the sauna were empty. The heat enveloped him, tried to coax him out of his rigidness. The silence seemed heavier here.

He wanted to call her name, but the words wouldn't leave his throat. He was afraid that once he turned the corner, he would find her, curled in a rictus like the Golgoth.

Diate couldn't bear it.

Not again.

He opened the door to the public bath, and let out a small sigh. The lights were still glowing. The remains of their breakfast still sat on the mat. The water was flat and unmoving.

The room was empty.

She had run away, just like she had done before.

She couldn't have known. She wouldn't have been so loving, so real if she had known.

But the Queen had used Carbete's poison.

Sheba's brother, Carbete.

His special poison.

Sheba had used Diate.

She had betrayed him.

The Queen was dead.

The Minister of Culture ruled.

A simple plot, conceived and executed with the help of Golga's chief of detectives. From beginning to end, he was implicated. He had slept with her in Rulanda. His name had been on the invitation. He had brought the suggestion for the Kingdom's participation to the Golgoth. He had slept with Sheba in the Pavilion.

He had slept with Sheba while the Golgoth died.

She had taken everything, and left him nothing.

Not even his self-respect.

Chapter 19

Diate didn't sleep for two days. He spent them investigating.

Sheba had left in an air shuttle, shortly after Diate had run from the Pavilion. Carbete was with her, as were the rest of the Queen's advisors. The shuttle arrived in the Kingdom to the greeting of a large crowd, who had cheered Sheba as Queen.

He discovered much of the information on the Golgoth's Vorgellian computer network, the rest through Kingdom informers. Sheba had seemed angry when she left, unwilling to go without Diate by her side. The informers had reported that sheepishly, as if they were embarrassed by Diate's relationship with Sheba.

He was not. He felt nothing at all. As each piece of information fell into place, his grip on his emotions grew tighter and tighter.

An examination of the poison confirmed that it was Carbete's special recipe. The remaining Kingdom personnel, mostly Talents rounded up from the aborted Festival, testified that Sheba was the Queen's favorite advisor, and could not believe that she would do anything to harm the Queen at all.

That left Carbete. He had much to gain from his sister's rise to the highest position of power. He could have laced the Queen's gloves and maneuvered the murder without Sheba's knowledge. Sheba would have been stupid not to follow through on the opportunity that her brother had handed her.

Diate had not left the palace. Occasionally, he would come out and note that the funeral proceedings were moving forward. He missed the funeral, Kreske's coronation as the new Golgoth, and the round of political meetings with other foreign heads of state.

Not until the third day after the Golgoth's death did he have enough information to call together both Kreske and Scio. They agreed to meet in Kreske's chambers, late at night, away from the guards and other ears.

Diate wanted it that way.

Kreske's chambers were located on the floor below the Golgoth's. They were the same size, but furnished differently. The floor was covered in thick carpet. The furniture was all wood with no cushions, and the fireplace looked like it had never been used. The chambers were cold and smelled faintly sweet, as if apples were beginning to turn in the back rooms. The thought of food made Diate's stomach rumble. He couldn't remember the last time he had eaten. Perhaps it was the meal with Sheba.

Scio and Kreske were waiting for him. Scio stood with his hands clasped behind his back in the center of the room. Kreske hovered near the empty fireplace. His thick red hair had been shaved off, giving his face an even more skull-like appearance. He wore the thick black robe of a Golgoth. It dwarfed him.

'Emilio,' Kreske said. 'What have you found?'

Diate stared at him, a slight dizziness catching him. He would have to get some food and sleep after this meeting. He also needed to get his arm checked. He had been unable to move the fingers on his left hand for the past two days. 'She's Queen,' he said. 'She arrived in the Kingdom to a rally celebrating that fact while we were still arguing about what to do with your father's body.'

Kreske shut his eyes and sank onto the cushionless couch. Scio didn't move. 'We could go after her,' Scio said. 'We're allowed vengeance. They murdered a head of state.'

'They probably expect that,' Kreske said. 'They figure that a new Golgoth wouldn't handle this right. That would open the door to a full-fledged war between us. My father would never have liked that.'

'It wouldn't seem right.' Diate walked down the two steps that led into the main room. 'He was murdered during the Peace Festival that he started. We can't go to war to avenge that.'

'We can't ignore it,' Scio said. 'We haven't done anything for days. We've already waited too long.'

'No,' Kreske said. 'We will not go to war. My father wouldn't stand for it.'

'Your father is dead.' The dizziness nearly overwhelmed Diate. He sat on the lower step. His body felt heavy and tired. The words came through a thick barrier deep inside him. 'The decision is yours.'

'I know.' Kreske's voice was soft. 'I don't know what to do.'

Scio glanced at him, alarm registering on his rounded face. 'You have to make decisions. That's your position.'

238

'There hasn't been war in this area since my father took over,' Kreske said. 'War would interrupt trade. It would ruin our economy. It might even hurt our long-term hold on imports and exports. I can't just order our ships to invade the Kingdom.'

'And you can't let her get away with this,' Scio said.

'Oh, but you can,' Diate said. 'If you do it right.'

They both stopped and stared at him. Kreske's eyes looked twice their normal size on his now-bald head. Scio took a step forward.

'This isn't a pro-Kingdom plot, is it?'

Diate glared at him. 'I won't even honor that sentence with an answer,' he said. 'This will benefit you, Kreske.' He couldn't bring himself to use Kreske's new title. 'It will show that you have done what you can.'

He stood, using the railing for balance. The dizziness was still there, but he was going to ignore it. He kept his left arm tight at his side, so that the others couldn't see that it had swollen to twice its normal size.

'You blame me,' he said.

Kreske was on his feet. 'You didn't do anything, Emilio.'

'You know that,' Diate said. 'Scio knows that. The Golgoth knew that. But who else? No one. All they know is that I had the new Queen of the Kingdom as a lover. Our relationship goes back to Rulanda. We hatched the plot there. When she came here for the Peace Festival, we met in the Pavilion and set it in motion. I danced for the Kingdom that morning. I was making love to her in the Pavilion when the Golgoth died. I came back here and killed the Queen – the only witness who could have confirmed my story. I have been maintaining my innocence ever since, but of course you don't believe me.'

'That story would have worked if you had left with her,' Scio said.

'I was supposed to,' Diate said. His good arm was shaking. It was bearing most of his weight. 'But the shuttle left without me. Or something like that. We can be creative. People have always believed that I was more Kingdom than Golgan. This proves it.'

'What would you have gained?' Kreske asked.

'I wanted to be Golgoth,' Diate said. 'Sheba was helping me. If we worked together, we would both head our respective countries, and unify the Kingdom and Golga again. But you stopped me, Kreske. You prevented me from killing you –'

239

'You would never do that, Emilio! Everyone knows that!'

'– and then imprisoned me. The coup becomes mine in this instance, and Sheba is exonerated. It makes the coup in the Kingdom an internal matter for them.'

'We don't want to exonerate them,' Scio said. 'She murdered the Golgoth.'

'Yes, but Kreske's right.' Diate leaned his right side against the railing. It was getting harder to stand up. 'We don't want to go to war. We can't.'

'What would we do to her, then?' Scio asked.

Diate smiled. 'Be patient. I came up with a plan to give Kreske the strength he needs to show as ruler without compromising our country. I can't think of everything else in just two days.' With no sleep, no food, and this damned exhaustion. He let go of the railing and walked to the couch, sitting beside Kreske. Diate wasn't sure how Kreske could enjoy this furniture. It was almost as uncomfortable as the stair.

'Emilio.' Kreske's voice was small. 'We can't blame you. We execute traitors. You didn't betray my father. I can't put you to death.'

'I'm not asking you to,' Diate said. 'I'm not that big a fool. You have to banish me. You have to send me away. For good.'

'We can't!' Scio whirled, his tonsure rising in the slight breeze. 'We need you now more than ever.'

'No,' Diate said. 'You don't. You saw the men after the Golgoth died. They didn't want to listen to me. They saw the Kingdom in me for the first time, and they'll remember that forever. You need someone new in my post. I would recommend Strega. He's young, he's smart, and he's good.'

Kreske put his hand on Diate's shoulder. 'We need *you* there, Emilio.'

Diate shook his head. The dizziness had grown worse. Black spots were forming in front of his eyes. 'No. You need me in the world. I'll be your eyes, Scio. I'll go where you want me to go, report on what you need to know. I can give you reliable information. You know that.'

'Why would you do this?' Scio said. 'You'll lose everything.'

Diate knew that too. He had thought it through as best he could. 'I owe the Golgoth,' he said. 'I owe him to make sure that this country remains intact, that Kreske has a successful reign. If you

240

don't need to go after Sheba, don't. She's smart and cunning and probably wants you to do just that.'

The black spots had grown to take most of his vision. He swayed, reached out with his left arm to catch himself, and missed, sending a wave of pain through him. He pitched forward. Someone's arms grabbed him and eased him to the floor.

'You have to listen to me,' he whispered as the darkness took him. 'It's the only way we'll all survive.'

Chapter 20

The Queen was small and lithe, with dark hair that ran down to her hips. Diate added a flourish to his bow, his feet nearly slipping off the mat. The room was large and cold, with ornate paintings on the walls. Paintings of naked people.

A dozen of the Queen's advisors sat beside her, larger than she was, but not dominating her. She smiled and beckoned to Diate.

He walked over to her, making certain that his spine was straight, his shoulders were back. Everyone watched him move.

She stood, extended her hand. He took it. Her fingers were cool in his hot, sweaty palm. He bent, kissed each fingertip in ritual greeting, and straightened. Her smile was wide, revealing small, painted teeth.

'You are Emilio Diate?' Her voice was soft.

'Yes.' He was pleased that he didn't stammer, that his nervousness didn't show.

'I remember watching you dance when you were a little boy. You have a lot of talent. More, I think, than I have ever seen.'

His cheeks grew hot. A bead of sweat ran down his back, itching as it went. He ignored the urge to scratch. 'Thank you.'

'Your father is also Emilio Diate?'

Diate nodded, catching his breath. His father had been producing pamphlets and selling them, hawking them on street corners to anyone who would listen.

'He is a naive man, your father. How many children are in your family?'

'Five,' Diate said.

'And you are the Talent.'

'He believes that the others have talent.'

She still clung to his fingers. 'Everyone has talent, but sometimes not the kind that can turn into profit. You don't believe your siblings have talent?'

He shrugged. 'The baby is too young. The boys don't try. My sister —'

He didn't want to say anything disloyal. When they danced together, his sister tripped him, stumbling too much herself. When he danced alone, he never stumbled and rarely fell.

The Queen touched a finger to his lips. 'It's all right. But your father is creating a disturbance. It will not do for him to continue.'

'I can't stop him.'

'You can,' she said. 'You must. Because if he continues to attack our rule, he will have to be dealt with. And sometimes that means dealing with family.'

Diate's breath caught in his throat. 'He won't listen to me. He thinks I don't understand.'

Her smile grew. The painted teeth gave an odd odor, of bitternuts and chicory. 'I think you do understand. I think you're scared.'

'What if I fail?' Diate whispered.

She let his hand drop. 'Then it is on his head.'

'Diate?'

Soft voice. Male voice. Not his father. Not his brothers. Who, then?

He didn't want to open his eyes and see. The bed was too warm, too comfortable. And his arm ached. A thin layer of sweat coated him. He was sick, couldn't they see that? Too sick to play. To sick to listen to anyone.

'Detective, you need to wake up. It's been too long –'

He pulled on his leggings and tied his shoes, keeping his back bent, almost hiding from the children. The dressing room was a large empty space filled with costumes and too many people. A year before, he had been with the children, waiting to perform, to see if his talent ranked. Now, he was to dance, to show them how a class A Talent looked.

He brushed long hair from his face and stretched his arms over his head. A woman stood beside him, her long hair curling around her shoulders. Small lines covered her skin and she didn't smile. A silver dot graced the bridge of her nose. Talent: magician.

'Young Diate,' she said.

He didn't move. His father said not to trust magic Talents because they abused their powers.

'Look behind you.'

He didn't resist, figuring the best thing to do was to go along. He turned around, saw rows and rows of children, some tying on toe shoes, others painting their faces, still others clutching bits of paper and art supplies as tightly as they could. One young girl sat alone on a stool, feet crossed behind the rungs. Her hair covered her head like a halo, but her face was in shadow.

'Yes,' the magic Talent said. 'She is your destiny. Choose well, young Diate, for your choices will remain with you for life.'

He took a step toward the young girl. Then another child tapped her arm, and she got off the stool. As she walked away, she moved slowly, as if she lacked the grace of a dancer. Her talent was something else then, something that didn't require movement.

He turned to ask the magic Talent a question, but she was gone.

His stomach rumbled. He put his good hand over it. His mouth was dry. He kept his eyes closed, but struggled to a sitting position.

Someone yelped.

The sound had come from his throat.

He opened his eyes. Grainy, no window, no light. But he was used to the darkness. A woman sat on a chair near the door. She got up, came to his side. 'We thought you were dying,' she said.

She seemed familiar, but he couldn't place her. She had long fingers, fingers of an Olean. She picked up the water glass, held his head, and helped him drink.

This time the water was cool and fresh. He finished the entire glass.

'I bet you're hungry,' she said.

He didn't nod, didn't move at all. The silence felt good. Not moving felt better.

'I'll be right back.'

She eased him onto the pillows and disappeared out the door. He resisted the urge to close his eyes. He needed food. He needed –

The door opened, and she entered, carrying a silver tray. It hooked onto the bars on each side of the bed, bars he hadn't noticed before. The prison wing of the Recovery Center? He hadn't done anything. They must have run out of beds. He tried to bring up his left arm, but the pain was too great.

A bowl of soup rested in the middle of the tray, with another glass of water beside it. Bread sat on a plate off to the side. The soup smelled of beef and spices. His stomach rumbled again.

'Can you get it or would you like help?' she asked.

He picked up the spoon with his good hand. It shook as he held it over the bowl. He leaned forward, slurped a spoonful of soup. The rich taste made his mouth water. He had never been this hungry before. Not since –

Not since he starved himself on the cruiser. Not since he escaped.

They must have put him in here then. The Vorgellian had helped him, and now the Golgoth had imprisoned him. But he didn't remember hurting his arm. Something must have happened in between. Something dangerous. Something that had wounded him.

Soup dribbled down his chin. The woman wiped it off with a towel. She pulled her chair closer. 'You're tired,' she said. 'Let me.'

She spooned soup into his mouth as if he were an infant. He put his right hand down beside him, grateful for the help. He had never been so weak. How long had it been since he exercised? He didn't know.

She sopped up the remaining soup with the bread and fed him the soggy pieces. The bread was light and flaky, the soup giving it a softness that he was surprised he needed.

He leaned back against the pillows. She wiped his mouth a final time. 'I wish you would talk to me,' she said. 'The infection isn't as bad as we thought.'

Perhaps she was familiar because she had spoken to him before surgery. Perhaps he knew her. He didn't remember.

He closed his eyes. Dreams were safer. No one died in dreams.

His legs were wobbling. He missed the leap, and his landing was off. Myla watched him, her hands crossed in front of her chest. 'Again,' she said.

The other students had gone home. The back office was dark. Only he and Myla remained. She had worked him for an extra hour, until his legs grew stiff and his body so sore he could barely move it.

'I can't,' he said. 'I've got to rest.'

'So the tireds hit you in the middle of a performance. You quit? No.'

'This isn't a performance.' He sat on the mat, its surface hard against his thighs. He ran a finger across the canvas, feeling the tiny threads binding the stuffing. 'They're expecting me at home.'

'No one expects you.' Myla turned her back on him. She grabbed his bag and tossed it to the floor, then sat on the chair where the bag had been. 'Go again.'

He bent his legs, feet meeting in the center, and stretched. The muscles in his back complained. 'I can't.'

'I instruct, and you will dance when I tell you to.' Her voice sounded odd, almost strained. She had never been this harsh with him before.

'Myla, I really ache. I just want to go home and soak.'

She sighed, and ran a hand along her face. 'You can't go home.'

He had had enough. He pushed himself to his feet, swaying a bit, then catching himself. 'I will go home when I want to. You can't stop me.'

'No,' she said. 'But I am supposed to.'

He tossed against the sheets. He didn't want to dream this. His dreams were safe. He opened his eyes. The dark room, no other occupant. He looked for a call button, for something, but couldn't find it. He leaned back against the pillow. Maybe if he thought about something else, the dream would go away.

He crossed over to her, stepping off the mat. His toe shoes felt odd on the wooden floor. 'Says who?'

She waved a hand, unable to meet his eyes. 'You're a great Talent, Emilio. An asset. Valued more than anyone.'

'Who says I can't go home?'

'Stay with me. I will train you and you will be safe –'

'Safe from what? What's going on, Myla?'

She shook her head. Her mouth was turned downward, her hands clasped tightly in her lap. The room had grown colder.

'What's happening?' he asked.

'I'm doing this badly,' she said. 'You're supposed to stay with me. Please listen, Emilio. It could be your life.'

His body froze. The warnings came back, the threats his father didn't always have time to hide. 'They're coming for my father, aren't they? They're going to get him, and they want me out of there.'

He stood for a moment, staring at his teacher, her body hunched protectively against him. If his father were gone, things would be easier. No one would complain about Diate's lessons. No one would worry that the other children weren't getting enough attention.

And no one would wrap an arm around his neck when people weren't looking. No one would whisper, 'I'm proud of you, Emilio.' No one would smile at him just so after a performance, a smile that praised, even while it condemned the process.

Diate's mouth had gone dry. 'They can't,' he said.

'Yes, they can.' Myla grabbed his wrists. 'They can do anything they want.'

He shook her off. 'You're part of it. You knew and you weren't going to *say anything. Just keep me here with you, as if nothing had happened. I'm going home, Myla. You can't stop me.'*

He danced away from her, pulled open the door, and ran outside. The heat was thick, the air almost unbreathable. The ground was hard, dirt cracking in the dryness. He could feel the cracks through his toe shoes.

Across the way, an old man was brushing leaves off his walk. He stopped when he saw Diate, put his arms on his brush, and watched.

He knew. The old man knew. They all knew but Diate.

Diate took a path through the woods, a shortcut he and his sister had found. His feet pounded against the dirt. Birds chirped overhead, stopping as they heard him come. The air was cooler here, but not much. Sweat poured down his body and the dryness in his mouth had grown.

The smell caught him first. Thick, coppery. He slowed to a walk and came out of the woods into the clearing where his house stood.

Flies swarmed over the yard. Blood coated the path, soaked into the grass. A hand lay near his feet, a big hand with a curving front knuckle and an oversized thumb.

His father's hand.

Diate had to swallow hard to keep his gorge down. He stepped around the hand, saw an arm, a leg, and finally the head, tossed casually beside the walk. He kept his gaze trained on the path in front of him. His father had to be the only one.

He mounted the steps, his toe shoes leaving bloody prints next to a series of other bloody prints. His sister was sprawled in her favorite chair, arms and legs wide, eyes open and empty.

He couldn't look at her. She was the reason it had all happened. Her father thought she had talent, and Diate never saw it. Never wanted to see it. He wanted to be the only Talent in the family.

The door stood open. Inside, the body of his mother was crumpled in a heap, the baby on top of her, its tiny neck turned at an odd angle. His brothers were holding sticks. They both had knives through the centers of their chests.

He had danced while they died. He had been dancing . . .

He sat up so fast that he hit his left arm on the rails beside the bed. His heart was pounding.

He had danced while they died. And what was dancing, but another form of making love?

Sheba.

The Golgoth.

The memories came back even though he didn't want them to.

He hated the darkness. He shoved one of the bed rails down, pushed the tray away, and got out of bed.

Dizziness so strong he had to brace himself against a table. He made himself take a deep breath, then crossed over to the door and groped until he found a light switch.

The light blinded him. He blinked, fell back, glad there were no more shadows. The room was simpler than he had thought, with a few chairs, a washbasin, a tray, and the bed. There was a window, but it was covered with a heavy cloth.

He was in the prison wing of the Recovery Center. The one reserved for special prisoners of the state. Kreske had taken Diate's advice. They were going to blame him. He would be banished, sent away from his second home.

This time at his own suggestion.

The door opened. The woman who had tended him before leaned in and blinked at the light. She gasped when she saw him.

'You're not supposed to be up.'

She put a strong arm around him and helped him back to the bed. He climbed between the cool sheets. It felt good to lie down. The trek across the room had exhausted him.

She brushed the hair off his forehead. 'Feeling better?'

He shook his head. After that dream, he was feeling worse.

She smiled. 'You have a lot more energy.'

With his good hand, he reached for the glass of water. She set it between his fingers and watched as he drank. 'You're waking up more frequently now,' she said. 'We'll be able to get more food down you, and maybe bring in some visitors.'

The water lubricated his dry throat. He didn't want visitors. He had had enough already.

She fluffed his pillow, and helped him lean back, taking the water from his hand and placing it on the tray. 'The doctor will be in in a little while. Why don't you get some rest –'

'No!' Diate sat up.

The woman moved out of his way, startled that he had spoken. 'Sleep is good for you,' she said. 'It helps you heal.'

He shook his head. His heart was pounding against his chest. He didn't want to go back to sleep. The dreams had turned ugly. If they showed him his family, they could show him even uglier memories.

He twisted away. The woman stood and rubbed her hands on her uniform. 'I'll get the doctor,' she said.

Her feet made clicking sounds on the floor. He didn't watch her walk away. He ran his right hand gingerly over the bandaging covering his left. Even the slightest touch left a slight burning sensation. The arm had been bandaged with white gauze and tape. A brown bloodstain marred the surface above the patch.

He flexed his fingers and they moved. Better than they had in those two days after Sheba left. Maybe he would get full range of motion back. He flexed them again, and winced as the pain grew worse. They didn't bend as far as he wanted them to. He leaned back, closed his eyes, then forced himself to open them.

No sleep. He couldn't sleep. Not with those dreams lurking in his subconscious.

His door opened. The surgeon who had operated on his arm came in. She wore a floor-length robe over her gray uniform. The robe trailed behind her and and made her look like she was flying.

'That's the last time I let you talk me into anything,' she said with a smile.

He smiled back, the old self peeking through. 'I'll talk you into anything I want.' His voice grated against his throat. It was clear he hadn't spoken in days.

Her smile grew. She sat on the side of the bed, one leg off the floor, and took his right wrist between her long fingers. 'Pulse is a little elevated. Durma said you had gotten out of bed. I'm pleased. You can start to move around a bit.' She set his arm down. 'Let me see the other one.'

He grimaced as he turned his left arm for her inspection.

'Hmm,' she said. 'That little movement hurts, huh? The bleeding is natural and not out of hand. We just have to change the bandage soon.'

She clasped her hands on her lap and looked at him. 'Durma says you haven't spoken in three days. When you said no a few minutes ago, you frightened her so badly she came and found me. Nightmares, detective? Is that why you don't want to sleep?'

Not nightmares so much as memories. Memories revisited, as vivid as if they were happening again.

'I can give you something so that you won't dream.'

'All right,' he said. He knew the fear was childish, knew that dreams couldn't hurt him.

249

She smiled and started to stand.

'Wait,' he said. 'How long have I been here?'

'Four days.' A small frown creased her forehead. 'We almost lost you that first day. Lots of hemorrhaging within the arm itself. I'm not sure what kind of use you'll regain. You may have to go somewhere where they specialize in repair. I did the best I could.'

He looked down at his injured hand and moved the fingers again. They twitched, but didn't really bend.

'After the bandages come off, we'll do some physical therapy with you, so that you can regain as much use of that arm as possible. I know you're not afraid of exercise. The more you do, the better the arm will get.'

'This is the prison section of the Recovery Center, isn't it?'

Her frown grew deeper. 'I tried to get you a good room in the center, but Kreske –'

'The Golgoth,' Diate corrected.

She nodded. 'He won't hear of it. As soon as you're well, he wants you out of this city. You won't be able to come back to Golga again.'

An ache flared in the center of his chest. Home. He had to leave home again. He rubbed a hand over his face. He was exhausted. He had made that suggestion to Kreske, and Kreske had taken him up on it. Diate had to play the traitor now. And he would, to keep everything here intact.

'I'm sorry,' she said. 'I personally don't think you did anything.'

He smiled, a sad little smile that barely curved his lips. 'I made a mistake. And some mistakes aren't forgivable, no matter what the cause.'

'I don't believe that.' She crossed her arms in front of her chest. 'I think you're blaming yourself for something that is not your fault. That little boy who thinks he's king is using you to absolve his own guilt.'

'That little boy,' Diate said softly, 'is king. And I don't think it's wise to talk about him that way.'

She nodded. 'I think it's almost time to leave the Port City. I have a hunch I won't be able to say many things I believe anymore.'

'Has Kreske made changes?'

She shook her head. 'Not yet. I've just watched the way he's treated you. The entire city knows you were raised as brothers. I have heard more people talk against Kreske, thinking that he's

250

treating you this way to get you away from him so there's no threat to his rule.'

Diate leaned back against the pillow. Exhaustion had hit him so hard he felt dizzy. 'I'm sure just as many think I planned this so that I could take over for the Golgoth when he died.'

She didn't answer, but her eyes flared a little. Surprise that he knew? Or something else? 'I'll send Durma in with some food and something to help you sleep.'

'I don't need help,' he said. 'Sleep comes.'

'But the dreams —'

'Are no less than I deserve.'

Candles burned all over the room, illuminating the tapestries on the wall. The one across from him, done in browns and reds, showed an assassin cutting off his father's head. The next, done in blues, showed the first man Diate had killed: A Kingdom smuggler who had assassinated a young girl. The tapestries progressed, each subject a death in his life, ending beside him with a silver and gold tapestry of the Queen, lying in a pool of her own blood.

The room smelled of candle wax, incense, and fear. It took a moment before he realized he was smelling himself.

A woman huddled in the corner, out of the flickering light. When she saw him, she crossed the room. Her feet were bare. A thin see-through gown flowed around her. Her recognized her even before he saw her face.

Sheba.

She carried a knife.

He sat cross-legged on a pillow, his detective's uniform brown with dried blood. She wasn't smiling as she walked toward him. The candles flickered, making the drawings on the tapestries seem like live things.

His family was dead.

But more Kingdom members had died at Diate's hands. Directly or indirectly. The Queen was only the last in a series.

Sheba held the knife by its hilt, arm upraised. She was going to kill him. He could stop her if he wanted. Two steps and she would be on her back, beneath him.

But he couldn't kill her. Even after everything, he couldn't hurt her. Not now. Not ever.

He gripped his ankles, leaned back, and closed his eyes. He held his breath. If he couldn't see her, couldn't smell her, his automatic reactions would be too late. He wouldn't be able to save himself.

'Open your eyes, Emilio,' she said. 'I need to look at you.'

The flickering candles reflected blue and green against his eyelids. His lungs ached for need of air.

'Emilio. Look at me.'

He opened his eyes –

– and she stood before him. Long hair flowing around her shoulders, hands clasped to her throat. She wore a long robe, covering everything except her head. The hood had fallen to her back, leaving her face open and vulnerable.

He struggled to sit up. Someone had turned out the light. The room had returned to its shadowy state. Only she had substance, as she stood at the edge of the bed, watching him sleep.

His arm ached, but he didn't care. Something inside him reached forward. 'Sheba.'

She smiled – or at least, he thought she did. She was hard to see in the dark. 'Emilio.'

He extended his good hand, wanting to pull her close. She ignored it, and sat on the edge of the bed, her slight weight barely making a dent. 'What are you doing here? They'll kill you if they find you.'

'They won't kill me.' Again that smile. He had missed her. He had thought she left him, left him to die.

'Yes, they will, if they know.'

'They won't know.'

Her smell, flowery and female, so distinctive, filled the room. 'What are you doing here?' he asked.

'I came to tell you to wait for me.'

He sat up, ignoring the dizziness in his body. 'You're not going to take me with you now?'

She shook her head. 'You're too weak, Emilio. They'd notice that you're missing. I have to do some things, and then I'll be back for you. I'll take you home.'

His vision blurred for a moment. He blinked, trying to clear it. He looked down. Something wet fell on his fingers. He wiped them against the sheet. He could go with her, couldn't he? That would still save Kreske, still prove that Diate was a traitor, still help Golga. And he would have a place to live. A home. 'I'd like to go now,' he said.

'Wait,' she said. 'It will be safer soon. I'll be back when you're better.'

She stood. He reached for her again, but she ducked out of his grasp. 'Let me hold you,' he said.

She shook her head. 'There's no time. I can't stay any longer. Just remember: I'll be back. I love you, Emilio.'

The words felt like a blessing. 'I love you, too,' he said.

She nodded once, and pulled the door open. He touched his bad arm, letting the pain roll through him. He was awake, and she had been in his room. She had gotten past the guards somehow, past all of them, risked her own life to find him. She hadn't abandoned him after all.

She would come back for him –

And he would be free.

Chapter 21

The smell of food woke him: sweet sauces and fresh-baked bread; the slightly bitter tang of hot cereal. He opened his eyes and saw a tray heaped with steaming bowls, each filled with a different delicacy.

Durma, the nurse who had been tending him, opened the curtain covering the window. Bright sunlight flooded the room. She smiled. Her face was almost pretty in the full light.

'We weren't sure what you liked, so we decided to try everything. It gets billed to the palace. They'll never notice.'

He pulled the tray closer. His hand was shaking with hunger. He broke a piece of bread and dipped it in one of the sweet sauces. The mixture of textures made his mouth water more.

'You never did this before,' he said.

'You never smiled at me before,' she replied.

For a moment, he lost his orientation. He hadn't smiled at her. Had he mistaken her for Sheba? Had Sheba not been in his room, after all?

He forced himself to eat slowly, remembering how awful food felt in an empty stomach.

'I'm glad that the dreams have eased,' she said.

But they hadn't. Sheba had been so real, and his reaction was not what he had expected. He had wanted to go with her. He had begged her to take him, and she had refused. He should never have wanted her. He should hate her for what she had done.

All he had wanted to do was hold her. He had wanted that so badly his body still ached.

'The arm still hurts,' he said.

'It will, for a while. It's not healing as quickly as we had expected.'

He finished the bread and the sweet sauce, and started on the hot cereal. A glass of water sat at the edge of the tray. He drank, letting its coolness prevent the tastes from mixing.

'You have a visitor this morning, if you're up to it.'

He stopped eating. A visitor? In this wing? It would have to be someone with clearance. Someone like Scio or Kreske.

His muscles tightened. He didn't want to see them after that dream. He felt as if he had betrayed them by still caring for Sheba. He forced himself to relax. 'I'm up for it,' he said.

She hovered near his tray. 'Are you finished?'

He took his water glass off and nodded. She picked up the tray and carried it to the door. 'I'll send your visitor right in,' she said.

He cradled the water glass in his good hand. He needed to talk to Kreske. Diate wanted to know how things were progressing, what the national reaction was to his attempt at a coup.

The door opened and Beltar walked it. He wore satiny red robes that swirled around his red slippers. The jewels on his fingers winked in the light.

Diate's breath caught in his throat. He thought he would never see Beltar again.

The door swung closed. 'They say you're a traitor,' Beltar said. He stayed near the wall, hands clasped in front of him. 'They say you killed the Golgoth.'

Diate braced the water glass on his leg. The glass's coolness radiated through the sheet. His body was tense. 'What do you say?'

'You loved the Golgoth.'

Diate looked down. The glass was half-full and smudged with his fingerprints. 'People kill people they love.'

Beltar shook his head. 'Not you.'

'How can you be sure?'

'Because I know you.'

Diate's grip tightened on the glass. 'People never really know each other.'

'I realized that,' Beltar said, 'when I saw you dance. I thought you had given that up.'

'I have danced every morning for my entire life,' Diate said.

Beltar bit his lower lip. 'I guess I don't know you then.'

'So you are wondering if I really killed the Golgoth.'

Beltar looked away. Loyal friends didn't mistrust the people they loved. Diate knew that even speaking of this went against Beltar's code. 'I think about it all the time,' Beltar said. 'I think about the warning you gave me, how you were going to work

255

closely with the Kingdom and how I needed to protect Martina, and then I think about watching you dance, and the way you held that woman afterwards –'

'Sheba,' Diate said quietly.

'Sheba. And I knew you told me you were going to do something you didn't want to. Something the Golgoth had asked you to do. I assumed it was the dance, until the Golgoth died and they blamed you. Did she make you do something you didn't want to do? Sometimes I think that's what happened. Then I think that you knew all along what was going on.' Beltar took a step forward. 'They say you're a traitor, Emilio. I don't even know how to defend you.'

Diate squeezed the glass. It made a small sound. 'You're not supposed to defend me.'

Beltar sighed. 'Just tell me what happened. You owe me that much.'

The words made Diate stiffen. He wasn't sure he could talk about this, but he had to. He did owe Beltar. Beltar had been his friend for nearly a decade. They had worked together. He had taken care of Diate's possessions, helped with Martina. He had always been there. A shoulder to lean on, someone to laugh with.

Diate set the glass on the tray beside the bed. 'You remember what I told you, how the Golgoth wanted me to convince her I would leave with her?'

'Yes. You said you weren't sure it would work. You said she might be using you.'

Diate nodded. 'It looks now like she was. She disappeared when the Golgoth died. Only my sources say she wanted me with her. So I don't know what to believe.'

Beltar sat down heavily in the chair. 'You set this coup business up. You want us all to think you betrayed us.'

Diate leaned against the pillows. 'We can't go to war with the Kingdom. Not now. Not with Kreske so new. If people think I tried to kill the Golgoth, they'll be less likely to demand military action against the Kigndom.'

'There've been people out in the streets, calling for your execution.'

Diate closed his eyes. He hadn't wanted to know that. 'Is it affecting you? People knew we were friends.'

'No one has said anything. I have kept my shop closed.'

That was the wrong thing to do. Diate opened his eyes again. 'You can't be involved in this. You need to stay clean. You have to go back and tell people about me and Sheba in Rulanda, how you stopped being my friend after that, when it became clear she was from the Kingdom.'

'I can't betray you, my friend.'

'You won't be,' Diate said. 'You'll be protecting yourself, and Martina.' He had to think things through. This might be the only chance he got to talk with Beltar. 'Kreske is going to banish me. I will never be able to come back here. But I don't want anything to happen to you. I may need you, Beltar.'

'You can't come back?' Beltar said.

'No.' Diate made himself smile. 'But you were right about a job. It looks as if I'll need one, if you want an assistant who knows nothing about wine.'

'Much easier to train,' Beltar said with an answering smile. The smile faded quickly. 'But it's not so easy, is it? We can't just have you work for me.'

'I'm not sure what I'm going to do yet,' Diate said. 'I might work for Scio. But I wanted to warn you. I may need your help, my friend.'

'You will always have it,' Beltar said.

They stared at each other for a moment, then Beltar walked to the side of the bed and took Diate's good hand. Beltar's fingers were warm and moist. 'I knew there was more to it. The official version says you masterminded the plan. Martina refused to believe it. She heard – well. It doesn't matter what she heard.'

Diate frowned. 'How could she hear anything? Did she leave her rooms?'

'Since you've been here, she's gone out everyday, trying to get news.'

Diate tried to imagine her on the streets, a slender crippled woman who looked three times older than her years. Did people look on her with pity? Or cast their eyes away from her deformities? 'What did she hear?'

'That you didn't care if you lived anymore. That you would never recover because you wanted to die.'

Diate leaned back in the pillows. Kreske and Scio were doing a good job. They were covering themselves in case he died in the Recovery Center. 'What did she think of that?'

257

'She's frightened for you, Emilio. She –' Beltar sighed. 'She loves you.'

Diate swallowed. He hadn't noticed. But it made sense. All that concern, all those light touches. Hearing that he had been with Sheba must have destroyed Martina. Thinking that he was betraying not just the country, but her with another woman. 'I never promised her anything,' he said.

'She knows.' Beltar let Diate's hand drop. 'She figured a man like you needed someone beautiful. And she knew she wasn't beautiful, at least not in that way. I guess sometimes we can't see beyond ourselves, can we? I think she's beautiful. But she doesn't care about me.'

'I'm sorry, Beltar,' Diate said softly.

He shrugged. 'It really has little to do with you. I know that you didn't lead her on, any more than I made my intentions clear. And I can't do that now, not with the way she's thinking about you. She wants you free, Emilio.'

'Is that why you're here?'

Beltar shook his head. 'I needed to know. I haven't been able to sleep. Every time I close my eyes, I see you dance for that woman. I see that paint on your face. I was wondering how I couldn't know a man like you – a man I had spent years with, talking about the things that concerned us, night after night.' He was silent for a moment. Then he asked, 'You going to keep that tear forever?'

Diate touched his cheek. He could feel nothing out of place. 'It's still there?'

'Yeah.'

The dye must have soaked in. Like a small tattoo, a brand. Perhaps he had used the wrong paint. Perhaps it was like the caste mark, something that would never come off.

'It should be gone by now.'

'It makes you look young,' Beltar said.

'I'm not young,' Diate said. He had never felt so old in his life. Old, tired, defeated. 'What would you have done if I really had betrayed the Golgoth?'

'I don't know,' Beltar said. 'I'm thankful that you didn't.'

He screamed, clawed his way out of a nightmare. The sheets were twisted against his legs, chafing his bruises. The bed felt too soft. He could stretch out. He was no longer cramped, no longer trapped.

He was in Golga. He had been there a week.

A light went on, revealing a bald man in long, flowing robes. He came into the room and sat on the edge of the bed. 'Are you all right?'

Diate nodded. He didn't want this man to know he had nightmares. He didn't want the man to know he had any weaknesses at all.

'Sounded like a particularly bad dream. Want to talk about it?'

'No,' Diate said. The word sounded too sullen. He couldn't sound sullen. The Golgoth would make him leave.

'Nightmares come from things we repress,' the Golgoth said. 'Talking about them makes the dreams go away.'

'My mother,' Diate blurted before he could stop himself. 'I dreamed I saw them kill her. They – They –'

He couldn't get the words out. Something choked him. He blinked and tears ran down his cheeks.

'They –'

Suddenly he was wrapped in big, strong arms. The Golgoth's robes were made of velvet. They smelled of wood smoke. The Golgoth rubbed Diate's back, making small nonsense sounds as he rocked him back and forth.

Great choking sobs racked Diate. He couldn't stop them, even though he tried. Every time he tried to hold back a sob, another came out, even stronger, even louder. All the pain and fear of the last few weeks shuddered through his body and found safety in the Golgoth's arms.

The man his mother had once told him was a killer.

No one was as he seemed. The whole world had turned around, changed, when he wasn't looking.

Finally, the sobs subsided. Diate could breathe again without the breath hitching in his throat. 'Sorry,' he said. His voice rasped.

'Don't be sorry.' The Golgoth stroked his hair, and didn't let go of Diate even though he had stopped crying. 'I've been waiting for this. You can't go on forever pretending to be strong. No one is that strong, Emilio. No one.'

Something woke him. He didn't open his eyes. He wanted the dream to return. He wanted the Golgoth to return. The Golgoth would live in his dreams.

A click signaled the door closing. Diate finally opened his eyes. The gray room had more shadows than usual. A hooded figure stood by the door. As he watched, two hands came up and pushed the hood back.

Sheba.

She was real then. The lift her presence gave him was real too.

259

'I didn't expect you back so soon,' he said.

'I couldn't stay away.' Her voice was soft, delicate. Her scent teased him.

'I've been wondering if you're a dream.'

'No, no dream.' The robe made her look as if she floated across the room.

'Where are you staying?'

'In the city. With friends.'

The memory of the Golgoth's arms still held him. He had tears buried inside now too. He wanted her to touch him. He wanted to hold her, to forget everything. 'Sheba, how are you going to get me out of here?'

'We're working on that,' she said. 'In the ports probably. People there will help me.'

As they had helped her before. The ports were always a little untrustworthy. No wonder the Golgoth's father had wanted to close them. The ports caused too many problems for Golga. Now Diate was going to be another of those problems.

'We don't have to do anything secret,' Diate said. 'Kreske will probably send me off in some ship. Any place we'll land will have transport to the Kingdom.'

'That might be better. I haven't worked out all the details.'

'You shouldn't be here,' he said again, the pleasure seeping into his voice. 'We can't do any of this if they catch you.'

She didn't sit down on the bed. She stood beside it, head bowed. 'You're not angry with me, Emilio? For setting you up?'

'You being here shows me that you didn't do it. You didn't know any more than I did. Sheba, what we have will get us through anything.'

'You thought I was gone for good. You thought I was never coming back.'

'I was wrong.' His voice echoed in the silence. 'Come sit beside me. I want to hold you.'

She shook her head.

He frowned. Something was odd. She had not refused his touch before the Golgoth died, and now she had done it twice. He held out his hand. 'Please. Let's forget the past, start over, make everything new. Please.'

She pulled her cloak tighter. 'I should go. I just wanted to see how you were doing.'

260

He reached for her, grabbed her wrist, and pulled her forward. Her skin felt coarse. It had ridges where it should have been smooth. He slid his hand up, took hers, and immediately dropped it. Her fingers were bony, sharp, and curved. Like a claw. Like Martina's fingers.

The hand that fell to her side was curved and fire-scarred. The hood fell back from her face, revealing black hair and a face with rigid immobile skin. Fire-scarred.

Martina.

'What —'

'I'm sorry,' she said. 'I knew you loved her.'

He sprang out of bed with an energy he didn't know he had. He gripped her shoulder with his good hand and pushed her back against the wall, holding her there. 'You knew I loved her. What were you trying to do, find out how much? Were you spying on me? Trying to see how far I would go?'

'No.' Her voice remained level, although her eyes had a wildness to them.

'What then?' He shook her once, careful not to bang her head against the wall. He wanted her to answer questions first.

'They said you were dying. They said you didn't want to live anymore. I thought if you knew she loved you, you might feel better. I thought —'

'You thought.' He kept his voice low. 'You thought I would fall for it.'

'You did,' she said, and cringed. He let her go. His left arm throbbed.

'How could you do that? I thought you were a music Talent.'

'I was,' she said, rubbing her shoulder with the heel of one hand. 'I told you there was magic in my background.'

'But you let me think you couldn't use it. How else have you lied to me, Martina?'

'I haven't lied.'

He whirled, facing her, his jaw set, eyes fierce. 'You're a magic Talent. You lied.'

'I didn't tell you everything, that's all.'

'What else didn't you tell me?'

'Nothing!'

'Is this what Torrie meant when she said she was glad you were working for them now?'

'Torrie?' Martina's face had gone pale. 'When did you see Torrie?'

'In Rulanda. She said she was happy you were alive, and finally working for them.'

Martina took in a deep breath. 'You didn't tell me.'

'I was afraid I'd scare you. I could keep the Kingdom away.'

Martina shook her head. 'No. You can't. She wasn't talking about the Kingdom. She was talking about the Rebels. They're trying to use you. They wanted me to manipulate you. They're all trying to use you.'

'Use me? What aren't you telling me?' He grabbed her arm, digging his fingers into her flesh.

'The Diate Rebels. They want you to lead them. They thought that if you felt betrayed you'd come back.'

'I feel betrayed, Martina.

'Stay away from the Rebels, Emilio. They only want to use you.'

'And you've been helping them?'

'I told you. I ran away from them. I hate them, Emilio. Please. You're hurting me.'

He let go. 'You lied to me.'

'No,' she said. 'Even about that, I told you what I thought you needed to know.'

'You didn't tell me you could shape-shift.'

'I can't!' Her voice rose. 'It's just an illusion that breaks with touch. That's why I don't go out in public. One person brushes against me in a crowd, and I change back. It's not like a shifting. I'm not that good.'

'You fooled me.' He sat down on the edge of the bed, feeling as if she had kicked him in the stomach. 'It fooled me.'

'But I was right,' she said. 'When you thought you were with Sheba, you were happier. You were getting better. If only you hadn't touched me.'

He let out a small laugh. 'Now it's my fault. You tricked me, I failed, and that's *my* fault?'

'No.' She bowed her head. 'I just thought if it could keep going for a while, then maybe you'd get better on your own.'

He looked away from her. He couldn't see that small frame in clothes he had thought belonged to Sheba. 'And you didn't think about what discovering you would do to me? I thought she had come back for me, Martina.'

'I know.' The words had such sadness that they almost sounded like a wail.

'She used me and abandoned me.' He let himself fall crosswise on the bed. 'You weren't the only one who fooled me, Martina. I've been a fool all along.'

'You couldn't have known,' she said. 'You loved her.'

'And that excuses everything? It excuses my mistakes? The Golgoth's death?' It hurt to speak. Something knotted his throat. His breath was coming in small gasps. He smiled wryly. 'I guess it does. If love excuses me, then it excuses you. What did you think, that you would get good enough so that I could make love to you as Sheba? Maybe you should have asked. Maybe I was desperate enough to have sex with you.'

'Stop it!'

'Maybe I would have felt enough pity to make the experience even pleasurable.'

'Stop it!'

'Hell, maybe I like fucking crippled women –'

'*Stop it!*'

His body was shaking. He couldn't believe the words had come out of him. He couldn't believe he thought them, let alone said them. But they hung in the air, and he was angry. Too angry to take them back.

'I was just trying to help you, Emilio.'

'You never thought this through, did you?' he said. 'Maybe I cared about you enough that having you here, as you, would have made all the difference.'

Her breath came in large, choking sobs. He made no effort to go to her. He didn't want her near him. He wanted her to leave.

The room still smelled of Sheba. Martina must have made some kind of perfume that mimicked Sheba's odor. Even that was false.

The door opened and the light came on. Diate sat up. Durma, the nurse, blocked Martina's exit. 'You're not supposed to be here,' Durma said. 'How did you get in?'

Martina licked her lips, and wiped the tears off her cheeks with the back of her hand.

'Show her,' Diate said. 'Show her how you got in.'

Martina glanced at him, her twisted hand still blocking her face.

'Show her,' he said as he stood up. 'Or I'll make you show her.'

Martina took a deep breath and then ran a hand down her entire

263

length. The air shimmered for a moment, and when it cleared, the surgeon stood before them, wrapped in a brown cloak.

'She's a magic Talent,' Diate said.

'The Kingdom.' Durma's voice held shock. She grabbed Martina's arm, and the air shimmered again. Martina returned. 'I'll take her from here. She won't harm you, detective.'

He walked over to them, and looked down at Martina. She bit her lower lip and stared at him. 'I could just let her take you,' Diate said. 'They would try you as a member of the Kingdom. They would figure you were here to kill me.'

Martina didn't move. Her eyes grew wider.

'But I won't do that.' He looked at Durma. 'She lives in Golga. She was under my protection. She came to the Center on a misguided mission to save my life. She startled me, and I nearly killed her. I'm not really happy about the entire incident, but when I calm down, I probably will feel the necessary gratitude.'

'What do you want me to do?' Durma asked. Her grip on Martina's arm had tightened visibly.

'Just let her go. And make sure no one comes to my room without being touched first.'

'No report, nothing?'

Diate shook his head. 'She thought she was helping me.'

'I was helping you,' Martina said.

Durma shook her. 'Enough. You can come with me.'

Martina put her free hand on Diate's good arm. 'Please. Forgive me.'

The smile that curved his lips didn't feel like his own. 'You don't know what you've done,' he said. He faced Durma. 'I don't want to see her again.'

He turned his back on them and walked back to the bed. It had never looked so inviting. He crawled beneath the sheets and pulled them over his body. His arm ached so badly that he checked it to make sure it wasn't bleeding again.

The door clicked. He glanced over. They were gone.

He felt a curious kind of emptiness. Maybe he should have let Martina stay. She had meant no harm. She had tried to help him.

Or so she said.

He leaned back against the pillows, sinking into their softness. It didn't matter. Kreske would banish him anyway. Diate was an exile.

An exhaustion rose from within him. He had thought that Sheba might have been a dream. But he had been hoping she wasn't. Martina was right; he needed something, someone. Martina had offered, but he had turned her away.

He closed his eyes, saw himself get off the bed and pin her to the wall. Just a bit more anger, just a little more loss of control, and he would have slammed her to death as he had done the Queen.

Martina hadn't deserved it.

But Sheba did.

He was angry at her for not being Sheba, but not angry enough to kill her.

Sheba was the one who had hurt him. Sheba was the one who deserved his hatred, not Martina. Sheba had betrayed him.

Or had she? Or had she been a victim as he was? Maybe she had planned part of it, but thought that Diate would be with her. She had looked confused when he ran out of the Pavilion. Maybe her confusion was fear.

Maybe she knew then that she had lost him.

Maybe she knew that he was going to die.

In that case, she could have done nothing to save him.

In that case, they both lost.

His body felt like a coiled spring. He ran, leapt, flipped twice, and landed, one foot back, the other beneath, braced. His breath came in small gasps. He had never done so well.

Myla left her position near the wall, her hands crossed in front of her thin chest. She got on the mat without taking off her shoes. The other students watched from the chairs lined up beneath the observation window.

'You didn't tuck,' she said.

'I did too.'

She put a finger to his nose, pressing hard. He wanted to turn away, but didn't. 'You didn't tuck. The flips were sloppy.'

'I landed square.'

'Doesn't matter when the flips are sloppy. Again.'

He made himself take deep breaths. 'I don't want to. It felt right.'

'Then you're learning it wrong. If wrong feels right, I am not teaching you.'

He was nearly as tall as she was now. Once he had thought her so big, so domineering. 'I did it right.'

She put her hands on his shoulders, fingers digging into his skin. 'You

265

have been determined class A. It is a ranking, a way so that the marketeers can sell your performances. It means you are good. It doesn't mean you are perfect.'

'You weren't class A.'

'That's right.' She let go of him, a small smile playing at her lips. 'They didn't have rankings in my day. But I still hold the record, Emilio. More people came to see me dance than any other performer in the history of this country. That means something.'

'It doesn't mean you were good. Just popular.'

Her smile broke into a laugh. 'I am sorry. But you have lived here all your life and you believe that? You are seriously misled, Emilio. Popular does not bring in crowds year after year.'

'If you're that good, why aren't you still dancing? Why aren't you competing against people like me?'

Her smile faded. 'I am too old, Emilio. The dance is unforgiving. All your life it stretches your body, pains you, makes demands you can't fulfill, and just when you understand it, it goes away. The body doesn't work any more.'

It was nearly dawn. A gray light had filtered into his room, marking everything in shadow. He had come awake suddenly, with the feeling that he was not alone.

After a moment, his eyes adjusted. A woman stood near the window. She was small and lithe, her slight movements graceful, her tawny hair pulled back away from her face.

He sighed, and rubbed a hand over his face. 'I thought I told you to leave, Martina.'

She turned. She wore simple leggings, and an open, ruffled blouse. A cloak draped over a chair. 'I'm not Martina.'

His breath stopped in his throat. Her voice was right. The inflection was right. It made him realize how far off Martina's illusion had been. Still, this could be simply a better version.

'Prove it,' he said. 'Come over here.'

She did, moving slowly, as if she were approaching a child. When she got within reaching distance of his right arm, he grabbed her and pulled her forward.

Her skin felt soft. She didn't change or vanish. She sprawled along the bed, her body brushing against his, her scent enveloping him. For a moment, just a moment, he allowed himself to breathe the sweet fragrance of her. Then he pushed her away.

'How did you get here?'

Sheba picked herself off the edge of the bed and brushed off her clothes. Her hands were trembling. 'We don't use the ports,' she said. 'We never have. And this area of the Recovery Center is very poorly guarded for a prison section.'

Scio hadn't thought he needed guards on Diate. Diate would have to correct him from now on. Catching the Queen of the Kingdom would have been a very big coup.

'You used the ports during the Festival. After you killed the Golgoth.'

She brushed the hair off her face. 'The shuttle port was convenient, and poorly watched that day,' she said. 'We needed to leave in a hurry.'

His heart was pounding against his chest. He pushed himself up against the pillows, conscious that he hadn't bathed in days, that his hair stuck up and he was unnaturally thin. 'Oh, yes,' he said. 'I forgot. You had a rally to attend, didn't you?'

'You sound bitter.'

'Bitter? What reason do I have to be bitter? You used me to help you murder a man I loved. That's not cause to be bitter.'

'I didn't kill him,' she said quietly.

'No. Your predecessor did, with your help. Nice move. Did you give her the gloves directly or did you have your brother do it?'

'Tonio acted without my knowledge,' she said.

Diate nodded. He wanted to believe her. 'That's why you allowed him to take you away after I had asked you to wait. That's why you greeted the crowd so easily. That's why we had one day – and one important night – together. Great alibi you had. The chief of the Port City's detectives. "We were together the whole time, gentlemen. I couldn't have laced the Queen's gloves with poison." '

Sheba's hands were clasped tightly in her lap. 'What choice did I have, Emilio? What Tonio had done was to ensure her death. If I didn't return to the Kingdom, I would have lost my chance at ruling. Someone else would have returned before me. Someone else would have taken over.'

'And that's important?'

'Of course!' She stood up. 'But so are you. I can't leave you here.'

'Or were you just feeling guilty because they want to kill me for your crime?'

She moved closer to the rail beside the bed. The half-light caught her face, placing shadows along her delicate nose, adding depth to her eyes. 'I came back,' she said, 'because I want you beside me, Emilio.'

'As what?' he asked. 'Another assassin?'

She shook her head. 'I want you to dance for me. You're still the best. You proved that. You have a few years left. You can finally achieve your destiny. You can dance for the Kingdom.'

He closed his eyes.

You're a great Talent, Emilio. An asset. Valued more than anyone.

They wanted me to dance for them, even though they had killed my family. As if it hadn't mattered. As if it hadn't mattered at all.

'What would I get from this?' he asked.

'Your life, for one thing,' Sheba said. 'You did me a great favor. We would also be together, Emilio. More nights like the one we shared.'

Like the one when the Golgoth died. 'No,' he said. He opened his eyes. 'No.'

He pulled back the covers and stood up. She didn't understand. She wanted to use him, just like the Kingdom had always wanted to use him. She *had* used him, and destroyed his second family, his second home. He could never forgive her for that.

'Get out,' he said. 'Get out before I call someone.'

She backed away from him. 'I thought we cared about each other,' she said. 'I thought we actually meant something.'

'We did.' He paced with her, length for length, backing her toward the door. 'That's why I'm giving you a chance to get out. Against my better judgment. You should die for the things you've done, Sheba.'

'Emilio,' she said, her hands up, 'you don't know what you're saying. I'm offering you life –'

'You're offering me a living hell. I've turned down this offer before, Sheba. You live in an evil place. You don't even see that what you've done is wrong. You don't even understand how much destruction you've caused.'

He had backed her against the door. She grasped the handle with both of her hands. 'No,' she said. '*You* don't see. This is how things are. The Kingdom stands for beauty and art, and you are part of that.'

'And murder.'

'She wasn't doing her job. Tonio did us both a favor, Emilio.'

'I don't care about her,' he said. His face was inches from Sheba's. If he wanted to, he could put his hands around her neck and squeeze until she was dead. But he didn't want to. He couldn't. He couldn't bring himself to touch her. 'In killing him, you sacrificed the one human being who had a real reason to destroy me, and who didn't. You have no understanding of what caring is, Sheba, and you never will.'

'Emilio –'

'Now get out.'

She reached for him. He dodged out of her way.

'Get out!'

She pulled open the door. 'You will always have a home with me,' she said.

'Get out,' he said.

She slipped into the hallway and pulled the door closed behind her. He leaned against it. He should call Kreske. He should call Scio. He should call for help, to prevent Sheba from leaving.

But what if she was right? What if Carbete had been the only one behind the plot?

It didn't matter. She still didn't understand. The Kingdom had destroyed his family twice, and twice had asked for his dancing in return. The Kingdom didn't stand for beauty and art. It stood for destruction and murder.

And no matter who led it, no matter who was in charge, things would always remain the same.

The problem wasn't the Queen. It wasn't Sheba. It was the Kingdom itself.

'I can't go with you, Sheba,' he whispered to the closed door. 'But I can make life better. For both of us.'

PART FOUR

One Year Later

Chapter 22

The heat shimmered. Diate pulled his surba farther over his head. His bald scalp itched with sweat. He missed his hair, but hair itched worse. All those years the Golgoth had wanted Diate to shave his head, and Diate had refused. Now that he was alone, he had done the Golgoth's bidding.

He hated irony.

Dust rose behind two overweight horses blocking the narrow street. People pressed against the mud walls of the buildings, trying to let the horses pass. The town smelled of dung and horse piss. Most of Ziklag smelled that way. Maybe things were cleaner in some of the other towns, but he doubted it. He doubted his source, too. No rebel in his right mind would stay in this country any longer than he had to.

Primitive, backward, close-minded. He had had to bed down in a stable the night before because his papers showed he was not native. Just as well. His money was running low, and no one in this smelly town would hire him for an odd job or two.

Not native. He was beginning to hate that phrase.

The sun reflected off the white garments, the brown buildings, the brown street. Only the horses, black and sweat-covered, seemed to absorb the heat.

The horses and Diate.

He pulled a kerchief out of his pocket and wiped his face. The kerchief came away dirty. At least the clothing was loose-fitting here, even if state requirements meant that all skin but the face, hands, and feet had to be covered.

Sheba would never last here. No one from the Kingdom would.

His source had to be wrong. Rebels would never come here, not even to escape the killing oppression Sheba's predecessor had imposed.

The horse in front of him raised its tail. He had learned enough to get as far away as possible when that happened. He turned down a side street.

A bit of shade covered the narrow walkway. He stopped to catch his breath. The kerchief was in his left hand. He squeezed three times, practicing as the doctors on Oleon had taught him. For the rest of his life, he had to exercise those fingers or they would lock up, like Martina's had.

Martina. Her name still brought up a bit of guilt. He had never seen her again, never had a chance to apologize. Beltar had promised to take a message to her, but Diate never heard if she had a reply. Probably a nasty one. Knowing Beltar, he hadn't wanted to repeat it.

At least Beltar had forgiven Diate those remarks, and had gone on to finance this campaign. Maybe, by the end of it, Martina would forgive him too. He had that to hope for.

But this was real. This was now.

In the distance, he heard a voice in the lilting cadence that he had come to recognize as a merchant hawking wares. He followed the sound, rounded two more corners, and found an open-air market. Men leaned over heaped tables, reaching for and cajoling passersby. The women sat on chairs behind the men, handing extra merchandise or money if the men needed it, saying nothing. Remaining invisible.

Diate had tried to speak to one of those women once. The men in the market had clubbed him and thrown him out of town. He never spoke to another woman again.

The tables were close together. Someone had stretched a thin, hole-filled canopy overhead in a vain attempt to keep out the sun. Diate passed table after table, looking at the soft, overripe fruit, the rancid meat, the bug-infested flour. Only the bread looked good. It smelled even better. The sun, falling on the loaves, released their scent, and that side of the market carried the odor of freshly baked bread.

'I will take one,' he said in his pidgin Ziklan.

The merchant held a dirty hand over the smallest loaf. Diate shook his head and indicated a larger loaf, near the front. It looked fresher. The merchant quoted a price and Diate dickered until the price was nearer to what he had paid in other towns along the coast. As he counted out the coins, the merchant touched his eyes.

'Kingdom,' the merchant said.

Diate squinted. The heat was making him tired, and he didn't understand the language very well. He brought a hand up to his own eye, touching the faded tear. 'Me?'

The merchant nodded. He spoke quickly. Diate only caught a few words. Kingdom and money.

'Please,' Diate said. 'Speak slower.'

'You might like more bread,' the man said. He enunciated clearly and spoke a bit louder, as if Diate were deaf as well as unable to understand the language. 'You are from the Kingdom. You must have extra money.'

Diate's breath stopped in his throat. He had never associated the Kingdom with money. He had always associated them with poverty. But the man had had some experience that led him to believe Kingdom members were rich.

'Yes,' Diate said. 'I am from the Kingdom. I am looking for some friends of mine. Have you seen other people from the Kingdom here?'

The woman behind the man touched his white trousers. He glanced at her. She shook her head, once, then looked down. The man pulled her hand from his leg.

Again he spoke too fast. Seeing Diate's confusion, the man slowed down. 'I have seen some. They buy a great deal of my bread. They said nothing about friends.'

'Have they said anything?' Diate had to translate the words as he spoke them. He wished he had a better command of the language so that he could ask sharper questions.

'They ask why bread is so costly,' the man said, and laughed.

Diate smiled. His heart was pounding. This was the closest he had come in months of travel. 'Do you know where they live?'

A hand took his arm. Diate looked down to see a young man beside him. The young man wore the white clothes of Ziklag, but instead of a surba, a thin gauze hood covered his head. Through the left side. Diate saw a red dot on the young man's temple. He was from the Kingdom. He was a Trader.

'We have been waiting for you, my brother. You are late,' the young man said in Ziklan. His voice still had musical tones of a boy. Then, in Lillish: 'Let's get away from here.'

'I am sorry,' Diate said in Ziklan. He let the boy lead him away. The merchant watched, hands on his hips. The boy hurried him to a side street and let go of his arm.

275

They were alone. The backs of mud-caked buildings surrounded them: no windows, no doors, no shade.

'What's your business?' the boy said in Lillish. His voice had taken on a rougher edge.

'I travel alone.'

The boy laughed. 'No one travels alone. Try again.'

Diate pulled off his surba, revealing his shaved head and his caste mark. 'I danced. Then I got injured and sent to Oleon. When they were done, they said I would never dance again. I kept my earnings, and have wandered the few months since. I don't want to go back. I don't know what they'll do.'

The boy ran a finger along the caste mark, then touched the tear that still decorated Diate's eye. As the boy looked up, Diate saw that a web of lines graced his face. He was older than Diate had thought. The boy took a step back. Dainty. Small-boned.

Female.

'No one comes here,' she said.

'You have. I have.'

'You were asking after us.'

Diate replaced his surba, bringing it low over his forehead. Sweat ran down the back of his neck. 'The man mentioned the Kingdom. I thought it might be that some others were here.'

She smiled. Her lips were thin and chapped from the heat. 'Who do you work for?'

'No one.'

She grabbed his arm and pushed up the white sleeve. His scar appeared, red, puckered, and ugly. She ran a finger along it. He winced at the pain. 'How does a man get this kind of injury dancing? Did you fall into a fence?'

'I fell into a party of assassins who didn't like the fact that I was investigating their Hoste glass collection.'

'Hoste glass.' She pressed on the scar and nodded when he grimaced. 'Hoste glass requires a patch like they use in Golga?'

He was holding his breath. He let it out slowly. 'No,' he said. She was too smart. She had caught him. 'Working for the Golgoth requires a patch. At least it did a year ago, when he died.'

She let his arm drop. His sleeve fell to his wrist, making the skin prickle. She licked her finger and wiped at his tattoo. Her fingers smelled of grapes. 'It's permanent.'

He nodded. 'I was a dancer. A class A Talent once. My family was murdered and I was forced to leave the Kingdom. A Vorgellian smuggled me to Golga, and the Golgoth made me his project, until he was murdered. Then his son kicked me out.'

'A class A dancer whose family was murdered.' She laughed. A man standing across the street looked up at the sound. She put her hand over her mouth. 'You are as priceless as Hoste glass, and nowhere near as intelligent. I didn't believe the story about the glass. I certainly won't believe that you're the son of Emilio Diate, the poet and rebel.'

Diate's breath caught in his throat. The trail of sweat running down his back itched. He hadn't expected to find the rebels he was searching for on the street of this small town. 'You may believe whatever you want,' he said. 'But you're the one who noticed the Golgan patch scar. How would a class A Talent get one of those?'

The man across the street adjusted his surba and took a few steps closer. The woman glanced at him, and sighed. 'Come with me,' she said.

They hurried down the street to a crossroads, then took two side streets. Here, the mud-brick buildings were cracked and hole-covered. Young children sat outside, listless in the heat. Small black insects Diate couldn't identify buzzed around their faces, but they did not brush them away. He reached in his pocket to toss them a coin, but the woman grabbed his hand.

'Don't call attention to yourself.'

She led him inside one of the buildings. The coolness was welcome after the afternoon's heat. The room was dark. Blankets covered the dirt floor, and a cracked water pitcher stood on the only table. She led him up two stairs into an even smaller room, with a cot and two chairs. The room had no windows, only the cloth-covered door.

'Wait here,' she said.

She pulled off her gauze shirt and white leggings, grabbing a black dress from the bed. Beneath the clothing she wore nothing, except a band of cloth binding her breasts. Her legs were thin and slender, her pubic hair a dark red. She unwound the cloth covering her breasts and slid the black dress on. Then she put on a woman's cap and veil and glided from the room, a different person entirely.

Her casualness convinced him where the caste mark had not. No woman from this land could have such ease with her body. He gripped his hands together and held tightly. The man had been watching her, expecting something, and she had felt it necessary to fool him.

Outside he heard footsteps. He held his breath. Any place else he would have heard conversation, but not here. Women and children had to remain invisible. To speak to them was the greatest of public sins.

Someday he would learn the history of these traditions, beyond the simple explanation the ship's captain had given him. *Religious nuts*, she had said. *I can't even leave the ship. You're on your own, detective.*

A rustling in the front room told him that someone had entered the building. He held his breath, willing himself to remain motionless. In the time he had been here, he hadn't learned whether men could just overrule a woman about her home. Judging from the things he had already seen, he suspected they could.

She came in and tossed off the veil. Then she reached back and let the cloth fall, covering the door itself. He opened his mouth to ask how it went, but she put a finger over hers. She pulled off the dress and left it crumpled in a heap on the floor. Then she reached over and tugged on Diate's shirt.

'Hey!' he whispered.

'Trust me,' she whispered back. She smelled good – sweat and grapes and a rich, female musk. Her skin was soft. He tried not to brush against it.

She pulled off his shirt, and reached for his trousers. He grabbed her wrist. She slid her other hand over his penis, felt the hardness he had been trying to hide. Her smile grew. 'Good,' she said in Ziklan.

He let her undress him. He was shaking. He hadn't been with a woman since Sheba, and he didn't want to be with this one, no matter how attractive she was, no matter how his body was betraying him. She took his hand and led him to the bed.

The curtain pulled back and the man stood there, a flush covering his cheeks. Diate finally understood. He whirled to show his arousal, pushed the woman onto the bed, and shouted in Ziklan: 'Get out of here!'

The man backed up, nearly stumbled, and caught himself on the table. The water pitcher wobbled. Diate followed him, repeating the phrases he had heard over and over since he had arrived in this barren place: 'Get out of here! Now, before I contact the authorities! Get out of here!'

The man pinwheeled out the door and ran down the street. The violence of his action interrupted the children's lethargy. They watched him go.

Diate's arousal was gone, although his heart was pounding furiously. The sweat was drying on his skin. He went back into the bedroom. She sat on the bed wearing only her gauze shirt. 'Did you think I was going to rape you?' she asked in Lillish.

He smiled for the first time since he had met her. 'You overestimate yourself.'

'And you forget how interested you were.'

He shrugged, and grabbed his pants, slipping them on and feeling relaxed. 'What does he want from you?'

'Proof that the boy he saw is a woman. For a woman to act freely in this culture is a capital offense.'

'You just gave him that proof.'

She smiled. 'Oh, no. We become a family with you here. The boy can look like me if he's my son.'

Diate smiled back at her. He liked her cunning. 'Strange place for you to be.'

'One of the few places no one will look for me. But I'm sure you know that.'

He sat on the chair. It creaked beneath his weight. 'I know very little,' he said.

'Yet you're here.'

He nodded, swallowed. She would be his only chance. He would have to talk with her, no matter how difficult it felt, how unused he was to confiding.

'Do you know Sheba?'

'The Queen of Tersis? How could I not know of her?'

'But you have never met her.'

The woman shook her head.

'I did, on Rulanda. I was working for the Golgoth as one of his detectives, and I let her seduce me. When she came to Golga a year later, asking to be part of the Peace Festival, I was supposed to fool her into trusting me and learn state secrets. Instead, she fooled me, killed both the Queen and the Golgoth in a single maneuver, and left me to die while she returned to the Kingdom to start her rule.'

The woman leaned back, curled her legs beneath her, and propped her head on one hand. 'You want revenge.'

'For that, and many other things.' He couldn't believe the calmness in his voice. His heart was beating so hard he could barely hear himself think. 'I heard that you are planning to act against Sheba.'

'And you found us?' She sat up.

He didn't miss the 'us.' He was in the right place. 'It wasn't as easy as it sounds. I spent months traveling from place to place, tracking down rumors. I was about to give up here, when I stumbled upon that merchant, and you.'

'You have found a woman, living alone in a hostile place. I too lost family, and I have no wish to return to the Kingdom.'

'I might have believed that if you hadn't been so adept at getting rid of that man, if you hadn't mentioned others.'

Her entire body froze in place. 'I asked you before if you were the son of Emilio Diate, the rebel. You didn't answer me.'

'You will doubt whatever answer I give you. I have a dancer's caste mark and a Golgan scar. I carry no other proof.'

'*The land drains you*
like a suckling child
empties a dying mother,' she said, quoting one of his father's lesser known poems.

'*You try to escape,*' Diate said, continuing, unable to stop until the poem was done,
'*but the land clings,*
convinces you
that you are the mother
and it the child.
Although its rich earth
covers generations of mother/children.

How do you flee
suckling land?
How do you abandon
a child older and wiser than you?

You leave it in the care of others,
shed tears of guilt
and relief as you run

– and hope
the welcoming arms of your new land
will enfold you gently
like an earth mother
protecting
another woman's abandoned son.'

The words left him dry-mouthed and pain-filled. He hadn't thought of the poem before, of the way the words could have been written for him, but weren't because his father had been dead when Diate had to flee.

He turned away, clenching and unclenching his left hand. Abandoned son of two lands, he didn't want there to be the third.

'How many of his poems can you quote?' she asked.

'All of them.' He kept his back to her, unwilling to look at her. 'As well as the opening to most of the pamphlets. You want stories from my childhood? My father's speeches over dinner?'

'No.' Her voice was soft.

'It's easy to memorize poems. Anyone who wants to infiltrate your group could learn my father's teachings and spout them back to you with reverence.'

'You had no reverence in your voice.'

That comment stopped him. He thought back to his recital. She was right; no reverence, only a confused pain mixed with anger. He turned back to her. She too had left her homeland, but she hadn't abandoned it. She wore it here, as clearly as Sheba wore her see-through dresses.

'I take it,' she said, 'that you are a Diate as well.'

He nodded.

She wiped the hair from her face. 'I'm Magdalena.'

He took her hand and kissed the fingers, remembering as he did so that this was the last act of the Golgoth. The irony didn't escape him. He made the gesture partly because he didn't want to give her his first name, thinking she would find it too much of a coincidence.

'What do you think we can do for you?' she asked, tucking her feet against her thighs and taking her hand back. Her movements were regal. Her caste mark, although that of a Trader, could also hide government connections.

The truthful answers were not the ones he wanted her to hear.

He needed a place, people to belong with. He needed time to think and the opportunity to take revenge if he wanted it. He also needed to find out how deeply involved Sheba was. 'I hope you can get me into the Kingdom with the minimum of fuss.'

She laughed quietly. 'We're hiding on Ziklag, and you think we can help you?'

'You are not hiding,' he said. 'You are planning, both your future and that of the Kingdom. When you're strong enough, you'll return, and I want to be with you.'

Her brown eyes measured him. She tugged the hem of the blouse over her hips, her hands betraying her nervousness. She clearly didn't know if she could trust him. He wouldn't, in her place. But he would be able to measure the maturity of their organization by their willingness to work with him. 'You must stay here,' she said, 'and not leave this room until I tell you. If you follow me, if you betray me, you will die. Is that clear?'

'Very.'

She sighed, and stood up. She pulled on her trousers, then pulled off the blouse, and took the bandage that she had used to wrap her breasts. She turned her back to him. The muscles in her arms and shoulders rippled as she wound the bandage around her ribcage. Then she pulled the cloth tight, and pinned it. She grabbed her blouse and the gauze hood, tucking it in as she went.

Then she faced him. The young boy who had found him had returned. 'I don't know when I'll be back,' she said, and left him alone in the cool darkness.

Chapter 23

He waited most of the afternoon and into the evening. At dusk, he crept out of the back room and drank from the cracked water pitcher. The water was stale and warm, but it refreshed his parched throat. He took a moment, ears cocked, to investigate the room. He found food scraps and a single gold piece that had fallen beneath a rug, but nothing else unusual or incriminating. He left the food and the gold where he had found them.

After he drank, he went back into the bedroom. He took Magdalena's dress and veil off the floor and draped them over a chair. Then he lay on the bed, arms supporting his head, and closed his eyes.

Most of the islands had their roots in ancient religions. The Vorgellians worshipped the science that brought people to Logos in the first place, as did the Oleans. Golga had been founded as a religious colony. So had Rulanda. But, being a resort community, it couldn't afford morality, and it let the practices go. When Diate was a boy, the stories of Golgan repression were far spread, and were the reasons behind the Kingdom's unusual liberties. But no one talked of Ziklag. Perhaps because no one had been there.

Magdalena had used sex to frighten off the man who had followed them. The entire incident had unnerved Diate.

Certainly no one would look for Kingdom members in this place. Most people would think that rebels would go to Rulanda or one of the other resort areas, or to empty islands so that they could continue their usual lifestyle. Here Magdalena couldn't even dress like a woman, let alone act like one from the Kingdom. The men must have had an easier time hiding themselves – or perhaps they didn't, judging by the bread merchant's comments. Kingdom rebels had money in Ziklag, an odd combination and one that made Diate suspicious.

The room grew even darker than it had been. A trickle of sweat ran down Diate's temple into the stubble where his hair had been.

She hadn't known how long she would be gone. Maybe if he slept, some of the oppressive heat would go away. Maybe the time would pass quicker.

He closed his eyes and let the darkness take him.

He woke once. The darkness was nearly complete. He couldn't see his hand in front of his face. It took a minute for him to remember where he was, and then he smiled. He hadn't slept on a real bed in a long time.

His shirt was matted to his back. He sat up, peeled the shirt off, and let it fall to the floor. Then he lay back down, on his stomach this time, and tucked a bunched-up blanket beneath his head like a pillow.

Then he sighed, and slipped back into sleep.

A knee pressed into his spine. Someone pulled his arms back so hard Diate thought they would snap out of the sockets. The scar on his left forearm ached. A hand grabbed his chin and yanked it back until his entire spine strained against that knee.

'Diate, son of Emilio Diate, dancer, detective. Sheba has no respect for us, and no respect for you.' The voice was male and guttural, even though it spoke Lillish.

Diate couldn't reply. The hand holding his chin kept his mouth tightly closed. A tremble started in the muscles in his back and neck.

'Let me give you the rules of infiltration for a rebel group. Number one, pretend to believe in the cause. Number two, have a personal heartbreaking reason for your belief. Number three, show evidence of squabbles with the authorities. Number four, do not claim to be the dead rebel leader's son.'

The hands holding Diate let him go. His body bounced against the bed. The knee lifted off his spine and he rolled away. Four men stood above him, with Magdalena beside them. The man who had spoken still knelt on the bed. His arms were thick and muscular, his upper torso distorted by his bulging muscles. The room smelled faintly of animal dung. One of the men in the corner held a lamp, and the dung inside provided the flame.

They didn't seem as rich as the merchant had said.

Diate resisted the urge to rub his chin. He sat up. The room, which had been so hot earlier, was cold despite the extra bodies.

Nights in the desert. He wasn't sure he would ever get used to them.

'I take it you don't believe me,' he said.

He stood in one fluid motion, making sure his movements were as dancer-like as possible. 'The five of you, judge, jury and executioner. You're no better than the people you fight.'

'You know nothing about us,' the man said.

Diate grabbed his shirt off the floor, his back to the man as if safety didn't matter. Diate shook the dirt off the fabric and then slipped the shirt on. It was clammy and still damp.

'I know quite a bit. You don't try to hide yourselves, except for Magdalena, who is a liability here because she's female. I know you throw too much money around, which means you feel safe. First mistake of a rebel, believing in safety. I found you easily. Imagine how easy it would be for one of Sheba's people to find you.' He adjusted his sleeves and leaned against the wall. The cool mud brick eased the shivering in his shoulders. 'I know you have no hope, no true game plan, no true desire to follow my father's teachings. If you did, you would have hurried back to the Kingdom upon the death of the old Queen and done what you could before Sheba arrived. You missed your opportunity.'

The thin light from the lamp cast odd shadows around the room. Magdalena's face was hidden. The other men had their arms crossed. The leader had gotten off the bed. His hands were clenched at his side, his beefy face red from too much exposure to Ziklag's hot sun.

'I am not trying to infiltrate. I used to work undercover all the time, and I have forgotten more rules than you will ever learn. I told Magdalena the truth because I thought it would get me farther with you people than any lie that I could conjure. I thought I needed you. But I don't need a group of inept so-called revolutionaries hiding in a country too poor to throw them out.'

Diate pivoted on one foot, his movement creating a bit of air that made the flame flicker. He pulled back the curtain, and found three more men standing in front of the bedroom door.

'We are not inept,' the leader said. 'We are training here. The Ziklan know more about guerrilla combat than any other people in the world. We have learned methods of fighting that haven't been tried in two millennia. Each of us knows ways to bring three men to their knees. You should feel honored that we decided to meet you

285

with a force eight strong. That shows our degree of uncertainty about you.'

Diate pinned the curtain back. He had nowhere to go even if he decided to leave. 'Why don't you join us in the bedroom, gentlemen? That way you can see better should anything happen.'

One of the men smiled, but they did not leave their posts. They were well trained. Diate returned to his spot on the wall. He mimicked the position of the others, legs apart, arms crossed over his chest.

Magdalena hadn't moved. He wished he could see her face.

'Honored, maybe. Curious, certainly. If you are as strong as you say you are, you should have left me to Magdalena and not worried.' Then Diate smiled. 'But there is the risk, isn't there, that I'm telling the truth.'

No one responded. He leaned against the wall, deciding he didn't like the combative stance.

'How long has it been since you've had contact with the outside world? One year? Two? Is that why you missed your opportunity, why you're still in this godforsaken place while Sheba consolidates her power?'

'I don't understand why the son of Emilio Diate would seek us out,' the leader said.

'I see,' Diate said. The smell of dung was making him woozy. He hated those lamps. 'Is that because you can't believe the son of a great rebel leader would seek out your pitiful tribe? Or did you bring that up to divert my attention from my suppositions about your competence?'

One of the men took a step forward. Magdalena caught his arm.

'Well,' Diate said, 'I will answer your question and the ones you haven't asked. You are, so far as I can tell, the only rebel group that actually fights against the Kingdom. The Kingdom was smart when it broke off from Golga. Give the people fame and wealth – or the opportunity for it – and they won't care what sort of government they live under. Seems a bit simple on the face of it, but since it has worked for over a century –'

'Do you always talk this much?' the leader asked.

' "Communication is the heart of revolution," ' Diate said with a smile. 'Or have you forgotten my father's teachings already?'

'We have no proof that Emilio Diate is your father.'

Diate cracked his knuckles, then let his hands drop to his side.

286

'We could go to Oleon for a DNA scan, provided, of course, that someone had the foresight to save my father's genetic records. Anywhere else, a simple blood test might convince you. But we're in Ziklag, the center of intellectual freedom in the entire world. You must trust my words, my memories, or kill me and live with the thought that you destroyed your rebellion for a lack of trust.'

The leader stared at Diate. The light flickered across the other man's face, making his eyes black and small. 'You have nothing to share with us.'

Diate's heart pounded against his chest. He had to work at looking relaxed. He hoped it didn't look like work to the others around him. This meant too much to him. He saw no other way into the Kingdom. He needed these rebels. 'Nothing?'

The leader shook his head. 'Even if you are who you claim to be, you ran away when your father was murdered. You lived in Golga. You are not of the Kingdom.'

Diate laughed. 'You are a blind man. The rest of you consent to being led by a man who cannot see?'

The men in front of Diate did not move. But he heard a rustle behind him.

'Get more light,' Diate said, and glanced behind him. The men had dropped their arms, but were not moving. 'Do it.'

'There's a lamp near the window,' Magdalena said.

One of the men left his formation and got the light. After a few tries, he lit it. Diate took the lamp from him. The glass was cool and greasy. He held the lamp beneath his face.

'You claim to follow my father,' he said to the leader. 'You must have seen the sketches my mother did on the flyleaves of his books. The Kingdom had posters of him posted all over the countryside as a warning during his last year. Even if I have nothing to contribute in the way of knowledge, I do have my father's face.'

'Magdalena says your scar bears the mark of Olean surgeons. They could have tampered with your face.'

Diate brought the lamp down. Its heat had burned his chin. 'I spent nearly two decades in the service of the Golgoth as a detective. We studied the Kingdom's weaknesses and strengths. I learned how to infiltrate groups, remain undercover, and I learned how to kill. I am, I would wager, the closest thing you have to a true assassin.'

'We have been training here. We know how to survive.'

'But not how to operate an offensive campaign. And that is what you must do, as rebels. I also worked with the Golgoth and his political advisors, balancing the use of force with the use of moral persuasion. I am, no matter what you think, my father's son.'

Diate switched the lamp to his other hand before that hand started shaking. This wasn't working. They didn't want him. He had never thought of that contingency. He had expected the rebels to welcome him like a long-lost son.

Magdalena glanced at the leader. He did not look at her.

'We do not need you,' the leader said.

'How can you be sure?' Magdalena took a step back as she spoke, as if she expected to be hit.

'He's certain,' Diate said. 'He's afraid that I will usurp his position as head of this small band. He forgets what I told you in the beginning. I am not interested in a rebellion. I am interested in revenge.'

'Revenge?' the leader asked.

'For the murder of his family,' Magdalena said in a tone that told Diate she was reminding the leader.

'I don't want leadership of anything,' Diate said.

The leader snapped his fingers. The men eased their positions. Diate tried not to let out a sigh of relief. 'If you try to usurp me, I will kill you myself,' the leader said.

Diate smiled and crossed his arms, standing at attention now that the others were relaxed. 'Your fear will be your undoing,' he said.

The leader shot Diate a quick glance, then turned to one of the men. 'Cover his eyes. We'll take him to camp.'

The man brought out a long kerchief, and walked toward Diate. As the man lifted the kerchief, Diate blocked it with his arm. 'Either you trust me completely, or I will remain here.'

'That gains you nothing,' the leader said.

'It gains you nothing as well,' Diate replied. 'And I'll be gone by morning. You'll never know whether I spoke to anyone about you or not.'

'I don't accept threats,' the leader said.

'Ah, the essence of leadership.' Diate smiled. 'You threaten, but will not tolerate the same behavior in return. No wonder you remain here. You're all bluster and no show.'

The leader took three rapid steps forward and grabbed Diate by the collar of his shirt. Diate felt small in the leader's grasp. The man lifted Diate off the ground. As the leader brought his fist back, Diate raised a foot and kicked forward with all of his strength.

His unbooted heel connected with the leader's groin. The leader yelped in pain. His grip on Diate's shirt loosened and Diate pulled away, kicking the leader again, this time in the chest. He fell backwards, stumbled against the bed, and nearly fell. The others watched, but didn't move.

Diate jumped on the bed, placed his knees on the leader's shoulders, and grabbed the man by his collar. 'I beat your former Queen to death with my bare hands about one year ago. Would you like me to try again?'

The leader did not reply, but his sweat took on a tangy fear-filled odour. Diate let the man's head drop.

'It's a shame I have no interest in taking over your leadership,' Diate said. 'It's clear that I could take it any time I wanted it. Rule one of leadership: loyalty at all costs. Obviously your people are not loyal. If they were, they wouldn't let me touch you like this.'

He got up and brushed his hands on his pants. 'I'm getting very tired of this room,' he said to Magdalena. 'Why don't you take me to your home?'

Chapter 24

They walked quietly, more quietly than any large group Diate had ever been with. It was as if they had all been trained to be dancers and light on their feet.

The village was quiet. No lights shone in any of the buildings. The streets looked wider without the tables for the bazaars. The air was cold, but still smelled of sweat and too many people. Diate rubbed a hand on his sleeve, wishing he had warmer clothes.

The streets became little more than a mud-caked path a short distance away from the last building. Rolling hills of sand looked like mountains in the darkness. Diate had followed that path into the village. He didn't relish walking it again.

After the third hill, they turned right. The trail they followed was almost invisible – a hardness under the sand where every place else the feet sank to the ankles, a bit of man-made rock beneath a wind-blown, sand-covered surface.

The sun was beginning to come up when the sand hills eased into a flatness that extended as far as Diate could see. A few trees rose near the last hill, and beyond them, a small pond and a spot of greenery so unexpected that at first Diate thought it a mirage.

Then he stepped a little farther and saw the tents surrounding it. This was camp. This would be home.

As they got closer, he saw that the tents sprawled for quite a distance. Two women huddled over a small fire. Men sat beside them, drinking hot liquid. The eight who had found him were only a fraction of the people who occupied the tent village.

'Quite a crew,' he said to the leader.

'Many people believe in what your father said.' The leader's tone had a trace of disapproval in it, as if Diate's actions showed that he hadn't trusted his father. And he hadn't. He had argued against his father's teachings.

'We have a tent for you,' Magdalena said. She took his hand and led him into the village. The smell of smoke and spices rose in the air.

The tent they had set aside for him was small and located across from the fire. Easy to protect and easy to guard. They had planned on bringing him back, but probably not with his freedom. They had probably planned on keeping him prisoner until they could figure out what to do with him.

He had to crouch to step inside. A pallet lay across the floor, covering most of the dirt, and a small table that reached barely to his calves was the other piece of furniture. On the table sat a large ornate jug and two glasses.

'It's not much,' Magdalena said, 'but it is all we have.'

Diate nodded. 'It will do.'

The people at the fire were watching him, their expressions carefully neutral. He got out of the tent. It was too small for two people.

'Why don't you show me the rest of the camp?' he asked.

She came out behind him. 'I really don't know –'

He turned and pinned her with a look. She took a step back. The confident woman who had used her body to scare off an intruder was gone. Good. Diate had frightened them all.

She sighed. 'I guess it wouldn't hurt.'

She didn't introduce him to the people sitting by the fire. Now that he was out of the tent, they were ignoring him, concentrating instead on the cups in their hands.

'Most of the tents are living quarters,' she said, 'but we do have one meeting tent.' She led him through the packed sand, away from the small pond. Two trees stood alone, like sentinels guarding the rear entrance to the camp. Two tents had been strung together. They looked like a long, fragile tunnel. Sand had coated the canvas, making it shimmer in the early morning light.

She pushed back the flap. Diate stepped inside – and stopped, heart in his throat. A large tapestry of his father hung from the far wall. The tapestry mimicked the portrait his mother had painted – the one that used to grace the flyleaf of his father's books. The colors were rich and fine – reds, yellows, greens, and blacks, as well as the skin tones that colored his father's face. Diate hadn't looked at the portrait in a long time. He had been right a few hours ago; the resemblance was startling. Even more so now that Diate matched his father in years.

Other tapestries covered the canvas sides. Most displayed his father's poems, the last poems, the political poems. Not even the best poems. Others had intricate designs around quotes from his father's political tracts. Diate stopped in front of one of the poems and ran his hand over the ribbed surface.

We trade poems
like secrets
whispered in the dark.

We wait for a hand
to caress our face
— a sign
of a secret understood.

We trade secrets
buried in poems,
coaxing them out of each other
like spies
with a reluctant traitor.

He had always hated that poem. It had seemed like a confession to him, an invitation to look inside the poetry, to find hidden, subversive meanings, to read into each line something his father may not have intended

Traitor. They had painted the word in blood on the living room wall. Diate had seen it, but had concentrated on his family instead. Yet the word had haunted him throughout his years with the Golgoth. From Golga's point of view, the entire Kingdom was made up of traitors, traitors who had left Golga to start a new country, whose entire focus was destroying the old. How could traitors assassinate people who betrayed them? How could they expect loyalty from anyone at all?

'Are you all right?' Magdalena asked.

Diate let his hand fall from the tapestry. He didn't answer her. He went to the next, and read the poem, one of his father's diatribes on revolution. Then he stopped before the next and the next, seeing the words of revolt, but no evidence of any action. In fact, the meeting room looked more like a temple than a hotbed of political activity. The focus was his father and his father's words, but the message seemed to be lost.

'How did you people find each other?' he asked.

292

He heard a sharp intake of breath. The question had surprised Magdalena. 'At home, there are societies, meeting groups, who are devoted to your father's teachings. The government tries to shut them down, but they travel from place to place. Rico wasn't our first leader. Santiago – you'll meet him later – he gathered those of us who felt that discussion was not enough. Then he brought us here, and put Rico in charge. Rico made us learn your father's words. Your father preached change, and change does not come just from studying the past.'

Diate turned. Magdalena stood near the tent flap. Her eyes glittered as she spoke.

'My father died because of what he preached,' Diate said.

She nodded. 'We were afraid that we would suffer for it too. We came here where we can talk freely.'

'Freely? In a tent village outside one of the poorest places in the world? That's not freedom, Magdalena. You're running away.'

She averted his eyes. 'Santiago told us to wait, and to learn. We have. Every evening we meet here, and read from your father's teachings, and plan our return.'

'How long? How long have you been making these plans?'

She walked over to one of the tapestries and adjusted it. The fringe floated toward her, absorbing her movements. 'We came here three years ago. Rico has returned twice to recruit more people.'

'Rico?' The name finally registered with Diate. 'The man who thought he could best me?'

'He is our leader.'

In name only. Diate said nothing. Since that evening, Rico would lead no one. They would all know that Diate could beat him. And Diate was the son of their hero, their true leader.

He suppressed a shudder. His father had hated this kind of hero worship. He had thought it a greater enemy of thought than anything the politicians did. His father would have shut these people down, taken away anything they had to believe in.

But Diate needed them. He would say nothing.

'You've lived here for three years.' He shook his head. 'That seems like an eternity. Has Rico a plan for your return to the Kingdom?'

'He says we'll know when the time is right.'

Diate let out a silent breath. That wasn't what he had wanted to hear. He wanted them to have a plan to return as soon as possible. He couldn't sit in the desert with fake rebels, listening to them recite his father's poetry like the word of God.

'You aren't the only one who thinks things should move faster.' Magdalena had lowered her voice.

'Oh?' He tried not to sound too interested.

'Lately even Santiago has become impatient. He thinks we should leave Ziklag, go back to the Kingdom, and see what we can do.'

Diate frowned. 'It sounds like I should met this Santiago.'

'You will,' she said. 'I'll make sure of it.'

She had an odd way of looking at him. She gazed at him through half-open eyes, not at all the alert, in-control woman he had met. It was as if she had decided to give all her power to Diate.

He was not going to play. He would treat her as an equal. 'How did Rico become your leader?'

Magdalena gave the tent flap a nervous glance. 'He knew the most about Diate's – your father's – teachings. He made us all study them, research them. He has led us from the beginning.'

Diate nodded. That was all he needed to know, for now. 'I would like to come to the evening meeting.'

She smiled. 'I think it would be impossible to keep you away.'

Diate went back into his tent. His interrupted sleep had left him exhausted. He lay on the pallet – nude so that his body would have some defense against the heat of the day – but his mind continued to jump.

He had expected a true group of rebels, dangerous, something Sheba had to fear. He had imagined going with them to the Kingdom, storming the palace, and –

– and there his imagination had always failed. He didn't know what he wanted. Sometimes he imagined himself taking her in his bare hands and killing her as he had done the Queen before her. Sometimes he would grab her and kiss her as he had at the ball. And sometimes they would stare at each other, waiting for the one of them to back down.

But he couldn't go directly into the Kingdom. After that last conversation, Sheba would wonder. She probably was wondering what he was doing anyway. He had told Scio of her visit, and Scio's men had found a small shuttle port just outside of the city. Martina had probably been brought there, as had countless other victims. The Kingdom had used that port as a base in Golga for decades.

The base was gone now. The first of many secrets that Diate had discovered, and had destroyed in his search for these rebels. He sighed. He needed these people. He had thought of bringing in his own force, but he figured that would take years. So he wanted to find an already existing force. And he had, only to discover that they were a group of misfits living in the desert.

Misfits who, despite their so-called training, were no match for him or his anger. They would certainly be no match for someone like Tonio Carbete.

He rolled over on his side, sweat dripping down his back. Somehow he had to train them. Somehow he had to use them as a cover for getting back into the Kingdom.

At dusk he awoke, feeling more tired and gritty than he had when he went to sleep. He used water from the pitcher to wash the sweat from his body. The water was warm, not refreshing, but the touch of it removed the first layer of grime. He would ask, when he could, if the small pond was also used for bathing.

He shook out his clothes and put them back on. He would have to go back into the town sometime soon for more clothing. He couldn't wear the same thing over and over, especially here, in the heat.

With one hand, he pushed the tent flap back and stepped outside. The sun had nearly set, leaving the air cooler than it was inside his tent. He decided to leave the flap up, hoping that some of the cool air would go inside. The ashes of the fire looked cold and untended, and the tent village itself was quiet.

They had gone off and left him alone out here. Alone to fend for himself, a year's worth of searching gone. Then he saw a light in the meeting tent, and felt a bit silly for his fears. He squared his shoulders, ran a hand over the stubble that had replaced his hair, and walked to the tent.

As he approached, he heard voices mumbling in unison. He strained to catch the words. Finally he heard the last stanza of the poem he had read earlier. Recited like a prayer. His father had put menace into those words, not reverence. That was one reason Diate had hated it. The menace gave the poem the extra layer that it seemed to miss in the text.

As he got older and read and reread his father's poetry, he understood why his father had been a class C poet and a first-class revolutionary. An occasional poem was wonderful, but none of them had the power that the great poets of the Kingdom had. Still, his poetry had something that inspired.

He ducked under the open tent flap and stepped inside. Thirty people sat in an oblong-shaped circle. Candles burned on trays beneath each tapestry. Across from the door, below the tapestry of Diate's father, Rico sat cross-legged, his hands resting palms up on his thighs.

'Magdalena said you were coming.' Rico's voice echoed oddly. The sound didn't deaden as much as Diate had thought. It merely flattened into nothing after one repetition. Rico turned to the group. 'This is the man we talked about, who claims he is the son of Diate.'

Diate let the comment pass. He walked around the group until he found Magdalena, then sat beside her. The group had to shift a little to make room for him.

He glanced around. His presence threw off the symmetry. Fifteen men and fifteen women, all about his age. None had more than a teenager's memory of his father, if they remembered anything at all.

In the corner nearest the door, a thin wiry man sat. The man had dark brown eyes and an intense face. Santiago. Diate didn't recognize him, but he knew just the same. Santiago nodded to him. Diate nodded back.

'For tonight's text, we turn to the *War Cantos*, page 65.' Rico held a small leather-bound book in his left hand. The *War Cantos* had been destroyed by the government. An existing copy was a rare thing.

Rico opened it and thumbed through the thin pages. The others watched him, except for Santiago, who watched Diate. Diate was motionless. Rico cleared his throat.

' "We were raised under the stench of death," ' he read. ' "My father went to war to hold our place on this small island; his brothers died to protect us, his sisters disappeared into the land we once cherished. Golga has been our enemy for nearly a century, they teach us. But Golga is merely a sign of our internal squabble. Half of our former whole. We took its creativity, its light, and its beauty, and tried to make a nation, and because creativity, light, and beauty are not enough, we had to take some darkness too. We teach our children to maim and kill, showing them that anything they do to serve our bidding and the bidding of the state is right – " '

Diate had heard these words before, over and over at the dinner table, spoken like a litany. It had gotten so that he would eat his dinner and bolt, leaving his father to preach to the family, and then later to the world. Diate had to clench his fists to keep the revulsion from his face. He had never expected to hear those words read like scripture.

' "– but Golga is not the problem. The problem lies in the division. For too long we have fought, been two parts of the same whole. Two unfulfilled parts, never to reunite. So we must find unity within ourselves. And sometimes the way to do that is to divide. For in dividing, we become another whole with sections that become the sum of its parts –" '

The statement had made no sense when his father first spoke it to him, and it made no sense now. His father's vision had always been a vision of duality. Act but do not act yet. Divide but unite. Strive for perfection, but let everyone be a Talent.

Rico set the book down. Diate sighed softly. Finally, they would talk about something important.

'What Diate teaches here,' Rico said, 'is that duality is part of our natures. In accepting our duality, we accept our wholeness, and until we can accept both we are nothing.'

Rico was preaching. He was using the *Cantos* as text. Diate couldn't take it anymore. He wondered how the others had stood this kind of nonsense for three years. 'What my father was saying,' Diate said with a quiet force in his voice, 'is that he wasn't sure if revolution was the answer. Revolution had left both Golga and the Kingdom crippled. He thought that their injuries might have come because they never reunited. So when he preached revolution, he preached the threat of division teaching both sides that they needed the other.'

'You have not been given permission to speak,' Rico said.

Diate pushed his sleeves up his arms. 'I think the others gave you permission to speak for too long.'

'You do not have an understanding of the text.'

Diate laughed. 'I lived with the source for sixteen years. I heard him refine his ideas night after night in conversations with my mother. I haven't seen that book since I was a teenager, but I

297

remember it. The next section discusses the duality of the individual and the ways that the Talent system ignores people who have many talents in small proportion in favor of the people who have one great talent.'

'You have no right to speak in this meeting,' Rico said.

'I think he has every right.' Magdalena spoke softly.

'He is the son of Diate,' Santiago said. 'That gives him right to speak.'

'There is no proof of that,' Rico said.

Santiago laughed. 'Just look at him. He is who he says he is.'

'Touch him,' another man said. 'Magic Talents can make themselves look like someone they're not.'

Magdalena put a hand on his arm. 'His appearance doesn't change, even in sleep. No Talent is good enough to cover for the subconscious.'

'I saw him asleep,' another man said.

'I want to hear him,' the woman across from Diate said.

Diate's hands were clasped in his lap. He was holding his breath. He let it out slowly as everyone turned to him. He glanced at Rico. 'I am sorry, Rico,' Diate said. 'I think you may have an understanding of my father's words that I cannot see because I was too close to him. I think the studies you have done have been valuable. But I think the time for study is long gone.'

The words didn't feel like his. They felt like his father's channeled through him. Diate usually didn't speak to people. He danced for them, or worked for them. He never led them. Not even his detectives. There he followed the Golgoth's orders.

'You missed your opportunity to fill a hole in Kingdom leadership when the Queen died. Sheba has had a year to consolidate her rule. The longer you wait, the more power she gains. The less chance you have of success.'

'How do you know what we want to do?' Rico asked.

Diate turned to him. 'I assume you want what my father wanted. Equality for all people. No talent judging, no privileges based on birth. An equality that everyone is born to. Am I wrong?'

'Our beliefs aren't that simple,' Rico said.

Daite waited, hands upturned on his thighs.

'We believe in equality, yes,' Rico said, 'and in the strength of the group. But we also believe that the rule of merchants, like Golga's, stifles the spirit. We believe –'

Diate held up his hand. 'What you believe matters in two instances. If you choose to stay here, what you believe becomes your business. You and your followers will live a sort of life based on your religion.' He couldn't keep the sarcasm out of the word 'religion.' 'If you choose to return, what you believe matters when you obtain power. Remaining here will not give you power.'

'We've been training here, learning to fight, learning how to survive.'

Diate smiled slowly. He made eye contact with Rico, watched as a flush built on Rico's florid face. 'You learned to fight? Then why didn't you defend yourself last night?'

'The circumstances were odd –'

'Yes, they were,' Diate said. 'Eight people against one man. I still managed to pin you to the bed, and no one came to your defense. You did not learn how to fight here. You have learned nothing, so far as I can see.'

'How important will fighting be when we return to the Kingdom?' Magdalena asked.

Diate shrugged. 'You may not have to touch anyone. It might be all you do. I have not been in the Kingdom in two decades. You people know what it's like there better than I do.'

People looked away from him, glancing at their hands. The candles behind him sputtered as breeze rose from the sudden movements.

Diate didn't like the feelings he was getting. Perhaps he would have been better off on his own. 'I need to know who you people are,' he said.

Santiago looked sharply at him. Diate's new tone of voice seemed to distrurb him. Diate ignored Santiago.

'You know who I am. You know what you're working with. I don't. When we're done, I want to talk to each of you. I want your name, your class, and your rank.'

'I thought your father taught that class and rank aren't important.' Rico matched Diate's sarcasm.

'You know my father's teachings as well as I do. Don't twist them,' Diate said.

'I am not –'

'My father believed that class and rank were important, but not the only thing of importance. He thought that we lost too much defining people by their best talent and ranking it. He thought we should continue the system, but determine what else a person was good at and not force people to live with the rankings but to make their own choices. Am I wrong?'

Rico looked down and shook his head. Diate thought he should feel compassion for the man – after all, Rico had led this group and Diate was usurping it – but he didn't. He needed these people, and he needed them to be a certain way. His father would have been embarrassed by them.

'Then I need to know who everyone is. Class and rank will give me a lot of information in a few short sentences.' Diate gripped his knees and leaned back. 'Look, I am sorry to take over your meeting. But when I heard that there was a group of rebels who followed my father's teachings, I finally thought that I would find a focus. I want to go home. I want to return to the Kingdom. My father always thought that, with followers, he could achieve his dream. Only he didn't live long enough to even try. When he reached a certain level of strength, he got murdered.'

'It could happen to us,' Rico said quietly.

'It will happen to some of you. That's the point of a rebellion – you fight for something that has so much value to you that you are willing to lose your life before giving up that right.' Diate took a breath. His heart was pounding. He had never made that kind of stand. He had never had anything – any cause – he believed in so much. He had believed in himself, and he had loved the Golgoth. But he had never lived the sentiment he had just expressed.

Things might have been easier for him if he had truly been his father's son, if he truly believed his father's teachings.

'You want to take us back, to overthrow the entire Kingdom government?' asked Santiago.

'Isn't that why you came here?'

'Yes, but –'

'But it's been what? Three, four years? That's longer than my father worked on his theories. He only spoke publicly for a few months. He developed his ideas over a space of three years. You have sat in the desert and studied him longer than he worked on this. I think he would find that odd.'

People shifted. The tent had grown stifling hot.

Magdalena touched his wrist. Her fingers were cold. They felt good. 'You're willing to lead us back to the Kingdom? To help us in our fight?'

'If I have to,' Diate said.

'What do you know about fighting? Or a rebellion?' Rico had straightened. His entire posture was rigid.

Diate stared at him. He couldn't believe Rico had asked the question.

Santiago leaned forward. 'This man's entire life has been a fight.'

'The question is still a valid one,' one of the women said.

Diate shot a quick glance at Santiago, wondering how much the other man knew about him. Diate didn't have time to find out right now. 'Yes,' he said. 'It is a valid question. But you already know the answer.'

'Just because your father was a rebel leader doesn't mean you know anything about rebellion,' Rico said.

'It's a start,' Diate said. 'I served as the chief detective under the Golgoth for eight years. I know how to quash rebellions. I know how successful ones start. I know how governments work, and I know when to use force and when to avoid it.'

'With so much skill, why did the Golgoth let you go?'

Diate's breath left him. The others watched carefully. They didn't know. They actually didn't know.

'Your Queen murdered him.' He felt like he was talking to children. They called themselves revolutionaries, and they didn't even know about the most important event in recent history. 'His son, who never trusted me, banned me from Golga.'

'So now you look for another place to be?'

'No.' Diate shot a glance at Magdalena. She had taken her hand off his wrist. She had said nothing about this, and apparently it had escaped the people who had tried to capture him the night before. He sighed. 'The murder of the Golgoth was the end for me. He raised me after my parents died. He supported me.'

The woman across from Diate grimaced.

'He was a good man,' Diate said. 'I owe him my life. He was working toward peace with the Kingdom when the Queen murdered him. That last bloodstain on my soul convinced me. I have had the training. I have the background. The Kingdom must pay.'

'Revenge? You're only here for revenge?' The woman asked.

'Why are you here? Altruism? You believe in my father's teachings solely and completely because of what he said? Or has someone in your family been denied a place among the class A

301

Talents? Has someone you know died stealing an artifact that should have remained with a country?'

She looked away. 'That doesn't make my beliefs less valuable.'

'No,' Diate said. 'It doesn't. It just makes them more credible. I would wager that no one here came just because of my father's teachings. My father spoke to a whole generation of people about injustice, injustice they have felt, you have felt. You came because you understand the injustice and want to change it.'

Some people were nodding. Others were watching Diate closely. Rico hadn't moved. He was biting his lower lip.

'Well, I was a class A Talent – the best ever in my division, they said – and I felt it too. You want to hear about injustice? My sister, who also danced but not as well as I did, got assigned to a cruise ship, with orders to watch whatever non-Kingdom members brought aboard. I helped her study the layout of the ship, the storage areas –'

He shook himself. He didn't want to talk about that, to remember how it felt, crammed into one of those small spaces, blood-spattered, frightened, and hungry, for three days.

'My father spoke out against it. He said my sister had other values to the Kingdom, values that would allow her to retain her integrity, and not become a thief in the night. No one in the government listened to him, but people around did. People like you, who had also experienced the injustices. And then, when he gained a following, the assassins came –'

Diate's voice broke. He swallowed and continued.

'The assassins came and slaughtered them all. Except me. They spared me, because I was a class A dancer, better than all the rest. More valuable. They expected me to dance for them, after all of that. To earn money for the Kingdom. And I couldn't. So I ran. And they tried to kill me then too, thinking me a traitor. I managed to escape, and a Vorgellian ship's captain saved me. I got sent to Golga, where I should have died, but the Golgoth saw value in me. He loved me until he died. At the hands of the Kingdom, who tried to pin it on me. Revenge. I think I have the right to revenge. And if, in that revenge, I can make my father's dreams come true, then I will.'

No one spoke for a long time. The candle across from Diate guttered and died. It cast a half-shadow on the people around him.

Finally Santiago moved a hand, as if to get Diate's attention. 'I can't speak for the others,' Santiago said. 'But I'm ready to go back. And I'll go with you.'

'So will I,' said Magdalena. Others echoed her. Only Rico didn't speak. Finally he stood.

'I hope you know what you're doing,' he said. 'At least thirty lives depend on it.'

He walked around the outside of the circle and ducked as he stepped through the tent flap. The others watched him go. Then Magdalena cleared her throat. Everyone looked at her.

'What do we have to do to prepare?'

Diate made himself look away from the open flap. He knew what he was doing – in theory. In theory, he knew better than Rico. But sometimes theory was not enough. He smiled at the group. 'I'll let you know how to prepare,' he said. 'But first I need to talk to you all, find out what has been happening here, and we can't do it all in one night. I assume there is a time for supper?'

Magdalena nodded. 'We begin cooking when the meeting is done.'

'Let's start now,' Diate said, 'and each of you can talk with me afterwards, let me get to know you. Then we'll talk about a plan.'

He got up, feeling cramped and dizzy from sitting in the same position for too long. He walked around the circle as Rico had done, and stepped out of the tent.

The air was cold and fresh. The darkness was not as complete as it had been the night before. Starlight gave it a blue opaqueness that covered the entire sky. A single light twinkled brighter than the rest. The Vorgellians said the bright lights slashing across the night sky were the colony ships that had brought everyone to Logos hundreds of years ago. Diate stretched, a shiver running through him as the sweat dried on his back.

He left the tent, not wanting anyone to catch him yet, and strode through the quiet main area. The sand was hard beneath his feet. The chill felt good after the stifling interior of the tent.

He stopped when he reached the last two tents. The trees beside them twisted toward the night sky. He put his hand on one. The bark was rough beneath his fingers.

'I thought you weren't going to lead them.' Rico's voice came from behind Diate.

Diate didn't turn. He wasn't surprised by Rico's presence. In fact, he had expected it. 'I thought you were going to kill me if I tried.'

'I said that when I thought you would take them over by force. They seem interested in what you say.'

Diate nodded. 'And I made that promise when I thought you actually led them.'

'I did,' Rico said. 'I just wasn't sure I wanted to lead them to their deaths.'

'So you let them live here? In this place? Is this life?'

'Yes.'

Diate finally turned. Rico stood behind him, a hulk of a man lost in shadow.

'You're a man who doesn't know how to act,' Diate said. Diate would never have let the situation get like this. He would have taken action long ago. He never would have allowed someone else to take over his position – at least not easily.

'I don't trust you,' Rico said. 'Despite your pretty speeches. I think you're using us for a different purpose altogether. If you cared about your father's teachings, you would have left Golga as a young man, founded a group yourself, and led the rebels into the Kingdom.'

'Leading a rebellion killed my father. I was afraid to die.'

Rico laughed, a bitter sound. 'Another pretty speech. Short, but the right words. Wrong sentiment. If you believed your father you never would have worked for the Golgoth, no matter how kind he had been to you. The Golgoth was the antithesis of everything your father stood for.'

'No,' Diate said. 'People rose in those ranks on merit and desire. They all started equal.'

'Not economically. The poverty in Golga is ugly.'

'Yes, it is,' Diate said. 'But at least Golgans don't kill and steal for their country.'

'No, they waste away their lives in small hovels, dying by inches from the moment they were born. They have no hope of improving their lives.'

Diate leaned his shoulder against the tree. The bark dug into his skin. 'Life on Golga turned out to be the right path for me. I stayed too long. I should have returned sooner. But life was easier for me there.'

'You would never have come here if the Golgoth hadn't died.'

Diate nodded. 'That's probably true. I might have stayed there the rest of my life. Because there I was fighting the Kingdom's system, in my own way.'

'I don't trust you,' Rico said.

'You never will.' Diate leaned his full weight against the tree. It bowed a little from the pressure. 'I took your leadership away.'

'I'm not that petty,' Rico said.

'Aren't you?' Diate let the thought hang in the air for a moment.

Rico didn't break eye contact. 'No,' he said. 'I'm not. I'm going to let you lead this group. I've been thinking about it since last night. You have strengths that I don't have, and a vision that may get us what we want.'

'You're backing down?'

'Not really,' Rico said. 'You're going to use us to get you to the Kingdom, to get your revenge. We may as well use you to get what we want too.'

'Use me?' Diate asked.

'You have fire. You have those leadership qualities that I remember your father having.'

At Diate's surprised movement, Rico smiled. 'Yes,' he said. 'I saw your father speak. Twice. The most moving experiences of my youth. I never forgot him, and I mourned when he died.'

Diate couldn't say anything. His heart pounded against his chest. His public father, the one most people thought was the man, had appeared again.

'You can help our group grow. You can make us strong, strong enough to take on the entire Kingdom government. I don't care why you do it, as long as you step aside should we win.'

Diate stared at Rico. Rico stared back.

'I make no promises,' Diate said.

Chapter 25

By morning, he had confirmed what he had suspected. Most of the followers in camp were class C Talents or lower. They, like his sister, did not want to work in menial jobs or as low-rent performers in small clubs, scooping out treasures for the Kingdom's treasury. A few were poets, the bulk musicians, and the rest were actors. Magdalena had no obvious talent whatsoever, and had been slotted for a government position from birth.

He had only one more person to talk to. Santiago.

The others held Santiago in a kind of reverence. He, more than Rico, was the leader of this group. The spiritual leader. The one the others relied upon to tell them what to do.

Diate cornered him after breakfast. Santiago was a small man, thin and wiry, the kind who looked as if he were all muscle and no fat.

'Walk with me,' Diate said.

Santiago hunched his shoulders together, a protective move.

'Come on,' Diate said. 'We need to talk.'

Santiago shook his head. 'You already know enough about me.'

'No.' Diate glanced around. Three people were cleaning up the remains of breakfast. One stayed to maintain the fire. The rest had gone to the far side of the tent village to practice defensive maneuvers they had learned. Diate had let that rest. He would teach them his own way later. 'We haven't spoken yet. The others value what you say. I want to talk to you too.'

The morning was already hot. The heat prickled through his clothes and covered his body with sweat. They walked in silence toward the twisted trees, where he had met with Rico the night before.

The trees provided little shade. Their limbs were overgrown and tangled, but spindly. Diate cupped a handful of water and drank. It was warm, but fresh and good.

Santiago sat beneath one of the trees, legs brought up against his chest, arms wrapped around them, as if he could make himself small enough to fit in the tree's shade. 'What did you want to talk with me about?'

'Magdalena told me that you're the one who put this group together.'

Santiago looked down at his hands. 'I believe in what your father said.'

'So did everyone else, but you seem like the only one who wanted to take any action.'

Santiago didn't move. He was hiding something, and not very effectively. He wanted Diate to find out.

Games. Diate suppressed a sigh. He hated games.

'Why did you let Rico lead them? Why the wasted years?'

Santiago tightened his grip on his legs. 'I was waiting.'

'Waiting?' Diate took the shade of the other tree. His long body didn't fit in the dark patch. His feet remained in the sun. The heat rose off the sand in waves.

'For you.' Santiago finally looked up. 'It took you a year longer than I expected. I was ready to give up.'

Diate swallowed. That light, trembly feeling he had had around Sheba returned. This was out of his depth. 'You were waiting for me?'

Santiago nodded. 'We have met before, did you know that?'

Diate peered at him. He had known who Santiago was last night, but that had been a combination of behaviors – the way Magdalena had looked at him; the deference of the others; and the way Santiago had held himself. 'I don't remember you.'

The air shimmered around Santiago. For a moment, he flickered in and out. Then he winked back in.

His shape hadn't changed. He was still small and wiry, but his face had a swarthiness that it hadn't had before. A scar slashed from his eye to the corner of his mouth. A silver spot glistened on the bridge of his nose – his caste mark, showing his position as magic user.

Diate let his breath out slowly. Another magic Talent. This one revealing himself easily. 'Do the others know who you are?'

Santiago shook his head.

'No one has touched you in all this time?' Diate said.

'One of the women tried for me,' Santiago said. 'I told her that I preferred men. She has stayed away since.'

'And none of the men have bothered you?'

307

Santiago shook his head. 'They're too concerned with their scholarship to think about demands of the flesh.'

'It takes a lot of effort to make an illusion that constant and good. You're class A.'

'Yes,' said Santiago.

'Then what are you doing here?'

Santiago smiled. 'I told you. I've been waiting for you.'

Diate stood. His feet slipped a little in the sand. 'You knew I was coming?'

'I can see forward a bit. I knew we needed you.'

'Why?'

'Because you're Diate's son. Because you have the charisma we all lack. Because you're the Rogue Talent. You can rally the people in the Kingdom. None of us can.'

'But you're class A. You have no need of my father's teachings.'

Santiago leaned back, revealing another small scar under his chin. 'Magic Talents are different. No one respects us. The old Queen wanted us banned from her court, and she could have used our help. Being a class A magic Talent is like being a class D dancer – people think you're only good for theft.'

The bitterness in Santiago's voice made Diate stop pacing. Santiago was clearly class A, and he thought it was important enough to be here. That was good enough for Diate, for now.

'I don't recognize you,' Diate said.

'Obviously,' Santiago said. He held out his hand. 'Let me remind you.'

Diate hunched in the sand. Santiago unfolded himself. He touched the bridge of his nose, then extended his palm. A small bubble rose in his hand. It grew and floated to Diate. Inside, nearly a hundred children milled in a lacquered room inside the palace. Diate saw himself, sitting on a stool, surrounded by other children, talking and laughing, secure in his future. His sister sat in the back, huddled like Santiago had been a moment before, tears running down her cheeks. A small, dark-featured boy crouched beside her and wiped a tear away.

Diate hadn't seen it. He didn't remember it. All he remembered from that day was his joy at being chosen and his father's anger over his sister's failure.

The bubble popped. Bits of moisture floated in the air. 'You were my sister's friend,' Diate said.

'She asked me, after I was chosen, if a class A magician could turn her into a class A dancer.' Santiago looked at his hands. 'I asked, but no one would tell me. And I experimented, never telling her. The attack on your family happened while I was still trying.'

Diate leaned against the tree, forcing himself to stretch the tension from his body. 'She once yelled at our father, telling him that someone really loved her. That was you?'

'I would have done anything for her.' Santiago raised a hand and then let it drop, in a gesture of helplessness. 'I still would. Am, in fact.'

'You're here because of her.'

Santiago nodded. 'When you didn't come, I was afraid that I had wasted three years. The longer you stayed away, the more hopeless it felt. I didn't know how to rehabilitate you, without you beside me. Most people in the Kingdom believe you're dead.'

The words sent a shiver down Diate's back. He wiped the sweat off his forehead. 'You would have rehabilitated me without me being there?'

Santiago smiled. The air shimmered around him again, and suddenly Diate was staring at himself. Santiago had the details right, down to the tear.

'Even this,' he said, 'is only a half-measure. It would still be me behind the mask. I can't make those heart-felt speeches like you can. And imagine what would happen if someone brushed against me in a crowd.'

Diate nodded. His hands were shaking. 'Change back please,' he said. He didn't like the implications. He had never thought about it. No wonder the Queen hadn't wanted magic Talents in her court. They could pretend to be her.

But Santiago wanted to use Diate. And Santiago gave him hope. With Santiago's help, Diate could arrive in the Kingdom unnoticed.

Santiago winked out, and then returned as the man Diate had seen the night before – no caste mark, no scars.

'If they think I'm dead,' Diate said, 'what of the Rogue Talent?'

'A rumor, a legend, a myth.' Santiago's eyes had grown bright. 'Something for you to build on. They believe that the Rogue Talent will return and save them.'

'Save them,' Diate murmured. 'I haven't even been able to save myself.'

Santiago put his hands behind his head and leaned back. 'You bring a different kind of salvation,' he said. 'The Kingdom needs something to believe in. The Talent system is too closed. Too few people are getting in. No one is safe any more. Even Talents receive public punishments for crime. All those people need to believe that they can be famous, rich, Talented, *and* that if they achieve their dreams, they'll be immune from the terror tactics of the government.'

'It sounds like you want me to lead a revolution.'

The smile played on Santiago's lips again. 'Isn't that why you came here?'

'I told you why I came here last night. Revenge.'

'Revenge is such a short-term thing,' Santiago said. 'The best revenge is to live well. You can live very well once we take over the Kingdom.'

The sand was burning through Diate's shoes. 'You make it sound so easy.'

'It's not easy,' Santiago said. 'Even getting you into the Kingdom will be a trick.'

Diate frowned. He had known that, but he had never heard anyone else confirm it.

'The island is completely closed to outsiders,' Santiago said. 'The rest of us have maintained valid papers. No one else is allowed in. A standing army patrols the ports, and the Vorgellians have given us a small fleet in exchange for valuables stolen specifically for them. Several nations have tried to breach the Kingdom's defenses, to regain stolen goods, to get extradition for murders. Nothing works. One nation even held performers hostage in an attempt to regain lost items.'

Diate had known this, but from a Golgan perspective. He had never put together what it would feel like to be inside the Kingdom itself. 'So the class A Talents are at risk.'

Santiago sat up. 'Everyone is at risk. A margin of safety exists only in the Kingdom or in protected areas like Rulanda, areas that require performance service for survival. Some of the class As are so talented and so popular that they can go anywhere. Their retinues act as an advance team for later groups. The smuggling has grown more dangerous and secretive. Fewer class Cs perform any more. Most of them go underground and work as they can, becoming better at lifting goods than performing routines.'

310

'And in the Kingdom itself?'

Sweat trickled down the side of Santiago's face, leaving marks. Diate wondered how that could happen on an illusion. 'You remember how many class As came out of that group of children,' Santiago said. 'Three. You, me, and an actress. Most families have no Talents at all. And most lose a child or two within the first decade of adulthood.'

Diate shut his eyes. He hadn't realized it was this bad. If it were, then Sheba would have trouble maintaining her government. No one would settle for those kinds of conditions for very long.

'Your father saw the future, and tried to stop it,' Santiago said.

'People put up with this?' Diate asked.

'They have no choice,' Santiago said. 'The Kingdom is as hard to leave as it is to get into, unless you have a mission. You could escape from any place they send you, but no outsider will help you or trust you. You condemned us for coming to Ziklag. But the Ziklans have nothing to steal and believe the performing arts are sinful. They're frightened of magic users. They have no use for the Kingdom, except for people like us. People who bring in money.'

The shiver in Diate's back had become a tremor which had moved to his hands. He had to learn so much. And now he had control of these people's lives. 'I'm going to need your help, Santiago.'

Santiago smiled. 'I knew that years ago.'

Diate stiffened. 'I don't know if I like being predictable.'

'You're not as predictable as I had hoped,' Santiago said.

'That should be a good thing.'

Santiago stood, slowly. The sand ran off his clothing like water. 'We'll see, Diate. We'll see.'

PART FIVE

(Six Months Later)

Chapter 26

Diate paced. He couldn't help it. He walked the length of the small shuttle, past the rows of seats filled with his comrades, past the windows reflecting the whiteness of clouds. Occasionally the pilot glanced nervously at him from her plush red seat up front. Since he had refused to sit beside her early in the trip, she could do nothing but reprimand him. And he wasn't doing anything wrong. She would tell them when to prepare for the landing.

He stuck his hands in his pockets. Pockets, for the first time in months. He dressed like a Queen's man now – tight leggings, an open blousy shirt that tied at the wrists, and calf-high boots with fringe. His hair had grown past his ears, and it had come in more silver than black.

His youth had finally left him. Now. Now that the Kingdom waited for him.

He made himself swallow. He really didn't want the others to see how nervous he was, but they couldn't miss it. He had tried to sit in a seat, to stare at the islands zooming by below like small toys, but he couldn't. It had taken him nearly a month on a ship from Oleon to go past these islands, stopping at each to check information, to search. Now they were passing over them in a space of hours.

They would land in the Kingdom soon.

The others ignored him. Most stared out the windows, faces pressed against the odd Vorgellian material. Magdalena had curled into the fetal position in the back of the shuttle. Eyes closed, hips drawn to her chest. She looked more like a frightened child than a woman.

Only two people watched Diate: Rico, with a look of anger on his florid face, and Santiago, whose features remained unreadable. Diate and Santiago had been fighting for the last week. Diate had finally won, but he wasn't sure where the victory had got him.

For the fifth time during the flight, he touched the papers stuck in the wide cuff of his shirt. Fake papers, identifying his as Tonio Carbete, the Queen's assistant. The Queen's assassin.

The Queen's brother.

Santiago had claimed Diate was taking too much of a risk, entering the country on Tonio's identity. But Diate had little choice. Santiago's magic would allow Diate to appear as any other person of similar mass and build. The problem was that in order for the magic to work, Diate had to know the person, had to be able to envision that person in his mind.

Most of the people he could envision in the Kingdom were dead or in prison in Golga. He could not masquerade as his own father; his father's death was too well known. He had tried to use other features, Kreske's, Beltar's, but they had a Golgan look that the other members of the group recognized right away.

They had been fooled by Tonio Carbete.

Tonio's presence was just slippery enough. No one knew where he was at any given time, and the old-fashioned record-keeping systems used within the country prevented anyone from cross checking. The key would be to get Diate inside.

'You can't walk us there any faster,' Rico said.

Diate stopped pacing, and glared at Rico. He had one of the seats closest to the pilot, offering more space and leg room. Even then he looked cramped.

Diate started to say something, but Santiago grabbed his arm. Diate felt a small pop as the illusion of Tonio disappeared. 'Save your energy,' Santiago said.

He wasn't referring to Diate's pacing. He didn't want Diate to fight with Rico. They had managed to avoid each other for a good portion of the training period, but when they did clash the entire tent village had heard it. And it got worse as they each became more adept at Ziklan fighting methods.

'Restore me,' Diate said.

'Not until we land. There's no reason for you to look like that man up here. You're making people nervous with all that pacing and that madman's face on your body.'

Diate nodded. He wandered to his seat and stared at it, unable to fold himself into it. He knew the emotions that warred within him. Terror. Terror that they would discover him and haul him away, murder him slowly as they had done with so many others. The due of a Diate.

Terror. And excitement. A part of him, a part bigger than he wanted to acknowledge, was looking forward to their arrival.

To going home.

'We're approaching,' the pilot said.

Diate walked behind her, holding the velvety softness of the seat back. The island rose before them, the low mountains looking like bumps on the horizon. The shuttle started its descent. As it got closer to the Kingdom, he could see the city of Tersis spread out like a fan in the lower valley. In the center, lights waved, marking the palace. Sheba was there. And she didn't know he was coming.

An odd shaking started inside his chest. His entire body felt lighter than it ever had before. If he let go of the pilot's chair, he would float to the ceiling and down again on the strength of this unnamed emotion.

Beyond the city were strands of trees and gatherings of buildings that marked rural villages. The coastlines were rocky, but with enough inlets to allow ships to dock. From this angle, he could see the gray-green buildings marking the army headquarters. Tiny black ships patrolled the outer waters, preventing any outsiders from entering.

'You need to sit down,' the pilot said.

Not now. Not when it was so close he could touch it. Not when his body was shivering from a dozen unknown emotions. He might look older, but he suddenly felt fifteen again – all arms and legs and uncontained energy.

He walked the three paces to his seat and strapped in, not taking his gaze from the windows. Condensation appeared on the glass, fogging it around the edges.

He was surprised at how small the Kingdom was. He had known that the Port City was larger than the entire island, but he had never realized what that meant. When he had left here, the Kingdom had been the entire world.

The shuttle bumped and listed to one side. Diate clung to his straps. He heard gasps behind him – inexperienced travelers. Most of the group had only traveled by ship to Ziklag. Diate had insisted upon the shuttle. He knew it was the best and safest way to get him into the country. He would avoid the military check-points as well as those black ships in the outer waters.

He still had internal customs to deal with, but he figured he could handle them.

He reached across the seat and tapped Santiago. 'It's time,' Diate said.

'I wish you would rethink this,' Santiago said.

Diate shook his head. 'I can't. My papers would be wrong if I did.'

Santiago sighed. He reached forward and pulled a strand of hair from Diate's head. The pinprick of pain made him feel alive. Santiago wrapped the strand between the forefingers of his left and right hands.

'Concentrate,' he said, 'on the man you wish to be. Think on him, remember everything about him. Think and remember.'

Diate closed his eyes again. Tonio Carbete's image rose in his mind: Colorless eyes, silver hair, the thin features of an aristocrat, a tall, reedy thinness that spoke of power. The air moved around Diate, then something as light as a sheet draped over him. He opened his eyes. Santiago was frowning at him.

'I hate that look,' he said.

Diate smiled. Santiago had had the same reaction the first time he had made Diate look like Carbete. If everyone responded the same way, Diate would be safe.

The pilot pushed a few buttons, and spoke to the ground. Buildings rose up beside them, suddenly life-sized. A blur of browns and blues crossed the front windshield before the port door opened and the shuttle settled inside. Once it stopped, the air temperature in the interior went up. The pilot made a few more adjustments.

Diate glanced at the group behind him and saw fear on most faces. He couldn't tell if the fear was for his new guise or for the return to the Kingdom. Probably a bit of both.

The plan was simple: they would all go their separate ways, like passengers in a standard air shuttle run. They were going to assemble later than night in Rico's family home near the ports.

The door swung open with a slight hiss, and the stairs folded down. Diate grabbed his duffel and swung ahead of the other passengers, careful not to touch them, just as he imagined Carbete would do. He strode down the steps and almost stopped, catching himself just in time.

The port smelled right – fumes, fuels, warm metal, and human sweat – but it looked all wrong. The walls were white tile with welcoming instructions blazed across them in calligraphic script.

Along the corners of the letters and in the blank spots on the tile, flowers sprouted. The floor mimicked the pattern, with the instructions in clearer script for the landing pilots. Etched glass windows overlooked the shuttle bay, and the stairs leading to those windows were also made of white tile. The railing had flowers looped through its wrought iron design.

He had never seen anything so beautiful or felt quite so welcome.

And so out of place.

He made himself walk without looking at the designs, as Carbete would do. Bay guards, wearing white decorated with ancient lions' heads over the sleeves, approached him.

'Mr Carbete, sir, we did not know you would be arriving.'

Diate nodded. 'One thing worked out right on this trip then,' he said, mimicking Carbete's clipped sardonic tones as best he could. Santiago has said the mimicry wasn't necessary – that people would hear as well as see the illusion – but Diate remembered the difference between Marina's illusion and Sheba. He didn't want to take any chances.

'The customs office is just under the stairs. We're honored that you've graced our humble port, sir.'

'Honored?' Diate raised an eyebrow. 'Well, I can't say I've ever been greeted with that word before.'

He slung the duffel over his shoulder and strode to the door under the stairs. It too bore a lion's head. Dangling from the mane were small jewels, all encrusted with the royal insignia.

Interesting. Sheba had chosen a lion, a creature of myth and fable, as her signature.

One of the guards opened the door. The room was small and stuffy. The smell of sweat was stronger here. A table with five chairs filled the front room. Another, smaller office hid in the back.

In here the walls were covered with simple tapestries. The chairs had matching covers. Two hand-blown mugs sat on a side shelf, still filled with dark liquid.

The guards were wary of him. They didn't believe that he was Tonio Carbete, but they couldn't doubt him either. Kingdom rules of decorum and simple fear kept them from touching him, from confirming their doubts.

He pulled the papers from his sleeve and tossed them on the table. One of the guards looked at his duffel. Diate pulled away. 'I would prefer you to check the documents first.'

They split the documents between them. Diate didn't watch. Instead he stared at the tapestry directly across from him.

It had been done in golds, browns, and russets on a white surface. The portraitist had caught Sheba in a fleeting moment, a half-glance that spoke of power not passion, strength not sensuality. Yet the passion and sensuality were there, in the eyes, in that mocking smile that always fluttered on the edge of her mouth.

He hadn't seen her face in over a year, and its impact on him was visceral. He wanted to touch the portrait, to lose himself in it, much as he had done the night he saw her in the Pavilion, as he had done when he saw her in Rulanda.

He had to control himself. She had killed the Golgoth, and she wanted him to dance.

'They seem to be in order,' one of the guards said, pushing the papers back across the table.

Diate made himself look away from the tapestry. He picked up the papers and returned them to their spot in his sleeve.

'Technically,' the other guard said, 'we are supposed to check the duffel.'

'I prefer my privacy,' Diate said.

'I'm sorry sir,' the guard said, 'but we are allowed to perform two of three tests. Document scan, luggage scan or body search. It is your choice.'

Diate shook his head as he tossed the duffel onto the table. 'I warned the pilot that any provincial backwater would do this. I will tell my sister that you are quite thorough here. Maybe she'll route more traffic to you, and then you won't have time to harass your betters.'

The guard touching the duffel had the grace to flush. His hands shook as they hovered over the clasp.

'Tools of the trade,' Diate said with a smile, 'and souvenirs of my trip. Be careful what you touch, or this meeting may come back to haunt you.'

'Is that a threat, sir?' the other guard asked.

'It's a warning,' Diate said. 'Since, if you plan to follow regulations to the letter, I cannot tell you what to touch and what to avoid.'

'It is against the law to transport dangerous materials.'

'I believe my documentation takes me above the law.' Diate's smile grew. 'This is a game, gentlemen, and we know it. I'll let you claim victory to save face if you let me out of this dingy room.'

'Forgive us, sir,' the first guard said, 'but if you're not Tonio Carbete –'

'Then it's your jobs, isn't it? Mean-spirited, low-level government positions in a small unimportant village. The only perks you have are the women who sleep with you to forfeit customs duty, and the hand-outs you get when you decide to play it a bit rough.' He leaned forward and put both hands on the table. 'I have no time for games, gentlemen. I have no patience for them.' He picked up the duffel. 'You had the time for your two tests. I have business to attend to, the first being a way out of this pissant place.'

He pushed open the door, steeling himself for the touch of a hand on his back. If that happened, he would run, placing himself on the mercy of his comrades. They stood in a line near the shuttle, while one beleaguered guard went through their belongings.

He turned his back on them, and went out the double doors near the bay.

Everything was white and clean. The sun seemed brighter here, reflecting off the buildings, shining on the port. Lush green trees cast thick foliage over the sidewalks, and flowers bloomed along the doorways.

As he stepped out of the shadows into the light, he noted that each building was decorated. With some, the decorations were simple: an ornate trim, fancy shutters. Others had murals on the walls, and still others had stained-glass windows on the ground floor. The random artwork gave the street a festive air.

He was surprised he had forgotten this. He did remember the Kingdom as a place of light and beauty, while thinking that Golga was dark, but the details escaped him. The house he grew up in had a rustic design, but the lawn had been full of ornamentation. His mother's sculptures hid in the trees and sat on the porch, like children.

He had forgotten it all.

People bowed a little and turned away from him as he approached. They wore flowing garments – mostly white – that revealed as much as they covered. Everything here had a free feel. Free and easy, belying the scene he had just experienced in the port.

That was truth. The harsh governmental policies hiding behind the beautiful facade. He had to remember why he was here.

He kept walking. They had chosen a small port, used mostly by

B and C Talents on return runs. Almost no traffic came through here. They hoped that the customs agents wouldn't be very efficient and that no one knew Tonio Carbete well enough to catch Diate. The shuttle pilot had made it sound as if they were landing off the main route because of some technical difficulties. If the customs agents thought they would have wondered why Carbete got off here and didn't ask for other transportation. Diate planned to be away from the town before the agents had a chance to act.

'I am behind you.'

Diate didn't move. His body didn't reflect the shock he felt. People didn't usually sneak up on him. But this was someone who knew enough not to touch Diate. He made himself turn slowly.

Santiago stood there. Diate recognized him by his build and the I'm-sorry shrug. Santiago's hair was blond and his skin dark. Only his eyes remained the same. They had a snappy brightness that Santiago couldn't hide.

'I was supposed to see you later,' Diate said.

'You were supposed to see the others later.' Santiago smiled. 'I promised nothing.'

'Any troubles?'

'None at all. We are all free to go.' Santiago's grin grew. 'I was wondering if you were going to go without us.'

Diate smiled. He still needed the rebels, although they didn't know how. They would find out that night. 'I need you,' he said.

Santiago shook his head. 'You did to get here. You're here now. You don't need us any longer.'

'But I do,' he said. 'Getting here was just the beginning.'

Santiago smiled. 'We have time then,' he said. 'Come with me. I have something to show you.'

Diate stared at him for a moment. He had thought to use these hours to get used to the Kingdom, to reaccustom himself to the way of life here.

The wind carried the familiar scents of pine and incense. The smells made his restlessness increase. He was still stuck in that panic that he had felt when he left the Kingdom. Still afraid that around any corner, someone would appear who wanted to kill him.

Good. It would keep him alert.

'All right,' he said. 'I'll follow you.'

Santiago led him through back alleys and a dozen quiet streets. The village was bigger on the ground than it looked in the air. Sometimes the houses were the size of Beltar's store, the artwork decorating them more ornate. And sometimes, they were tiny boxes, with children's drawings glued to the windows. The front exit from the ports opened onto a residential street. But the back, where Santiago led him, housed the pilots and the support staff.

Locked fences and barbed gates surrounded the compounds. These buildings were drab grays with no decorations at all. Some lawns had toys – apparently the pilots were allowed to have children – but the playthings were the only sign of disarray. A shudder ran down Diate's back. The Kingdom walled off the foreigners for a different reason: it didn't want to protect them; it wanted to keep them away from the community itself.

Just past the pilot's barracks, a glass building stood three stories high. It overlooked the rest of the town and towered above the trees that blocked a view of the ground floor. Diate had seen buildings like this before. As a boy, he had visited one for nearly a year. Government training centers. Talent Houses. The name varied from community to community, but the purpose was the same: to find and develop Talents, for the greater glory of the Kingdom.

'What's here?' he asked.

'You'll see.' Santiago led Diate down a narrow brick path. The bricks had been arranged by color – dark red near the sidewalk, tapering to a white by the door. Smart move on the designers' part. Not only was the look attractive, but it made the gathering of footprints easy. Unwanted guests could be tracked. Literally.

Diate followed Santiago up two wooden stairs to the front door. A young woman, her body flowing in mid-jeté – legs spread above the ground, torso arched, arms in second position, head thrown back in pure enjoyment – was etched into the glass. She was opaque, but otherwise so real that Diate thought he could touch her.

Santiago ran his finger alongside the doorjamb. The door swung open, revealing a carved oak hall. They stepped inside. The air was cooler here. The interior was done in glass and greenery. All of the glass was etched, all of the plants artfully arranged. Even the tiles on the floor were made of glass. Diate looked down, and saw the rooms below them like a scale model of a building. He looked up, and felt as if he were a small child hiding beneath the furniture.

As far as he could tell, they were alone.

'Come on,' Santiago said. He pushed on the glass, revealing a mirrored surface. With a flick of a finger, he touched the side of the mirror. It swung open, revealing a flight of wooden stairs.

Diate glanced around. No one could see inside this room. For all its surface openness, the building had hidden secrets. The smell of incense grew stronger, and voices echoed, deadened a little by the wooden walls.

The stairs creaked beneath his weight. As they got close to the bottom, Santiago reached up and took Diate's hand. Something popped as the illusion disappeared around him.

He gasped. 'Santiago –'

'We're among friends,' Santiago said.

But Diate had no way of knowing that. Had Santiago betrayed him? To what end?

Three steps from the bottom, he stopped. A dozen people were scattered around a small room. The room's walls were made of carved wood. The figures in it were all wearing long robes and had their hands reaching to the sky. The people inside the room also wore long robes, most a starry blue, and their conversation stopped when they saw Diate.

He scanned the faces. The ages varied, but they all had one thing in common. A silver dot on the bridge of the nose. He didn't recognize any of them until he looked at the last face. Torrie, the magic user. An old fear rose within him. 'I thought you said we were among friends.'

Torrie stood. She had been sitting on a cushion near the paneled walls. She looked the same as she always had. 'I am a friend, Emilio. You just never realized it.'

'Friend?' He said the word with such force that spittle flew from his lips. 'You had me captured on the Vorgellian ship.'

'Yes,' she said. 'A ship that was taking you to Rulanda, the Kingdom's favorite vacation spot. No one would have helped you there. They were all too afraid of losing their commissions. I knew Sehan. He wouldn't kill you, and I trusted the Golgoth. He wanted peace more than any of us.'

Diate's back stiffened. Santiago had stepped aside so that Diate could go the rest of the way down the stairs. Santiago looked like himself again. He felt no need to hide among these people.

'What am I doing here?' Diate asked.

'You'll see.' Santiago sat on the steps, his elbows resting on his knees.

'Join us, Emilio,' Torrie said.

His heart was pounding in his throat. This was the kind of thing he had hoped to avoid. Being trapped in a small place, with people he feared. He walked down the remaining steps. The light was brighter at the base of the stairs. Magic Talents. He had heard as a boy that they all knew each other and worked with each other, but he had never believed it. Other Talents competed and tried to drive each other out.

'I can't join you,' he said, leaving the sarcasm in his voice. 'I am but a simple dancer, and nothing – not even Santiago's illusions – will give me the power to join you.'

'You are not a simple dancer. You are the Rogue Talent, the only Talent to ever leave this place alive and do something beyond your destiny. Do you know what power that gives you?' Torrie waved her hand. The sleeve on her robe wavered as if it were in a small breeze.

'Where does that give me power?'

Torrie smiled. Her face cascaded into wrinkles. Suddenly her age appeared. She no longer had youth to buoy her up. 'You have the power of romance, the power of legend, the power of myth. We're prepared to help you use it, Emilio.'

'What do you gain from that?'

Torrie turned. A man sat on a stool in the back, one foot on a lower rung, one on a higher. Diate hadn't noticed him before. The man had long silver hair that flowed to his waist, and a beard that matched it in length.

'We are the underbelly of the Talent system,' the man said. 'The secret, misunderstood group that takes what bones the government throws us. We make no tangible art objects, we write no books, we give no performances. Our talent is subtle and feared.'

Diate knew that. He remembered the conversations, the hushed whispers as magic Talents walked through their public displays. His fear, when Torrie unmasked him, his fear that the magic Talents would find him anywhere. And –

You didn't tell me you could shape-shift.

I can't! It's just an illusion that breaks with touch . . .

325

You fooled me.

– his own anger based in fear. These people could be anything they wanted, do anything they wanted, hurt anyone they wanted.

'See?' the man said, a smile tugging at his beard. 'Even you fear us.'

Diate opened his mouth to deny it, then thought the better of it. He didn't know the level of Talent in the room. He had avoided magic Talents all his life until Santiago. And Santiago had not explained to him all that magic Talents could do.

'I don't understand what you want from me.'

'We have sideways abilities,' the man said. 'Some have the ability to see the future; others the truth of the past. A few of us can persuade, gently and convincingly, so convincingly that the subject believes it is his idea. And some of us can see into the corners of other people's minds.'

Diate crossed his arms over his chest. He didn't care that his body showed his fear. If they could read minds, they would know it. 'Who are you?' he asked the man.

The man smiled. 'I am you.'

Diate peered at him. The resemblance was there: the slenderness, the dancer's strength. The silver hair.

His shaking grew worse. 'I have no magic talent.'

'You have never been tested for them,' the man said. 'Your father feared magic Talents more than anything else.'

With justification. He would have feared them more had he known the kind of power they had had in his son's life. 'You cannot be me,' Diate said. 'I am standing right here.'

'And you cannot touch me,' the man in the corner said. 'For we are in different planes and different places. But I figured only I could be the one to convince you.'

Diate didn't want to be convinced. He didn't want to talk to this man any more. 'Of what?'

'To follow the path chosen for you. To stay in the light. If you go alone, you will die. If you go directly to the palace, you will lose yourself. Go to Rico's tonight. Listen to the others, here. They want to help you.'

Diate walked past the other magic Talents. Their robes brushed against his feet. He tried not to touch anyone. He didn't want more surprises. A few people cleared out of his way as he approached the man. Diate placed his hand on the man's shoulders, but his fingers went through as if the man weren't there at all.

'So now you believe,' the man said with a laugh. He raised the sleeve on his left arm, revealing a crooked silver scar.

'This is magic. Someone else is doing this.' Diate said. He whirled. 'Who is creating this illusion?'

No one answered. The man chuckled. Diate faced him again.

'It is magic,' the man said. 'But magic I control. Your eyes lie, Emilio, and they always have.'

The man faded like darkness before light. Even the stool was gone. Diate stood in the vacant spot. His shaking had grown worse. 'That made no sense,' he said to Torrie. 'What are you trying to do to me?'

'We're trying to get you to follow destiny.'

'In my father's footsteps?'

Torrie shook her head. 'Your father was a fool. He defied the authority of the state without understanding it.'

'Now you want me to defy it even though I understand it?'

'We want you to take it over.' Her voice was soft.

Diate leaned against the paneled wall. The curved wood dug into his back. He had never had any intention of ruling. 'You can see the future. You have sideways power. Why don't you do it?'

'Because we don't have your power. Santiago explained this to you. When you dance, Emilio, you woo the crowd. When you speak, you can do the same. It is a special kind of talent, one that goes unrecognized here because if it were acknowledged, the competition for leadership here would grow even stronger. But the Minister of Culture always tests for charisma as well as everything else. Your family wasn't singled out just because of your father, Emilio.'

The wood supported him even more. 'What do you mean?'

Torrie shrugged. 'You had talent in the dance, but you also had talent in leadership. If the government didn't separate you from your father, you might have tried to topple them as you realized your power. They thought, crudely I might add, that slaughtering your family would frighten you and make you do as they say. They didn't understand your strengths. They still don't.'

'If I work for you, what do you gain?'

'We gain a future,' Torrie said. 'Right now, we are bargain basement talents, our greatest skills ignored by the people who need them most. You would not rule as a dictator, but as part of a team. That team, for the first time in this country's history, would include us.'

'So I would become your figurehead.'

A man stood beside Torrie. She put a hand on his arm, as if to restrain him. 'No,' she said. 'You would do what this country has needed for a long time. You would change its economic base. You can't do that without us.'

Diate let out a small laugh. This situation had gotten too strange for him. The fact that he was listening to her babble frightened him. 'One man can't change the economic base of a nation. You realize that even if I could, it would mean economic collapse, poverty, starvation, not to mention the threat of take-over from Golga and other countries nearby.'

'We can prevent the take-over,' Torrie said. 'A country is vulnerable when it looks weak to the outside. We can raise an illusion, make this country look strong to visitors until the crisis is over.'

'But that doesn't solve the internal problems. People would starve, Torrie.'

She shook her head. 'Some of us can see various possible futures. We can prevent the bulk of the starvations. And the Kingdom has a treasure trove that the current government is unwilling to sell.'

Diate's hands were clammy. He pressed them against the wall and felt them stick. 'What?'

'The artifacts we have stolen over the years and made our own. Most countries have offered sizable rewards for those goods.'

'They wouldn't give those rewards to the people who stole the goods in the first place.'

'It wouldn't be the same people,' Torrie said. 'New government, new people. We would return them to show the corruption of the previous regime.'

'You're crazy,' he said.

'No. We're determined.'

'Why me? Why now?'

Torrie sighed. She ran a hand through her white hair. 'You have always been our greatest hope, Emilio. You and Sheba. We do not see the future. We see possible futures. Until Rulanda, we thought you were going to rule together. Then when the Golgoth accepted the bid for the Peace Festival, the old Queen would have died, you and Sheba would have taken over, the Golgoth would have lived, and there would have been peace between our countries, and a future for the Kingdom.'

He forced himself to breathe slowly. The strangeness, the manipulation, the interference in his life, was almost more than he could bear. 'Your meddling caused that,' he said. 'You said, "Your woman is dying," and I went to Martina, and Sheba thought I didn't care for her.'

'I meant to bring you closer. I meant Sheba. She was losing herself. She had lost herself.' Torrie said.

Diate stared at her for a moment. 'You're so effective, Torrie. If you can see the future, then you should have known that would throw us apart.'

Torrie looked down. 'I can't see everything.'

'No, you can't. And you make things worse,' Diate said. 'You went to see Martina, and I wouldn't let you in. You said, "We're glad she's finally doing her job." What was her job, Torrie?'

'Martina no longer matters to us.'

'Well, she matters to me!' Diate took a step toward Torrie. Immediately four magic Talents surrounded her.

'You're not going to touch me, Emilio,' Torrie said.

He stopped, and clenched his fists. 'So I do scare you.'

She nodded a little. The Talents moved away. 'I know what you can do.'

'Then tell me about Martina.' He was breathing heavily.

'All right.' Torrie leaned against a cushion. 'She left us. She had been a part of this group – we need all the class A magicians we can get – but she repudiated us. She didn't like the way we focused our energies on you. Ironic, isn't it, the way you became friends?'

'You planned that?' His voice came out as a whisper. 'You planned our friendship?'

'No.' Torrie clasped her hands together. 'I should have seen her on Rulanda. She warned you away from us. She was a true friend to you, Emilio. If you had listened to her, you wouldn't be here now.'

'Where you want me. Where you tried to manipulate me.' His tone rose with each word. 'You thought you could control me, but you were so inept that you tried to ruin everything. You're the one who destroyed my relationship with Sheba, Torrie.'

'I think you did that on your own,' Torrie said.

'No,' Diate said. 'She betrayed me, Torrie, and left me to die because of you. Because she thought I loved Martina.'

'Do you really believe that?' Torrie asked. 'That she left you because of love?'

Her words stopped him, even though he didn't want to hear them. 'What else could it have been?'

Torrie smiled. 'For all your living, you are naive, detective. She left you because she had business. She left you because you found her smugglers. She left you because, at the time, she didn't know how to use you.'

He was shaking. She had come back for him. That proved that she loved him.

'I had nothing to do with her,' Torrie said. 'I take credit for my successes – and my failures.'

Diate swallowed. He had to make himself move forward. 'You want me to believe that?' he said. 'You want me to work with you, with all of you, so that you can meddle with this country? I don't think so. The only examples I have of your work are bad ones. I see no reason to work with you.'

'We saved your life,' Torrie said softly. 'Twice.'

Diate made himself breathe. 'You saved my life once, Torrie. And I would debate your intentions. For all you know, the Golgoth would have killed me.'

'Believe what you want, Emilio,' Torrie said, 'but we need each other.'

'We do? You want me to agree to that, based on the words of an old man who disappeared?' Diate laughed. 'That man wasn't me. That was one of you, casting an illusion.'

'That was a possible you, speaking from a possible future,' one of the men said. Diate whirled toward him. The man held up his hands, but the expression on his face remained calm. 'We don't expect you to understand.'

'We need you, Emilio, as much as you need us. As a group, we have no power to topple the government. You do. You have many powers. You are famous here for escaping the system. You are a myth. You have the family lineage, the looks and the charisma to attract crowds. You have the need for vengeance.'

Diate stepped within inches of her. 'How do I know that you didn't kill my family to set these wheels into motion?'

'We can't kill,' she said. 'If we kill, we lose our abilities.'

'Then how did you manage to burn Martina?'

'We didn't kill her,' Torrie said.

The words hung between them for a moment. The picture became very clear. Martina had left them, and their schemes, and

330

had become a musical Talent. She got mixed up with an assassin, and the Kingdom brought her home, interrogated her, and set her free. She went to her family, and during the night, the magic Talents found her. They hurt her and set her free where Diate would find her, thinking she would help them now. She hadn't. She had been loyal to him.

The Diate Rebels. They want you to lead them. They felt that if you felt betrayed you'd come back. Stay away from the Rebels, Emilio. They only want to use you.

She had been his friend all along, and he had hurt her because he hadn't understood.

Diate crossed his arms in front of his chest. 'If you can't kill,' he said, 'then I couldn't have been that old man. I have killed, and I will do it again.'

'Yes, you will,' Torrie said. 'You will kill again. But that was you. The magic of power – your magic – only increases with danger.'

He pushed her away. 'Lies,' he said. 'It's all lies.'

She stumbled backwards, then righted herself. A smile crossed her face. 'Ah,' she said. 'Can you be sure?'

Her words made him shudder. He pushed past her and started up the stairs. He stopped beside Santiago. 'You should never have brought me here,' he said.

Santiago looked up at him. 'I have done nothing to hurt you. I have worked toward this from the beginning.'

'You burned an innocent woman. You manipulated people. You cost the Golgoth his life.'

'Burned an innocent woman?' Santiago froze. 'You have known me for six months. Do you think I'm capable of injuring Martina?'

'Your people hurt her and set her free, to make her meet me, to make her work with me.'

Torrie laughed. 'No, Emilio. Credit us for more finesse than that. Martina left us and our protection. We are guilty for that. But she was discovered to be a traitor after her interrogation, then burned and dumped. The government did that. We don't dare. If she had died, we would have lost all our powers.'

Torrie's words had a ring of truth. Diate forced himself to take a deep breath. He had to calm down and listen with his mind, not his heart. Torrie was right. They could use each other.

They wanted power. He wanted destruction. They had a gift of illusion. He had a band of troops.

331

Together they could create a future.

'How familiar are you with the Diate Rebels?' he asked.

Santiago grinned and visibly relaxed. Torrie shrugged. 'Familiar enough.'

'Good,' Diate said. 'Because we're all going to work together.'

Chapter 27

Diate sat in the electric rail car, clinging to the wooden hand-hold in front of his seat. Electric trains were different in the Kingdom. Here they were called trolleys and their bodies were made mostly of wood. Apparently the Vorgellians had wanted to make them metal, as they had in Golga, but the Kingdom had disagreed. They couldn't decorate the metal as well as the wood.

He sat alone in the back of the car, windows around him on all sides. The seats had large red cushions, and the walls bore carefully carved images the matched the car's name. The car, titled 'Memories,' had carvings of famous performers from the Kingdom's past. Since Diate had been on the car most of the day, he had played with the images, trying to remember as many of them as possible.

He tried not to look at himself. Santiago had disguised Diate as the old man he had met in the Talent Center. Diate had insisted: he couldn't get the image out of his head. The illusion worked, even for him. His hands were oversized and covered with age spots. The hair he wore just to the tip of his collar appeared to brush his chest. His voice, usually powerful, sounded querulous and old.

The car rumbled and shook along the rails, passing small groves of trees. Diate's hair blew in the breeze fom an open window. The air smelled of roses. Spring had just begun to touch the landscape. The riotous color only added to the beauty of the country around him.

In the past month, he had marveled at how deftly the Kingdom hid its poverty. Shacks were surrounded by trees. Artists covered any blank surface with drawings. Tiny homes had decorative banners hanging from the porch, and plants bloomed everywhere. Only when he saw the faces of the people who lived inside did he realize how few of them held hope.

Well, he would give them hope, had since he arrived. Although he hadn't left the small village, he had become an influence in the countryside. The Rebels had gone from place to place, describing him, repeating his father's words, saying that the Rogue Talent had returned. That they would finally control their own government again. That the Queen should worry about her throne. Twice troops went through the village, searching for him door-to-door. The last time, he had greeted them himself, in the disguise he wore now.

He was amazed at the Kingdom's lack of ability to flush out magic. All the troops had to do was touch him and he would be revealed. But touch followed particular rules in this culture. Most touch was considered sexual, and therefore not allowed unless each party made permission clear. Once permission was granted, touch became almost too personal. Diate's upbringing on Golga had not prepared him for Magdalena's friendly pats on the genitals, or the other rebel women's occasional hugs. He had to train himself to relax, to not take each action personally. He was better suited to Rico's rough treatment, and the battles the two of them still had.

At least Rico was working with him now.

Rico had coordinated the rebels. He had been the one to monitor their progress, to acknowledge that the level of hope within the Kingdom was rising. Sheba had commissioned more troops, in fear of some kind of action. Diate smiled. She would never expect what she was going to get.

He wasn't after her, although the Rebels thought he was. He was after the government itself, the Talent system, the economic system, and the tyranny that had marked the Kingdom since its inception.

The train swung around a wide corner and screeched to a stop. People left the car ahead of his, and more got on, a few entering his car. They saw him as a wild-eyed old man, looking feverish and crazy, huddled in the back seat, and kept their distance. He wanted that.

He was pleased it was working. He couldn't go places as Carbete any more. Carbete had caught on, and had ordered that anyone who saw him touch him to make sure he was real. Carbete had also issued a public threat, saying that anyone who impersonated him would die slowly and painfully.

Diate knew that Carbete meant every word.

The new people eased into their seats, backs to him. The train started again, slowly, then building up speed. Diate gazed out the windows. The trees were easing into more shacks, decorated with vines and poorly done art. In front of some of them, groups of people stood, talking excitedly. He had seen this sight all during his trip, and had overheard people say they were going into the city. If Rico had reached them, if they were going to see Diate, the numbers would be huge.

He made himself look away from the people and at the city itself. He hated this section of Tersis. As a boy, he had thought the city huge. It clustered against the best harbors, the poorest sections on the outer circles of the city, the wealthy sections, and the palace in the very center. Excitement ate at his stomach, and he could barely sit still.

The houses got bigger the farther into the city they went. This trolley didn't stop once they reached Tersis. It was designed for people who lived outside the city to travel to the center, for cultural events or minor Talent shows. No one from outside worked inside. The city's structure mirrored its social hierarchy. The poor circled and outnumbered the wealthy, and the wealthy circles were closed to all but the most talented and the most devious.

The trolley rattled as it went around corners. Diate's body shook. He had been on this thing for a long time. He had waited an hour before that to board. The others had left early, plans already in place. He hoped they knew what to do. If they betrayed him, he would die.

At least the final piece was in place. Beltar's ship had arrived in the harbor the night before. Magdalena had told Diate. She had thought it a supply ship, bringing weapons. Beltar had brought a few weapons, enough to fool Magdalena, but he had a different purpose.

At last, the trolley stopped at the station near the palace. The station was an old white building with bas-relief carvings all along its front. Diate had loved it as a boy. Inside, the ceiling had a huge mural representing all the art forms. The floor also sported a mural, this one of all forms of business practiced in other cultures. The murals met in a third mural that worked its way around the walls, portraying performers in other places, thieves plying their trade against businessmen in other cultures.

Diate had studied those murals as he went back and forth between dance contests. Even when he was alone in the station, he felt as if he had company.

The rails crisscrossed before the station. A huge crowd waited on the platform. They overflowed onto the stairs and down the sidewalks leading to the palace itself. He could see human beings trailing into the distance, so many of them that they lost their individuality. Sheba had to know. She had to be worried.

People got off his car before he did, and a few greeted others in the crowd. The rest of the crowd strained, watching the passengers disembark. They were waiting for someone.

He crept out of the back of the car and took the steps gingerly, as an elderly man would. The crowd ignored him, staring beyond him at the empty car. He glanced to either side. The other cars were empty as well. They weren't going to get to see anyone else this day.

Then he noticed the soldiers in the back, their white and gold uniforms blazing in the sun. Nearly fifty of them had spread through the crowd.

He didn't know a lot about Kingdom maneuvers, but he assumed they were similar to Golgan. If fifty soldiers were in sight, five hundred were hiding, with weapons trained on the station. His heart pounded in his throat. He made himself trip on a rail, then step over cautiously as if tripping were something he did often. When he reached the platform, a young woman reached down to help him up. He narrowly missed the touch of her fingers.

He wasn't sure how he would get through that crowd. Santiago wasn't with him, although Santiago had wanted to come. He needed Santiago at the palace, planted and waiting. He hadn't realized how dangerous it would be traveling in populated areas.

Diate smiled and shook his head at the woman. He wandered along the length of the rail until he reached a side staircase with only a handful of people on it. He grabbed the railing and hauled himself up slowly, avoiding the other people as he moved.

'Long trip, old man?' one of the soldiers asked him. The boy was young, his uniform new and shiny, his attitude as shiny as the clothing. The crowd shifted, sensing that something was happening.

'What's going on?' Diate asked, panting between each word to emphasize the effort of his walk.

'Rumors that the Rogue Talent is back.'

Diate made a dismissive gesture with his hands. 'That boy's long dead,' he said. 'I been telling my daughter that. It's all lies that someone is making up to excite the people.'

The soldier shrugged. 'Government can't be too sure. We can't face a threat like that.'

'From one man?' Diate asked. 'The government can handle one man.'

An older soldier glanced over, his face wizened and lined from too many hours in the sun. 'Not like this,' the soldier said. 'I've never seen crowds this silent and this hopeful. If this guy doesn't show up, I'm worried. If he does, I'm even more worried.'

The people nearby had turned away, finding the conversation dull. It probably repeated conversations that had been going on all morning. The crowd at the station was beginning to disperse, speaking in low whispers and avoiding the soldiers. People were pushing their way across the manicured lawn, back to the palace, to try to find a place to stand in the throng.

'He's not going to show up,' Diate said. 'That boy's been dead since they killed his daddy.'

'The crowd will get ugly if he doesn't,' the older soldier said. 'There's too many rumors, too much talk.'

Diate smiled a little. 'Sounds like you want to see him.'

'I've been hearing about him all my life,' the soldier said. 'I have often wondered what kind of man he is.'

'Yet you're here to kill him.'

The soldier shook his head. 'Crowd control. We're just supposed to make sure things don't get out of hand.'

Diate nodded. 'They won't,' he said. 'You mark this, boy. This'll be one of those days where everything'll be on edge and nothing'll happen.'

The platform was empty. He could just make it safely now. He started across, careful to keep his body hunched, his legs wobbling.

'Hey, old man!' the older soldier yelled. 'What are you doing here?'

Diate stopped, and turned slowly. 'I came to see my daughter,' he said. 'She ain't come to visit me in a long time. I figured I best see her.'

The soldier gave him a half-pitying smile. He understood. Too many children who made money abandoned their parents to the shacks outside of town. The children never wanted to look back. They never wanted to remember that they had been poor once too.

Diate surveyed the crowd. He could understand the soldiers'

nervousness. The crowd was silent, staring at the palace with an intensity Diate had never seen before. Most wore ragged clothing and no jewelry. Some carried small knives attached to their belts. The people rustled as they moved and low conversations were conducted in whispers. But had Diate not seen the gathering, he would have thought only a hundred people had shown up instead of over thousands.

Rico had done his job too well.

Diate couldn't face them yet. He needed a moment to himself.

He stepped out of the sun and went into the station. The murals were as he remembered them – perhaps even a bit more vivid, the browns darker, the reds brighter, the blues bolder. He stopped in the center and stared at it all. He had forgotten that the benches, water fountains, and ticket counters blended into the artwork.

He sat down on a bench that had been painted to look like a set of stairs that led into a jeweler's shop on the floor. The bench was as hard as the one on the train. He was shaking. He took a deep breath. He was only a few minutes away now.

He was ready.

Diate stood, feeling strong. He had waited all his life for this.

He walked down the marble stairs to the other side of the station, and looked out the plain glass windows. People were packed against the five oversized fountains that lined the walkway leading into the palace. The wide, tree-lined sidewalk that led to the fountains from the station was momentarily empty. The crowd must have assumed he was going to arrive some other way.

Diate left by the back door of the station. He stood on the thin concrete steps. People kept pouring in from the side streets, walking in family groups, sometimes holding hands. The early arrivals had staked out the fountains.

The fountains were huge, spewing water that caught the light and reflected it back in rainbow colors. The first two fountains were non-representational blocks of stone. The next two were half-uncarved and half-carved human forms appearing vaguely in the stone. The water ran off their arms and down their hair. The last fountain merged the half-carved forms into one form: a woman. The first Queen. She stood above the spouts as if she were making the water flow.

And she had for over a century.

She would no longer.

Four men appeared in the trees near the empty walk. As he glanced at them, they shimmered and changed into men as old as the one he appeared to be. Suddenly, Diate understood why the walk was empty. The magic Talents must have fooled the crowd into thinking this was not a place to stand. He breathed a sigh of relief. He was glad to see them. He had been wondering if he would have to do this part alone.

One of the men smiled at him and tipped an imaginary hat. Diate smiled back. He walked down the steps, using his true walk, no wobble, no pretended hesitation. He threw his head back and moved with the grace Myla had taught him, all the self-assurance the Golgoth had given him. He felt the power flowing through his body, felt like he could do anything.

And he would.

As he walked, he did as Santiago had taught him: he shed bits and pieces of the fake image. The long gray hair disappeared first, blown away by the wind. The age spots withered and sunk into his skin. His knuckles returned to their normal size. The wrinkles smoothed. By the time he had reached the first fountain, he looked like himself again.

People saw him and pointed. A cheer went up that echoed down the streets. Hands clapped. Heads turned toward him in unison, and in the back, the crowd strained to see him. A woman standing near him gasped and picked up the child at her feet. An elderly man nodded, recognition on his face. Three little boys in the front of the line started chanting: *Dee-ah-Tay! Dee-ah-Tay!* and the crowd picked it up.

He moved his feet to their rhythm, picked up his pace. The soldiers had moved to the edges of the crowd, the sun reflecting off their white uniforms. Behind them stood the palace, with its oversized unfinished mural depicting, in imagery, the history of the Kingdom. Two images had been added since he left: the first was a woman holding an eagle – the Queen he had killed. The second was almost finished. It portrayed Sheba, riding naked on the back of a lion. He stared at the image as he walked, seeing her idealized form, wondering if he would see her in person before everything began.

The chant was loud and overpowering. He had never heard so many voices speaking together. The rhythm they made was more potent than any music.

As the people chanted, he kept walking, head held high. The crowd parted to let him through. He stopped at the base of the fifth fountain, facing the wide marble stairs leading into the palace. As he approached the small wooden platform Rico had brought and set on the path, people scrambled off it. Diate climbed the two steps to the top and faced the audience.

The faces stretched even farther than he thought they had. Bodies were packed into the side streets. Children rode on the shoulders of adults. Other adults leaned out windows in nearby buildings. Only the palace windows appeared empty.

Scattered near the front of the crowd, he could see the faces of the rebels: Magdalena, Rico, Berto, and the others, including the people he had met since he arrived in the Kingdom. They were holding guns tightly against their sides.

He stood for a moment. The people were restless. They shifted as they saw him. His throat was dry. One word from him. All it would take was one word.

He was going to give them that word.

Santiago appeared behind him, half hidden by the fountain itself. Diate nodded when he saw him. The crowd's chant had grown. Diate raised his hands, and the chant eased into a whisper before dying out completely.

'It's good to be home!' he said and a large roar went up around him. The vibrations pounded him. He had only felt this a few times, when he had been particularly successful at the dance.

He waited for the cheers to die down. 'I see nothing has changed since I left. People are still killing for this country. People are still having their dreams destroyed. I bet there are hundreds of you out there who are very good at a lot of things, but were told you had no real talent at anything. Am I right?'

Heads nodded as voices shouted yes. Some people just stood and watched. Talents? Or guards? Loyalists? He didn't know. More troops filtered to the edge of the crowd. The troop numbers were half the size of the crowd's now, but he could see more people approaching, from the streets beyond.

He was shaking. Not with fear, but with a kind of elation. 'Some things have changed, though. There are more shacks on the edge of town. More of you seem to have no hope, no money, and no dreams.'

The people in the back couldn't hear him. A low murmur arose as his words were whispered from one person to the next. He raised his voice until he was shouting as loud as he could. 'I met a Talent on Golga – a woman who had been certified class A in both music and magic. She had been burned and left to die in a garbage bin near the ports. No wonder we have no hope! Not even our Talents are safe!'

'You survived!' A thin man with a balding head shouted. He stood up front, as close to Diate as he could get.

'Yes,' Diate said. 'I survived. I survived with the help of a man you were all taught to hate. A man your current Queen murdered. In the middle of a peace festival to which the Kingdom was invited. The Kingdom doesn't want peace. This government would die under an international peace treaty. This government that built these fountains, that palace. The wealth it has stolen from all of you!'

The crowd jeered and booed. People raised their fists in the direction of the palace. The doors at the top of the wide marble stairs were open and Diate could see the shadowy figures within. Sheba was watching. Her people were watching.

He wondered what she thought.

'We can stop it!' he yelled. 'That's my message to you. You have all heard of my father. You have heard the way he was killed because he spoke out against the government. You have heard that I escaped. I survived. I went other places. I learned to take control of my life, and you must take control of yours. No one has the right to tell you how good you are. No one has the right to make money off your talents and give you no choice about that. No one has the right to exploit you!

'I am a class A Talent, and I have only danced once in sixteen years. I made a real living without killing, without stealing, without robbing anyone. I broke away from the system, and still the system haunts me. It killed my family, and it killed my closest friend. It destroyed the woman I love.'

The words broke in his throat. He looked at the palace as he said that, wishing he could see Sheba's face. Torrie had been right all along. *The woman you love is dying.*

No, Torrie. The woman he loved was already dead.

The crowd was staring at him, rapt faces with different caste marks, different levels of hope, were clinging to every word.

'I broke away from the system,' he said. 'But I did it wrong. You can never escape the Kingdom, not as it stands now. The key is not to break away from the system. The key is to break the system itself!'

A cheer went up, so loud and deafening that he rode it. He almost didn't see the man run up the stairs, the long Vorgellian laser in his hand. Diate braced himself, but Rico was already there, grabbing the man, holding him down. Another Rebel took the pistol away.

So close. So very close. Santiago waved a hand, and a group of people wearing a uniform with Diate's face on the back appeared around the fountain. Their uniforms were black, their faces somber. They looked so real that, for a moment, Diate was as stunned as the people around him. But they weren't real. They were small bits of cloth, made to look like men, operating as a unit under the command of Santiago's right hand.

The toy soldiers were good. He hoped the other magic users scattered among the crowd would be as successful.

He glanced at the fake troops beside him, looking like real soldiers in the sunlight. 'My father spoke of revolution!' Diate cried. 'I'm here to make it! I am here to set you all free!'

Another cheer went up. The Kingdom troops snapped into position, guns raised above their heads. Diate froze when he saw them. Rifles of every make and model, from Ziklan to Vorgellian. Laser guns, all Vorgellian issue, and a few zap guns developed by the biologists on Oleon. Of course the Kingdom had excellent weapons. They stole from every place in the world.

Rico was right. This would be a slaughter. Diate hoped his plan would prevent as much bloodshed as possible.

'Are you with me?' he shouted.

'Yes!' The crowd answered with one voice.

'Then let's go.' He ran down the stairs, leading the crowd in its surge to the palace.

Chapter 28

Diate hadn't gone five yards before Santiago grabbed his arms. Up front, he could hear shouts and screams, the echoey reports of the older rifles shooting into the air. Hundreds of black-clothed toy soldiers led the charge, popping like balloons as lasers hit them, only to reappear an instant later. The Kingdom's soldiers shot blindly, not realizing that the advance guard were fake. Neither did the rest of the crowd. They cheered as they ran, ripping branches off trees, brandishing knives they must have brought, carrying rocks. They no longer saw Diate. All they saw was the mural, and the history of their own oppression.

Santiago held Diate back. 'You're not supposed to go with them.'

Diate glanced at Santiago. Santiago looked like himself, small and wiry, with his silver caste mark glowing in the middle of his forehead. 'Thanks,' Diate said. He had been caught in the moment, ready to storm with the rest of the people. His battle was not there. He had to get Rico and the others inside. To fight the true battle. With the guard.

And Carbete.

'This way,' Diate said. Santiago ran beside him, keeping a contingent of fifty toy soldiers around them. Diate protected Santiago with his own body. If a random shot got through, Diate needed Santiago more than the revolution now needed Diate.

The Kingdom's soldiers had moved into the crowd, clubbing people with the butt of their weapons, screaming as they did so. A woman lay on the path before Diate, trampled, her eyes open, her face covered with blood. He looked away.

Some of the soldiers were not fighting the crowd but moving with them. Most of these soldiers were young, not battle-scarred at all, able to remember the dreams they had lost when they put on the uniform. A bonus. One Diate hadn't thought he would get.

He and Santiago crossed behind the fountain. Some of the crowd had already split off and were heading to the back of the palace, just as Diate was. He wanted them to stop. He wanted the way to be free and clear, but he couldn't command that. The crowd was out of control now. He had turned it into a mob. He wouldn't be able to turn it back.

He moved with them, hoping that the plans of the palace he had taken from the Golgoth's headquarters were correct. The secret passages, the listening rooms: he hoped none of them had been changed in the year and a half since Kreske had given him the copy.

He needed everything to be accurate. He had not had a way to double-check this part of his plan, and it frustrated him.

They reached the back garden court. People had already breached the gate. The statues in the center area were draped with leaves, torn banners, and pictures of Diate himself. The grass was trampled, and the door into the palace stood open. Soldiers were shooting at people trying to enter. Guns hung from the windows and from the doors on the upper floors. A number of people lay dead in the grass.

'Santiago,' Diate whispered.

Santiago shook his head. 'We didn't plan on them being back here. I can't help them and finish what we need to do.'

Bile rose in Diate's throat. All his life he had worked to prevent this kind of killing. Even today's coup was designed to spare the most lives. He had never counted on this.

But if he backed down now, Sheba would remain in charge, and the slaughter would get worse. Every person *suspected* of participating in this would be executed.

As his family was.

As traitors.

The only way to make traitors into heroes was to win the war.

'All right,' Diate said. 'Let's go.'

Santiago nodded. He clapped his hands and the toy support troop disappeared. Then he touched Diate's face. 'You ready?'

Diate glanced at the guards fighting at the door, then closed his eyes. 'Ready.'

He felt the change. He was becoming accustomed to the subtle nuances of illusion. Santiago had told him that he was easy to convert, that there was magic blood in him somewhere.

Around him, people were screaming, pounding. He could feel

the battle through his bones. The ground beneath his feet vibrated from the force of it.

'Done,' Santiago said.

Diate opened his eyes and took a step back. Santiago stood before him, taller now, dressed in the white and gold of Sheba's soldiers. His features were heavier, his coloring dark, but he still looked like himself. Daite glanced down. He was dressed as a soldier too, but he had been concentrating on the older man he had met that morning. He hoped the disguise worked.

'We can't go through that mob,' he said.

'We can't stay here either,' Santiago said.

They ran the risk of being killed by their own people. Out of the corner of his eye, Diate saw more people arriving down the side streets and invading the government buildings near the palace. These people were prepared. They carried arms.

He followed the gate, crouching behind it, Santiago keeping an eye out for anyone coming from the other side. If they couldn't go through the main door, they had to try plan two. Diate held his breath as he moved. This had better work. He didn't like plan three. Plan three required them to revert to themselves and storm the door.

They reached the section where the gate met the palace wall. He felt along the side, his fingers finding only dirt and cool stone. A man flew over the gate, landing on his back. He let out an oof of air, saw Diate and Santiago, and tried to stand. Diate reached for the knife he had stored in his boot. Santiago pulled out a Vorgellian pistol. The man rolled away and scrambled in the dirt.

Something snapped in front of Diate, followed by the heavy scent of damp, decayed air. He turned. A section of the wall had moved. 'Come on,' he said, and slipped inside.

Santiago followed. The corridor was narrow, cobweb-filled and dust-covered. No one had used it in a long time. Santiago pulled out a small candle, and with a snap of the fingers, lit it. Diate grabbed the stone wall and slid it shut. He hoped no one had blocked off the other exits. Santiago had the ability to create fire and illusions, but he couldn't move anything larger than a book.

A set of stairs branched off to the left. Water dripped down them, from some kind of long-untended leak in the plumbing. The outside noise had diminished to almost nothing. The walls were too thick to admit any kind of sound.

345

If things were going well, Rico's group had breached the front door. In a few moments, Magdalena would work her way to the back. She might not need to provide any help. The soldiers guarding the garden already looked exhausted.

A door stood off to one side, but Diate didn't touch it. They were still too low. If they emerged here, they would become part of the battle. He didn't want that. He had done his part to storm the castle. The rest of this was for him.

The stairs took a sharp left, and Santiago's flame flickered. A cobweb brushed Diate in the face, and he had to stifle an exclamation. The stairs dead-ended in a corridor. The corridor was wide, with no dust, no dripping water, no cobwebs. It was used.

He felt the weight drop off him. Part of him had been afraid he was trapped for life.

When they reached the corridor, they turned right. Diate counted the doors they passed until he found the one he wanted. Santiago followed closely behind him. As Diate pushed the door open, he reached out and touched Santiago.

Their illusions dissolved with a quiet pop.

'Emilio!' Santiago said, raising his hands again.

Diate caught Santiago's wrists. 'No,' he said. 'No more tricks.'

The door opened into a room he hadn't seen since he was a child. It was done in gold leaf, with flowers entwined upon the floor, fake vines climbing the columns in the center. The portraits of all the Queens, which provided the room's only color, were framed by more gold flowers and vines. At the end of the room, on a dais, stood the throne, now done in black and decorated with small lions. This room, the center of it all, the cause of so much heartache.

'She's not here.' The voice echoed in the room's emptiness. Diate didn't have to turn, didn't have to search for the source. He knew who spoke. 'What did you expect her to do, wait for you here like a good lover?'

'Where is she, Carbete?'

'Packing. Looking for a way out. She's our most valuable asset. We're not going to leave her unprotected.'

Santiago stepped into the room beside Diate. Diate reached behind him and closed the passage door. 'You should have thought of that weeks ago. The palace isn't going to stand.'

Carbete appeared beside the throne. He looked even thinner

346

than he had before. He was wearing a ruffled shirt and tight black pants.

And gloves.

'It's just a building,' he said. 'Sheba is this country's center. She'll be all right.'

'If you can get her out of here.'

'I will,' Carbete said. 'But I knew you were coming, and I have the right to kill you first.' He walked down the two stairs in the middle to the floor below. 'No one, detective, absolutely no one has the right to impersonate me.'

Even in this room, the crowd noise sounded faint. The palace was built well. Only a few hard blows reverberated through the stone. 'This isn't the time to think of your honor,' Diate said.

'You don't frighten me,' Carbete said.

'No,' Diate said. 'But there are thousands of people below who should.'

'Thousands?' Carbete smiled, just a little. 'You overestimate your powers, detective.'

'Have you looked outside since this morning?'

Carbete shrugged. 'I've been waiting for you. I knew you would come for Sheba. You have that boyish sentimentality that confuses a good fuck with true love.'

'Was it your idea to wait for me, or hers?'

'Does it matter?' Carbete walked down the marble floor until he stopped before Diate. Something snicked. He slapped Diate across the face, sending a sharp ripping pain through him. 'You're not going to see her again.'

Diate felt something wet flow down his cheek. Blood. Carbete had cut him. He reached a hand up, half waiting for the poison to hit. But it didn't. Carbete hadn't infected him.

Yet.

With his other hand, Diate pulled the knife from his boot and held it in front of him like a shield. 'Stay away, Santiago. He can kill you with a touch.'

Santiago moved to the side, his brow creased with worry. Carbete and Diate circled each other. Carbete held a thin blade between his fingers. 'You remembered,' Carbete said. 'And I was beginning to think that you didn't love me anymore.'

He reached for Diate with his empty hand. Diate ducked, and rammed his head into Carbete's stomach, sending him two steps back to regain his balance. Diate stood up and shoved his knife into Carbete's chest.

Carbete lost his balance and fell onto his back. Diate straddled him, holding him down. Carbete didn't reach for the knife. Instead he brought a gloved finger toward Diate's cheek. Diate grabbed Carbete's wrists, and using all his strength, tried to force Carbete's right hand down.

They were equally strong. The pressure was bone-breaking. Diate couldn't move, but neither could Carbete. Diate could push away, but if he did, he lost his advantage. He couldn't grab the knife; he had to move quickly, or the poison would get into his bloodstream and kill him.

Suddenly an entire crowd of toy soldiers surrounded them. Diate started. Carbete flinched. The soldiers crouched down, each movement identical. The pressure on Diate's hand lessened just a bit. He forced Carbete's arms down, made them clutch the knife. Then he let go of Carbete's wrist, pulled out the knife, and slammed the knife back into place, pinning Carbete's gloved hand to the open wound.

Carbete screamed. The toy soldiers disappeared. Diate got up and stepped away as Carbete huddled into a fetal position. He began to shake, his eyes bulging, his skin turning black. Diate had to look away.

Santiago stood behind him, his face going gray as he watched Carbete die. Diate grabbed Santiago's arm and led him to the door. 'Good timing,' Diate said. 'Thank you.'

He pulled open the door, and suddenly the screams and shouts grew even louder. Thumps, thuds, and clangs echoed from below. If Sheba was still here, she was going to die. But she would wait, wait for Carbete, her right hand.

She had known he was going to kill Diate. She had done nothing. She had probably encouraged it.

Carbete had said she was packing, getting ready to leave. They hadn't expected the attack. They had expected Diate to appear, and then something benign to happen. They hadn't thought so many people would show up, and they hadn't thought he was a true threat to their government.

If they had, Sheba and Carbete would have been long gone.

At last, she had made a mistake.

If she was still here, there was only one place she could be. A small, secluded room off the tower that led to the passageways. Carbete would have found her without going through the hallways. Diate would do the same.

'Come on, Santiago,' he said. 'More stairs.'

Chapter 29

The sounds of fighting were beginning to lessen. The shouts were not as frequent, the bangs not as loud. If everything had gone according to plan, the lower half of the palace was taken. If it had gone according to plan, hardly anyone had died.

Diate hoped so. The fact that some of Sheba's soldiers had joined his side so easily encouraged him.

He didn't have time to focus on what was going on below, however. He and Santiago had gotten back into the passageway and were heading for the tower. This was the way Carbete would have gone had he won. Diate didn't want Sheba to suspect that anything would be different.

The passageway narrowed as it filtered into the tower, becoming a series of very small, thin steps. The steps twisted at sharp angles, and he had to hang onto the cold stone wall to keep his footing.

'What do you need?' Santiago asked as they neared the top.

'Privacy,' Diate said. He hadn't realized until now that was what he wanted. He had no plans yet, no idea how he would deal with Sheba. 'Why don't you go down, see what's happening. I will meet you there shortly.'

Santiago paused, biting his lower lip. 'No toy soldiers? No illusions? No disguises?'

Diate shook his head. 'This one has to be just me.'

Santiago didn't move. Diate touched his shoulder lightly. 'She's not expecting me,' he said. 'She's expecting her brother.'

'But she could kill you.'

Diate nodded. 'She could. But she won't.'

'You don't know that, now that you've killed her brother.'

'I don't know that,' Diate said. 'I do know that I'm the physically stronger of the two of us. I'll be careful, Santiago. I promise.'

Santiago's lips pressed tightly together. 'You'd better,' he said. He clung to the wall as he turned around. He stomped down, not looking back.

Diate waited until he couldn't hear the footsteps anymore. Then he finished the climb.

The stairs ended at a narrow stone door with a single wooden knob. He took a deep breath and turned the knob, opening the door, stepping inside, and closing the door in a single movement.

The room was small and round. Oversized pillows graced the walls and the floor, covering the soft red carpet with their shapes. Tables with food and wine stood in the center of the room. Sheba ignored all the luxuries. She was facing the oversized windows, staring down at the fighting below.

'Most of our soldiers have surrendered,' she said as she turned, her voice trailing off when she saw Diate. She froze. 'Emilio.'

He nodded once, as if they were meeting across a crowded dance floor. 'Sheba.'

She was beautiful. Her hair frizzed around her shoulders, and her cheeks were flushed. She wore the same ruffled blouse and tight leggings that her brother had worn. But she was not wearing gloves. She had a Vorgellian laser pistol attached to her belt. No other weapons. The room was that secluded. People who didn't know about the passages couldn't find it.

'I killed Tonio,' Diate said.

'Obviously.' Her voice was tight. She swallowed. 'Me next?'

'That's up to you.'

She took a step toward him, hands out, shaking. 'What did I do, Emilio? For the last month I've been wondering. I wanted to take you with me. I wanted us to be together. I never meant to hurt you.'

'I know that,' he said. Almost against his will, he took her hands. Her palms were warm. He pulled her against him, holding both her hands with his right, and cradled her with his left. After a moment, he brought his left hand up and stroked her soft hair. She smelled good. He could hold her forever. 'But you did hurt me,' he said, softly. 'It's this place. It's who you are. What I want to know is whether or not you can be someone else.'

'Away from here?' She pulled out of his arms and went to the window, hugging herself. 'The soldiers are yours now. I was watching. A lot of them defected right away.' She shook her head. 'I have nothing now.'

'I know.' He came up behind her, and took the Vorgellian pistol from her belt. Below, people swarmed, picking up weapons, helping the injured. Some young boys were drinking out of the fountains. He opened the window and tossed the pistol out. 'The question is whether or not you'll be content with nothing, or whether you'll try to take the Kingdom back.'

Her body was warm against him. She hadn't moved, even though he had stolen her protection. 'What are you offering me?'

'Freedom. A future. Somewhere away from here. Away from all this.'

She ran a finger down the length of the window. 'You killed Tonio.'

'He tried to kill me. You were going to let him.'

'I thought you hated me. I thought you were coming after me.'

'If I wanted to kill you,' Diate said, 'I would have done it in my hospital room. It took courage to come for me, Sheba. Don't think I didn't appreciate it. I did. I just couldn't live here. And I couldn't let this government slaughter more families, and destroy other countries for its own whims.'

'So you had to be the conquering hero.' Her tone was dry. He could feel the loss in it, the beginnings of grief.

'There was no one else,' he said.

'You expect me to love you, now? Be your mate? Raise your children?'

'I don't know.' He walked away, unable to touch her. 'I didn't know what I would do until I got here. This is your only chance, Sheba. If you leave with me now, you can get off the island. You can live.'

She turned. A single tear traced a path down her cheek. 'Then I don't have much choice, do I?'

'You could stay, and see what comes of it.'

Her smile didn't reach her eyes. 'I know what comes of it. A long and public trial. Then they'll shave off my hair, strip me naked, and fry me for a traitor. You offer the better deal.'

He held out his hand. 'Let's go.'

She clasped hers behind her back. 'I would like to get a few things. Tonio wouldn't let me bring them here in case we had to run. We don't have to run, do we, Emilio?'

'No,' he said, although he wasn't sure how he would get her through the mob without Santiago's help. He just hoped they had calmed enough that they would listen to him when he said that he was taking her prisoner. 'But I'm coming with you.'

She opened the door to the passageway and started down the stairs. Diate followed. He knew where they were going: they were going to her rooms in the next wing. They stopped on the first landing and took a dark passageway to the right. When she reached the door, Diate pushed her aside. He opened it, and listened. The fighting was still continuing, but sounded quieter. Things had gone smoothly. The planning had paid off.

'All right,' he said.

She slipped past him. The corridor had stained-glass walls. The lights were hidden behind the glass, making the paintings look as if they moved. Then he stopped, touched the glass. The images swirled toward him, filled with terror. He took his hand away as if he had been burned.

Hoste glass. The corridor was filled with Hoste glass.

Sheba didn't see his startlement. He took a deep breath and followed her. The palace predated her. The glass could have been there for a long time. He didn't recognize any of the patterns. They weren't among the ones he had seen.

She opened the door to her rooms and he followed her inside. Hoste glass chandeliers, planters, decanters stood on the tables. The walls were also inlaid with Hoste glass, as was the ceiling.

He stared at it all as she rummaged, remembering Tellen's words. *We used to have Hoste glass everywhere, but then it started disappearing. I didn't realize it was stolen until I went to the storeroom.*

Sheba's file was as thick as Beltar's. Dating back to the days before the glass started to disappear.

That first night, she had hurried into her cabin before him, and thrown a rug over a piece of glass. He had always hoped the glass was a mirror. Now he knew for sure. She had covered Hoste glass.

The images saw him, swirled, pounded to get out. *Free us,* tiny lips mouthed in Lillish. *We want to go home.*

She was packing some of the decanters, rolled in her clothes. 'What are you doing?' he asked.

'We're going to need money,' she said. 'We need things to sell.'

'They're not ours to sell.'

'Emilio, if we're going to survive, we're going to have to take risks.'

She didn't even think it was wrong. She didn't understand at all. He hadn't understood either. To become Queen of the Kingdom, a person had to absorb the Kingdom, make it her own. Sheba had become what the rebels said she was: the Kingdom itself wrapped in one person.

She might promise him that she wouldn't try to come back. But she would leave him, steal something precious, and mount a campaign. The Kingdom was small. The next government would be shaky. It would be easy.

The deaths would start again: first Rico's family, then Santiago's, then Magdalena's. Kreske wouldn't be safe, nor would Beltar and Martina. The peace that the Golgoth wanted would disappear forever.

Diate had to kill her. It was the only way everyone could be safe.

He touched her hair, and kissed the top of her head. A simple movement down to her neck would be all it took. He let his hand slide down. His thumb rested on her pulse.

She brought her gaze up to his, looking like she did when he first saw her in Rulanda. He had never stopped loving her.

He took his hand off her neck.

'Let's go,' he said. He took her clothing sack from her and carried it. He slipped his free hand into hers. She let him.

Hand-in-hand they walked out of her room, past that beautiful glass, and down to the real steps. These steps were marble inlay, and wide. They descended like a king and queen surveying their nation. As they walked past levels, people stopped and watched, no one speaking, no one moving.

The fighting had indeed stopped. A few guards were trussed up, some injured people were getting their wounds bandaged. Mostly, the rebels wandered from room to room, surveying a wealth they had never seen before. They had a look of awe, as if they were visiting a museum.

Diate found Santiago on the first floor. He was standing with Torrie near the main door, counting the dead, his face pale. When he saw Diate, he paused.

'I thought you were over her,' Santiago said, a sadness in his voice. 'But when it took you so long, I found myself wondering if it would come to this.'

Diate swallowed. He pulled Sheba closer, enjoying her warmth.

'I never planned to run this place,' Diate said. 'It's yours. Yours and Torrie's. There's a lot of Hoste glass upstairs, begging to be returned to Rulanda. Please do that. I'll inform the authorities that it's here. You were right, Torrie. You can get a lot of good will if you return all these things.'

She nodded. 'It would be better if you stayed. It would be better if she died.'

Sheba's hand tightened in his. Diate didn't look at her. He couldn't. She might see what he was planning. 'I can't stay,' Diate said. 'You have dreams of fixing this place. I only had dreams of tearing it down. I can't manage a government. I don't want to. It's time I lived my own life, not the life my past dictated. I'm leaving.'

He took a deep breath. Leaving the Kingdom was not hard, but this next part was. He let go of Sheba's hand and slid his arm around her back, pushing her forward. 'Sheba is staying with you.'

She turned and grabbed for him. He moved out of her way. 'You promised!' she said. 'You promised to get me out of here.'

'You swore to me you had nothing to do with the Golgoth's death. Upstairs you let me think you could reform. Then you put Hoste glass in your pack, because we might need money. You don't even know what you're doing is wrong, Sheba. How can you change?'

'I will,' she said. She ran a hand along his cheek. 'I love you, Emilio.'

He took the hand and let it drop. 'No, you don't,' he said. 'You don't love anyone. Just things. And just this place, as it was, not as it will be.'

He leaned forward and kissed her on the mouth, sampling her rich taste for the very last time. Then he let her go. 'She's yours, Santiago,' he said, handing over her pack. 'Use her however you need to.'

'Emilio,' Santiago said. 'I don't understand.'

'Maybe not yet,' he said. 'But Sheba does. She would – and has – done no less to us.'

'He'll kill me.' Sheba's voice was measured. She stood empty-handed, unarmed. Her weapons were in her pack. Diate had watched her put them there.

'He might kill you,' Diate said. 'If that's what it takes.'

He turned his back and walked away, not listening to her cries, Santiago's calls, trying not to see the hands reaching for him, the people asking his advice as he passed. He took the steps out of the palace and down to the fountains, leaving the Kingdom in ruins behind him.

Chapter 30

By the time he reached Beltar's ship in Tersis harbor, the sun was setting. The ocean was bathed in a red-gold light. The air smelled faintly of rain.

The ship was small, more of a yacht, built for only a handful of passengers. The crew had been instructed to wait below. Beltar sat on the deck, arms crossed over his chest. Martina sat beside him, nearer to the door, ready to bolt below decks if she had to.

Magdalena had said nothing about Martina. Diate stared at her. In the twilight, her scars were nearly invisible. The shadows on her face gave her an eerie beauty.

'I was getting worried,' Beltar said. 'Both Rico and Santiago had said it would be loud, but we hadn't expected this. We could hear the screams from the palace.'

'We were afraid they would kill you.' Martina spoke softly, not looking at Diate.

He stepped onto the deck. The boat rocked beneath his feet. 'After what I did to you,' he said, 'I didn't think you would care.'

She shook her head. 'I was wrong,' she said. 'I shouldn't have tricked you.'

'And I shouldn't have said the things I did.' He crouched beside her and put his fingers under her chin, raising her head. 'We're family. And family is something I value above everything else.'

'I know that, Emilio,' she said. 'Why do you think I'm here?'

'She's here because I couldn't keep her away,' Beltar said. He got up and walked to the edge of the deck, looking into the city. The murmur of a large crowd washed over the air. The battle must have sounded terrible. Beltar glanced at Diate. 'Is she dead?'

Diate didn't have to ask who she was. 'I don't know,' he said. 'I left her with Santiago. It's his decision.'

'You should have killed her,' Beltar said.

Diate ran a finger along the wooden rail. He was shaking. The stress was catching up to him. 'I couldn't touch her.'

Beltar gave him a measuring look. 'No,' he said after a moment. 'I don't suppose you could.'

Lights had gone on in the buildings near the port. The darkness was spreading across the water.

'What will Santiago do with her?' Martina asked.

Small red lights moved in the street. Torches. The people were still gathered, still waiting. 'I don't know,' Diate said. 'If he's smart, he'll make an example of her. Before he kills her.'

The last four words barely escaped his throat. The shaking had grown. He gripped the railing hard. 'We should shove off.'

'I'll let them know.' Martina got up and slipped below deck. He watched her go. He had missed her steadiness, her even understanding. Her forgiveness startled him. He had never expected to see her again.

'We killed – a lot of people today,' Diate said. His voice came out husky. Something was caught in his throat.

'How many?'

'I don't know. I counted fifteen near the fountains as I left.'

'You knew that would be a risk.'

'I didn't want it to happen to anyone.'

'No,' Beltar said. He gripped the railing, not looking at Diate. The ship rocked beneath their feet. 'I hate to sound cold. It's not meant to be cold. But better those fifteen than all the families that would die like yours, better them than the Talents that would have their bodies destroyed because they disobeyed a small law, an unjust law. Better people who knew and believed in what they were fighting for, than a strong, good man who was working for peace.'

'Maybe,' Diate said.

'Emilio,' Beltar said. 'Those fifteen are the end of it now. Rico, Santiago, Magdalena, they won't allow things to get out of hand again. Trust your friends.'

Diate put his hand on top of Beltar's. 'Oh, I do,' he said. 'I do.'

Chains clanked as the anchor rolled in below them. The ship rocked some more, then a roaring echoed as the engine fired up. Diate squeezed Beltar's hand and let it go. Diate walked away from the rail, turning his back on the Kingdom, and stared out into the ocean.

It was vast and dark, completely unknown. He would sail into it with two friends, and no magic around them. No manipulation, no threats.

The Kingdom he had hated was gone.
For the first time in his life, Diate was free.